USA TODAY bestselling autho[...] writes emotional contempora[...] of sparkling banter, sizzling heat and uplifting endings—perfect for readers who love to escape with empowered heroines and arrogant alphas who are too sexy for their own good. When not writing, you'll find her wrangling her four children, three cats, two goldfish and one dog…and snuggled in a heap on the sofa with her husband at the end of the day. Follow her at natalie-anderson.com.

Canadian **Dani Collins** knew in high school that she wanted to write romance for a living. Twenty-five years later, after marrying her high school sweetheart, having two kids with him, working at several generic office jobs and submitting countless manuscripts, she got The Call. Her first Mills & Boon novel won the Reviewers' Choice Award for Best First in Series from *RT Book Reviews*. She now works in her own office, writing romance.

Also by Natalie Anderson

Revealing Her Nine-Month Secret
The Night the King Claimed Her

Rebels, Brothers, Billionaires miniseries

Stranded for One Scandalous Week
Nine Months to Claim Her

The Christmas Princess Swap collection

The Queen's Impossible Boss

Also by Dani Collins

One Snowbound New Year's Night
Cinderella for the Miami Playboy
Innocent in Her Enemy's Bed

Four Weddings and a Baby miniseries

Cinderella's Secret Baby

The Secret Sisters miniseries

Married for One Reason Only
Manhattan's Most Scandalous Reunion

Discover more at millsandboon.co.uk.

CARRYING HER BOSS'S CHRISTMAS BABY

NATALIE ANDERSON

WEDDING NIGHT WITH THE WRONG BILLIONAIRE

DANI COLLINS

MILLS & BOON

First published in Great Britain 2022
by Mills & Boon, an imprint of HarperCollins*Publishers* Ltd,
1 London Bridge Street, London, SE1 9GF

www.harpercollins.co.uk

HarperCollins*Publishers*
1st Floor, Watermarque Building,
Ringsend Road, Dublin 4, Ireland

Carrying Her Boss's Christmas Baby © 2022 Natalie Anderson

Wedding Night with the Wrong Billionaire © 2022 Dani Collins

ISBN: 978-0-263-30105-2

11/22

MIX
Paper | Supporting
responsible forestry
FSC™ C007454

This book is produced from independently certified FSC™ paper
to ensure responsible forest management.
For more information visit: www.harpercollins.co.uk/green.

Printed and Bound in Spain using 100% Renewable Electricity
at CPI Black Print, Barcelona

CARRYING HER BOSS'S CHRISTMAS BABY

NATALIE ANDERSON

MILLS & BOON

For my dreamers and adventurers.
Go for it.

CHAPTER ONE

Halloween

ROMAN FRASER STRODE through the deserted atrium, struggling to avoid the Halloween decorations strewn across the floor. The party had clearly been a success. He should be heading to another party himself now—one more wild than the one in his company headquarters. But he'd avoided this one and he was probably going to skip the next as well.

As CEO of Fraser Holdings, he was too busy overseeing a wide assortment of companies and interests. The merchant-banking arm was insanely busy, the group's hotels were at the highest occupancy rates they'd been in years while the luxury goods and accessories arm was growing at a phenomenal rate. Built upon the legacy of his great-grandparents, the Fraser name was synonymous with finance, luxury travel and now had the global success Roman had long sought.

Tomorrow he'd head overseas to check in on the subsidiary companies and some of the hotels, but right now an enormous pair of wings lay in his path. They were snowy-white and sparkling, though one wing was broken. Frowning, he hoisted them up from the floor and slung the harness over his shoulder. It wasn't fair for the cleaners to have to lug them out. It was tough enough, having to work through the small hours, let alone having to deal with this extra mess, especially when they were so heavy. He wasn't surprised the angel who'd worn them had decided to ditch them. Not that there were angels, of course. Demons, on the other hand? Roman knew there were plenty of those. He had more in his head than were running around Manhattan tonight.

Halloween heralded the slide into the festive season. Upbeat, jingling songs would soon be on endless repeat. The expectation to socialise would skyrocket even higher than normal. It was the start of the sharing season—the time to give and receive, to eat, drink and be merry. To kiss beneath mistletoe and again at the stroke of midnight. None of which Roman wanted to do.

He was bored. Jaded. Ready to retreat into work. Not even the prospect of beauties in skimpy witch or nymph costumes tempted him. This time of year simply sucked. So he was out of here. On a plane first thing tomorrow. Yeah, he was a grumpy Grinch who wanted to be alone. He wanted to be alone *always*. Most especially now.

Violet Summers was late locking up. She'd been enjoying the vibe of people walking past, dressed up to party—the costumes were something else. Halloween wasn't as huge at home in New Zealand as it was in the US and here in Manhattan—like everything else in the city—it was next level. Some of the sizzling costumes and special effects make-up on people going past the window were stunning.

She was working alone late at night in a teeny-tiny macaron store in the heart of Corporateville—the store being small, that was, not the macarons. She giggled to herself. If only her over-protective parents could see her now. She'd even managed to engage the alarm without accidentally setting it off. She turned back from securing the door, stopped and stared. While she'd had her back to the street, an angel had fallen and landed just five feet away. A tall, broad-shouldered, beautiful angel.

He paused on the pavement, looking as though he didn't know where to head next. He had an enormous set of wings. One of them was broken. Honestly, it only added to his not-of-this-world look. He was the most classically handsome man she'd ever seen and, since arriving in New York a fortnight ago, she'd seen a lot of stylish, good-looking people. They walked past the shop all the time. But this guy? Maybe it was just the lighting—the harsh streetlights overhead hollowed and highlighted the planes and edges of his face, giving him a sharply sculpted look and his skin an unearthly pallor. He'd be perfect inspiration for an animé artist. He *was* perfect—attractive to anyone with a pulse.

She froze, afraid he'd disappear if she blinked. She wanted to enjoy the magic for as long as possible. But she laughed at herself again. Was she really ogling a guy in the street? She was used to men—four brothers and all their friends had done that. But this guy should have been in a superhero, supernatural mash-up movie. Vaguely she acknowledged that moments like these were rare. Mostly she just enjoyed the view.

He still didn't move. He just gazed into the middle distance as if he wasn't really present—was he lost in troubling thoughts? Her appreciation gave way to curiosity and then concern. He looked as if he was bowed beneath a burden far bigger than the enormous wings he was shouldering.

She stepped forward into the middle of the footpath and softly called to him. 'Do you need some help?'

He turned. The distant look evaporated, instantly replaced with alertness. He didn't smile but his all-encompassing gaze grew mildly incredulous. 'Are you talking to *me*?'

The sharpness in his tone shaved an edge off his handsomeness. It was a shame. Not just a fallen angel but a bitter one.

She swallowed. 'Yes.'

'What makes you think I need help?'

'You looked…' She was embarrassed but at the same time his lack of grace fired her spirit. There was no reason for him to be rude to someone simply reaching out. 'You looked like you were lost.'

'Lost?' he echoed sardonically.

'Yeah. Like you've landed in a place you don't belong.' She winced inwardly.

'A place *I* don't belong?'

Well, okay, it was obvious she wasn't from around here. But still. 'And your costume is—'

'Costume?' His eyes widened.

'The wings are great, by the way. The broken one works really well with your whole…' She trailed off, realising too late as she took in the fine black suit. 'You're not in costume, are you?'

He shook his head and there was a softening at the edges of his mouth.

'Holding the wings for someone else?' she asked.

He was probably waiting for his date to emerge from that swanky building next door. In moments, a car with a chauffeur would arrive to take them both to some exclusive Halloween party.

'No. I found them.'

'So you're out here looking for the owner?'

He stepped closer and Violet simply stared. His vibrant eyes weren't quite perfectly blue—one had a patch of another colour. She'd have to get closer to determine it. Part of Violet really wanted to get closer.

'It isn't you, is it?' he asked.

'Do they look like they'd fit me?' She'd topple over if she tried to wear those wings. 'I'm more elf than angel.'

His gaze dropped and he slowly scrutinised her scarlet velvet dress. She was suddenly so engulfed in heat, she had to look down. Which meant she was faced with his stunningly muscular physique.

'Alternatively,' he said huskily. 'You're a sweet-looking but inherently dangerous demon.'

'Demon?' Her gaze shot back to him.

But his attention was gone. He glanced behind her and his frown suddenly returned ten-fold. 'Watch—'

She was abruptly jostled from behind. 'Oh!'

As she was almost knocked off-balance, he swooped. Violet gasped. There was such strength in his hold as he lifted her and turned them both. He pressed her back against the glass store-front and stood in front of her, sheltering her from the… She didn't even know what. Instead she gazed up, fascinated by the glower in his angel eyes. The angle of his jaw was even more defined as he gritted his teeth. There was literally a stampede of people rushing past them. Actually, they were not really people.

'What the…?' Violet was shocked. *More* shockingly, he was pressed against her. Those wings were lifted above him like a protective umbrella and she didn't want to move. Ever.

She would have giggled at the ridiculousness of it, only adrenalin surged as if she were in real danger. As if this really were serious. The crowd ran past them in a groaning, amorphous mess of limbs, body paint and excitement. She'd not even heard them until they were upon her.

'Zombies.' He shook his head slightly.

There had to be a hundred if not more. A zombie rampage.

Violet didn't care if they were zombies, vampires or werewolves. Her attention was sucked straight ahead of her. It wasn't just his heat but the pulsing strength of his muscles. He was bodyguard-built and, shockingly, she was more than melting. She was almost purring like a kitten curled up on a lap feeling all safe and cared for. She should wriggle a little, step aside, because this proximity was too intimate. Yet she didn't move. She didn't want to breathe and break the spell.

'Zombies?' She'd been so focused on figuring out the peculiarity in his eyes that she'd not heard the noise rising behind her. 'I didn't think they were supposed to move so fast. I thought they were supposed to be slow and fall over their feet.'

'Maybe they're vampire zombies,' he muttered. 'Either way…you okay?' He stared into her eyes and his annoyance morphed into something else. 'Sorry if I crushed you.'

But he didn't step back, even if he too had realised that they were in a clinch that was no longer necessary. It was an incredibly comfortable clinch. Their bodies moulded together, fitting snugly, as her size and his strength matched somehow. It ought to have been impossible, given he was huge and she was petite, but it worked—dangerously well.

And now she knew that patch in his left eye was brown. Topaz, really. It almost had a glow to it. It was uneven, imperfect, intriguing. Mesmerised, she couldn't stop staring.

'You moved fast,' she muttered, dissolving just like that into a breathless female.

'Instinct.'

Yeah. He was naturally protective. She'd been around protective people her whole life and she wasn't supposed to want to sink against someone and simply…stay. Only that was exactly what she wanted this second—to take shelter in his arms. But in a swoop of his lashes that sentiment changed—to take even more appreciation of his strength, of the spark between them. She lowered her gaze, almost dazed. She couldn't take the heat in those gorgeous, striking eyes.

But then she saw it. Instinctively, she put a hand on his chest where the crisp white shirt was now stained. 'You're bleeding.'

'It's fake. And it's not mine. Don't worry, I'm fine.'

She looked back up to his eyes. She didn't believe him. She'd lied in the exact same way so many times.

I'm fine.

The blood was fake but there was a real wound there. A deep one. She could feel his strong heart beat beneath her palm. His solid, hot muscles had flinched at her first touch. Not a zombie. Not an angel either. He was all man and she simply couldn't lift her hand away from him.

This should have been too intimate but those wings were like a barrier from the rest of the world, enclosing them both in a safe haven. Her back was against the glass and with him pressed against her she felt a whisper of temptation. The urge was so out of character for her, it should be shocking. But if he lowered his head now she would kiss him.

'The wings have lost more feathers,' she said breathlessly, distracting herself, because this was a total random stranger. 'It's a shame. It would've taken someone a lot of time to make them.' They were cardboard, glue, feathers and a few million diamantes to make them sparkle.

'Except they discarded them before midnight,' he pointed out.

'Did they, though? What if they weren't left? Maybe

someone was going to come back for them. You've effectively stolen them.'

'Good point.' He stilled, then the slowest of smiles spread across his face. 'My bad.'

There should have been a clap of thunder…lightning should have lit the sky ablaze—at the very least a wolf should have howled in the distance. This moment was portentous—a blink in which life irrevocably changed. Just like that, Violet Summers became a different woman. A tsunami of sensual awareness swamped her, wreaking changes deep within—softening, heating, as hunger stirred. All because of one gorgeous smile.

'Maybe you should put a sign up on the building,' she suggested desperately. '"Broken wings found—apply within".'

He nodded. 'They're actually pretty heavy.'

'Do you think being an angel was too much hard work and that's why they ditched the wings?'

'Must be pretty burdensome. Always having to be good.' There was an edge to the word. A wicked glint in his eye.

She smiled. 'You get sick of that?'

'I get sick of everything.' He gave a rasp.

Honesty that time. Yeah, the guy was not 'fine'.

'What do you do, then?' She breathed. 'When you're sick of everything…?'

His gaze held hers. 'Not angelic things.'

Another low admission that shot an electrical pulse along her veins. 'Oh?'

There was a tilt to his lips now and her brain wasn't working at all any more.

Do not fall for a moody, damaged dude.

She'd been the damaged one. She was looking for whole and healthy fun. To live in the moment and make the most of everything. This was her chance. She was finally on the other side of the world from her loving but ever so slightly suffocating family that she truly adored. But she needed to escape it to do all the things she wanted. Having four over-protective older brothers, and parents who constantly worried about her even though they tried to pretend they didn't, wasn't easy. They all pretended they weren't helicoptering around, making sure she didn't do anything that might put her at risk…

Until now, she'd needed just a little space to breathe. To figure out her own life. To prove she was as capable as her hale and hearty, mega-brain brothers and not have them joke she needed to marry well to secure herself a reasonable future…

She was hardly about to marry well when she'd hardly even flirted before. When she'd barely been allowed out to experience anything much with a man at all.

Her breathing quickened. But then, something changed.

His intense eyes narrowed and he shook his head. 'What's a woman like you doing out on the street alone late at night like this?' He glared at her.

A woman like her? What did *that* mean? She felt indignant. 'I've been working in this shop since early this morning.' She lifted her chin. 'What are *you* doing out on the street late at night like this?'

His eyes widened. 'I was working too. Now I'm supposed to go to a party but I…'

'Don't know the way?' she guessed. 'It is hard to get taxis round here sometimes.' She nodded. 'You could try the subway?'

He blinked. 'Subway?'

'Yeah, you know? Underground trains,' she said.

'I do know. But I haven't ridden it much.'

'Me neither,' she acknowledged.

'Because you're not from around here. That's not a local accent. Yet you think you can help me somehow?'

'Two heads are generally better than one,' she said a little defensively. 'And I am pretty good at helping people, actually. A lot of my customers are tourists who come in looking for directions or suggestions. I've got good, even though we don't even have any subways in Aotearoa.'

'Aotea…?'

'Aotearoa, New Zealand. Yeah.' She saw the perplexed look on his face. 'Am I talking too fast? I'm probably talking too fast. It makes me harder to understand. And I'm talking too much,' she muttered, but it was as if a valve had been released, and it was better than staring at the guy fixedly as though he was the best-looking thing she'd ever seen. Which he was. But he didn't need to know that, because he was a bit of an arrogant grump, so she just babbled.

'Don't get me wrong, I love New Zealand, but I really wanted to come abroad. Especially to New York. It's a big city, you know? This is my first time—'

'First time, huh?' he interrupted and his mouth twitched.

He was mocking her. A flush crept over her skin. 'Nothing wrong with that.'

'Oh, no. Not at all. Everyone needs a first time and it should always be special.'

She paused, suddenly tossed back into that tumult of attraction. She desperately tried to stop herself thinking things he sure wouldn't be. This rapid descent into desire—into craving someone she'd barely met—was insane.

'You're not from here either,' she said pointedly. He couldn't be, if he never rode the subway.

'Actually, you're wrong. While I'm originally from upstate New York, I live in Manhattan most of the time.'

How did anyone live in Manhattan 'most of the time'

when they had at least one other place to live some of the time? Fallen Angel here was no cash-strapped tourist like her. Fallen Angel wasn't wearing a costume. He was wearing a suit that had probably cost more than six months' salary. He was…not someone she'd usually be talking to unless he was buying something in her macaron shop. Which he wouldn't, because she just knew he was more exclusive than that. And then, to her intense disappointment, he stepped back a couple of inches and lowered the wings to the ground.

'What are you going to do with them?' she asked.

'I haven't thought that far ahead. I just…'

'Wanted them as a last-minute costume because you forgot?'

'No.' He gave a wry sigh. 'They were left in the middle of the floor in the atrium of my building. There'd been a Halloween function earlier and there was a mess. Turns out they're really heavy, and I didn't want the cleaner to have to haul them away and try to find somewhere to put…' He drew a breath and shook his head. 'I have no idea why I'm telling you all this.'

'Because I asked,' she pointed out reasonably.

'Yeah, but I don't normally—' He broke off.

'Talk to random strangers on the street? Or women like me? Or…'

His lips twisted. 'I don't normally have random strangers on the street offering me assistance.'

'Everyone needs assistance sometimes. Even fallen angels in suits.'

'Fallen…?' His jaw dropped again. 'What assistance do you really think *I* need?'

She gazed up at him. He was serious. Gorgeous. Serious. So very serious.

'Light relief?' she ventured. 'Something to make you

smile?' She cocked her head to study him impishly. 'Have you actually smiled today? Before you met me, that is.'

He didn't just smile this time, he actually chuckled. 'You think that's your specialty? Light relief?'

'Not just speciality, super-power.'

'Is that right?' He stepped closer. 'You think *you're* the hero now?'

'Sure.'

'Then why did you need me to save you from being trampled by speeding zombies?'

'Who says I did? You moved before I—'

'Before you got trampled because you hadn't even noticed them. You know it's okay to acknowledge that. It's also okay to say thank you.'

She didn't want to say thank you. Perversely, she felt like *not* doing as he suggested. 'I didn't need you to rescue me.'

'Maybe that's not what I'm doing now.'

A sizzle shimmied down her spine and she didn't quite know how to respond. 'Why aren't you going to go to your Halloween party?'

'I'm avoiding people.'

'You don't like people?'

'Let me guess—you do.'

'Sure. Especially when it's holiday nights. Customers give big tips to people working on a holiday.'

The topaz in his eye glittered. 'Not so angelic after all.'

'Not completely naïve.' Contrary to what people always thought. 'I'm working in retail, but I'm going to get a position as a travel guide, and holidays are the best.'

His eyebrows lifted. 'You're going to be a guide in a country that's not your own?'

'Why can't that work? I've discovered lots of things and can pass on the tricks. Plus, I know what a lot of tourists

like to see and do because I am one. And it's a way of seeing the country myself.'

He was staring at her and his expression was grim. She
didn't know why he'd returned to serious and grumpy.

'I'm talking too much again.' She grimaced.

'Did I say that?'

'You didn't need to. I read your expression.'

'Then you read it wrong. I wasn't thinking that. I
have—'

'A resting grumpy face?'

'A what?'

'Well, maybe not grumpy, as much as closed off,' she
revised.

'Closed. Right.' He drew breath. 'Well, you were wrong.
I was enjoying listening to you. You have a delightful way
of rolling your "r"s.'

'The Southland roll.' She nodded.

'The what?'

'Very bottom of the South Island,' she explained. 'It's
a regional thing.'

'What is?'

'The Southland rolling of the "r".'

'Right. The bottom, huh?'

'Of the *island*.' She shot him a look.

His smile returned, widened—and devastating.

It was her *eyes* that she rolled this time. 'I'm going to
be quiet now.'

'Is that even possible?'

'Occasionally.'

His gaze dropped to her mouth and she felt a shiver of
sensation, as if she knew exactly what he was thinking
about how she could be quietened. By being silenced by
his mouth, with his smile upon hers. But he shook his head

again, and now there was a self-mocking smile on his face. Then there was distance. Too much distance.

She watched as he hailed a taxi. So much for transport being a problem at this time of night.

'Are you going to go to your party?' she asked.

'I don't think so, no.'

'You're avoiding socialising.'

'I think that's best. Yes.'

She frowned. 'Not necessarily best.'

'You're a romantic who believes in connection. In hope.'

'You're a cynic. Born alone, live alone, die alone.'

'Oh, sure, strike the blade home. I knew you were dangerous.' He opened the door to the taxi and stood back for her to get in. 'The cab will take you wherever you need to go. No matter the distance, the fare's covered.'

'You don't need to do that.' But she couldn't afford the cab fare herself, and there was a scaredy-cat bit in her that didn't want to walk these streets alone. Not with all the zombie vampires running around grabbing all the cabs first.

'No. But I want to.'

'And you always do what you want.'

His smile flashed, illuminating his face, making his fascinating eyes sparkle. 'I'm afraid I do.'

'Why be afraid to admit that?' she challenged him. 'Life's too short not to take what you want.'

'You take what you want?' He looked sceptical.

He was right to because, no, she didn't. She was still working up the courage.

'You're too sweet to walk these streets alone—certainly this late at night,' he said. 'If you're not careful, real demons might jump out and bite.'

'They'll regret it if they do. Maybe I'm not as *sweet* or as soft as I look.'

'Is that so?'

'Don't patronise me.'

'Don't tempt me.' He sent her a scorching look and lifted his hand to cup her jaw. 'This…?'

She held her breath, insanely happy to be close to him again.

'Not a good idea, Angel. Not for you.'

Anger flared. 'What makes you say that?' Protectiveness? That she did *not* need. 'You don't know anything about me. I don't want or need *protection* from you.'

She'd never pushed before. Never been brazen. She'd never wanted to. But this was midnight, this was Halloween and she was away from home, finally free to assert herself. She was in a dreamscape with a fallen angel at her feet.

His lips twisted into a beautiful, broken smile. 'Of course you do. Everybody does.'

CHAPTER TWO

Thanksgiving

ROMAN FRASER STALKED through the empty atrium. He'd returned after just over three weeks visiting the major city offices of the Fraser empire this morning, and then had worked through another nationwide festival, catching up on things he'd missed while away. The offices had been pleasingly devoid of life the whole day. Everyone else was with family or friends. He figured they'd have watched the parade—plus highlights on repeat—feasted, had fun and be stretched out on sofas in food comas by now. He grimaced. Fortunately, work provided a never-ending list of things to focus on.

Except one thing kept rising to the top of that damned list. She wasn't angel or demon, elf or ghost, yet ever since Halloween she'd haunted his days and nights. One petite brunette in red velvet with breathless chatter and a smile that reached places he'd thought safely sealed for good.

Protection?

He was the one who really needed it. Temptation twisted a tighter hold on his willpower, calling him to sate the curiosity that had been consuming his concentration with increasing ferocity for days. Was she working on a holiday again, selling sweet treats to late-night tourists and revellers in the small shop in the building next door?

Memory hit of the magic of that meeting, the soft sweetness as he'd sheltered her from that stampede of outrageously dressed, screaming partygoers. The intimate atmosphere, as they'd pressed together to escape the crowd in a feathered bubble of their own, had been dizzying.

Rationally, he knew the baseline sexual attraction had been inflated by the fantastical elements of the night—a trick of lighting and mood making it into something more. He'd gone from bored to blinded with lust in seconds, and resisting the instinct to invite her with him—to seduce her—had been almost impossible.

Because she was a novelty, with her Antipodean accent, her rushed honesty and the mutual fascination she'd been unable to hide even as she'd tried. She'd merely been an unexpected diversion on a night when he'd needed it. If he saw her again, he'd probably find he wasn't that drawn to her after all. Reality was like that. Things were never quite as one remembered. Moments like that could never be repeated. Gut feelings couldn't be trusted. After all, he'd been brutally betrayed by instinct before.

But *this* instinct was very basic, very singular and very blunt. And what would it matter if he indulged it? Where was the risk? There was none for him. Because he wasn't the one who'd needed help or directions. He was the one who knew the score.

Of course, she wasn't a fool. She was smart—hustling, working on a day everyone else took off. But she was too sweet for him. Too sincere. Too small-town, with her wide-eyed, wondering way of looking at the world. She'd been covering as best she could, but basically she'd been quivering before him And, yeah, he'd been right to warn her off and walk away.

Still, he wondered about her. Apparently playing the gentleman had only made him want her more. He gritted his teeth. That he was this obsessed after a brief interaction showed how bored he'd become. Roman Fraser generally avoided any return to the past. But tonight he was too tired to resist.

Two minutes later, he paused on the pavement. Through the glass of her shop, he watched her animatedly conversing with a customer. She looked as though she'd teleported from the nineteen-sixties in that flared red velvet dress. Her hair was loose—long, straight and glossy, it fell just below her shoulders, while the heavy fringe framed her sweetheart face. Her wide eyes gleamed, each topped with a flick of black eyeliner. Her lips were pink and perfectly made to be teased with gentle kisses.

Kisses he wouldn't be able to keep gentle for long. The sharp edge of sexual hunger sliced, releasing a flare of jealousy as she smiled at someone else. The possessiveness was utterly unreasonable. Maybe it hadn't been exaggeration when he'd said she needed protection from him.

He meant to move away. This was stalker-like. He did not do this with any woman at any time. Only, the customer turned and his Halloween angel glanced up and caught sight of him at the window. Even from this distance he saw her eyes widen and colour swirl across her skin. She couldn't hide her physical response and it was so much stronger than simple recognition. He was walking before he realised it. Suddenly he was standing at her counter and he'd somehow lost a few moments of time altogether.

'Working again?' His voice was husky and he tensed.

Her gaze dropped to his unbuttoned wool coat and the suit beneath. There was a twist to those plump lips and, even with the black high heels, she was a full foot shorter than him.

'Avoiding socialising again?' she countered.

'Always.'

'Why? You don't like people? Someone hurt you?'

He smiled as it hit—how *much* he'd missed her sharp chatter.

Her eyes widened. 'Is that actually a smile? So soon?'

He put his hands on the counter and leaned across it. 'Yeah, it is.'

Her pupils dilated and she swallowed. She'd lost her words and it was because of him. Good.

'Someone once told me not to be afraid of admitting what I want,' he said.

Her teeth pressed on her lower lip for a second. But then she couldn't resist asking the question he'd set. 'And what do you want?' She was breathless already.

'You.' He paused, intently observing the effect on her and following up with a whole-body smile of satisfaction. 'To have supper with me.'

But, despite the excitement blooming on her skin and making her eyes sparkle, her slim shoulders squared. 'I thought I needed protecting from you.'

So that had stung… It had been a throwaway line because at the time he'd barely been able to think. His instincts had been warring—to push away or to pull close. He'd gone with caution and pushed her away. He'd been rewarded with sleepless curiosity and insatiable desire. So. Time to change the play. Time to pull close. But only for long enough to ease the ache.

'I've been wondering if I wasn't wrong about that.'

'Wondering for a while?' she asked.

Oh. Had she been counting the days too?

'I've been criss-crossing the globe since November first,' he said.

'Is that supposed to impress me?'

He smiled again. 'I'm saying I've been unable to see you again until now. I'm saying I only returned to Manhattan this morning and—'

'You're saying you're jet-lagged and you want distraction.' Violet looked at him.

'I know a place. They do the best pumpkin pie. You ever had it?'

She shook her head.

'First time. Better be special.' There was a glint in his eye. 'You're about to close up, right?'

Violet stared at him. He'd timed his arrival perfectly. *Deliberately.*

And had he really been away all the time? Could she believe him? Or was she too naïve to think that she could take him at face value? Going for a drink with a random stranger she'd met around midnight on the streets of New York City? Her parents and brothers would warn her it was too dangerous. But they weren't here to tell her not to go. And pumpkin pie would be in a diner. It would be public.

She might not have qualifications coming out of her ears but she could look after herself. Although, she *had* encountered some luck. She'd not realised her store was right next door to the headquarters of a massive hotel conglomerate. Not until she'd begun chatting to one of her regulars who came in for her daily macaron fix. Turned out the woman was a manager there and, when she'd found out about Violet's tourism training, she'd encouraged her to apply for a temporary steward position on one of the trips they specialised in—some fancy train journey.

Violet was considering it and yet, despite the positive prospects of the last fortnight such as this one, the bereft feeling inside her hadn't faded. To have become so intrigued by a man in only a few minutes was shocking. Being inexperienced and sheltered was bad enough but what sort of *fool* was she? Yet never had she regretted not taking a risk more. She'd pushed, but not enough. He'd walked away with some throwaway, dramatic line suggesting he'd somehow be dangerous for her.

For a while, she'd wondered if she'd dreamt it all and he was a figment of an over-active imagination. That their narrow escape from the zombie crush had been like a flash in an alternative reality—one she didn't fit into. But now he was back and she wasn't going to make the same mistake again. Yet nor was she going to embarrass herself.

'Pumpkin pie sounds interesting,' she said, trying not to sound too keen.

His smile teased. 'Come on, then, we can walk.'

In only a few minutes he directed her to a large building. A liveried man opened the door for them and held it with a nod as they walked through. It was the kind of building that could double as a magical portal in some sci-fi or superhero movie, all carved stonework and curving windows. There were crystal chandeliers and sumptuous velvet furnishings. It was opulent yet somehow not over the top. Somehow it all worked.

'This is definitely…a place.' She couldn't help staring in amazement. 'Where angels go for peace and quiet and escape the demands of the humans who need their help at inconvenient hours…' It seriously felt as though she'd stepped into a parallel universe—a secret side of Manhattan only the elite knew existed. 'I thought you meant some diner open all hours across the street.'

'Do I look like I hang out at diners?'

She laughed. 'No. More like a champagne or whisky bar.'

'So do you want crowds or space?' he asked.

'You prefer space.'

His lips twitched.

'You really don't like people?'

He hesitated. 'I don't like people watching me. I like privacy.'

She glanced around the lobby and realised everyone *was* watching him—the woman behind the reception desk, the man on the door. A couple seated at a table. They were discreet but observant all the same. They were surreptitiously staring at him with the kind of awed attentiveness reserved for the very elite—as if they were absolutely wowed, but also knew he was not approachable. Yeah, well, the 'resting grumpy' vibe ensured that.

Who *was* this guy? She didn't even know his name. She almost didn't want to. Maybe she'd be better off not knowing those details—it allowed another kind of honesty between them. She wouldn't be overwhelmed by his achievements or intimidated by his power.

Well, maybe she already was a little. But not enough to silence her.

'Then let's have privacy,' she said. 'This place is a hotel, not an apartment building,' she realised aloud as he led her to the lift.

He nodded and looked into a small screen and pushed the button at the top of the lift's electronics panel.

'Are you staying here?' she asked, a little confused. 'You said you live most of the time in Manhattan.'

'I live most of the time here.'

'In a hotel?'

'Yes.'

Her curiosity deepened. 'Because you work here?'

He shook his head. 'I work in the building beside your shop.'

That hotel and tourism company? She didn't want to tell him about the manager she'd met. She had the feeling this guy was more *senior* management than she was. 'You're really wealthy, aren't you?'

'Are you going to be nicer to me if I say yes?'

She shot him a scornful look. 'I'm not a gold-digger.'

'Never thought you were.' He suddenly laughed. 'I've met a few in my time and you don't come across that way.'

'Oh?' He'd met a few gold-diggers? Had they tried to trap him? She was unaccountably jealous. 'How do I come across?'

He sent her a long, considering look. 'I think you are infinitely more dangerous.'

She gaped at him for a second then shook her head. 'Rot. I'm the least threatening person you're ever likely to meet.'

His chuckle was soft. 'I strongly disagree.'

Her pulse lifted. She shouldn't feel empowered. The guy didn't even mean it. Yet her gaze was drawn to his. And his, while amused, was also serious and very, very intense. Those eyes of his were *such* seductive weapons— that blue, that patch of mystery. All he had to do was look at her. Was it his beauty that distracted her? No. It was the steely quality beneath. The assurance that oozed from him.

'Why?'

'I can walk away from other women.'

His words stole her breath. 'You can't walk away from me?'

'Apparently not.'

'Then I guess we're stuck here,' she murmured. 'Because I can't walk away from you either.' A husky, shy admission.

The lift door slid open and wordlessly he took her hand. A series of sizzling sparks shimmered up her arm. A rush of desire for more. He didn't say anything more, nor did she as he led her into the suite.

'I promised you pumpkin pie.'

'Isn't it too late to order from the hotel kitchen?' she asked.

He chuckled. 'You're in the city that never sleeps. Midnight might as well be midday.'

Except there was something more magical about midnight. The lights weren't on but the curtains weren't drawn, so the light from the city illuminated the space enough for her to see. And she'd never seen anything like this suite—the furnishings were muted but luxe and light glinted on crystal and silver finishing. Then she noticed a trolley by the plump sofa.

'The pie is already delivered?' she asked.

'Amazing service in this place.'

She shook her head at him. 'Were you certain I'd say yes?'

'If you didn't I'd be miserable, so then I'd comfort-eat all of it myself…'

A giggle bubbled from her. She sat down on the sofa and watched as he lifted the lids, then she simply stared at the sculpture on the plate. '*This* is pumpkin pie?'

'This is an award-winning pastry chef's spin on pumpkin pie, sure.'

It didn't look like *pie*. It was a gold-dusted orb with steam rising from a decorative dish below the plate. 'How do I go about eating it?'

'However you want.' He showed pure amusement.

She shot him a look and picked up the small silver fork. Slicing through the smooth, perfect exterior, she marvelled at the complex layers revealed. It was such a delicate *entremet*, it melted in the mouth. 'It's exquisite…it's…'

'Unforgettable?'

'Definitely that.'

He didn't use a fork. He just picked his up and ate it all in one big bite, his gaze on her the whole time.

'It's so smooth.' Violet's taste buds were so happy, she could barely mumble. 'I…don't have enough words to describe it.'

'Do you always talk so much you end up breathless?' he teased.

It wasn't the talking making her breathless, and from his amused expression he knew it.

'You weren't sorry to be working on Thanksgiving?' he asked.

'I don't have family here.' Her spine prickled with awareness of a predatory glint in his eyes. There was an edge that hadn't been there at Halloween when he'd walked away from her. But tonight the way he watched her made everything zing inside. 'You've been working today too.'

'Yes.'

'No big dinner, family event or thing to go to…?'

'No.'

'Alone again, then.'

'Not now.'

He watched her so intently, it made her feel as if he could see into her head. Which made her blush burn hotter, because the images scrolling through her mind were appallingly inappropriate. This second—right here, right now—was the most exciting of her life. And, yes, she knew that was a little tragic. But what did it matter? This was what she'd wanted, right? Adventure. A life a little more… *wild*.

Energised, her pulse raced as she met his gaze. They might've fallen silent but the communication didn't end. And those thoughts she was having—the crazy, indecent ones—he was having them too. She'd bet her life on it. But she was not having those regrets again. This time she was saying yes to everything. But not just saying yes— she would ask. Maybe even take.

'This is really…' She couldn't think of the word any more. Not when he watched her with such heat in his eyes. Eyes that had been so remote the first time she'd seen him.

She wanted everything. On her terms. And here— with a man she barely knew yet instinctively trusted— she wanted to release the truth. She felt oddly able to be honest with him.

'I've not done this before.' She breathed.

'Eaten pumpkin pie? Celebrated Thanksgiving? Gone back to a hotel room with a man?'

'All of the above.'

He stilled. 'Why now? Why with me?'

The suspicion in his eyes made her laugh. 'Have you looked in the mirror lately?'

'You're saying it's a superficial thing?'

'Pretty much. I'm having a shallow moment.' She nodded. 'You're…dazzling. And, honestly, I've been very sheltered. I haven't had the opportunity to do *any* of these things until now.'

'Why so sheltered?'

She paused. 'I come from a lovely family. They're the best. Loving parents. Four older brothers. But…'

'Four.' His lips curved.

'They're all alpha types too. Or they think they are. Brothers can be very over-protective.' She glanced at him and laughed. *'You'd* be an over-protective big brother.'

His smile froze. The chill was instant.

She bit her lip. 'I didn't mean to offend you.'

'You didn't. You're just wrong, that's all.' He drew a breath and his smile returned, but it was a little forced. 'Your brothers are all back in New Zealand, right? They're not going to burst down the door and lay into me for being alone with their baby sister?'

She shook her head with a smile. He was even bigger

than her brothers. He could hold his own. 'You're okay. They're all back home.'

'Why are they so protective? Is it just because you're the only girl?' His brow creased. 'Sounds like the old-fashioned double standard.'

'It's a little more than that.' She paused, debating. She'd wanted to escape the controls of her childhood, but at the same time she yearned to be able to be honest. And she was free to be so now, right? So, despite the risk, honesty won out.

'I was sick for a while. Cancer. But I'm all good now.' She braced herself. If he was scared off by that, then he wasn't the man she'd thought he was.

'When?'

'I was seventeen when first diagnosed. I had chemo. Radiation. All the things for a while.'

'That must have been tough.'

'We all get tough stuff to deal with.' She nodded jerkily and then forced a smile at him. 'Don't feel sorry for me. I'm fine now. But that's why lots of things are new.'

She didn't regret telling him. Complete honesty was liberating. Because she was sure there was something elemental in this connection. Something far deeper than *superficial*. And, as he gazed at her, the sharp scrutiny in his eyes slipped away to reveal sombreness...and suddenly her own emotions rose.

'I was orphaned at ten.' The bald sentence was roughened with huskiness. She was sure he didn't say that often. 'Don't feel sorry for me.'

She was certain he didn't say that often either. 'Okay.'

Orphaned at ten. No wonder there weren't any big Thanksgiving feasts. Did he have siblings? Aunts or uncles who'd taken him in? She didn't think so. Was that why he lived in a hotel suite most of the time? But he offered nothing more. Instead, they measured each other thoughtfully.

'You're not going to ask me anything more?' she eventually asked.

'You'll tell me if you want me to know anything else,' he said. 'You're not curious?'

'I'm crazy-curious but I'm trying to hide it.'

'Failing.' He grinned. 'So now you're on the other side of the world.'

'Living in the moment.' She nodded. 'Seizing the day and the opportunities each brings.'

'That's what this is, an opportunity?'

'Definitely.'

'For what?'

'An experience.'

He leaned forward. 'You don't even want to know my name?'

He was so strong. So much bigger than her. With his size and strength, he could crush her. But in that moment, when they'd fitted so close in the alcove of the building, the rest of the world and all its dangers had simply disappeared. He'd been strong but gentle. Maybe it was madness but she knew she was safe.

'Does it really matter?' she whispered. 'Will it make any difference to what happens?'

'None at all.'

An illicit thrill shivered through her. This was a risk, yet in her bones she knew it was okay. He wasn't just the protective sort. He'd once been broken too.

'Then, no. Don't tell me.'

CHAPTER THREE

ROMAN KNEW HE shouldn't have brought her here but, now that he had, the empty sensation he'd battled for days eased. He wanted to watch her. He wanted to listen to her rushed speech and see that delighted smile flash. He wanted to scoop her close. He should tell her his name, but he didn't want to. He should ask her what hers was, but he didn't want to do that either. He didn't want to muddy this intensity with details that didn't matter. Because she'd told him something deeply personal, something she didn't tell everyone—he'd seen the flash of vulnerability in her eyes.

And he? Since when had he ever talked to anyone about his past? He hadn't. Not even a little. Most people he met already knew—the 'tragic family past' of the supposedly 'eligible billionaire' was regularly rehashed in trashy socialite articles online. He loathed it. He didn't want pity. He certainly didn't appreciate people prying, as if they could somehow make it better. As if they could ever understand. He had everything but he'd lost everyone. He'd been in the accident that had killed his parents instantly, the one from which his baby sister had gone missing, never to be found. He'd been left alone. And nowadays alone was what he liked to be.

But not tonight. Not now.

This was a mercurial, magic moment. One that was not

going to last—things *never* lasted. And, besides, he wasn't going to seduce her. He was *not* going to seduce her. He was not going to…*stop her from seducing him*…which was apparently what was happening. Like a beautiful witch, she drew him closer until somehow she was only a breath away. But he was the one who'd moved.

'Is that okay?' She placed her palm on his jaw.

It was the sweetest whisper. Was she seeking his consent to her touch? Or to anonymity? What did it matter? It was always going to be yes.

Roman wasn't normally lost for words or moves to make. But for a split-second he was paralysed. He gazed into her eyes, taking a mental snapshot, struck by the irrevocable realisation that *this* was a moment he would always remember. He savoured the surprise and satisfaction flowing through him. But then she blinked and he saw a flicker of insecurity. He wasn't having *that*.

'Is it okay if I kiss you?' he countered gruffly.

Her gaze shot back to his and that gorgeous colour filled her face. 'Yes.'

'Yes' was the best word in the world.

He leaned closer, gently tasting the silken softness of her mouth. *This* was what he'd been craving all the days and nights since he'd first met her. What he'd wanted then and what he wanted even more now.

He felt a jolt of recognition. This burgeoning excitement had a deeper origin than pure lust. This was special. But he immediately shook off the fanciful thought. It was the jet lag. The delight in seeing her again. In holding her close this time. But he couldn't resist spending a long time just kissing her, delighting in the building heat of her response. It was perfection. Until it wasn't. Until he needed more. And, given she was breathless and stirring, so did she. He wrapped his arms around her and lifted her closer until she was sprawled across his lap. Her hair was mussed, her eyes gleamed and her mouth was deliciously full from the pressure of his.

'We should have done this sooner.' He growled.

'We're doing it now. Now is all that matters. Now is all there is.'

He lifted his gaze, seeking depth to her meaning, understanding.

'I'm leaving,' she added breathlessly. 'Train trip.'

'Train?'

'You don't like them?'

She didn't know his name, let alone know the train his grandfather had had built. So he teased. 'Stuck in a small compartment for days at a time?'

'You don't think the rhythm of the track would be soothing?' she murmured distractedly.

'Oh.' He smiled at her. 'You like a soothing rhythm?'

She flushed and there was another flash of sweet uncertainty in her face. He kissed it away. He kissed her and kissed her until she stirred restlessly again in his arms. He loved the way she couldn't stay still, that she couldn't resist arching towards his touch. He pushed the bodice of her dress down and drank in the view of her lace bra. Then he unhooked it, unapologetically determined to see her bared. She had perfect breasts. He cupped them, loving the way they spilled into his hands, the softest feminine treasure. He lifted her easily, repositioning her to face him and pulling her forward so she was explicitly astride him.

Her eyes widened and her mouth parted, and he couldn't resist a second longer. He teased each soft breast in his hands, then bent to taste her. The slide of his tongue elicited groans from her. Each deep, throaty moan of pleasure and need drove him wild. He teased her tight nipple between finger and thumb—a pinch, a release, a blast of heat as he then sucked her breast into his mouth. He repeated the treatment with her other nipple, feeling her arousal build with every caress, until even her groans faltered as her breathlessness increased. She was sensitive to this. *So* sensitive. So very nearly undone.

Violet writhed, unable to stop herself from moving in sheer pleasure. His strength was all about her, his scent, his size. She sighed restlessly, seeking more of the huge, hard ridge of his erection beneath her. There were too many layers between them. Even so, she squirmed on his lap—she was so close to release. And, facing him this way, her breasts were exposed to his hungry gaze, to the torment of his fingers, to the rough lash of his tongue. She was desperate for him to assuage the hot, wet ache between her legs, but right now her nipples were so tight and sensation was screaming along her veins, deep into her belly as he alternated between soft, gentle suction and tiny bites.

'Let go.' His words were low and slurred.

An invitation. An order. A plea. Who knew? It didn't matter. Her answer would be the same regardless of his intention. Because it was but a breath. A moment that would disappear if she didn't breathe back.

'Yes.' She arched, jutting her breasts further forward, pressing her nipples hard into his palms. His mouth then teased hers, his tongue a mere taste of the full possession she ached for. His hips rocked beneath her, giving just enough rhythm to rub where she was wet and aching, teasing her with the promise of so much more. Teasing her until she could take it no more. Paroxysms of pleasure shook her and she cried out as the ecstasy hit.

When she finally opened her eyes, he was so much closer. His eyes were darker, that amber patch startling in intensity. She felt his energy coiled about her.

'I'm taking you to bed.' He stood, easily lifting her with him.

She wrapped her legs around his waist. 'Yes.'

Moments later he placed her in the middle of a large mattress. The room was big and lush but she didn't care. She had eyes only for him. And he didn't leave her for a second. She trembled as he tugged her dress down and suddenly she was clad only in her panties. His gaze basically glowed—and somehow he heated her skin just by looking at her.

'You're sensitive,' he murmured. 'Very, very sensitive.' His fingertips skated up her thighs.

She couldn't stop staring at him and her mouth dried. She reached up and fumbled with the first button on his shirt. Fumbled so badly he stepped back and stripped himself for her. When he moved back close, she saw a massive scar on his upper thigh. The skin was horribly puckered from past trauma.

'You were hurt,' she muttered.

'A long time ago. It's not sore.'

She reached out before realising it might be too invasive. But they were beyond secrets, right? There was only truth. 'Do you have any sensation left or feel nothing?'

'Nothing,' he said quietly. 'It's just a mark.'

She didn't ask more. Medical histories were deeply personal. Instead she moved her hand higher. To see a big man like him racked by a shiver of need… His eyes were hungry, watching for her touch. Letting her lead. And she did, discovering an intensely luxurious deliciousness in making love to a near stranger. Yet he wasn't a stranger. Not now. There were things she now knew.

'You come off cold. But when I touch you   when you touch me—you're so *hot*,' she said.

'I thought it would be good but this…' He arched, his words morphing into a growl. 'I need to get protection.'

She'd known he would. He was that sort—not promiscuous necessarily, though maybe, but protective. He would ensure her safety, and of course his own. He was definitely the sort who would protect his own. Always.

She felt the heat in her core as excitement pooled there, even as she felt a qualm at the size of him as he rolled the condom down his length. He glanced up, catching her staring, slack-jawed, at the size of him. He grinned. 'Don't worry, I'll make sure you're ready.'

She flushed even more. Had he read her mind? And then he moved over her, nudging her legs that little bit further apart to make room for his powerful body.

'Sweetheart?' He drew back, suddenly frowning—that fallen angel again. 'When you said you'd not done this before…did you mean at *all*?'

Oh, hell—had it been that obvious? She shivered, cold and cross at the loss of contact and the humiliation of her inexperience. 'I already have too many over-protective people in my life. I don't need you trying to protect me too.'

His frown didn't lessen. 'Are you a *virgin*?'

Well, he didn't need to say it as though it was some disease. Emotionally charged, she couldn't help challenging him. 'What I am is a fully functional person who can make her own decisions. For herself.'

He silently glared at her.

'What does it matter whether I've slept with one or one hundred men before?' she added.

'But it's not one or one hundred. It's *none*.'

She winced. 'Can we not…?'

'Tell me your name,' he interrupted.

She glared back at him. 'How is that relevant?'

'My name is Roman. You should know the name of the

man you're giving your virginity to. And I want to know the name of the woman giving her innocence to me. It's my first time taking this from someone.'

Heat flooded her again and she felt that softening deep in her sex. 'So you're not going to stop?' Oh, it was a desperate whisper.

'Not unless you want me to.' He paused, still braced above her. 'So, if you don't want me to stop, tell me your name.'

'Violet.'

'Really?' He suddenly smiled. 'As in a small, pretty flower?'

'As in the colour of the bruise you're going to get if you keep patronising me.'

He laughed, then sobered. 'Are you *sure* about this?'

She felt a boldness flow through her. 'Do I feel sure?'

His jaw locked. 'You can change your mind any time. Okay?'

'I know that. But I'm not going to. Please.'

He kissed her and moved. Closer. So much closer. It was unbelievably intimate. She'd never imagined that she would feel this intimate with someone. As exposed or as vulnerable. He was barely breaching her body with his— only with the blunt head of his thick length, pressing ever so slightly in and back, again and again. It was so tantalising. So teasing. And she was increasingly hungry for more. Much more. And somehow she was searingly hot.

'Roman.' She was so glad she knew his name now. *'Please.'*

'I know,' he muttered through gritted teeth. 'I know... I know...'

'I need more.'

His grip tightened on her hips, stopping her rocking up and taking him deeper. 'Soon.'

'Now.'

His jaw locked even more tightly. 'It might hurt.'

'I'm ready. You know I am.'

His pupils blew and his grip dug. She drew a breath and a moment later he thrust hard—finally pushing his hot length all of the way inside her. He was so deep inside, so wide, and she cried out at the stinging, shocking sensation of literally being pinned by him.

He stilled, his gaze fierce and intent as sweat slicked his unbearably handsome face. 'Violet?'

'Yes,' she hissed as the flicker of pain subsided and pleasure spiked in its place.

She had him. Her hands were greedy—she palmed then pressed his butt, pushing him against her. Keeping him deep in place. She arched her neck, savouring the sensations smashing down on her. He rocked, still locked so deeply inside her. It was so intense. So good.

'Oh, my… Oh…' She couldn't speak, couldn't breathe. Just like that, she paused, already on the precipice.

'I like making you lose your words.' He growled. 'I like making you come. I'm going to make you come again. Again. And again.'

His thrusts literally punctuated his promise—deep and fierce. And it was so easy. So instant. So fantastic. She shuddered in his arms.

'Sweet Violet.'

But his words were strained and now another kind of pleasure rippled within her as she realised he was at her mercy in the way she'd been at his. To see someone so strong, shuddering uncontrollably because of her heat, her touch… And when she clenched her body hard on his…

'Violet.' His focus blurred and his voice strained.

'Harder,' she whispered a sultry command, instinctively

knowing it would make him lose control completely. 'Take me harder. Make me yours.'

Whatever post-orgasm hormones were called, they were raging. Violet had thought sex was supposed to make you sleepy, but instead she was wide, wide awake. She needed to get out of here and process everything that had just happened. And somehow she had to do this without making a fool of herself.

All the anxiety she'd not felt, all the uncertainty... Now it hit. *Hard.* She swallowed and slithered from the bed, wondering where her dress and panties had been flung.

'Where are you going?' A growl came from the tousled, handsome length of masculinity still panting in the middle of the bed.

'I should go, right?' Guiltily, she paused. 'I don't want this to be awkward.'

She didn't know what to do. Would he want her to stay? To leave right away? That had been so intense for her, she didn't know where to put herself.

'Has it been awkward at all already?' he asked.

'No.'

'Then why would it be now?'

'I don't know how one-night stands normally end. Or when. Or anything.'

He stilled. 'They normally end at the end of the night.'

She gazed at him warily. 'You want me to stay the night?'

He was the guy who avoided holidays and people, and who lived in a hotel suite where there was little that was personal. It was so far removed from her family home, filled with photos and papers and chaos.

He threw back the sheet and left the bed. She couldn't look at his body.

'Oh, Lord.' Embarrassment overcame her. 'I'm sorry about the stain on that lovely linen! I hope it's not marked for ever.'

Roman watched the fierce colour swarm her face and half-laughed, even as she devastated him with her candour. As for marked for ever? That was him. He was never going to forget this.

'Don't be embarrassed. Come on. Come with me.' He took her hand and led her towards the bathroom.

She was trembling. He wasn't surprised. Right now, his limbs felt wobbly too. That had been the most intense sexual encounter of his life. His every defence was gone. All that mattered to him now was ensuring her comfort, soothing her sensitive system down from the exquisite power of that experience.

But as he walked that keening hunger rose in his body. She was an enchantress and she was his. He could help her explore all the ways in which she could enjoy sex. He wanted to know all the ways—not because he would have stopped. *Nothing* would have stopped him once she'd said yes. He wanted to savour every second. He wanted to go slower still. He could go slow again now.

But she was still, watching him with big eyes. Her attention dropped to the arousal he had no way of hiding.

'You don't want this again?' he asked.

'Of *course* I do.'

There was no coy pretence. No flirtation. Just the sweetest honesty and a sigh of such delight. A thrill like no other. He closed his eyes as the purest pleasure rippled through him. He didn't want this to stop. He could do this again and again and again. He'd focus on making her shake so damned hard, she wouldn't refuse him again. He'd make it too good to say no to.

'Then stay longer,' he tempted. 'Don't retreat now.'

She'd been so brave. So open, vulnerable and honest.

'You know it's probably best I get out of here. The moment is over.'

But she was breathless, her focus was distracted and as he touched her her tone wavered.

'No, I think we could have a few more moments.'

She didn't argue. She shivered in his arms even as the hot water streamed over her.

'You should be more greedy,' he said.

She was like warm wax in his hands, leaning back against him as he gently caressed her with warm, soapy hands. He kissed her and stroked her and held her so she rested against him. There was such sweet comfort in supporting her soft body with his.

'It's—it's too good,' she whispered brokenly.

'Don't you think you deserve good?'

'I…do…' She paused. She sounded damned unsure. 'But more than this isn't what either of us want. Not yet, for me.'

And never for him. There was nothing he could say to that. It was true.

'We're from really different worlds,' she said. 'And I think ultimately we want different things from life.'

She was right. Her leaving would be for the best. There was no future in this, in anything. There was just now.

He reached for a towel, wrapped it around her and picked her up in his arms again. 'You're a romantic.'

'I'm an *optimist*,' she corrected with a small smile. 'Whereas you're an isolated grump.'

He carried her through to the spare bedroom. The first time the place had ever been used.

Ultimately, she did want permanence—as she should. And he was very determinedly not imagining her in the future with a husband, family and a laughing smile on her face as she excitedly chattered to them. He was *not* picturing that. He'd made a mistake in seducing her. He was making another mistake now by taking her again. But his hold was tight and his hands slid to places he ached to touch again. He couldn't resist.

'Please make it easy for me to leave,' she whispered even as she spread her legs to let him touch her. 'You've made everything else so perfect.'

'I'll make it easy for you,' he promised. 'Soon.'

She released a husky laugh. 'I can't stay, anyway. Tomorrow's my last day. I have a new job as a tour guide.'

'You're going to work Christmas?'

'Of course.'

'Good for you.'

Her eyes turned smoky. 'I'm not going to regret this. Not ever. And I'm never going to forget it either.'

His heart shattered. 'So let me show you one last thing before you leave.'

That sceptical look entered her eyes again. '*One* thing?'

Sensual amusement whistled through him. 'Maybe a couple of things.'

As she gazed up at him, her eyes widened and glazed. As his fingers stroked, her lips parted and she sighed. 'Okay.'

It was the hottest, sweetest surrender.

'*Yes.*'

CHAPTER FOUR

Five days before Christmas

'VIOLET? VIOLET!'

'Yes?' Violet looked up from where she'd been stowing ornate silver salt cellars into a specially built container. 'Frankie?'

The chief steward appeared in the compartment, looking utterly frazzled—a highly unusual state, given the guy was the master of efficient service.

'Can you dash to the Presidential Suite?' he asked. 'We have a VIP boarding and we have to get rid of the Christmas decorations in there immediately.'

'Get rid of the Christmas decorations?' Bemused, Violet stared at Frankie. Each private compartment had been decorated with the most stylish decorations she'd ever seen. 'Are we going to have a Grinch on board for Christmas Day?'

'Apparently.' Frankie chuckled. 'No tinsel allowed. Can you gather all the bits quickly? Colson's gone into overdrive.'

'Of course.' Violet bit her lip to stop her smile.

Colson managed the train service and was the most officious man Violet had met. As for tinsel, there was none of that. The offending decorations were vintage hand-made ornaments—blown glass, carved wood, moulded silver. Each of the private compartments had a set, suiting its unique geographically themed decor.

Servicing the Presidential Suite was way above her pay grade, so she was excited to get a chance to check it out for longer than the sneak peek she'd got during her training.

She was stationed in the dining and lounge car, plus she serviced a couple of the smaller compartments. All were unbelievably luxurious with gleaming brass, polished wood and lush furnishings. It was as if the train had time-travelled from the nineteen-twenties, but with modern conveniences added in. Slickly concealed panels hid touch screens which closed curtains, adjusted thermostats and placed orders direct to the prize-winning chefs working in the galley. One of only a few private trains in the States, this Christmas week it would be taking a slow, scenic route from east to west coasts through the beautiful central states, past the lakes and mountains of Illinois, Iowa and Colorado and eventually finishing in San Francisco.

Violet couldn't wait. She mightn't have all the qualifications her brothers had, but she worked hard, she liked people and she liked seeing people having a nice time. She wanted to *help* them have a nice time, and she was good at it. Plus, she got to see the sights herself, and no way would she ever have got on board this train otherwise. A one-way journey cost thousands and this Christmas run cost even more. It was like a polar express for adults with endless champagne fountains, high quality linen and fine dining, and only the financial elite had the bank balance even to consider such a thing. This transported people for whom time was a limitless luxury and where the destination didn't really matter—the slow serenity of the trip was the whole point. Passengers on this train had no need to get to the next place as quickly as possible. This was about stepping back to a gilded age of splendour and sumptuousness.

But behind the serene scenes it was busy. While the wealthy sat sampling delicious *petits fours* at leisure, the trio of chefs in the galley worked in sync. The stewards had to achieve everything immediately in a tiny space and with a genuine smile. Since her training, Violet had done a two-day run with guests on board as part of a charity deal and she'd loved every second. She was living in the moment and refusing to remember the night to end all nights again and *again*.

Except she did. All the time.

As she walked the length of the train, she reminded herself once more it was good she'd left Manhattan so quickly, otherwise she'd have been tempted to return to that hotel and ask for the guest named Roman who resided in the penthouse suite. That would've been a bad idea. They were from different worlds and wanted different things. So it was *really* good she was about to help others enjoy their trip of a lifetime. Even for those used to luxury, this would still be an amazing adventure. She'd memorised the list of passengers and knew there were celebratory events aside from Christmas—a birthday and an anniversary. But, while some wanted to celebrate, others demanded discretion, and of course not everyone celebrated Christmas, hence the required removal of the ornaments.

She smoothly slid open the wooden carriage door. She drew a breath as she stepped into the antechamber and picked up the first carved ornament hanging from a gleaming hook. This was next-level luxury, created for sultans, princes and, yes, presidents. The textured wallpaper was gold but not ostentatious. The space was sleek and sumptuous and there were cleverly hidden recesses to maximise what was limited space. But when she walked in to the main compartment it was already occupied. A tall man stood at the desk with his back to her.

Shoulders back. Smile in place. Speak slowly. Her training whizzed through her brain. 'Oh, excuse me, I do apologise…'

The man turned and her jaw dropped. All her training left her.

Roman?

'What are *you* doing here?' She stared, full of accusation. She forgot entirely that he was apparently a paying customer and she was here to *serve*.

His perma-frown deepened but the impact on his devastating looks was negligible. His black tee-shirt and black jeans were too casual an outfit for a guest, yet she knew with utter conviction that he belonged here. He emanated not just control, but power. And that tee-shirt was pure distraction. The way it hugged his muscles, the ones she'd sprawled over a few weeks ago… Her mouth dried and her body heated as, with appalling timing, her brain went AWOL and she remembered just how big and powerful he'd felt beneath her. And then above her. And then…

It was a good thing the ornament she held was wooden, not glass. It would have shattered by now from the way she gripped it.

'You shouldn't be here,' she muttered desperately. 'You really shouldn't.'

He didn't reply. He just stared. His gaze travelled over her uniform, making her uncomfortably aware of the collared white blouse and the royal-blue knee-length skirt that sat just a little snugly over her bottom. Not to mention the ugly black shoes with the non-slip tread and no high heel that made her feel even shorter beside him.

'Passengers aren't scheduled to arrive for another forty minutes,' she added. 'You are a passenger, right?'

His frown didn't ease, rather the edges of his jaw tightened as he strolled towards her. It wasn't just awkward—it was *frigid*.

'You can't be my steward for this journey,' he said grimly.

The rejection stung. 'I'm not assigned to this carriage.' She mustered dignity. 'I've only come to clear the Christmas decorations.'

But she put the ornament down on the nearest surface, deciding he could put them out of sight himself. What was he doing here? Was he really a passenger? 'I thought you planned to work through Christmas.'

'I am.'

She couldn't stop herself from looking into his eyes, fascinated once more by the brilliant blue and that singular patch of topaz…

'Violet?' Frankie's voice summoned her.

Never had she been so thankful for an interruption. 'Excuse me please.'

She turned and fled, aware he'd stepped forward to stop her. But she didn't let him. She just ran.

Frankie met her halfway along the corridor of the preceding carriage. His eyebrows lifted at her breathlessness. 'You okay?'

'Um… Fine.' Violet dragged in much needed air. 'What do you need? I haven't had a chance to—'

'We've been called in for random drug-testing. They do it every so often. This time it's because the boss is boarding, and Colson's switched into ultra-efficient manager mode—which basically means he's panicking.'

'The boss?'

'Of the whole company.' Frankie gestured for her to follow. 'Come on, we have to get this done now or the departure will be delayed.'

Violet didn't have time to dwell on the total disaster that was the fact that her fallen angel had just landed on her train. She followed Frankie to the employee office inside the station. Colson shoved pages still warm from the printer into their hands.

'It's in your contract, but here's the permission form,' he said. 'We double opt-in every time. Standard health and safety protocol. No drugs that can impair performance or other conditions that might cause safety issues.'

Frankie sighed. 'So much admin.'

Violet skimmed the form, signed her name and handed it back. Poor Colson was really living on his nerves. She flashed a reassuring smile at him before joining the queue at the bathroom. It was somewhat embarrassing to take the small plastic container to a medic waiting in the office with a selection of dipsticks assembled on the table in front of him.

'What a job,' Frankie murmured in an amused tone as they returned to the train.

Violet wasn't concerned about the test. She hadn't touched alcohol in the last few weeks. The price of cocktails in Manhattan was prohibitive, and she was flat broke. She'd even had to dip into her return-trip fund, which was why a job that included bed and food was perfect. But now Roman was on board. And that was too awkward.

'I'll sort those Christmas decorations,' Frankie said. 'You get back to the dining car.'

'Sure.' She was so relieved not to have to return to his compartment.

Ten minutes later, she pointlessly wiped the already gleaming silver handles and tried to rationalise it. She could avoid him, right? She wasn't working at that ultra-elite end. But the train wasn't huge. There were only ten carriages in total.

'Violet?' Colson came up behind her.

'Sir? Is there something you…?' She frowned. The poor guy was sweating even more than before.

'Look…ah…you can't come on the journey.' He sighed, a gust of pure stress. 'I don't know where I'm going to…but you can't stay on board for this trip. It's against the rules.'

'What rules?' Violet was shocked. 'Why not?' What had she done wrong?

He ran a hand under his collar. 'Your test—'

'Should have been fine.'

'Showed you're pregnant.'

Their simultaneous statements clashed but she still heard what he'd said.

Pregnant?

'That's not possible.' Violet broke the sudden silence. 'The medic must have mixed up the samples.'

'He repeated the test.' Colson couldn't hold her gaze.

'It *can't* be right.'

'We need to offload your gear—'

'What's the problem?' Another voice interrupted. An authoritative, arrogant voice.

Violet wanted to disappear. Why was Roman in the dining car? Why was he here at all—and listening in? She glared at him. It was easier to get angry than absorb what Colson had said. She wasn't having Roman involved in this mix-up. That was all it was—a mix up.

'Mr Fraser.' Colson went from shocked to terrified. 'Nothing that need concern you, sir.' He pressed his lips together.

Roman looked from Colson to Violet. His gaze narrowed and he stepped forward. 'I would like to understand the problem.'

Violet stared, thrown by the double whammy of discoveries. Mr *Fraser*? Fraser, as in Fraser Holdings, the logo of which was on the paperwork she'd signed only minutes earlier?

Frankie's words came back to her: *the boss is boarding.* Surely not? But Colson's reaction… If it was true, it meant technically he was *her* boss. And she'd had *no* idea.

Meanwhile Colson had no trouble throwing her under the bus. 'Ms Summers hasn't passed our final health and safety check.'

'Your final health and safety check is wrong,' she muttered.

'That means she'll disembark immediately,' Colson added, ignoring her.

'Leaving you a crew member short for this journey?' Roman queried.

Violet glanced at him but his mood was impossible to determine. He had his frozen face on.

'We have contingency plans. But we cannot have someone on board who—'

'It's *not* possible,' Violet gruffly interrupted and glared at Colson. If he dared disclose that result to anyone!

Colson swallowed, nervously shooting a glance between her and Roman. 'This needn't concern you, Mr Fraser. The test is an operational matter. Violet, let's go into the station office and sort it out privately.'

'Would you like to retake the test?' Roman asked as if Colson hadn't spoken.

One tiny bit of her brain had been assimilating the result, denying its plausibility. It *wasn't* possible. Except for the fact that it *was*. And the reason it was possible was standing three feet away, staring at her with sombre judgment in his eyes. So, no, right now she did *not* want to retake the test.

Because what if it was right? *Could* it be? That tiny bit of brain panicked. She didn't yet know whether her cancer treatment had impacted on her ability to get pregnant. That wasn't something she'd thought she'd have to explore for a while. She was supposed to be travelling, all carefree adventure...

But a huge amount of unexpected hope suddenly hit, and belief followed. Maybe it was intuition or an innate awareness but, now the prospect had been raised, *was* it possible? Or was it simply wishful thinking because the possibility of a fertility struggle had been something she'd buried?

As the thoughts occurred to her too slowly, too confusedly, there was suddenly an image in her mind that shouldn't be there: an adorable cherub, a dumpling delight of an infant. A boy with blue eyes with a singular brown patch, with unruly dark hair and a devilishly charming smile. It melted her heart and broke it all at the same time. She couldn't let that thought in. She just couldn't.

Stricken, she stared at Roman.

'Would you give us a moment?' Roman said firmly to Colson, but his gaze on Violet was unwavering.

'Sir?'

'Violet and I are acquainted. I'll handle this.' He offered no other explanation.

Violet turned in time to see Colson's eyes all but pop out of his head.

'Of course.' He couldn't get out quickly enough.

'I suggest you enact those contingency plans,' Roman called as the manager headed out of the carriage. 'She will not be working this trip.'

Violet gaped. Was he going to throw her off the train? That meant she had no place to go. Manhattan had run her travel fund down to dire levels. Her parents had warned her that she hadn't saved enough when they'd wanted to stop her travelling. They'd been right. And now?

She glared at Roman.

He gazed back watchfully. 'Drugs, Violet?'

'Not drugs.' Her voice came out horribly husky.

He didn't respond. He didn't help her out at all. He just waited.

'Apparently they also test for…for…' She couldn't actually utter the word.

He still stared at her. Waiting.

'You don't even *know*?' Scared, she let anger rage. 'It's your company and you don't even know all the things they test for?'

'Crew compliance is an operational issue,' he said. 'So if it's not drugs…?'

'Pregnancy.'

His eyes widened. 'What?'

She couldn't cope with talking about it. Not yet. She needed confirmation of other things. She needed time to think about what the heck she was going to do. 'Why did Colson leave when you asked him to? Are you his boss? Why are you even *here*?'

'You're *pregnant*?'

Her throat tightened and then she couldn't speak at all.

He ran his hand through his hair and suddenly stepped closer. 'You're pregnant with *my* baby.'

His savage certainty shouldn't have made her shiver but shiver she did, a trembling, head-to-toe shudder in response to the raw possessiveness in his tone.

She twisted her fingers, trying to hold it together. 'It can't be right.'

'You didn't know?'

'Of course not.' She threw him a shocked look. 'Not until just now.'

'We'll need to find out for sure,' he snapped.

'And I will.' *She* needed to get away from him. She

needed space and time to think. But how was she going to get that? Her anger sparked back. 'Meanwhile, it shouldn't stop me from working.'

She could think while working. When doing mundane, repetitive tasks, she'd be able to process this slowly and somewhat privately. She wouldn't spiral into a full-blown panic, which frankly Roman's presence only aggravated.

'You're on a moving train with movable parts. There's a higher risk of falls and injury,' he said coldly. 'Besides which, it was in the contract you signed.'

The fine print she hadn't read closely enough. 'So you terminate the employment of any pregnant employee?' She flared angrily.

'Of course not. Pregnant employees are assigned to other duties for the duration of their pregnancy,' he said. 'No one should ever feel the need to hide their status from us. We also have a period of paid parental leave. We're a leading employer on that issue.'

'Oh, wow, ten points to you,' she muttered. 'But what about short-term contract workers?'

He hesitated.

Yeah. She wasn't a permanent employee. She'd been hired only for this month. Temporary cover. Only because she'd met that manager and they'd got talking. 'How do you expect them to get another steward in such a short time? They were short as it was. That's why they hired me.'

'I'm sure Colson is capable of working it out.'

But *she* really had nowhere else to go and not enough funds to generate options. Plus, she'd *wanted* to go on this journey. She'd wanted to experience—even in a back-room way—the luxury of the train and see the majestic views of this vast country...

And then there were the ramifications of the result that

she couldn't bear to think about just yet. *Pregnant?* That image of a cherubic infant swam before her eyes.

'Sit down,' Roman said sharply.

'No.' But the ground beneath her feet had turned to jelly.

She heard a feral mutter and next minute she wasn't just swaying, she was being swung in the air, and then the world went black.

It took a few moments for her to realise the blackness was because her face was pressed to his broad, black-tee-shirt-covered chest. His arms were strong and he was carrying her as if she were weightless. He marched along the corridor, shoving the doors back with more force than necessary. Illicit delight surged. She tried to deny it—and him.

'I can walk,' she said. 'Put me down.'

'I don't feel like it,' he growled.

'You can't just do whatever you feel like doing.'

'Watch me.'

He carried her all the way back to the carriage she'd entered less than half an hour ago.

'You're really staying in the Presidential Suite?'

'Of course. I'm the president of the company.' The door closed behind him.

But he still didn't put her down. He took five more paces and sat on the sofa, keeping her in his arms, so now she was across his lap, his hold was still strong and she hadn't the resistance to push away from him. Heaven help her, she felt safe. And she felt...

'You can't be the boss of this,' she snapped, sucking back her concentration. 'You can't own all of this.'

'Why not?'

'You're too young.'

He gazed at her intently. 'You really didn't recognise my name that night?'

'Why would I?'

'You were working in a store right next door to Fraser Holdings. You know, the really big building? You didn't work it out?'

'You only told me your first name. And I…wasn't in any state to make connections at that moment.'

His mouth quirked ever so slightly. 'I live in a hotel that I own. Around the corner from another building that I own. In Manhattan. How many random guys do you meet in New York who can afford to live in a hotel like that?'

'I don't know. It's New York. Aren't there billionaires on every corner?'

He stared at her. 'Seriously?'

'Of course not seriously! Honestly, it's beyond the realms of possibility in my world. It never even occurred to me that would be your…situation. It's not *normal*.'

He stared at her for another moment and she felt his muscles tense.

'How did you get this job?' he asked. 'Did you know who I am all along? Have you just been playing me?'

'What? No!' She was outraged but his grip on her tightened. 'I had no idea who you were. You never told me you worked in that building until I was at the hotel and I already had this job by then.'

'How did you get it—this job?'

'I met a manager who worked in your building. Only I never knew it was *your* building. I never knew your name until…' She breathed hard and made herself say it. 'Until you told me when you had me naked and beneath you in your bed.'

Emotion flared in his eyes at the reminder. The rigidity of his body beneath her wasn't something she could consider but her body responded regardless, melting against his even as she argued with him. Deep within she ached for even greater closeness—for the clothes to vanish. It was appalling—especially considering he was now accusing her of…of…she didn't even know what, exactly. But it wasn't nice.

Breathless, she talked even more quickly than normal. 'She was a regular and we got talking. Her name's Sasha. She's lovely. She asked about my past. She suggested I apply. And I got the job. On my own merit, I believe. Not because I slept with you.' She glared at him. 'Unless *you* knew about this position and *you* engineered the whole thing. Maybe *you* made Sasha talk to me and offer me the job. Maybe you orchestrated my being here.'

His mouth compressed. 'I would never use my position to influence someone's employment status. Why would I?'

'So you could…could…'

'Seduce you again?' he said silkily.

'Yeah.'

'We both know I could have seduced you again in seconds if I'd set my mind to it,' he whispered fiercely. 'Instead I respected your decision to end it that night. The idea that I set *this* up isn't just far-fetched, it's ridiculous.'

'Right. Just as ridiculous as the idea that I'd get this job here purely to get closer to you.'

They couldn't get much closer than they were now. And now they were *both* breathing hard.

'No one even knew you were coming on this damn train,' she snarled.

Grudging respect dawned in his eyes but still he didn't let her go. Still she didn't try to move. There was something paradoxically comforting about being this close to him. It was just like that moment at Halloween when they'd stood locked together far beyond the duration of any outward danger. They'd stayed close because it had felt good, *too* good to deny.

'You really know nothing about Fraser Holdings?' he eventually asked. 'About the family?'

'What is there to know?' she asked acidly. 'Is there some terrible curse or something?'

A shadow darkened his eyes before he blinked. 'So you don't know anything about me.'

'Well, I know you're awfully fond of demonstrating your brute strength.'

His lips twisted. 'You don't want to know more?'

She hesitated. 'I already do. Your job tells me much more.'

'Such as?'

'You're the boss. You're a billionaire. Which means you're used to getting what you want.'

'Life doesn't work that way, not even for stupidly wealthy people.'

She regarded him sceptically. 'But I bet you're used to everyone saying yes to your every whim.'

'Should I pay you, then? Treat you like one of my employees?'

'Of course not. I can't be bought. I won't let this baby be bought either.'

'What makes you think we're going to be in opposition regarding the child's future?' he asked softly. 'Maybe we'll want the same things for her.'

Her? Was he thinking of a daughter? She'd thought of a son. A mini-Roman. Holder of her heart. Breaker of it.

Violet's brain could move lightning-quickly sometimes and now it was fast off on a fantasy. She had visions of a toddler already, a youth…smiles and laughter. She wanted it with such sudden ferocity, she didn't recognise herself. Equally suddenly, she was so, so afraid of losing it. This might be her one—and only—chance. She had to fight.

For her freedom, for her control. She'd waited so long for both those things already.

'We don't even know for sure that I am pregnant,' she said.

'Not sure you can get false positives.'

'It shouldn't be possible,' she muttered. 'You used protection. I saw you.'

'I know. I'm sorry. I don't know why—'

'And even if you hadn't I…' she interrupted, and then took a deep breath. 'I'm not sure about my fertility. I don't know if the treatment…'

He shook her gently in his arms. 'We'll get you seen by the best doctors. That's one thing I won't compromise on.'

'You don't need to—'

'To what?'

Wrong move. She heard the ice in his question and glanced at him warily. She saw a glimpse of ruthlessness. She paused. She didn't want to fight with him.

But she already knew what she wanted to do. She had no idea how she was going to make this work but she was having this baby and she didn't want him—or anyone—taking over *her* life. She could manage this.

'It's a miracle,' she said quietly. 'I'm keeping it.' Suddenly she couldn't look at him. 'You don't have to…'

'To what?' He said it quietly again. Too quietly.

'I don't want anything from you.' She breathed. 'I don't expect anything from you.'

'Too bad, you're going to get it. Furthermore, I expect things from you too.'

She glanced back up and saw something flicker in his eyes. *Not that.* He did *not* mean that. How could she be confronted by life-changing news yet be so easily distracted by thoughts of kissing him? But he was so close—he was literally surrounding her. His arms were like a cocoon and it would take nothing for her to tilt her chin, press her mouth to his and feel that heady pleasure again.

'My baby too,' he said softly, his all but magical eyes boring into hers. 'My decisions too.'

She swallowed, thinking through her options. She could go home. Only, she didn't even have the air fare for that and she didn't want to ask her parents for help. To go home less than six months into her big adventure and pregnant to boot? While her parents would welcome her, they would want to take care of her, give her such *cosseting* care. Over-protectiveness would become smothering and make her feel as if she couldn't manage on her own...

And maybe she couldn't. Turned out she couldn't have a one-night stand without messing that up. But Roman was over-protective too, bossy and authoritative. He was going to take over. She couldn't let that happen. She needed to breathe. She needed her space.

'I need to go.' She wriggled on his lap.

'You're not going anywhere. Not without me.' Roman didn't want to release her. Now he had her in his arms again, it was the only thing that felt right. Holding her was the only thing soothing the unruly emotion flaring inside right now—and the way she was moving against him... His arms tightened all on their own. And she stilled, staring up at him with her beautiful eyes.

He'd not realised how angry he was. And now that anger was pushing at the walls of his self-control. He wanted to kiss her. Kiss her long, slowly, hard and deeply—until the only word that she could breathe was *yes*. He'd been shocked to see her, and even more shocking had been how much of a turn-on that uniform was. He wanted to carry her to the bed and sate his pent-up desire like some cave-man not even bothering to get consent.

Not going to happen.

She'd run about two seconds after first seeing him here on the train. Then he'd watched from the window, observing the flurry of activity outside the office. He'd had to find out what was going on, and thank goodness he had.

Pregnant.

She was pregnant with his child. He raged against the idea but at the same time he felt possessiveness like nothing he'd ever known. The knife-like need to draw her close and keep her by his side shocked him. He breathed, determined to work this through rationally. People had children all the time, there was no need to feel this instant terror.

But most people didn't have the assets he had. This child would be the heir to a fortune. This child would be a target. So would Violet. Roman knew all about fortune-hunters and fraudsters. He knew first-hand the lengths people could go to deceive if they thought there was serious money in it. They didn't just lie, they did almost anything—like the woman who'd disguised her daughter to trick him into thinking she was his lost sister. She'd gone to such insane lengths...

He took another slow breath and pushed away the memory. First up, he had to ensure the baby was even his. His immediate reaction had been to claim it, and even now his gut instinct curdled at the thought the child might *not* be his. But his instincts couldn't be trusted.

Evidence was essential—again, something he'd learned through bitter experience. In his search for Eloise—in the desperate depths of his determination to find her—he'd been fooled almost completely. He'd been blind because it was what he'd wanted more than anything. He'd had such hope. Such futile, stupid, naïve hope.

And part of him deep inside wanted this to be true with Violet now. To believe her baby was his. In his bones, he did. But she was right. He'd used protection. He was always careful. So it shouldn't have happened. He had to be *certain* of everything. It wasn't that he couldn't trust her, he couldn't trust himself. He'd been so wrong before. It wasn't happening this time.

But he also knew about loss and he was never going to have anything of his taken away again. Nor any*one*. That was the overriding instinct now. The old wound ripped open and deep inside his chest the ache seeped, leaking acidic guilt. He never should have taken Violet back to the hotel that night. Once again, he'd failed someone innocent with his selfish desires. He'd let her down.

The uncertainty in her eyes—the very real distress when she'd mentioned her treatment—deepened his guilt. Violet needed care. He would ensure she got it. This *was* all on him. But there were only a few short days until Christmas and many people were already on holiday. He'd liaise via phone and learn what information he could. This train provided the perfect place for them to finalise a personal plan. There was no one to interrupt them, no press, only absolute privacy.

Good. Because he couldn't fail again. Not himself. Not her. Certainly, never their child.

'Stay on board with me,' he said huskily.

Her faced turned pink, then pale. She wriggled to get off his lap and this time he let her go.

'I'm not sleeping with you.' She walked away from him.

A fireball burst in his belly at the challenge she'd just thrown. He'd felt her breathing. He'd seen the stark hunger in her eyes only moments ago. It was no surprise *this* was the first thing she'd thought of. And it brought him immense pleasure that it was top of the mind for her. It was for him too.

But he drew breath and replied coolly, 'Have I asked you to?'

'I can't stay in the staff compartment now, not now they'll all know that test result. And the other guest compartments are full.'

He tensed, realising she was right about the remainder of the train staff knowing. He'd need to deal with that. 'As I said, you're going to stay on board with *me*.'

'In this compartment?' Her eyes widened. 'Haven't you noticed there's only *one* bed?'

'You're not that big and that bed is fairly large,' he said lightly. 'I'm confident we can manage.'

But her eyes were telling him the opposite. The rise of colour in her cheeks added emphasis. She was remembering moments of their night together. So was he.

'I don't…'

'What are you going to do, run away?' he asked. 'What's the point? I'll only follow. We need to face this together, so why not work it through here and now? You have all your things with you for the journey. So do I. It is the simplest solution for us to stay here.'

'It's embarrassing. I was supposed to work with those people.'

She was concerned about what others thought of her, about them knowing her condition. Roman didn't give a damn about what anyone thought of him but his status meant there'd be a hell of a lot of speculation about her and this situation. Which meant he needed to act to protect her—physically and emotionally.

'You don't have to leave this compartment at all if you don't want to,' he said. 'We'll have all our meals delivered. That was my intention anyway.'

'You were going to *hide* on board for Christmas?' She stared at him.

He wasn't hiding. It was practical. Privacy was one of the greatest pleasures and not always easily achieved.

'You don't want to mix with other passengers?' she added.

'The other passengers won't even be aware I'm on board. That is why I am here so early now.'

She gaped.

He shrugged. 'I have reports to write.'

'You're writing reports for Christmas.'

She made it sound like the saddest thing in the world, when it really wasn't.

'It's a good opportunity to get quiet time when everyone else is on holiday. There are no interruptions and I can focus.' He looked at her and pointed out the obvious. 'You were planning on working too.'

'Because it's a way of seeing more of the world. Because it's different. It's not what I do every year. Do you work every Christmas?'

He didn't understand her point. This really was the least of their problems.

'You hate it,' she said slowly. 'The people. The celebrations. Is that why you wanted rid of all the Christmas decorations?'

He realised she really didn't know much about him. Not his past—the accident that had destroyed everything. Right now, he didn't have the equilibrium within to enlighten her. 'I needed the space for my work.' He passed it off glibly. 'I've a bunch of files with me.'

'So you've got plenty to occupy *you*. What do you expect me to do while I'm stuck in here all day?'

Violet paced around the compartment. As luxurious as it was, it was too small to be in with *him*. Although, to be fair, a full-sized athletics arena would also be too small to be alone in with him. The man wasn't just magnetic, he rearranged her insides—melting her muscles, scrambling her brain. He was her personal kryptonite.

He leaned back in the sofa, watching her with an increasingly wicked smile. 'You can keep the uniform on if you want. I don't mind.'

'You want me as your attendant?' She shot him a look. 'Like a hand maiden?'

'Pouring my champagne and turning down my sheets…'

'Not happening.' Except she was wrought with temptation, such temptation.

'That's probably for the best.' His smile faded. 'You know I wouldn't have stepped on board had I known you were working this service.'

Wouldn't he? He didn't want to bother her. That shouldn't hurt, yet somehow it did. What had he been doing these last few weeks? Had he seen someone else since her? She had no right to know, let alone be jealous. But she was. And she was very glad he was travelling alone here. It would have been horrendous if he'd had a woman with him.

'But it's a good thing I did or I might not have…' He trailed off. His frown fully returned.

'I would have told you,' she said, but his frown didn't lighten. 'You think I would have kept it secret from you or something?'

He didn't acknowledge her words.

Her legs felt empty. She sat in the arm chair opposite to his sofa. 'Don't you trust people?'

'I'm always cautious of the reasons why people seek my company.'

She blinked. He couldn't be serious. 'Well, you are insanely good-looking, and people like looking at pretty things. Plus, you're wealthier than pretty much anyone else on the planet.'

'Superficial things, Violet.'

'No, you fool.' She shook her head. 'Maybe people seek your company because you're a nice guy.'

'I thought I had a "resting grump face".'

'Sometimes, sure. But actions trump everything. Even looks and money.'

'Actions?'

She drew a breath. 'You were nice to me.'

'Because I gave you multiple—'

'No.' She flushed. 'Not that. You were nice to me at Halloween. Even when you didn't want to be. You helped me escape the zombie crush.'

'Because I *wanted* you. It was entirely self-serving.'

'Are you trying to tell me that beneath that charming, frowning facade you're a total jerk?' She shook her head. 'I don't believe you for a second. I was vulnerable and you were a gentleman. And, anyway, that first night you walked away, so you didn't even want me all that much.'

His mouth dropped. 'I didn't *what*?'

'You let me go without so much as—'

'Just because I didn't assault you doesn't make me a nice guy.' He pinched his nose and muttered an oath.

'Well, it's a start, isn't it?' With a chuckle, she shook her head. 'You tried to warn me off that night too. Why? What's so bad about you?'

'What's bad?' He dropped his hands and fixed her with a firm glare. 'Be warned, Violet. I won't stop until I get what I want. I've experienced the worst failure imaginable and I'm *never* putting myself in that position again.'

'That doesn't sound bad, that sounds determined.' She looked at him, feeling both cautious and curious. Curiosity won. 'What was the failure?'

She was sure it wasn't money he was talking about. Nothing to do with the business. This was something deeply entrenched and far more emotive—more raw than something simply material. This was something that had wounded his soul.

But he'd stilled, that flare of emotion subsiding as swiftly as it had risen.

'It's irrelevant to this,' he said. 'But you can be sure I won't fail again. Not you. Not our child. That's why we're getting married as soon as it can be arranged.'

CHAPTER FIVE

'WE'RE NOT GETTING MARRIED.' A fierce kick of rejection made Violet speak immediately.

That was what he wanted? Why on earth would he want that?

'Sure we are. It's the only sensible thing to do.'

'Sensible?'

'You're not an American citizen. You're here on what— some sort of temporary visa?'

She fell silent.

'Doubtless you could get sent out of the country awfully easily,' he added. 'I can't have my child—'

'Don't…' she breathed. She couldn't cope with the 'child' concept being uttered aloud yet.

'Plus, how are your family going to react?' he pivoted with remorseless precision. 'Surely those brothers of yours wouldn't want their baby sister left pregnant and alone? Won't they fully support my plan? And your parents— they'd want me to do the right thing, wouldn't they?'

'Don't use my family to persuade me. You don't even know them.'

'That's true. So you tell me what *they* would want you to do.'

They'd be impressed that he wanted to 'do the right thing', and he was the ultimate 'marry well' groom. But they also wouldn't want her to marry him if she really didn't want to. They'd always try to protect her from anything tough but they believed their way was the only way. And that was the problem. 'Go home to them,' she said. 'Right away. And they'll take care of everything. Of me. And my baby.'

'*Our* baby.'

'Doesn't matter. They'd do anything to help me.'

He paused. His gaze narrowed. 'But you don't *want* their help. Or mine.' He inhaled sharply. 'What happened to make you so determined to have your independence?' His jaw tensed. 'Were your parents more than over-protective? Did they keep you on such a short leash…?' His focus zeroed in on her. 'Your inexperience stretches beyond the sexual.'

So what if it did? She was not discussing any of that with him. Nor was it the time to revisit the claustrophobic upbringing that had constrained her so much.

'Yet you care greatly what others think of you,' he added.

Heat flamed her face. Of course she cared about what her family thought, what anyone thought. What had happened between them was supposed to have been her own secret. But to have had a one-night stand and fallen pregnant, after all the warnings her family had issued…?

'Are you ashamed of consorting with me, angel?' Roman asked. 'Am I not the kind of man a woman like you marries?'

The ridiculousness of that statement made her shake her head. He was the ultimate catch—a supremely successful businessman, gorgeous to boot. Who *wouldn't* want to marry him?

Well, Violet, actually. She didn't want to marry anyone.

She wanted her freedom. She'd waited a long time for it. She wanted adventures and independence.

Roman might be amazing, but he'd also be super-bossy, and for her protectiveness had always been a kind of imprisonment. Besides that, there was the small fact that she barely knew him. And the other small fact that she wasn't in love with him. In lust—absolutely. But love?

Her heart smote and her lungs tightened. Happily ever after—the thought of being together with Roman *for ever*... She shivered, sinking inside. She'd deliberately made plans only for travel experiences, for adventure, because she hadn't dared dream too *far* into the future. She'd not been able to bear the hope she might meet someone, want them always and that her body—her health—would let her have that. Have it all.

'We don't need to decide *anything* yet,' she said quietly. 'We don't even know if...'

He frowned. 'If...?'

Her heart pounded. 'If it's even real. If it's even going to...' A rush of fear swamped her.

Motherhood wasn't something she'd allowed herself to consider. At the time of her cancer treatment, her doctors had encouraged her to check in with them when she was thinking about starting a family. She knew it might not be easy for her to conceive—if at all. But apparently she'd conceived *his* baby. Handsome, intelligent, suave Roman Fraser, who would also be far *too* easy to fall in love with.

'It's ages before the baby is due.' She determinedly pushed on from the topics that frankly terrified her. 'So we have plenty of time to work things out. A shotgun marriage is so last century. Let's get our immediate problems sorted.'

'Yes. Let's,' he mocked as he pulled his phone from his

pocket and tapped the screen. 'I need you and the head steward in my compartment immediately.'

In less than two minutes, Colson appeared, flanked by Frankie, who immediately shot Violet the serious side-eye of concern.

'I wanted to inform you both that Violet will be remaining on the train as my guest here in my compartment. If you could bring her belongings from the staff quarters, we would appreciate it.'

Colson's eyes bugged. Frankie's jaw dropped. Violet wanted to sink into the floor.

But apparently Roman knew no shame. 'I know you're aware of Violet's condition and by now you'll have connected the dots. Obviously, we would appreciate our privacy. If your discretion is assured, there'll be a sizeable bonus for both you and the rest of the train's staff at the end of the journey. However, if this leaks, then there'll be consequences.' He nodded dismissively.

He was *buying* their silence! Violet didn't know whether to be outraged or impressed.

'Of course, sir. We completely understand, and you can rely on us. Thank you.' Colson didn't even look at Violet, he just escaped.

But Frankie remained. He frowned at Roman before facing her. 'Are you happy with this plan, Violet? If you're in trouble and need help, then let me know. I'll…'

Engulfed in a flush of embarrassment mixed with gratitude, Violet glanced at Roman and saw cynical amusement flash in his eyes. She turned back to Frankie to reassure him. 'I appreciate your concern but, honestly, I'm fine.'

Frankie didn't look appeased. 'But—'

'I want to stay here.' She was mortified and somewhat grumpy. 'Truly.'

'You know he has a reputation?' Frankie slowly looked

from Roman to her and back again. 'You know he was just voted Most Eligible Bachelor in New York in a magazine?'

Violet blinked. *He what?*

'No longer eligible, I'm afraid,' Roman piped up dryly.

Frankie's eyes widened. 'So this is…?'

'Personal,' Roman finished.

Frankie stared hard at Roman, who simply didn't move. He didn't need to.

'It's okay, Frankie.' Violet made herself smile.

Frankie reluctantly turned. 'If you need anything at all…' He finally left the compartment.

A sharp smile played around Roman's mouth as he watched Violet pour herself a glass of water. 'You've known him how long?'

'Almost two weeks.'

'And he's already very protective of you.'

She sipped the sparkling water to soothe the irritation burning her insides. 'Perhaps he's wary of you.'

His smile broadened, like a shark's. 'I don't think you really appreciated his concern.'

She drew a breath. It was kind of someone to worry about her, especially given this extraordinary situation. 'It took courage for him to check on me in front of you. Of course I appreciated that.'

'But it still annoyed the hell out of you.'

'Well, at least he *asked* me if he could help and then *accepted* my answer. He didn't just try to railroad me into whatever solution he thought best, like some power-hungry bully.'

'You think that's what I'm doing?' Roman positively smouldered.

'Isn't it?'

'What's your solution, then?'

'Time,' she said bluntly. 'I need time to get my head

around all this.' Frankly she didn't have any solutions yet. She was still processing the simple facts. 'This wasn't supposed to have happened. We were temporary. One night.'

His jaw locked. 'But now you're having my baby.'

She shifted uncomfortably. She still wasn't thinking about that too closely. It was like a secret inside her. A massive, overwhelming secret that she couldn't yet look at directly because it might burn her eyes. It terrified her because she wanted it so very much.

'I don't think these are the best circumstances in which to begin a relationship,' she said.

'Nevertheless, we now have to. But I don't want to marry you because I'm in love with you, I'm proposing an arrangement to preserve all our best interests. Security and stability.'

She stared at him disbelievingly. 'You're okay about celibacy for the foreseeable future?'

That topaz patch in his eye gleamed. 'I think we have some options that we could consider. Later. When you're ready to talk about it.'

Options? Later? No, she was clarifying his intentions now. 'You think we should sleep together again.'

He half laughed. 'Does that really surprise you?'

'You think you can seduce me into saying yes to you. Yes to everything.'

'I'm not that arrogant.'

'Yes, you are.'

'I think we have unfinished business in that arena.'

'That's unrelated to the long-term problem.'

'It's kind of related. But, for now, let's relax and enjoy the journey. You get to be the tourist you wanted to be. You can sit and watch the landscape.'

Well, she *wasn't* going to look at that bed but she really had little choice. He was right. There was no point going somewhere else to sort this out. They had time and privacy here. She just needed to think about it all herself first.

As the train departed the station she felt a flutter of excitement. She liked to be on the move, not bogged down in one place. She'd been looking forward to meeting the other passengers, but equally she could appreciate the chance to sit and take in the view, especially in such incredible luxury. She curled her feet up beneath her and fixed her attention on looking out of the window. Except her mind whirled. She'd wanted independence—the freedom to travel and explore and decide what she wanted to do and when and where and with whomever she chose. She'd only just got it. And now?

Now there was a miracle. An absolute gift. But it dragged Roman Fraser right behind with it—powerful. Determined. Successful. He was so beyond her league and she had no idea how to handle him or how to handle the fact that she was still crazily attracted to him.

There was a knock on the door and she saw Frankie had brought her bag into the antechamber. She went to fetch it but Roman beat her to it.

'You don't need to do that,' she said awkwardly as he brought it into the main compartment for her. 'It's a small bag.'

'It's a stupidly small bag—are all your clothes in there?'

'Yes, and clearly I can manage it all by myself.'

'You can't accept even a common courtesy?' He raised his brows. 'You don't think a pregnant woman ought to be cared for?'

She was barely pregnant and her need for independence flared. 'There's a difference between caring for her and being over the top. You think I can't even carry a bag? That a pregnant person can't even work on a train? I think a woman should choose to do whatever she wants to.'

'Physical safety matters. Tiredness matters. These things are real. Hormones, chemicals, affect the way a person feels, maybe even thinks sometimes. You can't deny that there's an impact just because you fear being perceived as weaker. That you're less strong somehow.'

That wasn't it. It was some dinosaur idea of looking after the little woman.

'Hormones and chemicals don't affect everyone the same way. Why penalise anyone pregnant with an arbitrary, blanket rule?' she asked.

He just laughed. 'People don't want to be served by a heavily pregnant woman pushing a heavy trolley. They're naturally concerned and want to help them. It's not relaxing to sit watching a woman struggle.'

'Struggle.' She glared at him.

He smothered a smile and shrugged. 'I can't help—'

'Having an inflated sense of chivalry?'

He crouched before her, putting his hands on the arms of her chair and boxing her in. 'It's normal human behaviour. You give up your seat for the pregnant woman on the bus. It's instilled in you from childhood. Isn't it a sign of respect? That she's doing something important?' He leaned close. 'It is literally *vital*. It is the most important, most precious thing. So, yes, I'll do whatever I have to do to care and protect both her and the baby and ensure both their safety.'

She stared into his eyes, touched yet wanting to rebel against him at the same time—tempted to fall forward and force him to embrace her. She'd snuggle in and want to stay there. That couldn't happen. She knew he wanted the best for her but his power scared her. Not the power of his money or his resources but the power *he* had over her. Him as a man. He made her crave the one thing she'd fought so long to escape: *security*. But to have someone wrap her in cotton wool...

'I don't need you to do that. I can take care of myself.' She needed to understand him and to help him see that she could manage alone.

'Yeah? Well, you don't have to.'

Hours later, it was a huge relief for Violet to escape into the bathroom to get ready for bed. The train she'd worked on in New Zealand hadn't been an overnight train and there'd been no private bedroom compartments. She'd never actually slept on a train before. And to have to sleep next to Roman Fraser—like that was going to be possible. It would be too tempting to turn towards him and seek out his touch. He could make her feel so good. Memories flitted. Fantasies formed.

She furiously brushed her teeth, her hair and scrubbed her face clean. Then she braved the lion's den. But she stopped in the main compartment.

'What are you wearing?' She glared at him.

He glanced down at his boxers. 'Be grateful I'm wearing these. I don't normally wear anything in bed. But in the circumstances...'

'You went with tight knit briefs? That was so considerate of you.'

'Well, I can see you put a lot of thought into your attire.' He eyed her pyjamas severely.

'I was meant to be in a staff compartment. Have you seen them? They're very small. Four stewards to a cabin. Narrow little bunks.'

'So having half of this bed will be luxury for you. So much more space.' His lips twitched. 'Or, if you would prefer, I can take the floor.'

'I'm sure you'll be a gentleman and stay on your side of the bed.'

He mock-bowed, then eyed her brushed cotton pyjamas again. 'Christmas themed?'

'They were on sale.'

'I am not surprised.'

Yeah? Well, he could handle the disappointment. She figured the lack of sexiness was a good thing.

'What are you doing now?' he asked as she strode to the wall.

Violet tapped the central control panel, super-glad she'd had the training. 'Turning down the thermostat.'

'You're feeling hot?' Roman asked. 'Or you want more of a winter vibe because you're used to sun in December?'

'I'm hoping you'll get so cold you'll cover up. Jersey. Sweatpants—baggy ones.'

He chuckled. 'You're not kidding, are you?'

'Not in the least. I told you, I'm very superficial when confronted with your…'

'Oh.' He patted his chest and mock-preened. 'So you're breathless again?'

She climbed into bed and with a flounce rolled to face the other direction to glare at the beautiful gold-pressed wallpaper. Even with the thermostat blasting frigid air she was hot and bothered.

'Sleep well, Violet.'

She heard the dry amusement in his voice. Then there was silence. She waited to hear his breathing deepen. But, like her, he was *too* still, *too* quiet. She could barely breathe. Not even the rhythm of the train riding the tracks could lull her to sleep. It felt like for ever, and despite her spinning the thermostat she was only growing hotter and more uncomfortable.

Finally, she sighed. 'Why are you still awake?'

'Why are you?' Amused tones came back at her in the darkness.

She rolled onto her back and stared up. Despite the chill of the compartment, she was melting. 'Well, I'm trying to process my unplanned pregnancy. Plus, the fact the father of my baby is a virtual stranger, and now I'm stuck on a train in very close confines with said stranger and it's super-awkward. I'm low on money so I can't just run away anywhere, other than home to my parents, and I don't want to do that anyway. Plus, people must be wondering—'

'Awkward?' he interrupted. 'Because we're lying here like mannequins, too scared to relax in case we inadvertently touch each other instead of touching each other the way we really want to?' He rolled towards her. 'Remind me why we aren't kissing right now.'

Heat flared. Kissing? Her whole body quivered at the mere thought. It would be so easy to say yes. But she feared, once she started, she wouldn't be able to stop. She'd say yes to *everything* he wanted, and she had to retain *some* control of her life. It had taken so long to get it.

'Because we still want different things,' she said.

It sounded weak. *Touching...the way we really want to.* Which meant he still wanted her, and now her cells were singing the 'Hallelujah Chorus'. But it was a distraction. A complication.

'I think we still want some of the *same* things,' he argued. 'I think we still want each other. And you know we're good together.'

CHAPTER SIX

ROMAN WANTED TO bite back the words but that breathless way she had of speaking whatever was in her head just made him want to tease her more. It would take nothing to move closer. To touch and forget everything for lush moments. He ached to do it.

But she was pregnant. She was vulnerable. She'd obviously been through hell in the past. Was she even up to the physical demands of pregnancy? Roman didn't know. So what the hell was he thinking? All he wanted was to bury himself in the pleasure of her body again—selfish jerk that he was.

'Roman.' A husky murmur. 'I—'

'I'm sorry,' he interrupted her harshly, inwardly cursing his own weakness. Since when had he been so unwilling to exert his self-control? 'I shouldn't have said that. Go to sleep. You need rest. It'll be okay.'

This wasn't only about *him*. He mentally berated his cravings—he was too used to pleasing only himself. That was going to have to change. Guilt burned off the desire. It had been a stupid idea to stay on the train with her. But he'd had her in his arms, and he'd wanted to keep her there, and the train had seemed the perfect solution. All that had happened was that he'd put himself into a torture chamber. So close but unable to touch her.

Now she didn't argue with him, and then it truly was awkward as they both lay still and silent. When had he last shared a bed with anyone to actually *sleep*? He hadn't. Ever. And to think he'd proposed marriage! Didn't that mean sharing a bed for the rest of their days?

Eventually he heard the gentle deepening of her breathing. But, though he was pleased she was resting, *he* couldn't relax. This wasn't what he wanted. He'd deliberately stayed single because he never wanted a family. For almost two decades he'd put his focus into finding Eloise, his missing sister. But he'd failed—time and time again. He didn't want any more emotional responsibility. He didn't want a wife or children. Didn't want the burden of keeping them happy or keeping them safe. He'd not been able to do that even in the little way required as a brother.

His thoughts muddled, swirling towards darkness, towards the past. Familiar images haunted him. He knew he was dreaming but couldn't wake from the horrors and stop it screening in his head. He was unable to move—just as he'd been unable to move all those years ago. There were flashes: still images, loud sounds. Snow in the headlights. Tearing metal. Spinning. The unbearable pressure on his leg. The scream of his mother. Blackness.

Then words he couldn't understand. Voices he didn't know. Eloise had been near. He remembered her little woollen jacket and her bright-white blanket because a light had been shone on her. A thin beam from a torch. He screamed at them. To stop. To stay. But he heard only silence. Because not only could he not move, he couldn't make even the smallest sound emerge. He watched that hand reach towards her. But he couldn't do anything. He couldn't even concentrate. He closed his eyes for a moment. Only a moment. And when he opened his eyes she was—

Roman thrashed as he jerked awake. In a blink he remembered he wasn't alone in the bed and he froze, hoping he hadn't just woken Violet or, worse, inadvertently kicked her. Hell, maybe he *was* a danger to her. But as the deafening, panicked roar of his pulse in his ears subsided, he realised Violet was still fast asleep, curled in a ball beside him. *Close* beside him. Her glossy hair encroached on his pillow and a subtle citrusy scent wafted towards him. It was practically edible. He wanted to bury himself in it. In her.

No. He rubbed his chest, feeling the slick of sweat despite the chilled air, and reminded himself to breathe, slower, slower, slower until the panic fully subsided. Grimly, he gave thanks he hadn't ended up sleepwalking.

It shocked him that the terror had returned. A decade ago the relentless recurrence of the dream had got so bad he'd ended up using alcohol, sex or both to effectively knock himself out with exhaustion. He'd not done that in years, and neither was an option here. Not with Violet.

Kicking out with that once-maimed leg, being out of control of his own limbs... He didn't trust himself. He eased out of the bed, quietly moving to the desk so he didn't wake her. He would work—that had become the replacement for those other two more self-destructive options. He would work and he would research. He knew next to nothing about pregnancy. He needed to find her a specialist—especially given her health history. He needed to find out everything he could.

He tried not to watch her sleeping in the dim light cast by his laptop. He tried to ignore the ache calling him to crawl back into bed and curl around her. But hours later, when she finally stirred, his heart lifted.

'Why are you up already?' She pushed her hair out of her eyes. She almost glittered with fresh-woken radiance.

'Work.' It wasn't entirely a lie. He had a ton to do and

he'd got nothing done yesterday when he'd ended up just watching her looking out of the window.

She nodded slowly and stretched. His skin tightened.

'I'll order breakfast,' he muttered. 'You feeling okay?'

Did she have any morning sickness?

'I'm fine.' She got out of bed and went into the bathroom.

He'd never imagined he'd find bright-red, Christmas-stocking-stamped, brushed-cotton pyjamas attractive but it seemed there was a first time for everything.

The breakfast trolley arrived while she was still in the bathroom. Roman poured fresh orange juice into a crystal glass for her. Frustration locked his muscles when she emerged looking revitalised. Her hair was damp, her skin glowed, her faded jeans emphasised the curve of her hips and the white tee-shirt ended tantalisingly near to her narrow waist. His fingers itched to slide underneath it and then up to those gorgeous breasts of hers. How he wanted to see them again. To stroke them. To…

'I think we need to understand each other better.' She took the chair opposite the desk and reached for the glass he offered. 'So let's talk.'

Her business-like demeanour was a cool shock to the steaming resurgence of his desire. Talk? He suspected it was going to be more like an inquisition.

'You want to interview me?' he asked irritably. The last thing he wanted to do was *talk*.

'Might as well.' She shrugged. 'It's a better way to spend the time than arguing, don't you think?'

He was tired. Frustrated. Confused. There was no way he could stand much more time in this tiny compartment with her.

'You want to get off the train?' he asked. 'There's an excursion to a lakeside town today.'

She paused, then shot him a look. 'Am I allowed?'

He glared back.

She blinked, all innocence. 'I thought you had reports to write. Orders to issue. Weddings to plan.'

'I can do all that tonight when I can't sleep because I'm too close to you and you're too hot.' He was too grumpy to cope.

Colour filled her cheeks but she frowned. 'Or are you just avoiding my interview?'

'Am I so transparent?' he murmured, pleased to see the effect his words had had on her. She'd been looking far too undisturbed. Now she was flushing again and her breathing had quickened. 'Shocker.' He cocked his head. 'I guess there are other ways I could try to distract you from your inquisition.'

She swallowed, now avoiding his gaze. 'Escaping the train for a little while could be good.'

'Yeah.' It would be a *very* good idea.

But then he saw her take in a determined deep breath.

'Meanwhile, we might as well talk over breakfast.' She took a sip of orange juice.

But it was a challenge he couldn't ignore. 'You really want an interview? Why don't I just give you the highlights?'

She reached for a croissant. 'Go right ahead.'

He gritted his teeth. 'I was the first born. Heir to the family conglomerate comprised of an investment banking arm, a collection of hotels and luxury goods manufacturers. I received an elite, private education. My early childhood was good until my parents died in a car accident when I was ten. Then I went to boarding school for yet more elite education. As soon as I was done I went into the company—the banking side. I took complete control in my twenties and have worked to ensure its success in all areas.'

She stared at him. He braced. He knew she had a million more questions about all those things.

'Is it what you always wanted to do? To run the company? You didn't have other dreams?'

'Honestly, no,' he said flatly. 'It's in my blood.' And, because of that, he would never let his company down. It was on him to continue the Fraser empire, in the corporate world at least. He wanted to ensure everything held strong so that if—when—Eloise was ever found then she would have everything. But she hadn't been found and she never would be. And all that remained in Roman was that need to keep the business going well. He didn't want anything more.

'And why are you such a closed book? Why don't you want people to get to know you?' Violet gazed at him frankly.

'I don't want people's pity. People think…' He didn't want to think what they thought.

'Pity because of the accident?'

'I don't want people around when they're only interested in my money.'

She looked sceptical. 'Is that really the only reason why they're interested?'

'Apparently one or two are only interested in my looks,' he jeered lightly. 'But usually it's the money.'

'And women?' Her colour was high again. 'You like sex. You're good at it.'

He caught his breath. She floored him with that honesty sometimes.

'I'm good at a lot of things, Violet.' He was soft but so insolent and her colour rose even more.

But it didn't please him the same. Because he was not good at some other things—things she might really want—and he never wanted to be good at them, such as real, deep relationships. He needed to make her understand that somehow. 'For a while in my early twenties, I partied hard. But I grew up. Got a little jaded.'

There was more to it, a nuance—the reason *why* he'd partied hard. He couldn't tell her that. He'd had foolish hope when there could be none and losing it had almost destroyed him.

She fiddled with a silver knife instead of buttering her croissant. 'So what happened with me…?'

'Was the first in a while. There hasn't been anyone since.' The truth just slid out and for a second he felt as shocked by his admission as she looked.

Why there hadn't been anyone else?

The question flickered in her eyes but he didn't answer. He only knew he'd not been able to shake her from his mind. He'd not even noticed other women these past few weeks. He'd not wanted to. And, even though he was no longer the player he'd been a while back, it was weird. But that night with her hadn't just been intense, it had been emotional—touching something within that he didn't think could easily be repeated. He didn't want to settle for less with someone else. He didn't want someone else at all.

The blush now blooming on her face was scarlet and every cell inside him was swamped by satisfaction. Yeah, it *mattered* to her. To him too. He couldn't stand the thought of her being with anyone else. The irritation he'd felt about his fixation with her evaporated. It was all he could do not to vault out of his chair, cup her face and kiss her—everywhere—to help her release the surfeit of sensual tension he just knew she was struggling with right now. She'd been pleased to hear that from him and he ached to please her so much more. To satisfy the ache they were both barely enduring would ease everything.

Instead he pushed the instinct down. 'Enough to go on for now?'

She nodded and shifted from the chair opposite his at the table to the larger, more comfortable arm chair by the window.

He was rendered useless to work again. Instead of focusing on number crunching, he surreptitiously watched her curled up on that chair, looking at the view out of the window. So beautiful, and unbelievably quiet. Where had the breathless chatter and tease gone? The wide eyes were still there. He wanted to know what she was thinking. He wanted to share how she experienced the world.

He tensed. What kind of whimsical wish was that? His untrustworthy, frankly fanciful, instincts were overriding any actual thinking right now. He needed space and time to work all this out, but honestly it was too huge to contemplate. Knowing they were aligned in having the child was good, but navigating arrangements for co-parenting? He feared it was going to be impossible. So the relief when the train finally slowed to pull into the station was intense.

'Time to escape,' she said lightly.

Yeah. She felt it as keenly as he did.

The station was in the centre of a pretty little lakeside town. They could opt for 'ye olde horse and carriage' to transport them, but it was only a three-minute walk to the waterside, and Violet was walking before he could even ask her. He chuckled ruefully. It seemed she didn't want to sit near him even for a few extra minutes.

As the collection of timber booths decked out in festive finery came into view, he gritted his teeth and cursed himself for the idea. The Christmas market sold handmade wooden ornaments and decorations, spiced wine, deep-fried dumplings, sleigh rides, sparkling lights and festive trees. And there were people. Lots of people—

families, couples and older folk, all smiling and excited. It was everything he avoided in a one-mile radius. But in the centre, right beside him, with a bigger smile than anyone was Violet. So he avoided all the Christmas kitsch and focused on her.

'It's beautiful,' she murmured.

Vitality and energy shone in her eyes as she chattered to the stall holders. She was curious, engaging and skilful in getting people to open up to her. They beamed, plying her with samples of cake and chocolate, or slivers of the soaps they were selling. She had genuine enthusiasm for hearing other people's stories. No wonder she was good at customer-facing roles—she'd be an amazing tour guide. She was charming and guileless, this petite woman with an impish smile and irresistible freckles. She brought everyone's protective instincts out the second they saw her.

Except for Roman's. He—hungry beast that he was—just wanted to drag her back to his bed, cover her soft mouth with his own and keep her all to himself. Because he knew the stormy passion that lay beneath that sweet surface. He'd seen the challenging sassiness in her eyes and he'd felt her heat. She was a complex creature and he couldn't get enough.

Now she was at a booth selling fine wool products, inspecting brightly coloured hats. There were tiny, knitted baby hats—Christmas-themed ones—and he couldn't look at them.

'Are they all hand-knitted?' she enquired. 'They're exquisite.'

The stall holder smiled but Roman had frozen. Years ago at Christmas he'd been given a woollen hat like the ones on display here. Hand-knitted and exquisite and made with love.

'You like them too.' Violet glanced up at him.

He realised he'd been staring at the hats for far too long.

'I had an awesome beanie collection a few years ago,' she added.

'Beanie?' He couldn't resist running his hand through her tresses. 'You lost your hair during treatment?'

His heart ached as she nodded.

'You'd never know,' he said gruffly. 'It's so thick and beautiful now.'

Pleasure sparkled in her eyes. 'Thank you. I like it too.' She bit her lip and amusement deepened. 'In fact, I'm really vain about it. My hair appliances take up most of the room in my bag. That's why I don't have many clothes.'

He chuckled and ruffled her hair. He loved the silkiness of it—and the way she responded.

'Hey.' She ducked, only to then reach out and rumple her fingers through his. 'How do you like it?'

'I like it a lot.' He caught her close. 'Go ahead and mess me up a little. I deserve it.'

'Do you think?' She grew serious and he knew she was thinking about the baby. 'I don't blame you. I was there too. Don't diminish my responsibility. I'm every bit at fault—in fact, I think I was the one who started it.'

She gave him a little push, turned and walked away from him through the pretty market. But Roman still didn't look at the stalls. He followed her, thoughtful, aware he'd just disappointed her in a deeper way than he'd intended. Her little flare told him something more about her. Something she'd been trying to tell him from the moment they'd met.

I don't need you to rescue me.

Now he needed to understand why she'd assumed he'd even been trying to. She assumed *everyone* had that in mind where she was concerned. Maybe she had reason to. Frankie had wanted to rescue her. Hell, Roman also wanted to protect her. Of course he did. But what was so wrong with that? She didn't want to be treated as less than responsible or less than capable. She asserted her independence, repeatedly insisting she didn't need protecting. She was afraid of him being too powerful and exerting too much control over her life. Was that something she was used to?

'Tell me about it,' he said as he caught up with her as she passed a stall selling hot spiced wine.

'About what?'

'Your family. Why they're so over-protective. Why you don't want to go home even now you're in "trouble". Was it because of the cancer?'

Violet walked to a gap in the line-up of wooden stalls through which she could view the lake gently lapping the shore. She probably needed to explain everything so he'd understand why she wasn't exactly thrilled about his whole 'I'll marry you and take care of everything' vibe.

'It started way before the cancer,' she said bluntly. 'I was premature. An unexpected fifth child and the first and only girl. I was born five years after my youngest brother. I was precious and wanted and loved. And I appreciate that, I do.'

He faced away from the lake. Faced her. 'But?'

'I was small from the start, of course, so they were super-protective, super-worried. But that worry never eased—not even when I was bigger and healthier. At the first sign of any cough or cold, they'd keep me home. I didn't go to pre-school or anything. Later, a lot of the time I didn't go to school.'

'Because you were sickly?'

'I was always undersized but not as sickly as they thought. I could have…' She could have gone to school more. She could have played outside more. She could have strived and then thrived a little more. Instead she'd been cosseted and constrained and, even when she'd been older, healthier, the limits had remained. 'They worried about me. A lot. Too much.' She drew a breath. 'They treated me like a porcelain doll.' And she'd hated that. She hated being petite, being thought of as incapable or lacking in strength. 'But in missing a lot of school I slipped behind academically. And in never doing much sport I didn't get very strong.'

He nodded slowly.

'My brothers are all engineers. They're super-smart guys. Successful in other ways too. Like sports. But I wasn't like them, and they all always said not to worry, it didn't matter... But in reality Mum did so much worrying, she stopped me from...' She gazed at the lake and felt that old frustration begin to burn. 'They stopped me from doing everything. This might go wrong, or that might go wrong—they were full of all the "if"s and "but"s and "you shouldn't". She saw so many possibilities—all the risks that were never worth taking. I didn't have the resources or the strength, and then I didn't have the smarts...'

'Violet—'

'I know I'm good at some things,' she interrupted. 'I can talk to anyone about anything and I'm curious about everything. And now I want to see everything. Do everything. I want to soak *everything* up,' she said fiercely. 'I want to feel free and travel and live. I love that they love me, and I know it sounds so ungrateful to moan about them, but...'

She inhaled deeply and admitted at last, 'In my teens I started to lie about how I felt just so they wouldn't stop me from doing something. Because I wanted to go out, you know? I wanted to go on adventures with my friends. But they wouldn't even let me go on school camp. They said I wasn't strong enough to carry the damned pack. And then...'

She hated remembering this time.

'The cancer,' Roman said softly.

'I *should* have told them sooner.' She shook her head as her eyes stung. 'That was the lesson. I'd hidden that I'd been feeling lousy. That I'd lost some weight without intending to. Then I found a lump on my neck—a bit more than the usual swollen glands, you know? I was sure it was just going to be some other virus but it turned out it was Hodgkin's lymphoma.'

'Oh, Violet.'

'Bit unlucky, right?' She swallowed hard. 'But then, super-lucky at the same time, because we caught it early and there was aggressive treatment and a good prognosis.'

'But there was a rough time to go through with that aggressive treatment.'

Yeah, it *had* been rough. 'I dropped out of school.' She nodded. 'I didn't go to my school ball or anything, and that was okay, because I was so, so tired and I felt…' She flushed. She'd felt unattractive—losing her hair, then the impact of the steroids later on.

'When I was finally improving, my family wanted me to relax, not worry and just take my time. They didn't want me to go to uni. They wanted me to stay at home for ever, where they could keep me safe. Mum wanted to make everything so perfect for me. Especially Christmas. But it can't be perfect, you know? And, honestly, I just wanted to travel. I wanted to be free. I wanted to have some *adventure*, have some fun now I was finally well enough to.'

'So you should. Life's for living.'

'Right.' She flashed him a grateful smile for understanding. 'I did a tourism paper at the polytechnic. Then got a guide job down the road—just part-time. I did another paper, and tried to get my family used to the idea, because I didn't want to hurt them. I know they love me.

I know they just want to protect me. And I slowly saved up enough money to buy my ticket overseas.'

'But they still didn't want you to go?'

Violet's heart ached. He was too astute.

'I couldn't wait,' she said huskily. 'I didn't want to struggle through another family Christmas.'

'You really don't like Christmas?' He frowned. 'You were wearing Christmas pyjamas last night.'

'I told you, they were on sale.' She gazed up at him. 'Christmas is the worst, right? There's such expectation, always making everything perfect. It sounds so spoiled of me—not to appreciate that they would go to such lengths. But it was stifling. It didn't matter to me. I wanted to relax and just enjoy being with them and having some fun. Instead there was this underlying, fraught element. Mum was so afraid all of the time.'

She sighed. 'They want nothing but the best for me—to protect me. And they did. I don't mean to make them sound awful or for me to sound ungrateful. They're wonderful. They love me and I do love them.'

'It's okay if things aren't perfect, Violet—if you struggle with them. It doesn't make you a bad daughter to have a moan or to regret the way some things were. It makes you human. Everyone has issues with family.'

'Even you?'

'Yeah, well, I don't have family. I guess that's an issue in itself.'

Violet looked up at him, but he turned to focus on something beyond the lake.

'You're used to being alone,' she said.

'Yeah.' He nodded. 'I guess I'm not quite sure how to cope with the unexpected family we now find ourselves with.'

She wasn't sure either. And the irony of it… Embarrassment slithered across her skin but she told him anyway. 'It's the family joke that I'll need to marry well because I'm not going to have some massive money-making career like them. But that it won't matter because I'll have some guy to "look after me". Because I bring out everyone's protective instincts because I'm small and a bit stupid.' She watched the tension enter Roman's stance as she spoke and then shrugged. 'Yeah, they're going love you. They're going to think you're just the best thing ever!'

'But you don't,' he said. 'You're worried I'm going to stop you from doing all the things you want.'

For sure, the man was too smart.

'That's not what I want to do, Violet.' He studied her and that frown of his returned. 'Why did you tell me about the cancer that night? Didn't you think it might scare me off completely? Or make me all over-protective? That I'd treat you like you're more fragile because of it?'

'But you didn't,' she said softly. 'I knew you were decent at heart, but to be honest you're also kind of ruthless. You were anonymous and bold. My past didn't matter to you. It wasn't going to stop you from…'

'Taking what I wanted,' he said huskily.

'Taking what I was offering. And giving me what you could. Which is all I wanted.' She faced him, unable to stop herself admitting the deep truth. 'I wanted to be able to be *honest* with someone—especially someone I was literally going to open up to. If you'd handled it differently, I would have stopped. But you didn't just accept it, you told *me* something too, and then neither of those things mattered to what was real right then in that moment. But they did make it *more* somehow. I didn't want to hide anything. I wanted just to be me. And you let me.'

And she was still grateful to him for that. 'I want to be able to tell the truth about how I'm feeling without someone immediately taking drastic steps to try to *fix* it. Sometimes you just want someone to listen, you know? Just to be there and listen and keep you company while it all washes through.'

'Right.' He breathed out, a gust of tension escaping him. 'Okay.'

'So maybe we could keep being that honest?' she suggested.

He regarded her steadily. 'Sure. I'll try.' He hesitated before reaching out and toying with a strand of her hair. 'And your health now?'

'Pretty good. I try to take care of myself.' She nibbled her lower lip. 'What about you?'

'Me?' His eyes widened, as if he was surprised she'd asked. 'I try to take care of myself too.'

'Good.' She smiled up at him. 'I'm glad.'

He stared into her eyes for so long, she lost track of her thoughts. All she registered was the warmth deepening within. It wasn't only the flirty kind, it was more potent, more poignant—and the wisp of tenderness in his gaze stole her breath away.

He suddenly inhaled sharply, as if he too had gone without air for too long. 'We'd better get back to the train or it might leave without us.'

CHAPTER SEVEN

VIOLET HADN'T BEEN up to much dinner. When they'd returned to the train that afternoon, they'd retreated to opposite sides of the compartment by unspoken agreement. Roman had worked at his desk—all executive focus—but the stubble on his chin emphasised that cute dimple and the jeans and tee gave him a more rugged, younger look. Violet had never seen him look so handsome, nor had she ever been left so unable to do anything. The *distraction* of the man!

Now she stood in the bathroom and could barely look at herself in the mirror. Her cheeks were flushed—their colour practically matching her pyjamas—and her eyes were sparkling. She looked drunk. Talking to him at the Christmas market this afternoon had stirred memories up and made other parts of her hungry for other things. There was no denying it any more, and she didn't want to. She wanted to live. She wanted Roman.

She walked out of the bathroom and went straight to the control panel.

'You adjusting the thermostat again?' he asked.

She glanced over and gulped. 'Well, you're wearing very little to bed again.'

He stood in the middle of the compartment in nothing but those briefs. Violet's temperature soared. She wanted to feel good. She wanted to forget the problems they faced. She wanted to live in the moment. *This* moment. And Roman Fraser was excellent at making her forget everything but his touch. It could be searingly simple and she was fed up with the frustration. It had been so good, that night when she'd been bold. The memory emboldened her now. She walked towards him, unfastening the top button of her pyjama top.

Roman remained standing stock-still. 'What are you doing now?'

Nerves shimmered through her body but his reaction fired her confidence. She abandoned unbuttoning her top, took a big breath and shimmied out of the pyjama bottoms—right there, just like that. 'What do you think?'

His jaw dropped. 'I think…' He cleared his throat. 'I think…'

'I think you should forget about thinking. Just for a little while. That's what I'm going to do,' she said as she walked towards him.

'Last time the thought of more than one night made you run. You know if we do this it will be for more than one night, Violet.'

'Things are different now,' she muttered. But her self-preservation instinct sounded. He was the bossy, protective kind who'd want to constrain her life, and she'd been constrained for too long. So she needed to clarify things. 'I'm going to sleep with you. But I'm not agreeing to your marriage plan. You know it's unnecessarily old-fashioned and complicated.'

'I don't think giving the baby the security of my name is complicated.' He put his hands on her waist and pulled her closer, but not flush against him the way she really wanted.

'The baby can have your name. We don't need to be

married for that. The baby can have all your money too. I don't need it or want it.'

'So you don't want to marry me, but you'll sleep with me.'

'A couple more times. Yes.'

'A couple…' He trailed off.

'You don't want to marry me,' she reasoned. 'You don't want to marry anyone.'

'What makes you say that?'

'If you wanted to get married, you would be already. There're so many perfectly wonderful women you've met already, and the fact that you haven't got one already… *You* can marry anyone you want.' She knew that to be deeply, deeply true.

'Except you, apparently.'

'Because we're…' She paused. 'We don't even know each other. There wasn't supposed to be anything more between us.'

'But now there is,' he argued. 'Now we get to know each other. You said that yourself this morning. We have no choice but to work this out.'

'Not in a rush, though,' she said.

He regarded her speculatively. She wasn't sure she wanted to know what he was thinking.

'You're right,' he said. 'I don't want to marry anyone. Which is why it's perfect that I marry you.'

'Pardon?'

He laughed at her. 'This way I get a ready-made family without all the emotional baggage. That's obviously what I'm avoiding.'

'Obviously.' She began to feel grumpy.

'We can have a more level-headed arrangement and I can take care of you both.'

Her hackles rose. 'How many times do I need to tell you? I don't need taking care of.'

'You're pregnant. On the other side of the world from your family. With limited funds. You need a—'

'*Friend.* Not a husband.'

He bristled.

'And, let's be honest, you're not exactly comfortable with either of those concepts,' she pointed out.

'I have a friend.'

'Really? A close one?' She didn't believe him. And now she felt hot and angry and she wanted to deal with it. 'That doesn't matter. And none of it means that we shouldn't still release this chemistry.'

'Chemistry?'

'I'm swimming in early pregnancy hormones,' she snapped. 'You're...'

'I'm...?'

'A virile man with needs.'

'Needs?' He gazed down at her. 'You mean like an appetite that I can't suppress?'

'I—'

'Because, sweetheart, I can suppress it.'

She glanced down at the very rigid evidence of his desire in his briefs. 'I'm not saying you're an animal without any control. I'm just suggesting...'

'Suggesting what?' He acted mystified. 'Please do carry on.'

'That there's a reaction between us. That, like all reactions, it will work out, pass through...whatever.'

'Because you're so very experienced in such matters,' he said sarcastically.

'No. But—'

'You think this reaction is purely pregnancy hormones for you?'

'Maybe...' She trailed off and couldn't look him in the eyes any more. 'I don't know.'

'You really think it's superficial because you like looking at me?'

What did it matter? 'What do you think, then?' She growled at him, irritated that he seemed to have slowed down when they could be kissing already. 'Seeing you do have vastly more experience in these things.'

'Not in pregnancy, I don't.'

'In lust, though.'

'Lust.' He inhaled deeply. 'Frankie referred to my "reputation".'

'The edible bachelor thing?'

He shot a stunned look at her.

'Eligible!' she corrected hurriedly. 'Whatever. It's hardly a surprise. You admitted it yourself. It's no shock that a man like you—'

'Good-looking and wealthy.'

'Confident and assured,' she corrected, even more irritated. 'Draws attention and is popular.'

'Violet...'

'Could you just kiss me, Roman?' She glared at him.

'Are you sure?'

'What else are we going to do?' she flung at him furiously. 'I don't want to fight it any more. Neither of us can sleep. It might help with that.'

'So might a glass of milk and a cookie.'

'We can have that too. After.' She breathed hard.

To her annoyance, he suddenly chuckled. But then he lifted his hands from her waist and deftly undid the last of her pyjama buttons. Wordlessly holding her gaze, he opened the top, and now she was bare-breasted and bare-bottomed, there for him to study. And study he did. As his gaze lowered, his amusement sank beneath stark hunger. She wriggled her shoulders so the top fell down her arms to the floor. His gaze flickered and he cupped her breasts. She shuddered as desire shot tension deep within her body. She'd ached for this for too long.

His smile flashed. 'You like it when I do this.'

His hands were big and warm and strong, and sending delicious shivers through her body as he stroked closer and closer to her tight nipples.

She groaned. 'Am I not supposed to?'

A low laugh escaped him and he bent close, his breath warm on her sensitive skin. 'I love seeing you like this. Feeling you…you're so beautiful.'

'Can you just kiss me?' she muttered.

'Sure,' he promised. 'In a moment.'

His thumbs circled her tight nipples. She needed him to caress their tips but instead he teased in ever-decreasing circles, still not stroking the aching buds. 'Tease.'

His face flushed as he watched her body's reaction to his touch.

'Kiss me,' she whispered.

But Roman dropped to his knees.

'What are you…? *Oh*…'

He *was* kissing her. Kissing her inner thighs. Kissing her…*there*…long and lush and deep, and she was overcome. Her legs trembled. He caught her, tumbling her down to the plush carpet, and then she was on her back, her legs spread and he was still kissing her—there. Savouring her intimately, desperately. She stretched her arms out, her palms down, sliding her spread fingers through the intricately woven wool. She could feel the vibration of the train riding the tracks beneath her. Her hips lifted as sensations surged. She wanted *him* to ride *her*.

'Please…please…'

'I want to taste your pleasure, Violet.' He growled. 'It's been so long.'

'Oh...'

It didn't take long at all.

With a triumphant laugh, he lifted up only to shuck his briefs. Holding her hips, he pushed her legs wide with his knee so he could take his place between them.

'Are you sure you're okay with this?' He growled.

'I'll be less okay if you don't hurry up.'

That smile again. 'Are you trying to boss *me* around?'

'Is it working?' she murmured.

'Oh, yes.'

And then he was there. She groaned in guttural, animal pleasure as he pushed deep. 'Roman.'

He stilled, locked inside as they both gasped.

'How good does this feel?' He gazed into her eyes.

She wrapped herself around him. Holding him tight, she rose to meet him, rocking her hips, pushing them both faster, deeper and so desperately until she screamed with the searing pleasure of her release and his shout of ecstasy echoed in her ears.

And then she was in another realm altogether, so limp, so blissful, she couldn't move.

'Feels better, right?' she muttered dreamily, still floating.

'Better?' he echoed with amusement as he picked her up and carried her to the bed. 'Feels like we've barely begun.'

CHAPTER EIGHT

VIOLET WOKE, INSTINCTIVELY AWARE something wasn't quite right. Behind her Roman's breathing was irregular and his body tense. He made a sound—almost a choke—and his big body flinched. This was no restful sleep.

'Roman?' Gently she put her hand on his shoulder and felt the blazing heat of his skin. 'Roman?'

He jerked, instantly awake. 'Did I wake you? Sorry. Restless sleeper.'

She rolled towards him, wishing she could see his face, but the light in the carriage wasn't bright enough. 'That was a little more than restless.'

He slid out of the bed. 'Work stress. Sorry. Go back to sleep. I'm going to get this stuff done while I'm thinking of it.'

'But it's…' She raised up and pushed the button to illuminate her watch. 'Not even four in the morning.'

'Yeah, you go back to sleep.'

Violet paused. He was avoiding talking to her about whatever the hell had been going on in his head. His uneven breathing was still audible but now wasn't the time to push it. She'd broach it later.

But later on in the morning, while she ate pastries for breakfast, Roman kept his focus firmly on his computer screen. Feeling fidgety, she explored the compartment and discovered a hidden cupboard in which there were some beautiful hardbound books and intricately carved games and puzzles.

'They thought of everything on this train,' she murmured with delight.

He glanced up and watched her carry a couple of puzzle boxes to the small table by her comfy arm chair. She went with solitaire first.

Ten minutes later, Roman finally spoke. 'You're good at that.'

'I'm good at entertaining myself alone for long periods of time,' she said lightly.

His lips twisted in a rueful smile. 'What other games are there?'

'Chess, of course. And checkers. Do you know how to play?'

'Neither, I'm afraid.'

'Shall I teach you?'

He leaned back in his chair. 'How do you know how to play if you were always entertaining yourself alone?'

'I spun the board and played against myself.'

'Oh?' He looked arch. 'What else did you do to entertain yourself *alone*?'

She shot a look at his saucy tone and felt that delicious warmth deep inside. 'I painted my nails and I plaited my hair. And I'm not joking. I mastered all sorts of cool styles with my wigs.' She leaned forward. 'But I don't like that I have to play by myself *now*.'

He opened his arms. 'Come play with me, then.'

Finally. She sauntered over to him and straddled his lap. Looking deep into his eyes, she saw that lingering tiredness. He'd been awake for hours.

'I think you need to go to bed.' She brushed her lips against his.

'You think?'

'I know.'

'Only if you come with me.'

'Oh, I intend to. Repeatedly.'

He chuckled and stood, lifting her easily. Violet wriggled and wrapped around him in delight. This chemistry they had… She was beginning to think it had an eternal source of fuel.

'I've been researching on the Internet,' he said hours later after they'd eaten a lazy dinner and were naked and reclining on the bed like debauched demigods from antiquity.

'Is that wise?' She looked at him askance. 'There's a lot of rubbish on the Internet.'

He chuckled. 'You don't bother?'

'Never.'

'You haven't typed in my name?'

'No.' She really didn't want to see what the world said about him.

'Well, I've been looking at some obstetricians. You want to look over their details? Then maybe we can make an appointment for next week back in Manhattan.'

She wrapped her arms around her legs. 'If we must.' But she appreciated that he was asking her, not just making the appointment without even informing her.

'You know we must, Violet. Don't let fear stop you from doing what's right.' He inhaled. 'We're still going to need confirmation of everything. All counts.'

'All counts?' She frowned, puzzled, and then narrowed in on his wariness. 'Do you mean you still want to get a paternity test?'

He nodded. 'My lawyers will require evidence of the relationship between the child and me.'

'Your word isn't enough?' Shock then anger rippled

through her. 'Don't *you* believe I was a virgin that night? Do you believe I've had sex with someone else since? A whole lot of someone else's? Unprotected sex, even?'

How could he even ask this when they were lying naked in bed *right now*? She sat up and tugged the top sheet, wrapping it around her and not caring at all that she'd left him exposed.

'I apologise if it offends you. I'm not questioning your integrity.'

'Of course you are. That's exactly what you're doing.' She frowned. 'I told you. At the time. I trusted you enough to tell you and then to let you…' She was hurt that he wouldn't believe she'd been honest about that. 'The only person I've ever had sex with is you. But you don't believe me.'

'I do believe you,' he argued gruffly. 'Other *people* won't. It is in both our best interests for everything to be proven. For the baby too. It'll stop the worst conjecture.'

'What do we care about conjecture? I don't care about what strangers think about me.'

He scoffed. 'You were worried just yesterday about the stewards knowing. You care.'

'I care much more about what *you* think about me. Because if we're going to work together—and the word is *work*—then we need to trust each other.'

'Right. So can you trust my experience in dealing with this?'

She sat still, remembering his response when he'd first found out yesterday that she was pregnant. His immediate reaction had been raw and primal. That first instinct had been to believe her. It was only now he'd had time to *think* that he was doubting her. She didn't really mind that his lawyers would want evidence but she wanted to know why he was suddenly cautious and so careful to give it to them.

'Can you tell me what that experience actually is?' she asked. 'Have you been in this position before?'

'Not this exact position.' He drew in an irritated breath. 'But I don't want you to be attacked.'

She didn't think this was about that. There was something more bothering him. 'How many times do I have to tell you that I don't need your protection?'

'You're naïve to think that you won't. Violet, I'm one of the wealthiest men in the country, if not the world. People find out you're pregnant with my child, you're a target for abduction. Or worse.'

'You're trying to scare me.' And distract her from whatever his *actual* experience was. He needed evidence. Proof. Certainty. Why?

'Yes. Because I'm trying to make you see sense. You want to walk away from me? You're going to need a bodyguard. You were right when you said we lived in different worlds.'

'But you don't need to drag me fully into yours. I can still be independent. You know that.'

'You can't live on the other side of the world from me. I can't let that happen. I can't let you out of my sight.'

She stared at him. 'Your *sight*?'

He rolled his shoulders. 'I'm sorry. It's not negotiable for me.'

'You want to completely control my life!' She blinked, confused. This wasn't the understanding man she'd opened up to only yesterday—who'd encouraged her to speak honestly. The generous one who only minutes ago had done everything in his power to make her shake with unbridled ecstasy. 'Why? What's happened?'

His reaction seemed so extreme. She took in the tired expression in his eyes, the desolate edge to his voice. This was more than him being tired from their night together.

It was that dream—or nightmare—she'd caught him having last night. He'd barely been sleeping. There was something going on. Something beyond her. And he needed to let her in on it.

But he wouldn't look at her and he didn't answer her. It hurt. She'd been honest with him yesterday. She'd trusted him on many levels. She'd thought the barriers were coming down and they were truly getting to know each other. But they weren't at all. *He* was still so very reserved.

'Tell you what, Roman. I will marry you,' she said. 'In fact, I'll marry you this second if that's what you want. Go get Colson. He's probably got his celebrant's certificate or something.'

His eyes narrowed. 'On what condition?'

Because he knew there was one. It couldn't be that she'd realised her love for him.

And he was right.

'That there's no pre-nuptial contract,' she said.

He stiffened and just stared at her.

'No pre-nup. No lawyers. Nothing.' She leaned closer to him, suddenly confident. 'Which could mean I'd stay married to you for as long as I could be bothered and then grab as much of your money and assets as possible.'

'Out of respect for my employees, you know I can't agree to that.'

'No? Because of your employees, you say?'

'Violet—'

'I believe we're at an impasse.' She cut him off. 'You won't marry me without a pre-nup. I won't marry you *with* one. What are we going to do?'

His jaw locked. 'You're going to get it together and be sensible.'

'Or maybe you're going to get it together and realise you can trust me. Just a little, Roman. Right now you don't trust me enough to even tell me what's going on with you!' she said angrily. 'So why on earth would I *ever* agree to marry you?'

'I don't want to admit that I've been conned before!' he exploded, equally angrily. 'No one ever wants to admit that they've been taken for a god damned ride.'

'For money?' She gazed at him in amazement. *'How?'*

Roman's tension was unsustainable. He'd slept poorly. Not because he'd been making love with Violet most of the night, but because he'd then been wary of falling deeply asleep and having those dreams again. And he had, of course. And she'd caught him. And now she was looking at him with those big eyes of her and he couldn't stand it. 'It's a long story.'

'Fortunately for you, this train is slow.'

He half laughed but his whole body was aching. 'Why couldn't you do even a little Internet search? Just to understand the basics.'

'Honestly, I don't want to see the "edible bachelor" photos. They probably have a line-up of potential bachelorettes linked in the article. That would make me feel very grumpy.'

He chuckled again. 'Oh, Violet…'

The way she could make him laugh… But her jokes were laced with honesty, always honesty, and it mattered to her much more than he'd realised. She deserved full honesty from him. She'd trusted him with her truth. He owed her the same.

'I was an only child for a long time.' He sighed. 'My parents had fertility struggles. I know a kid shouldn't know too much, but Mum would get sad, and Dad told me it was because there wasn't a new baby. I tried to be there for her. Be enough.'

But he hadn't been. She'd wanted more. While he kind

of understood that now, his eight-year-old self hadn't. His eight-year-old self had felt inadequate. And, during those times when his mother had got too sad, he'd gone to stay with his grandparents.

'Did they struggle to have you too?' Violet asked.

'I don't know. Never had the chance to ask.' He closed his eyes. 'Although, probably. They were married ten years before they had me.' Now he thought of it, the maths was simple and the conclusion pretty obvious. 'Anyway, it finally happened. Mother got pregnant, and she was so excited. She talked to me all the time about the new baby coming. Dad was happy too and when she finally arrived she was the cutest thing.'

Violet shuffled fractionally closer. 'What was her name?'

'Eloise.'

'So.' Violet looked wary. 'Where is she now?'

'She was in the accident.'

'The one that killed your parents?' Violet drew a pained breath. 'Roman, I'm so sorry.'

'She was in the back seat with me. Mum and Dad died instantly. But Eloise—'

'*You* were there too?' she whispered.

Roman paused. Hadn't she realised that? He drew a breath. He wasn't used to explaining that had happened. It was all publicly available information. His acquaintances knew. People who wanted his investment knew, because it cropped up in the due diligence they did on him. But Violet was from the other side of the world and she'd never heard of his family. She'd not put two and two together even when she'd known his name. She'd not looked at the stories on the Internet. She knew nothing. It was an odd feeling. But, though he never discussed it, now he had to.

And he found he almost wanted to. He wanted her to *understand*. 'Yeah.'

'The scar on your leg. Of course. I should have—'

'I never talk about it,' he assured her when he saw the flush slide over her face. 'Without looking me up, you weren't going to know.'

She nodded.

'We were in Scotland. It was late at night and we were going into the Highlands. I don't remember what happened. But one moment we were driving, the next...'

'Then what happened?'

'I flew back to the States on a private jet. I convalesced for a while, then went to boarding school.'

'You had no family to take you in?'

'My grandparents had both passed earlier that year. There was no one else.' He couldn't look at her as he admitted that. 'A few months later, there was a formal memorial service. They included Eloise in that. The only explanation they could come up with was that her safety belt hadn't been fastened properly, so she'd been flung from the car. Only they never found her body.'

'Never found her?' Violet looked horrified, and then perplexed. 'But she was just a baby, right?'

Right. That was the thing. Roman bowed his head. 'I have snapshots of memory. I couldn't move. My leg was pinned. Eloise was in the back with me. I know she was there with me. Someone came to help. I could *hear* Eloise crying. So I know she survived the accident. But they took her and I couldn't stop them. I couldn't speak. And then...'

'What do you mean "they" took her? You think someone came along and took Eloise?'

He sighed despairingly. 'I was certain of it. But I couldn't give the police the details they wanted. After a while, they began talking to me about whether perhaps I'd been dreaming. And I didn't know. I couldn't remember *anything* clearly. The more I tried to remember, the less clear it became.'

'It must have been awful and so confusing.' She gazed at him worriedly. 'You were so young.'

'They mounted a massive search but there was no sign of her. She'd just vanished.'

'And you were all alone.' Violet breathed.

He rolled his shoulders. Pity? No, he didn't want it. 'I met Alex at school.'

'Alex?'

'My friend.' He flashed her a small, teasing smile. 'The one who has the Halloween party.'

'The party you skipped.'

'Because sometimes I don't feel like socialising,' he admitted. 'At least, not in large groups.'

'But one to one is okay?' She smiled at him sadly.

'One to one is okay if the one is you.'

'That's an awfully charming thing to say. You'd best be careful or I might believe you.'

He smiled. 'You believe me already. You take things at face value.'

Her nose wrinkled. 'You're saying I'm naïve.'

'I'm saying you have faith in the world.'

'But you've lost yours.'

Her words sliced him open. 'I just know there's no happy endings, Violet.'

'And you know this because of Eloise.'

He nodded. 'When I was older, I couldn't shake the belief that she was out there. I launched several private searches. Eventually I even offered a reward for information, you know? A big one.'

'Oh, Roman.'

'It was highly publicised and lots of people came forward. None of the information gathered was helpful.' He rolled his shoulders. 'It kept an assistant very well-employed for a long time. I decided to focus my energies on the company and ensure Eloise's inheritance was intact— if not better—for when she was found. But one day, about a decade ago, a woman came forward. She had a young girl, the right age, the right…'

'Okay.' Violet looked worried. She was right to.

'You might not have noticed the patch of colour in my left eye.' He gestured to his face.

'I've noticed.' A half-smile.

'It's called sectoral heterochromia. It's a genetic thing.'

'Meaning it runs in families.'

'Yeah. So this girl had my coloured eyes, and she looked just like I'd imagine Eloise to look. She was the right age and everything…'

'So you believed it was her.'

'I didn't want to listen to anyone who doubted it. I was happy. I *really* wanted it to be her.' He'd wanted it more than anything.

'Of course you did.'

'But Alex made sure the science was done. He insisted, and he was right to. It was a fraud—a simple contact lens in her eye and a whole sequence of avoidance to reel me in and not question the discrepancies. They'd said the contacts were for short-sightedness. My grandmother was short-sighted, and I just wanted to believe it was her so badly, I overlooked everything that was blindingly obvious. But she wasn't her. Eloise was dead.'

'You must have been devastated.'

'I didn't handle it well.' Understatement of the century. He'd been wrecked. 'It was easier to drown everything.'

'In women?'

'And parties and drinking. Everything in excess.' He

stared down at the endless expanse of white sheet. 'Sometimes I wonder if she was even real. If I just made her up because I knew how much my parents wanted her. But I didn't. I know she was there…and then all of a sudden she wasn't. They've never found any trace of her. I should have called out. I should have stopped them.'

'Even if she was taken, you never could have stopped whoever it was. You were badly hurt and you were all alone. You were a *child*.'

Yeah, that was what Alex had said. It was Alex who had told him to pull his head in when he'd been partying too hard—who'd told him he couldn't let the accident destroy his life. Alex who'd convinced him it was time to let go, move forward and that he had to build something for himself. And finally, after that terrible hoax, he'd listened. He'd stopped searching. He'd had to. He'd accepted he was never going to find Eloise. She really was gone.

'It must hurt to be the only one left.' Violet looked concerned. 'Carrying the burden of the family company.'

'It's the only thing I can do for them. I want to keep some of their dreams alive.'

He'd realised he couldn't let everything be destroyed. Instead he'd vowed to make the company—the family name—bigger and better. It had given him meaning and purpose in these last few years. And there was a tiny, tiny spark of hope buried deep that, if Eloise ever were found, then he knew it would all be waiting here for her. Not that he ever acknowledged that spark.

'Like this train.' Violet waved a graceful hand at the gleaming interior.

'Right.' But truthfully the train had never been for the money. The thing ran at a loss. But it had been his grandfather's passion and Roman wanted to keep it going purely for him. He wanted to be a success at something—anything—that had mattered to his grandparents. He wanted to honour them.

'It's other people too—their livelihoods.' He cleared his throat. 'Other people's memories. We give them a magical experience.'

And of course it allowed him a lifestyle that most people barely dreamed of. He had no right to be unhappy. He had it all. He'd done it all. Except this—he'd never got a lover pregnant. Never even had a 'scare' before. And he'd never felt this confused or this out of control. It felt like the past and the present were colliding and creating a future he couldn't cope with.

'You don't have any hope of finding Eloise now?' Violet asked.

'I've delegated any of those enquiries to Alex.' He avoided answering directly. 'He protects me from any chancers who turn up claiming to be her. Occasionally they still do. But they never are.'

'Alex sounds like a good friend.'

'Guess we all need one, like you said.' He suddenly laughed. 'He was runner-up in the "eligible" list this year. He's quite put out about it. He won last year.'

'But you toppled him?' she teased.

'We take turns.' Roman turned serious. 'I'm sorry I haven't been a good friend to you, Violet. You trusted me that night, and I wanted to honour the gift of your trust, but I let you down.'

'It was an accident. Accidents happen.' She met his gaze squarely.

'Yeah. They do.'

And they could have devastating consequences.

'I don't want your money, Roman.'

'I know that, angel.'

They had far bigger issues than that.

Roman knew babies—or the lack thereof—caused strain in relationships. He'd never wanted to board the rollercoaster of conflicting desires and disappointment when people didn't get what they wanted in a marriage. He'd always wanted to remain alone.

But the stupid thing was, he didn't want to let Violet go. And he could. He could set her up in an apartment. She could have security, staff, all the safety mechanisms in place. They'd barely have to engage with each other at all. He could still be involved in their child's life. Violet need not give up her dreams—they could have the best nannies and she could travel if she wished.

But he'd turned selfish. He liked having her here in the chair opposite his with her feet tucked up, a book in her hand and her gaze on the window, watching the world race by with that curious vitality shining in her eyes. A possessiveness he'd never felt before burgeoned. She was his. And he wanted her to be his alone. And honestly he didn't have much that was his. Things, yes, but not a person.

You can't have a person. You can't keep a person.

People moved in and out of his life. Of everyone's lives. That was the point. There was no such thing as 'for ever'. He knew that intimately. They left—through travel, through death. He would lose her. He would lose this child. He was suddenly certain. He couldn't let it happen—but he knew he couldn't stop it. Things—and people—could be lost or destroyed too easily. They could disappear.

Violet came from the other side of the world. He'd lost his sister on the other side of the world, and his parents. He'd come back home alone. Having Violet and the baby on the other side of the world wasn't going to happen. He had to convince her to stay with him and he'd do it by whatever means necessary. She thought she couldn't be seduced into marriage—he'd see about that. Failure was an unacceptable, impossible outcome.

So he pulled the sheet from her, moved over her, relentless and ravenous in his quest to secure her acquiescence. Nothing mattered more in this instant than being with her—honest and hot. She was like quicksilver in his arms—pliant and pleasing, so willing. The sweetest, steamiest of lovers, increasingly adventurous and increasingly ravenous too. She met him, matched him. Vanquished him.

But afterwards he lay awake, listening to her gentle deep breathing. He couldn't hold on to her. He *shouldn't*. Because, while he could get her to scream *yes* to him, while he could satisfy her between these sheets…for how long would she actually be happy? Not long at all. Because this wasn't what she wanted. He wasn't what she wanted.

He slid out of bed but didn't turn on the lights, not wanting to wake her. He sat in the chair and tried to think his way through the impossible problem. But he was tired and his head wasn't working right.

Telling her about the past hadn't helped in any way. And they certainly hadn't got rid of any of that chemistry, even though he'd lost count of how many times they'd had sex today. He tried not to watch her sleeping. It was too much of a 'freaky stalker' thing to do. But she looked so beautifully relaxed, he was almost jealous. He was sorely tempted to curl beside her. To pull her against him felt like the only way he would ever get rest again. But the dreams hadn't just returned, they were worsening. And he couldn't risk her hearing him or him kicking out again.

Indulging in physical pleasure was satisfying but ultimately pointless in terms of sorting their future. They were merely treading water. And he couldn't sleep with her—actually *sleep*.

Which meant they couldn't stay on this train.

CHAPTER NINE

Christmas Eve

'VIOLET? YOU NEED to wake up.'

Violet stirred and rolled over with a reluctant sigh. She smiled and opened her eyes—expecting Roman to be beside her. But he wasn't.

She sat up and saw him fully dressed and back behind that wretched work desk. 'What's wrong? Didn't you sleep again?'

'I'm okay.'

She knew he wasn't. He'd talked to her and they'd had an amazing night but he wasn't okay. Something felt wrong—worse, in fact. This was like the calm before a storm. Then she realised there was a literal stillness that hadn't been present in days. 'The train isn't moving.'

Roman didn't look surprised or concerned.

'What's happening?' She brushed aside the curtain to peek out of the window. 'We're in a siding. Roman, you should see the view from here. It's stunning. Are we in Colorado? It is *beautiful*.'

She could see snow, huge skies, mountains. And there was another sound, growing louder. She watched round-eyed as a helicopter landed in the field beside the railway tracks. She turned and looked at Roman's expressionless face. 'That's for us, isn't it?'

'Yes. So you need to get dressed. Okay?'

She didn't want to get dressed, she wanted to understand what was going on. 'Where are we going?'

'I think we need space.'

His words stabbed her heart. He wanted distance from her.

'I can't think clearly when you're this close,' he said.

'Do you need to think?' Weren't they just…living day by day through this? Wouldn't they work it all out eventually?

'Always. But especially now.' He drew in a breath. 'Plus, you get to see a little more of the country. That's a win, right?'

She nodded. But she couldn't help a small worry from growing.

'I should have talked to you first before arranging everything but you were asleep.'

'You didn't sleep well again.' She gazed at him. 'Bad dreams?'

He hesitated and there was the briefest flicker of vulnerability on his face. 'I haven't had them in a long while.'

'But these last few nights you have.' She slid out of bed and quickly pulled on her clothes. 'What happens in the dreams?'

He didn't answer for a long while and when he did it was so soft she had to stand still to hear him.

'I can't call out. Can't move. I'm stuck and silent but inside I'm screaming. No one hears me. No one helps.'

He abruptly stood and pushed the button to open the curtains fully. Violet moved to stand beside him.

'I wish I could help,' she said wistfully. 'But you know I can barely handle my own issues…'

To her relief, he suddenly smiled. She smiled back and linked her fingers through his to let him know she didn't really mean to leave him alone. 'I guess this…situation… is stressful, huh? Makes all the old worries come alive,' she said. 'Even the ones we thought were gone for good.'

He looked down at her and returned her grip with a tighter one of his own. 'What are your worries?'

'All of them. I have all of them. I'm a big chicken.'

'Not the first adjective I'd pick for you.'

'I thought I was brave. I thought I was ready to take on the world. But I hear the voice in my head the whole time: *Don't take the risk…you shouldn't…be careful…now look what you've done…* All the possible bad things flash through my mind. Never the possible best things. I try to ignore and push past. But it's hard.'

'I think you're being a bit hard on yourself. You're here—doing all these things. It might be scary but you're doing it anyway. Even coping with me.' He turned, lifting his free hand, and brushed back her hair. 'Maybe this baby *is* the best thing.'

Her eyes suddenly filled. 'That's definitely the best thing. But it's also very complicated.'

'Life is.'

'Yeah. To tell you the truth, I've never been in a helicopter.'

'Really? Well, I'm glad I can provide you with another first-time experience,' he teased.

'Are you saying this is going to be as good as that?'

'Not quite as good. But, still, perhaps a thrill.'

'Okay.' She gazed at him. 'I trust you.'

He looked at her and then back to the helicopter. 'Right. Then let's do this, okay?'

The helicopter wasn't anything like Violet had imagined. They had a compartment in the back that was plush and *quiet*. And the views from the windows were incredible.

'Where are we going?' She couldn't stop staring at the scenery.

'We have a lodge in the mountains.'

We.

While she felt exhilarated as the helicopter flew towards the enormous mountain range, Roman looked a little pale.

'Are you okay?' she asked.

'I needed to get off the train for Christmas Eve.'

'Oh?' she suddenly teased. 'Did you want to make sure Santa knows exactly where to find you?'

His eyes widened and a small smile broke his tension. 'I forget you don't know.' He shook his head. 'No. The accident was on Christmas Eve.'

'Oh, *Roman*.' She felt terrible for her silly joke. 'I'm so sorry, I didn't mean—'

'I know.' He squeezed her hand. 'I like that you make me laugh even when I'm…'

Her heart broke and she didn't try to finish his sentence. No wonder he didn't like Christmas. That was the saddest thing. She stared out at the vast mountains, this time barely noticing the snow-covered trees and the wide blue sky above. She was imagining a very lonely, scared little boy stuck in a smashed-up car with his deceased parents, knowing his sister was missing. How could anyone bear that?

'You need space tonight,' she muttered.

There would be space in a lodge in the mountains. Knowing him, it would be a big house with lots of room.

'You understand?' he confirmed.

'Of course I do.'

So much now fell into place. She would be there beside him if he wanted, just silent, saying something stupid if he wanted distraction. But he didn't. He wanted distance. He always wanted distance.

And she didn't blame him. Some wounds were too deep ever to be healed.

Half an hour later, Violet stared slack-jawed at the massive stone and wooden lodge, with its enormous deck and lights that twinkled warmly even now, in the middle of the very cold day. Through the left set of windows, she saw a huge Christmas tree inside, gorgeously decorated.

'It's been in the family for years,' Roman said. 'My great-grandfather built it. My grandfather added on to it.'

'It's…' She couldn't think of the word—any words.

'Roman?' An older woman bustled out from the building, a stunned look on her face. 'I had no idea you were coming.'

'I know, Linda. It's okay.' He smiled as the woman raced down the stone steps. 'Violet, this is Linda. Linda, Violet.'

The woman nodded kindly at Violet but the concern didn't leave her face as she quickly glanced back to Roman. 'Your suite is ready, of course.' Now she looked even more anxious. 'You remember…it's the ball tonight? It's Christmas Eve.'

Roman stilled. There was the slightest of caught breaths before he replied. 'Of course. I…'

'Should I cancel it?' Linda wiped her hands again. 'I can—'

'No. Definitely not. That wouldn't be fair to everyone.' He pushed out a smile but Violet saw the tension in his stance. 'I'm sure you'll have done a wonderful job with the preparations.'

Linda's eyes suddenly filled.

'I'll show Violet the rest of the lodge,' Roman said quickly. 'Give you time to double-check our rooms. I know you'll want to ensure they're perfect, even though I also know they already will be.'

Linda flashed a tremulous smile.

Roman hesitated. 'I'll…stay in the upstairs wing tonight.' His voice was husky. 'Won't encroach.'

'Of course.'

Violet's heart ached as Roman led her up the stairs. It was Christmas Eve, he wanted to be alone and there was going to be some big party here?

'I forgot there was the Christmas Eve ball,' he said as he guided her across the deck and then into the vast entrance of the lodge.

'You've had other things on your mind,' Violet said lightly. 'Is it a thing here?'

'A tradition my grandparents started a long time ago. It's a celebration and a fundraiser for the local community. Linda does it all every year.'

'She's lived here a long time?'

'They've looked after the lodge for longer than I've been alive. She and her husband Dennis live in the gatehouse we passed at the edge of the property.'

That would be the gorgeous gingerbread-house building she'd seen. She'd thought *that* was the lodge, but it was tiny compared to this. This place was like one of his hotels, only it was private.

'They raised their family there,' Roman continued. 'They have grandchildren now. One's a formidable snowboarder.'

Were they almost family, then? Violet's heart ached even more. This was someone who'd known Roman a long time. Who'd known all his family too. Yet there'd been an obvious strain just now. Linda clearly cared about him but she also knew better than to make a fuss. Roman's preference for isolation was deeply entrenched. That knowledge made her anxious. How was he really going to feel about fatherhood?

'This is the reception room.' He led her through vast double doors.

'Oh, my.' Violet turned on the spot. 'My mother would melt in a heap at the sight of this room.' She shot him a sideways look. 'How did they get the lights so perfectly strung on those trees? How did they find *three* such perfect trees?'

'I thought you weren't that into Christmas.' Roman looked both amused and wistful.

'So did I. But it turns out I'm fickle like that…because this is *beautiful*.'

'There's mistletoe.'

'There's also…' She suddenly froze, staring beneath the central tree, too scared to move. 'Is that a bobcat or something?'

There was literally a giant ginger beast skulking out from beneath the Christmas tree and heading towards them with a murderous gleam in its eyes.

Roman burst out laughing. 'That is Linda's cat, Bruce.'

'That's a *cat*? He looks…' Where were the words? 'Majestic. Really majestic. And terrifying. He's huge.'

'Stop, you'll inflate his ego. He already thinks he owns the place.'

Violet watched the enormous cat leisurely stretch then stroll towards Roman, imperiously allowing him to scratch beneath his ears. It was obviously something he'd done many times before.

'Of course he does,' Violet muttered.

She was blown away. This was a place that was a *home*. This had photos of his family.

'Do you spend much time here?' She couldn't contain her curiosity.

'I come skiing for a week, later in January. To check in on Linda and Dennis and make sure they have all they need to keep the place up.'

Just one week in the whole year? She would have been here so much more than that. 'What other properties do you have to keep up?'

'There's a big house in upstate New York. An apartment in Manhattan.'

'But you stay in that hotel when you're there.'

'It's nearer to the office.'

And it was opulent. But it was also impersonal. Unlike this place, which was utterly opulent but also *very* personal.

'Everything is ready upstairs for you, Roman.' Linda reappeared.

'Thanks, Linda.' But he turned away as his phone pinged. 'One moment.'

'Thank you so much for welcoming me,' Violet said shyly to Linda. 'I'm sorry we're a surprise arrival on such a busy day for you.'

'No, I'm thrilled you're here. Especially that he's brought you. He's never...' Linda smiled awkwardly.

Violet just nodded. She didn't want to ask the older woman anything private. That wouldn't be fair on her or on Roman. But Linda stilled, her expression serious.

'He's not been here for Christmas since the accident. I never thought...' Linda looked at Violet with worried eyes. 'Should the ball still go ahead?'

Violet was the *least* qualified person to make that call. 'It sounds like it's a really important tradition.'

'But for Roman, Christmas Eve is—'

'Still Christmas Eve,' Violet said gently. But he wanted space and she needed something to do. 'Can I help at all?'

She turned to Linda impulsively. 'I'd really love to be able to help.'

Linda's expression widened. 'You're...'

'Going to let Roman be upstairs,' she said. 'But, please, if there's anything that needs doing, I'd really like to help out. I've waitressed—I can carry heaped trays without dropping *hors d'oeuvres*.'

Linda laughed. 'This is Roman's home and you're *his* guest. But it would be an honour for me if you came along tonight as our guest.'

'No, I don't want to intrude.' Neither upstairs in the private wing nor down here at the ball. 'I just wanted to...'

Linda's expression softened. 'Don't worry, its not a "table settings" sort of night. It's a "stand and nibble, drink then dance" kind of night. There are so many people coming, one more guest won't be noticed. It'll be marvellous.'

Violet was tempted. Really tempted. And she'd rather feel slightly awkward down here with a group of strangers than really awkward upstairs avoiding Roman, who wanted nothing more than to be alone. 'Maybe I could just help out the back?' she asked one last time. 'Or is that too awkward?'

'You don't want to come to the ball?' Linda looked disbelieving, but then her gaze dropped to her jeans. 'You didn't have much luggage with you.'

'No.' She felt so awkward right now. She just had that little overnight bag that Roman had scoffed at.

'Some of my daughter's clothes are stored in the cottage attic. She's taller than you, but we might find something that'll fit if you don't have anything formal to wear.'

And now the temptation was too much to stand. 'Are you sure?'

Linda was the kind of person for whom nothing was a

problem. Who wanted to make things nice. Violet knew the sort and could appreciate her.

'I always need help with tying bows on the bannisters. They tend to go wonky on me.'

'I can do ribbon.' Violet squared her shoulders. 'And I would love to come tonight. Thank you.'

Linda smiled. 'Then go and settle your things upstairs and come down when you're ready. We'll have plenty of time to sort the ribbons and fix up a dress.'

Violet turned to where Roman was still talking on his phone. But his gaze was locked on her.

'Okay?' Roman asked curiously once he'd finished the call. 'I see you've hit it off with Linda. You get on with everyone instantly, don't you?'

'Not true.' She followed him up the wide staircase, marvelling at the wood panelling and the high vaulted ceiling. 'But I did ask her if I could help her out this evening.'

'You want to attend?' Roman paused on the step above hers and looked back at her. 'I thought you didn't like perfect Christmases. There'll be decorations and amazing food and well-dressed people. You could just stay up…' He cleared his throat. 'There's a den up here with satellite TV…' He trailed off awkwardly.

'You might want to just zone out in front of it.' She kept climbing up the stairs past him. She would stay out of his way. 'I'd like to go. It's not going to be one of my usual claustrophobic family Christmases with everyone on eggshells, hoping everyone else is having the Best Time Ever. I can help out in the background and observe a fancy party on my first winter Christmas. That way, you get your space and I get to experience something new.'

Roman was silent as he led her into the large private wing on the first floor. He couldn't quite cope with being back here. He'd forgotten about the ball when he'd made the plan to fly to the lodge. He'd just wanted to get off the train to ensure he got more space from Violet at night-time because the dreams weren't easing. Because it was Christmas Eve and he needed to be alone. But there was the ball, and he'd not just forgotten that, but how this place looked at Christmas. It had been so, so long.

But it was almost exactly as he'd remembered. So many memories assailed him. The scent of the fir, of the candles. The spices in the *gluhwein* that Linda always made. Linda, who opened the house up to let people celebrate. Who kept all his grandmother's traditions alive. And starry-eyed Violet was now standing beside him. Her appreciation of the place—the snow, the festive settings—made something thaw inside. It hurt as he saw it all as if for the first time. Like Violet was doing. Only it wasn't the first time for him. And it meant so much.

'This room is amazing.' Violet gazed up at the cathedral-like ceiling. Floor-to-ceiling windows spanned two walls, giving a view of the mountains in the distance. It faced away from the nearby village—only snowy mountains, trees and sky stretched for miles. It was utterly private.

Violet turned from the view outside to the few framed pictures on the wall.

'Your family?' she asked, then stopped by one photo. 'You?'

He was wearing a hand-knitted beanie. It had been a gift from his grandmother.

'And that's you on the train? As a child?'

'It was my grandfather's crazy dream to restore it. It's one of the few private trains in the country and only runs a few routes each year. Usually for charity.'

'Crazy dream? Did they want to recreate the halcyon days of train travel?' she said.

'I guess. Maybe. Yeah.' He suddenly smiled. 'He and my grandmother Joan travelled on it together. He oversaw the refurbishment. She chose the coverings.'

'They made it extremely beautiful,' she said. 'They were romantics. And it's romantic of you to keep that dream alive for them both.'

He couldn't resist her. He inhaled the effervescence she exuded and her breathless, wide-eyed chatter, the way she made friends in moments... He leaned closer to her and the discomfort eased. He always felt better when he stood a few inches too close to her to be polite. Oh, the irony that, the second he'd got them to a place where they could actually be apart, he couldn't bear to be more than an inch from her.

'What are you going to wear tonight?' He tugged at her top, trying to distract himself from the emotion threatening to overwhelm him. 'That train-steward skirt is cute, but it's not appropriate for a formal celebration, and as far as I can tell you only have jeans...' He unfastened those jeans.

'I'll figure something out.' She shrugged.

He wondered about that. He could ask Linda if she could find something. But Violet stopped him as he reached for his phone.

'Don't,' she said. 'I can sort this.' Concern entered her eyes. 'Unless you don't want me to mix with the guests? I promise I'll be good. You don't need to worry about me.'

'You'll be wonderful. They'll love to meet you. But you don't have—'

'Don't think you have to give me a makeover. I can figure something out. I can be creative.'

'Creative?' He grinned at her. 'Prove it.'

Violet looked up into his eyes but she didn't smile back. 'I'm sorry this is such a difficult day for you, Roman. I'm sorry you have to suffer alone through all of this.'

Her words sliced him open and he suddenly couldn't speak. But he wasn't alone right now. He was with her. And he didn't want to see that look in her eyes. It wasn't sympathy. It wasn't pity. It was something else. Something he refused to recognise yet couldn't resist.

He pulled her into his arms. But it wasn't like the times with those other women years ago—when sex had purely been about avoidance and orgasm. Violet's touch was too soft, then too firm. She held him so close, so tight. And he had no choice but to close his eyes. He had to bury his face in her neck and breathe that citrusy scent as she swept her arms around him in an embrace like no other. And he lost himself, completely lost himself, in the safety of her hold.

Three hours later Violet stood in the bathroom attached to one of the guest bedrooms, trying to hold her leaking heart together. It was spilling bits of empathy everywhere but Roman didn't want that. He wanted to be alone. And that was fair enough. She would totally respect it. She wasn't going to fall into the trap that her mother had—wanting to make everything all better for someone. That wasn't possible. It was Christmas Eve, she was going to have some fun for herself and that was okay.

She twisted to the side and executed a little shimmy jump to get the zipper of her dress done all the way up. It was long and silver and she really quite liked it. The only shoes she had were the ballet flats that she'd folded up in her small bag—her emergency evening shoes. They would have to do. She'd done what she could with the sparse make-up supplies she had with her, but then she'd shamelessly taken her time with her hair. She hadn't seen Roman since she'd left him in his room that afternoon, and honestly she rather wished he could see her right now. She thought she'd done okay pulling together an outfit for a fancy Christmas ball last minute.

A knock on her door made her heart leap but, when she opened it, it was Linda.

'I thought you might like to borrow these.' Linda held a small box. 'If you wanted to add a little sparkle.'

The diamanté drop earrings were fabulously theatrical—a chain of stones in an almost architectural Art Deco style. They'd be a perfect contrast against the simplicity of the silver dress they'd found this afternoon.

'Oh, I couldn't.'

'They're inexpensive crystals,' Linda said briskly. 'Please wear them. They'll go so well with your dress.'

Violet took in the green silk caftan Linda was wearing, the diamond-studded tennis bracelet on her wrist and the gold rings on her fingers. This was a bling event. This was Christmas Festive.

'Are you absolutely sure?' she double-checked.

'Yes.' Linda watched Violet put the earrings in and smiled. 'You look lovely.'

'So do you.' Violet smiled back and then laughed. 'Thank you so much for including me in this.'

She walked downstairs with Linda, blinking when she saw the crowd in its elegant evening wear. She'd not realised so many guests had arrived already.

'They arrive on a big coach all together,' Linda explained as she took her arm. 'Now, come on with me. You need to meet my Dennis.'

CHAPTER TEN

ALMOST TWO HOURS LATER, Violet was chatting with the local vet, who was entertaining her with tales of Linda's cats. She was sipping lemonade from a cut-crystal glass and chuckling with delight when she realised there was someone standing in the far doorway. Someone was watching. He was half in the shadow and he wasn't smiling. She wasn't sure how long he'd been there, but suddenly it was impossible to breathe. She'd seen him in a tuxedo the first night they'd met, but this was different. So very different.

She excused herself from the conversation and quietly walked towards him, meeting him in the shadowed entranceway.

'Roman.' Her concern grew when she saw the sharp edges in his face. 'You didn't have to come down.'

She couldn't quite tell if his response was a smile or a grimace.

'I'm okay,' she added. 'You didn't need to check on me. I can handle this.'

'I know you can. But I…' That expressionless mask suddenly dropped to reveal stark desolation in his eyes. His shrug was small.

She rose up onto tiptoe so she could hear him, so she could get closer, to encourage him to finish what he'd been going to say.

'What else was I going to do?'

The query was almost inaudible, but she heard the thread of pain and longing.

'I thought you wanted to be alone,' she whispered.

'I did. I thought that too. Until…' His sombre eyes didn't waver from hers. 'Until I didn't.' He swallowed. 'I don't want to be alone.'

Her heart simply burst.

'I thought I'd come find you instead.' His breath was the softest warmth brushing her forehead.

'Okay.' She slipped her hand in his and swallowed. 'Okay, then.'

She glanced about, suddenly aware that people had noticed his arrival and that he looked awkward. Roman didn't do awkward. Roman was suave and confident. But now he gripped her hand.

'Did you have that suit on the train?' She smiled up at him.

'I have a whole wardrobe here.' He stared at her. 'Where'd you get your dress?'

'It's Linda's daughter's old prom dress. The theme was The Golden Age of Hollywood. I feel like I should be in the nineteen-twenties. She shortened the straps for me.'

'Prom dress, huh?'

She chuckled. 'Yeah. I finally got to wear one.'

'And the earrings?'

'Linda's costume jewellery.'

'That's what she told you?'

'It is. Isn't it?' She put her hand to her ear. 'The crystals are too massive to be real.'

A gleam entered his eyes and suddenly she was suspicious.

'Are they not costume?' She was shocked—and then appalled. Was she wearing something unspeakably valu-

able? 'How do you know?' Her eyes narrowed as she realised. 'You deceived me.'

'I've said nothing.' He shrugged.

'Omission is still a lie.'

'Don't be angry. They're beautiful on you.'

'I thought…'

'They're kept here. Family vault. They haven't seen the
light of day in years.'

They really were real! 'What if I'd lost them?' She
breathed.

'At least they'd have been worn one last time.'

'Why did you do it?'

'You'd have said no if I told you. I just wanted to do
something nice for you without any…' He trailed off.

'Drama?'

He suddenly laughed. And that was what snuffed out
any annoyance that might've lit inside her. He was smiling and she was so pleased to see it.

'You're the dramatic one,' she teased him, mock-bale-
fully. 'Secretly passing me priceless jewellery.'

He'd wanted to do something nice for her. Something
fluttered in her chest. Something both dangerous and devastating and tempting her to believe in it.

'We can just hang out in the background,' she said. 'No
one is really interested in talking to me.'

'That's not true. I was watching you for a while before you saw me. That guy was super-interested in talking to you.'

That flutter in her chest grew stronger. 'He was talking
to me about Linda's cats.'

'I think…' He suddenly sighed. 'That, seeing you're
wearing a vintage prom dress and vintage jewels, I think
that we ought to dance.'

'Are you sure?'

'If we're dancing, everyone else will leave us alone.'

Violet had seen Linda watching them from the doorway and seen the protective lift of her chin. She wouldn't let anyone interrupt them. And the guests smiled but stayed back, giving him the space. The older ones were all aware of his past. There was a hint of curiosity, of course, but they were too well-mannered and too compassionate to intrude. So Violet and Roman danced at the back of the room in the shadows, as lost in the crowd as it was possible to get.

He moved stiffly at first, but she wrapped her arms around his waist and leaned in. Then he softened. He wasn't really a grump—he was prickly because he was protecting himself. And, given all the losses he'd suffered, she didn't blame him.

He couldn't seem to take his gaze off her. She certainly couldn't look away from him. Lazy jazz music played—Christmas tunes somehow blended into easy-moving melodies. The pianist was talented, as was the singer. They were barely moving to the music, but he was safe, warm and not alone, and it didn't matter if they weren't terribly social.

'They all leave at eleven,' Roman muttered eventually. 'There's a service in town at midnight for those who want to attend. Others go home and open presents.'

'On Christmas Eve?'

'Well, it's Christmas Day by then. But yes.'

Roman's whole body ached. She looked like the angel on top of a Christmas tree. A perfect, petite thing dressed in silver. She'd been laughing when he'd first spotted her. Of course she'd been laughing, as she'd chattered away to the group of people surrounding her. She entranced everyone—most especially him.

Her beautiful glossy hair was partially tied up in an intricate plait from which the length then fell at the back. The style exposed her fine features—those high cheekbones and the heart-shaped face and dainty ears from which, he noted with immense pleasure, the diamonds hung. Radiance shone like silvery light from her. Stars sparkled in her eyes.

'Are you okay?' She broke into his thoughts. 'You look a little ferocious.'

'I'm okay.'

Oddly enough, he was. He rubbed his eyes with the back of his hand. Being here like this, he had feelings both of happiness and heartache. So many memories converged on him at once. He only wanted to recall the good.

'I remember so many balls here. Joan—my grandmother—would let me choose one present to unwrap before sending me to bed.'

Violet's smile deepened. 'She spoilt you.'

'She did.'

'What else did you do at the balls?'

'Lots of the things you see here. Linda's kept up all the traditions she knew. The lights in the windows are there to invite everyone in and so Santa couldn't possibly miss the lodge. Reindeer feed outside. Cookies.'

'Did you have a stocking?'

He nodded. 'Always got a new woollen hat to keep my ears warm. Joan knitted it. But I'd always lose it some time in the ski season.'

'A hat like the ones we saw at that market?'

He nodded and she pressed closer to him.

Everything ached. 'Is it okay if we go upstairs now?' he asked.

'You want me to come up with you?'

He didn't bother answering, he just kept hold of her hand.

Up in the private wing, he'd left the lights off and the curtains open, so now the view was nothing but stars. He drew her to the sofa with him. The fire burning in the grate cast heat and a glow that made her even more radiant.

'I'm glad you have happy memories here,' she said softly. 'But sometimes it's the happy memories that hurt most.'

She was awfully right about that. She was, he realised, awfully wise.

'This was always my favourite place,' he admitted. 'I've not been back here for Christmas in all this time. Twenty-one years.'

She simply looked at him. And that was all it took for the words he'd never spoken to fall.

'Joan died in July, just a month after Eloise was born. She had a stroke out of the blue. My grandfather was heart-broken and he grew very frail, very quickly, and lasted only a few months without her. I was…' He shrugged. His heart hurt too much and he had to look away from the deepening compassion in Violet's eyes. 'They were my go-to when my parents were down. I'd wanted to be enough for them. I was happy, and I couldn't understand why they weren't, why they wanted more. But then they did, they had Eloise. I'd been so spoiled by my grandparents and in less than six months I'd lost them both.'

'Children should be spoiled,' she said softly. 'I was spoiled too in a way.'

Not like him. 'I didn't want to come back here for Christmas that year. I couldn't face it without them.' He stared at the fire burning low in the grate. 'It was my idea that we go to Scotland for Christmas.'

Beside him, Violet sat very still. 'They wouldn't have gone if they didn't want to.'

'I know. It was a way of checking out a possible hotel purchase. I even framed it that way to my father when I suggested it. I knew he'd say yes to that. My mother didn't want to take either a nanny or a driver. She wanted it to be the four of us because she felt our family was finally complete.'

'You can't blame yourself for the accident, Roman. It wasn't your fault.'

Couldn't he?

'Those were decisions made by adults,' she added. 'You were ten.'

'But I'd been born into the business. I knew they'd say yes.'

She didn't try to argue. She took his hand and held it between both of hers and remained wordless. Because sometimes there was nothing anyone could *say*. Sometimes you could only *stay* with someone. And eventually Roman's breathing eased, slowed and deepened as Violet stayed, watching the stars and the sparks in the fire and holding his hand in hers so he wasn't alone.

For once Violet was the one wide awake while Roman was fast asleep. And it wasn't because of her rumbling stomach. She was still wrapping her head around what he'd told her. He'd suffered so many losses that year, no wonder he was so protective of his heart. All she wanted was to wrap around *him*. To love him.

Because she loved him already.

Violet froze—still curled up with him on the sofa—as she realised the truth. She was already completely and utterly and totally in love with him. And it wasn't just that he was gorgeous, he was funny and kind and smart and unbearably sexy. But this was the last thing he wanted. He was serious and focused on work and he got bored easily with women. He'd be bored with her soon enough. Eventually he'd see sense and relinquish the wedding idea. He'd install her in some fancy house and ensure she and

the baby had everything. But she didn't want everything.
She just wanted him.

Which meant she could never, ever agree to marry him
now. *That* would destroy her. She'd made such a mistake.
It wasn't that she rejected his protection. Her heart was
his prisoner. And she was going to be shackled to him for
the rest of her life because of their baby. Their baby, who
she wanted more than she wanted to breathe. For whom
she would do anything and everything—who *she* wanted
to protect. She understood that too.

She loved them both with everything she had. And now
she was tense with anxiety. She wished she could control
everything…but everything important, everything fundamental, was beyond her control. When one lived, when
one died…they would happen when they happened. One
could only love with everything one had while one could.
One had to accept it and enjoy it for as long as it lasted.

But finally she understood her mother. She'd always
understood it on a rational basis—wanting to make things
perfect for someone you loved, especially when that person
was vulnerable. She'd been vulnerable and her mother had
wanted to make everything fabulous. But now she really
understood the *emotion*. The irrational, almost desperate
desire to make everything so much better than okay. But
it wasn't possible. Perfect didn't exist. Like the perfect
Christmas—what did it matter if the 'right' gift wasn't
bought, if the food wasn't cooked on time, if there'd been a
variation on the old recipe or if the tree lights were strung
at a wonky angle? The perfect Christmas was time with the
people you loved. Letting them be, loving them for who
they were, supporting them in the things they wanted to do.

Trying too hard, thinking too much, worrying too
much… Those things all made everything awkward. So
she had to let this go. She had to let what would be, be.

She had to trust that it would be okay. Because there *was* a little trust there in her heart. Because he'd turned to her today. He'd sought out her company because…

He liked sleeping with her? Yes. But tonight it hadn't been that at all. Tonight had been more. It was so complicated, so confusing, she could barely breathe. She felt hot and flustered, too stupidly hopeful. Suddenly she needed fresh air. She needed to clear her head.

You had to have the courage to obey. Because that was
a battle. It was the harder, braver, more intelligent course
of action. And it might mean victory.
Or it might mean war. Well, for him the conflict hadn't
lessened. It had only gone deeper... Every step towards
compliance met a second impulse to battle back. Silence
came to reinforce rebellion, to remind him of the futility of
resistance, of open defeat...

CHAPTER ELEVEN

ROMAN JOLTED. HE FROZE and took mental stock as adrenalin shocked him into a hyper-alert state. His muscles were
stiff, his shirt stuck to his skin. Memory returned. They'd
fallen asleep on the sofa in front of the fire. Now the flames
had faded to embers and, not only was he cold, he was
alone. He hauled himself together and stood, aching all
over. Violet must've gone to bed. He'd join her there. But
the big bed in the adjoining room was empty. He flicked
the lights on to double-check, blinking at the brightness.

She wasn't there. He paused and listened. It was a big
house. And it was very, very quiet. His pulse lifted. He
checked the nearest guest bedroom. And the one after that.
Then the next one. All empty and undisturbed.

'Violet?' He walked along the corridor to the stairs.
'Violet?'

On the ground floor, he stared. The front door was ajar.
Cold air curled in, sinking the core temperature of the
house. His pulse pushed his blood so fast, it thundered.
He could hear nothing else.

She's gone.

'Violet?' Surely she wouldn't go out in the middle of
the night? Why would she?

Fear...irrational, uncontrollable fear...surged. He strode
outside, uncaring that he was dressed only in his trousers

and shirt. The almost moonless sky emphasised the infinite number of stars stretching above him. He peered into the shadows, the snow-laden trees. Why would she have gone? Where? Had she been alone or had she been taken? He went down the stairs to the path. How could he not have noticed? How had he not woken? Why hadn't he done anything? His whole body was shaking now.

'Violet!'

He hadn't been able to stop his sister from disappearing. Now Violet had gone too. What kind of father was he going to make? What kind of *brother* had he been?

He paced around, finally spotting footprints in the snow, and a return set. He went back in to the lodge. He checked the reception room. The lights were still glowing on the tree. He went beyond to the kitchen and had to put a hand out to the doorjamb. She was there. She had her back to him. She was in those ridiculous red Christmas pyjamas. She had a couple of plates on the counter in front of her.

'What are you doing?' he muttered.

But she didn't respond.

He stepped closer and put his hand to her shoulder. 'Violet?'

She was startled, her eyes widening. 'Roman?'

'I've been calling you.' He sagged against the counter as he realised. 'You have your earphones in.'

She pulled the little wireless buds out of her ears. 'I was listening to my family's Christmas message.'

Her what?

'The front door is open,' he said confusedly. 'I thought…'

She stared at him for a long moment. 'That I'd gone?' She slowly shook her head. 'I went outside to get a photo of the lodge. You know, with the lights, under the stars in the snow. Have you seen how beautiful it looks? I forgot to do it earlier. But Bruce got out. I thought I'd leave the door open for him to come back in.'

'You could have got lost.'

'I didn't go any further from where I could see the lodge. It was too cold.'

Roman couldn't make sense of it. 'And now you're eating? At three in the morning?'

She looked embarrassed. 'I didn't eat much last night and I couldn't sleep, my stomach was rumbling so loud. I'm surprised it didn't wake you. But you were *really* asleep.' She cleared her throat. 'I forgot to phone my family last night. I was distracted. But it's Christmas Day there, so I sent them a photo of the lodge. I hope that's okay.'

He nodded.

'They've been sending some silly videos back.'

His throat felt tight. 'Did you tell them about the pregnancy?'

'I didn't think it was an appropriate time. It'll be better to tell them in person.'

He stared, barely processing what she'd told him. The relief? It didn't come. He needed physical proof—not just to see with his own eyes but feel with his own fingers that she was safe and well. But he couldn't seem to move.

She lightly pressed the back of her hand to his cheek. 'You're freezing, Roman.' Concern etched deeper in her eyes. 'How long were you out there looking for me?'

It had felt like for ever. And he'd have felt a fool if he didn't feel so damn feverish. Maybe it *was* the flu—or just the remnants of the night terror that had morphed into a mess tonight. The past, the present and the future were all muddled up. She'd been gone. Tonight of all nights. A desperate wave of emotion shook him.

'Roman, you need to warm up.'

Both her hands were on his forehead now, smoothing the frown. But he was frozen.

She bit her lip. 'Maybe you ought to go in that hot tub.'

'No.' He shook his head. 'You can't while you're pregnant.'

She looked confused.

'I read an article online,' he muttered.

Her hands felt even softer now. 'You've been reading pregnancy advice?'

Yeah, of course, he'd wanted to take care of her. But he didn't think he was doing a great job of it.

'You really need to get warm, Roman.'

He couldn't do anything other than look at her. Her cheeks were flushed, her hair was a thick, glossy mess about her face and he knew she'd be warm and soft. Usually sex made him forget everything. It was a distraction, a relaxant. But not with Violet. It had always been more with her. Even that night, when they'd not known anything but each other's first names. It was too much. Too personal. He couldn't trust himself to touch her this second. He'd unravel completely. He had yesterday, hadn't he? He couldn't let that happen again. He didn't want to feel *this*. He didn't want to feel anything. He hadn't for so long.

Last night she'd kept him company, kept him warm. But when he'd woken she'd been gone and it was the worst possible thing. All over again, he'd thought he'd handle it. Hell, he'd even made it through that party last night well enough. But he wasn't over any of his loss. He never would be. And he couldn't handle the prospect of any more.

'Roman?'

She saw it. She sensed the rejection. 'I'm sorry,' she whispered. 'I didn't mean to scare you.'

Wild rage flared in his chest—denial and rejection. He didn't want this—her understanding.

'Roman—'

'Leave it,' he snapped and stepped back.

'No.' She walked towards him, keeping close. 'I'm fine, Roman.' She took his numb hands and put them on her waist. 'I'm here. And I'm fine.'

His fingers tightened. He didn't mean for it to happen but he couldn't stop any of it. She was real and strong before him.

'I'm not,' he muttered. 'I'm not fine.' He was finally releasing the truth. 'I'm angry.'

She nodded.

'I thought…' He closed his eyes tight. He couldn't cope.

But she stepped closer still, holding him. And then somehow she was guiding him. Leading him. He was too tired to resist. Too tired to feel any of this any more. He just followed. He felt her push and there was softness beneath his back, his face. He was so confused, he didn't know if this was all part of a dream and he'd not woken at all. Because she was here now and she was warm. He was sick of being cold and alone. He didn't want that any more. The anger and adrenalin evaporated, his energy and strength sapped too. She burrowed tight beside him. He managed to raise his arms and wrap them around her. They were probably too heavy for her…they felt too heavy for him. But she didn't complain. Her fingertips swirled, softly skating over his chest.

'I'm tired,' he muttered. He couldn't think straight any more. He couldn't keep his eyes open.

'I know,' she murmured. 'It's okay. Go to sleep.'

He began to drift. 'Don't go.'

She was back with him. Right where he needed her. And he was almost asleep.

'I won't.'

He listened for the words he wanted and it was the sweetest of dreams when she spoke.

'Not ever.'

CHAPTER TWELVE

Christmas Day

ROMAN BLINKED AGAIN at the computer screen. His eyes were dry and scratchy and he couldn't concentrate on reading more than two sentences. He shouldn't be so tired. He'd slept for hours—far into the day. He'd stirred when Violet had slipped from the bed at mid-morning but to his subsequent amazement he'd fallen back to sleep for another few hours, meaning it'd been early afternoon before he'd fully roused.

He'd found Violet had left a note on the pillow, telling him she'd gone downstairs. Was that so he didn't freak out when he saw she wasn't beside him again? He winced at the recollection of his middle-of-the-night terror and fought down the sick feeling that returned with it.

But even though the day had half-gone he hadn't then gone down to see her. He'd showered and dressed, then sat at his desk. He'd figured that if he worked for a while he might get himself back on track.

Three hours later, it still hadn't happened. His pulse was still irregular. His equilibrium was off. Maybe it was caffeine deprivation. After all, he'd missed both breakfast and lunch and it wasn't far off dinner time. He shut his laptop and finally went downstairs.

Violet wasn't anywhere to be seen but the sight of the kitchen counter reminded him of her midnight snack there. He recalled the softness of that conversation—felt again the stress in his voice, his body. And his sudden exhaustion. He'd basically collapsed in her arms when they'd finally fallen back to bed. Grimly, he opened the fridge, somewhat stunned as he took in the contents. Linda had left masses of food for them. Of course she had. But he shut the door. He had zero appetite.

Then Violet appeared in the doorway and his whole body lurched.

'Hey.' She watched him warily. 'Merry Christmas.'

Hell, it was late afternoon already and he'd not even remembered. She'd been alone all day. His brain was like mush. All he could process was that she looked sexy as hell in the oversized sweater and leggings she must've pulled from her Tardis-like overnight bag. He felt the prickling instinct to back away.

'Do you want some help?' she asked.

He knew she meant prepping food but his pulse veered and his first instinct was to say no. He rolled his shoulders and tried to relax. 'I'm sorry about last night.'

He gritted his teeth as he recalled the extent of his confusion. He needed to sort himself out. How did he think he was going to create some semblance of security for Violet and the child if he couldn't keep his own head together?

'No, I'm sorry. I—'

'You were hungry.' He forced a smile, determined to downplay it. 'I just had another bad dream.'

'No, you—'

His phone rang and he'd never been more grateful. He glanced at the screen: Alex.

'Sorry,' he muttered to Violet again. But he didn't bother

moving out of the room. Violet would meet Alex soon enough.

'Hey,' he answered on the third ring.

'Roman. I've got news.'

Roman tensed, instantly picking up on Alex's tone. He didn't sound quite right. 'What's wrong?'

Had people heard about Violet's pregnancy somehow?

'I've found Eloise.'

No preamble. It was not what Roman had ever imagined Alex would call to say.

'It's really her,' Alex continued. 'I waited 'til I had the results. But they're clear. She's your sister.'

Alive? For the second time in less than twelve hours, Roman's body emptied of all strength, as did his brain.

'Where?' His mouth was suddenly so dry, he had to cough out the rest. 'Where is she?'

'Manhattan. I—'

'I'm on my way.'

'You don't want to know how…?'

'Later. I have to see her.' His heart and lungs stopped. 'Give me the location.'

'Roman…' Alex's intake of breath was audible and harsh. 'We need to talk when you get here. I'll send through confirmation now.'

Roman ended the call and stared at his phone. It wasn't possible. It just *wasn't* possible. Two seconds later, the screen lit up. An address and an attachment. He opened it. It was a letter from a laboratory. Letters, numbers, analysing, comparing, DNA codes… Sample one. Sample two. Relationship confirmed. The irrefutable scientific proof Alex had always insisted on.

Roman's empty stomach roiled. The stress of sleeplessness and the strain of emotion over the last few days all swirled together and clouded everything in his head in a mass of confusion.

What the hell...? What the hell had just happened?

'Roman?'

A soft voice. He turned, startled.

'Is everything okay?'

Violet. Standing at the kitchen counter with two plates. She'd retrieved some of the things from the fridge.

'I have to...' He'd forgotten everything in the adrenalin rush. The only way to cope was to concentrate on one thing. To compartmentalise.

'Alex found Eloise,' he said.

He had to go to Eloise. See her. But he'd been wrong. So wrong. Nausea swirled in his gut, burning up his chest. She'd been out there lost in the wilderness for *years*. And what had he done? He'd stopped looking for her. He'd given up.

'What?' Violet put the plates down and pressed her hands on the counter.

'Alex found her,' he repeated flatly. 'She's alive. Apparently, it's her.'

'He's sure?'

'DNA-test sure.' He clenched the phone, trying to stop the sickness spilling out.

Violet's eyes widened. 'How...?'

'He had authorisation. I left it to him to deal with the occasional people who...' He shook his head. 'Turned out this one wasn't a fraud. She's real.'

'Oh...' Violet breathed. 'Roman, that's just amazing.'

He stared at her. She'd lit up as though it was the best thing. And it was. But at the same time a crevasse opened up inside him. Horror and guilt and fear spewed up. He was a volcano of regret. 'I have to go.'

He had so many questions. Was Eloise okay? Had she been hurt? How had she survived all these years?

'Of course you do.' Violet nodded. 'Right away.'

He phoned his pilot, immediately feeling both awful and unapologetic. It was Christmas freaking Day and the guy was in the midst of his own family celebrations. Roman would have flown himself but his hands were shaking and, besides, the helicopter was back in town with the pilot an hour away. He'd expected to be here a few more days with Violet. Violet, at whom he couldn't look. He didn't want her to witness him shaking like this. Not again. Not after...

'It's going to be okay.'

Her voice sounded behind him, calm and quiet. He couldn't let himself look at her. Because she didn't know that. No one could know that.

'My pilot will be here in an hour,' he said tersely.

'Good. That's good.'

It gave him time to...to...he didn't know what. He couldn't bear to think about all the ramifications. Who had Eloise been with all this time? How had she managed? She had to know she would never have to struggle again.

'I need to get the paperwork sorted,' he muttered.

'The paperwork?'

'For the trust. Her trust.' He finally glanced back at Violet.

She looked worried and he couldn't cope with the concern in her huge eyes.

'Her inheritance,' he explained shortly. 'Her rights regarding the company. She needs to understand it's all here for her.' He'd focus on that. He'd not allowed the lawyers to break it up. It didn't matter if the world had declared her dead, he'd kept her share safe. He'd never wanted to touch it. Instead, he'd grown it. Now he needed to get it to her and make sure she understood she'd get her full inheritance—the properties, the shares. Hell, she could have more if she needed it. He'd give her everything. 'She needs to know all that's in place.'

But it wasn't worth anything, really. How could it ever heal the years in which she'd been isolated and alone? He'd not protected her. He'd not found her. He'd effectively abandoned her.

'Maybe she just needs to see you,' Violet said. 'Know *you're* here for her.'

He blanched at that. Because he hadn't been.

'Maybe *you* just need a moment.' Violet moved towards him. 'This is a lot to take in.'

He did not want a moment. He did not want to think beyond the neatly delineated constraints of contracts and papers. 'Not all of us need for ever and a day to grasp something so fundamental,' he snapped.

Hurt flashed in her eyes and she stopped a few feet from him.

Good. That felt good. He could breathe a little better. Violet shouldn't want… She shouldn't be near him. Suddenly he was filled with a driving need to push back from her, to push *her* away.

Violet had wanted time to process the pregnancy and how they would handle it. He hadn't needed time. He needed solutions to problems and then he'd move on, knowing everything was okay. Just as he did in his business every damned day. He liked things to be clear-cut. He needed this—*everything with her*—to be clear-cut too. He needed it all fixed and certain. And *contained*.

'Well, it's amazing you've finally found her.' Placating softness… She'd ignored his cruel outburst.

And made him feel worse. Suddenly he was angry. How was he ever going to be a good enough father, a good enough husband? Because he'd *never* been a good enough brother.

'But I didn't find her,' he snapped. 'I failed her. All these years and I couldn't even be sure of what I'd *seen*. And she's been surviving who knows what this whole time. Away from her birth right. Alone.'

'You were alone too,' Violet said quietly. 'You were both alone. And it wasn't either of your faults.'

Roman flinched. Violet was wrong. So wrong. He'd told her he was to blame. She'd not listened. And he would always regret what he'd done.

He didn't want her *understanding*. He certainly did not want her forgiving him in this moment. He deserved neither. And he certainly didn't want her indulging his emotional *weakness*. He had to claw back his emotional control, focus on what and how he could actually help. Not just Eloise, but Violet too, and the baby. And the only thing he could truly offer all of them with any degree of certainty was financial security. Physical safety was barely a maybe. So he needed to push this back where he should have put it in the beginning.

'All that matters now is that I ensure she understands what I have set aside for her.' He looked at Violet steadily. 'Same with you.'

Violet leaned back against the kitchen counter for support. Roman was shutting down before her eyes. The man from last night had gone—the hurt, lonely human who'd come seeking solace in her company—and the remote isolationist was back, more prickly than ever.

Last night she'd been so sleepless—adrenalin, excitement and worry surging as she'd realised the extent of her feelings for him. The hunger she'd wanted to fill had really been a distraction activity. As had the idea to step outside into the starry night and take a Christmas selfie to share with her family. She'd not wanted to wake him. He'd been sleeping so soundly. But he'd woken and found her gone. He'd frozen. And the extent of that fear had shocked and scared him even more. While he'd warmed up physically, there was a coldness within him today that was new.

Frankly, now that chill was spreading to her as she saw the deadened look in his eyes and the emotion she'd just watched him suppress. It was scary, the degree to which he could control it. He broke her heart. She knew that over the years he'd grown defences to protect that hurt heart of his. He'd been so hurt, he didn't want to lose anyone again—which meant he wouldn't put himself at the risk of that happening.

'We should have something to eat before we go,' she suggested distractedly. 'Shall I...?' She hesitated as she saw his flinch. Then she realised. 'You don't want me to come with you.' She swallowed, mortified. But this wasn't about her. 'Of course you don't. This is very private.'

She wasn't part of this for him. He wanted to face this alone.

'There's nothing there for you to do,' he said gruffly.

Except be there alongside him. To wait while he went. To quietly offer support when he returned. It wasn't that she wanted to intrude at all, but she'd like to be there for him later. But he didn't want that. Not from her. And that hurt. Because last night he had. Last night he'd asked her not to leave him. Last night she'd started to *hope*. And to dream.

She knew how scary it was to be alone through difficult things. How hard it was when you didn't have someone you could talk to openly about how you were feeling. Someone with whom you could admit your fears and then forget them for a few moments while you had a little laugh.

She'd yearned to have that deeply human connection with one special person—the ups, the downs and all the in-betweens, all of which could happen within one hour when life was throwing its fullest at you. Which it currently was, at them both.

And for a little moment there she'd thought she'd found that with him. She'd been able to be honest with him in a way she'd never been able to be honest with anyone else. And then she'd even begun to believe that he might feel able to do the same with her. But it had lasted mere seconds. Now, in the light of day, he was pushing her away. Hard.

'I need you to promise me you won't leave while I'm gone,' he said shortly.

Shocked, she stared at him, her hurt swiftly deepening. 'Of course I won't.' She would never, ever do that.

'You promise?'

Did he really have to double-check and demand an oath? That hurt burgeoned and built into something more. Anger spread along her veins. He still didn't trust her. Not at heart. Not when it really mattered. He didn't feel as if he could count on her. And he didn't want to. That broke another chunk off her heart. Would he ever learn to trust her? Because without trust, without honesty and belief in one another, there couldn't be love.

'You want me to sign a contract? Or do you want to leave me with an armed bodyguard?' she asked testily. 'You think I'd walk out when you're in the middle of a massive personal crisis? What kind of person do you think I am?'

He threw her a furious look. And she knew then this was what he'd wanted—to vent and rage.

'I get that you don't want to talk about it,' she said, struggling to keep control of her own emotions. 'I'm not going to make you. But that you think I'd walk out at a moment when you're so vulnerable? You really think that little of me?'

'I expect the worst.'

'Well, you shouldn't from me. Not *ever* from me.' Her eyes filled. 'Roman, I will be here for you. I will always be here for you.'

'I don't want that,' he snapped. 'That's not what I want.'

She stared at him.

'This has been a mistake,' he said. 'We shouldn't have—'

'What? Fallen for each other?'

'That's not what's happened.'

Her heart stopped. 'You don't have to face everything alone, Roman.'

He stared at her for a long moment, calculating something behind his eyes that she couldn't guess at. But it wasn't good.

'I'm not alone,' he said gruffly. 'I have Alex.'

'And I just heard your conversation. You guys might be close but you don't exactly communicate.'

'We don't all need to express every inner emotion with endless talkfests or journal entries.'

She blinked. 'No. But expressing a few aloud mightn't hurt. Better than bottling them up until the only way they can emerge is when you're asleep.'

His mouth compressed. 'I don't need your support.'

The last thing he'd said to her last night had been a request not to leave him. But now he'd flipped back—from the solace of warmth to flames of fear. *She* couldn't let fear hold her back from what she really wanted. Not this time.

'No? Like you didn't in the middle of the night?' she challenged him. 'Last night you asked me not to go. Not to leave you.'

'I don't recall,' he said grimly. 'I was barely awake.'

Last night had been like a fairy-tale—those glamorous guests, the decorations, the delight in everyone's eyes. It had been lovely. But when she'd seen him walk in she'd been stunned—not because he'd looked so unbearably handsome, but because she'd known it had been a supreme act of courage, the choice *not* to be alone in that moment. Especially when he'd explained everything. But today?

'Then let me remind you,' she said huskily. 'You were brave last night. When you realised you didn't want to be alone. When you came to find me. That took courage. Now you're pushing me away. You're running, retreating back to emotional isolation, because you're hurt and you don't want to be hurt any more.'

She knew it wasn't the time to be saying any of this. To lay this on him when he had a big enough emotional burden to deal with today. But Violet had lost her ability to control her emotions. She felt for him too much. And she didn't want to see him shut down from her again. She was terrified he'd never come back. Not the way she wanted him to.

'That's not what I'm doing,' he said.

'It's exactly that.'

'Last night was the result of a lack of sleep, and the fact is I sleep better alone.' He huffed out a breath. 'Look, we need to appreciate the reality. You're pregnant, but you're right—we shouldn't get married. It was an old-fashioned impulse that's taken me some time to untangle. We'll live apart, but I'll obviously support you both. But there won't be anything more between us.'

Violet gaped. Then it hit—bursting the remnants of her heart apart. 'You're a zombie. An actual, bloodless zombie just going through the motions of life. You have no warmth. No heart. You don't just want to shut me out.

You shut everyone out—Linda and Dennis. Are you going to do this to your sister too?'

'I'm going to apologise to her.'

'For what? You really think you could have stopped what happened? You really think you're responsible for everything? You were *ten years old*. Not strong. Not powerful. And even now you're super-wealthy, super-successful, super…' She shook her head. 'You're not in control of everything and everyone. *No one* is. Accidents happen. Illness happens. Bad shit happens. You can't claim credit for all of it.'

He threw her a furious look.

'Deal with it, Roman. Accept that it happened and it was awful. Just awful. But move forward, live life, because there's only the one.'

'Like you do, you mean?' He scoffed. 'Your goal of "living in the moment" is simply a way to avoid making any really difficult decisions. You're terrified of putting faith into any future plans.'

Maybe that had been true earlier. Before he'd given her confidence in her self—in her choices, in her ability to fight. Before she'd realised her own feelings. 'I would have put my faith in you,' she argued. 'In us.'

'There *is* no us.'

'You think these last few days have meant nothing?'

He stood very still.

'I know you, Roman,' she said. 'I know you in a way that's—'

'Sexual.'

'Far deeper than that.'

'You said yourself—more than once—that this is superficial.' He shut her down. 'This is sexual chemistry that inadvertently created a long-term problem.'

'A *what*?' All the emotions escaped, especially rage.

Because this rejection hurt. It was as if she'd been thrust into another reality from the one in which she'd lived these last few days. 'We are so much more.' She pushed back. 'We could be everything.'

But maybe she was wrong. It wouldn't be the first time. Her family had always chuckled when she'd got 'the wrong end of the stick'. Maybe she'd read all kinds of things into something that really was simply sexual chemistry. But her emotions had spilled over now and she couldn't pull it back together.

'I'm scared too, Roman,' she said softly. 'The truth is, I'm terrified. Of not being there for this baby. Of wanting you for ever when for ever can never be guaranteed. We both know that so deeply. But I'm willing, I want to try. I want to fight. This is worth it, Roman. *You're* worth it.'

'I don't want that kind of relationship with you. I never will,' he said flatly. 'I'm sorry that our sleeping together complicated things for you.' He was like a machine, stuck on a loop, and not going to concede an inch. 'I'm not the person you want me to be.'

'And what do you intend to be for our baby? A father or a financial institution?'

He flinched and closed his eyes. And when he opened them, all her hope died.

'I know this isn't easy,' he said grimly. 'But at least we've cleared the situation.'

Cleared the situation? The man had gone for the nuclear option and she felt burned alive.

He paused in the doorway on his way out. 'Violet, you know if you leave, I'll track you down.'

In the distance, she heard the approach of the helicopter coming to take him away. 'You really do always believe the worst will happen. You can't believe someone would stay for you. Well, *I'm* going to stay. I have the courage both to compromise and admit how I'm really feeling. I'm going to be honest now, Roman. I'm always going to be honest. Even if you can't be.'

She pushed away from the counter and walked towards him. 'So, here's the truth—I am here for you. I know you don't want that. Hell, you probably don't even believe me. But it's true, and I'm only saying this the once. So don't worry, I won't embarrass you by expressing my unwanted feelings towards you again. I won't continue to throw myself against the brick wall of your *fear*. I'll get over you, and I'm going to live. That means taking chances—and I'm taking this one last chance with you. So, here it is—I love you, Roman. I've fallen in love with you, okay?'

He stood still, silent, then turned away.

And it wasn't okay.

CHAPTER THIRTEEN

Boxing Day

ROMAN GRIMLY WAITED at the front desk. Every second dragged his tension tighter. Alex had messaged him the address but the reality still shocked. A *hostel*. Not even a halfway decent hostel. He dreaded to think what her life had been like these past two decades with those…abductors? Guilt sluiced through him—followed fast by acidic doubt. Was it *really* going to be her? The guy behind the desk was shooting him some wary side-eye but Roman couldn't scrub the glower from his face. Even in his heavy wool coat he felt cold, sick and angry. But then his spine prickled and he swung round.

Emotion roiled to the surface. It *had* to be her. He made himself move. She'd frozen to the spot and was growing paler by the second—a brunette with startling blue eyes. But he couldn't trust that colourful patch that matched his. That had been faked once before. But the DNA test couldn't be faked. Alex wouldn't put Roman in this position if he didn't really believe this woman was Eloise.

Besides, this time there was more. Roman's instincts flooded, rendering his brain redundant. She was the spitting image of his grandmother. A colour replica of the old black and white photo of Joan that was in his private lounge at the lodge. The one that had never been published. The one he'd glanced at the other night with...

He gritted his teeth. *Not Violet. Not now.* He couldn't think about anything beyond what was in front of him. One issue at a time. He was the king of compartmentalisation. He'd worked for years to focus on the current priority. Admittedly, that was usually work, but right now it was...

'Eloise.' His voice hardly worked. 'You look just like Grandma Joan.'

'I'm Ellie,' she answered in a strained but strong Scottish-accented voice. 'Eleanor MacGregor.'

He stared, scared that if he blinked she'd vanish again. He'd blinked all those years ago and she'd been there one moment, gone the next. Those memories flashed then— the ones he'd not been able to trust. The ones he'd hated. The darkness. Surely it was impossible that she stood before him now? That this stranger was his sister? She was obviously as thrown by the idea as he was. Wariness, defensiveness, *hurt* had bloomed in her expression as she corrected him.

'Of course,' he murmured. 'I'm Roman.'

'I know, I recognised you.'

The break in her whisper tore at his fragile composure. She did? How?

'I saw your picture on the Internet,' she added.

Not gut instinct, then. Of course not. Conflicting emotions soared—his ability to trust his instincts had been severed, but now his instincts were screaming at him. He'd screwed everything up.

'Right.' He glanced around the hostel's lobby, his unhappiness with the shabby surroundings mushrooming. This wasn't a safe place for her. Especially now. 'Grab your stuff and I'll take you to my hotel uptown. You can stay in a suite there for now.'

His brain whirred. He'd spoken before thinking—because she might not want a hotel, she might want a *home*. And she *had* a home. But she'd not been there in decades. 'Or you can move into the Fraser mansion on the Upper East Side,' he offered. 'I keep it fully staffed, but I'm not there much myself, so that will give you your own space.'

He wanted her to understand all that he'd kept for her. All that was *hers*. It was so important that she understand. 'We'll meet with the legal team tomorrow to settle the inheritance. Then you can take your pick of the other properties owned by Fraser Holdings.' He hesitated. Why was she frowning?

'Or simply buy your own place,' he swerved, trying to give her choices, trying to read her mind so he could supply the right options. 'Whatever works for you. But I don't want—'

'Whoa, wait.'

Roman paused, desperately trying to pull out some patience.

'I'm not going anywhere today. And I don't want to speak to any legal team tomorrow.'

She…*what*?

'Why not?' he asked. Why didn't she want to speak to the lawyers? Did she mean she had something else to do tomorrow, or did she mean she didn't want to speak to them at *all*?

There was a rebellious expression in her eyes. One he recognised with a sinking feeling.

'Because I live here—this is what I can afford. And I have shifts working in a bar in Columbus Circle today and tomorrow.'

What she could afford? Working in a bar? But she didn't have to do that any more. Never. He could help her. He *had* to help her. He was her brother, her only blood relative. And, in this way, this was all he could do. 'Eloise, I don't think you understand—'

'Ellie.'

He blinked at the soft, implacable reminder. 'Right, Ellie.' He drew a breath, trying not to be patronising but knowing he was failing already.

If Violet were here she'd be rolling her eyes right now, then softly steering him. Telling him not to focus on the damned finances. But they were important. Their existence was going to impact Eloise's—Ellie's—life completely. Roman wanted her to have everything she'd been denied for so long. This was the only tangible thing he could do for her.

'You're now worth upwards of five billion dollars in real-estate dividends, share options and a trust fund set up in your name twenty-one years ago,' he tried to explain. 'You can afford to live wherever you want. And there's no charge to live at the hotel, or at the Fraser mansion, because those places belong to you too—you're my sister.'

He gritted his teeth the second he'd said it. Simultaneously, she flinched.

Yeah: *sister.*

It was strange to him—he had no other sisters, no brothers either. But did she have other siblings in that family that had stolen her? Rage swarmed, clouding his vision. She was so precious. She had been so tiny and she'd been *taken*. The protective urge overwhelmed him. He had to ensure the failures of the past would never be repeated. 'And no way am I letting you continue to work in a bar,' he growled.

'Excuse me?' She glared at him. 'Who made you the boss of me?'

Roman froze, realising his mistake too late. The boss. The bully. He winced inwardly as once more Violet's words echoed. Emotional control…he'd lost it already. He'd lost it the moment he'd fallen apart in Violet's arms and he couldn't get it back no matter how hard he tried.

Could he have made more of a mess of this?

To his absolute horror, Ellie's expression slowly crumpled. He watched as she furiously worked, blinking back tears that escaped her eyes regardless.

'I don't think you understand. I don't want the money.' She sniffed. 'I don't want any of this. I'm not ready to meet you, to deal with all the lies they told me…'

She wasn't ready to meet him.

He didn't know how to make any of this better. He'd been unable to reach out and rescue her all those years ago and he was helpless—*useless*—once again. He absorbed the hit as calmly as he could, trying to stay composed. But compartmentalising wasn't working. Feelings flooded. He needed a moment, just like Violet had suggested. She'd been so damned understanding.

He blinked. *Understanding?* He could only try. Eloise had been through hell and he was bossing her—pushing too fast—even though he thought it in her best interests. But even if it was, was he never going to learn? He needed to listen. He needed to engage. Or at least try.

So he nodded, swallowing but unable to push the hard rock in his throat. 'I'm sorry, you're right.' He spoke slowly, trying to quell his anxiety about ensuring her protection and that she understood all the things he'd set aside for her. She wasn't ready for any of it—certainly not to listen to all his damned arrangements.

Because this wasn't about *him*. Not about what he'd *done*. That wasn't going to make *her* feel better. It wasn't what she needed from him right now. Right now, there was simply their meeting to deal with. The shock of it.

Violet had been right. When it came to emotion—*all* of

the emotions—he was inept. They weren't just impossible to control, he didn't know how to express them. He'd always tried to suppress them. Ultimately, recently he'd discovered that didn't work. So what the hell did? He stared at the ground. What would Violet do?

Try again. Because Violet had courage. And Violet didn't give up. She would pause, breathe, smile…and she would also be honest. But honesty was hard.

'How about we start over?' he said to Ellie softly, trying to ask, not just inform or straight-up railroad her into agreeing. 'Find somewhere private to talk. We have a lot to discuss.'

Together.

Ellie looked at him searchingly. 'Really?'

'Sure. I've got my car parked out front.' Illegally, like the entitled ass he was—expecting everything to work for him the way he wanted. Instantly. He grimaced ruefully. 'We can sit in there. If it hasn't been towed already.'

A little laugh burst from her. The sound softened the rock in his throat ever so slightly.

'Would it be okay if we went for a wee walk instead?' she suggested. 'Central Park is only a block away.'

Roman hesitated. There were risks to that—risks she maybe hadn't yet realised, with her change in status. First up, simply to be seen walking with him would generate speculation. And, when their true relationship was revealed, there was going to be an *insane* amount of attention. There'd be press, there'd be predators. He knew. He'd run the gamut of it all more than once. He'd been duped by con artists wanting access to his money, and they were sophisticated in their attempts. Ellie was going to need support whether she wanted to acknowledge it yet or not. But it also meant maybe this was the one chance they did have to walk in the park in peace. So, despite his misgivings, he nodded.

'Sure, if that's what you want.' He pulled his phone from his pocket. 'I'll just get that car moved and we can go.'

She shot him a small smile and turned away.

But, despite finally having managed something to mitigate the awkwardness to even a tiniest degree, his tension wouldn't ease. Because if they couldn't talk about the financial plans and security he had in place for her, then there was only the past. It rose like a spectre. And a kaleidoscope of emotion meshed with memories swirled. He had so many questions. So much regret. He didn't know how or where to begin. Eloise had been in the wilderness for *twenty-one years*. Away from her family home, from her birth right. And it was his fault.

'I'm sorry,' he muttered as they walked into the park.

She glanced at him, eyebrows lifting.

'I should have stopped them,' he added dully. 'Said something. Done something. I should have...'

There was a silence.

'Are you talking about the accident?'

He nodded.

More silence. 'Alex said you were going in and out of consciousness,' she said. 'You must have had a head injury. You had to be cut out of the car, right?'

What did that matter? His injuries weren't the point. 'I should have said something. I should have called out at the time.'

'You were ten. You were a child, in shock, badly hurt. It's a wonder you were still breathing.' She paused on the path and frowned at him. 'You don't seriously blame yourself?'

Again, making it about him wasn't what he'd intended. He was so frustrated with how this was going down. He should have said more to the rescuers who had found him. Pushed to be heard by the police at the time. He'd been confused, easily convinced what he'd thought he'd seen was wrong. He'd not been strong enough. And as a result Ellie had been raised by strangers and now had to live in hostels and work in bars because she didn't have much money.

'I just want you to know, I'm sorry.' His tone was clipped.

'You don't need to be.'

He gritted his teeth. But it wasn't just that it had been his push to go to Scotland, that he'd not called out at the time, that he'd not been able to move and be able to stop those people from taking her. He'd *given up*. He'd lost faith in his own instinct, in his own memory, in the search for her. He'd all but stopped these past years. And in doing that he'd let *her* down. He could *never* make that up to her.

But he wasn't going to burden her with more emotional baggage in asking for her forgiveness for that too. She had enough to be dealing with right now. He needed to focus on what *she* wanted and needed. He needed to ask her what that was instead of assuming that he somehow already knew. He rolled his shoulders, trying to do better. 'What can I tell you? What do you want to know?'

Eloise—Ellie—glanced at him. 'Everything.'

'Sure you don't want a waffle to go with that?' Roman asked as he handed Ellie the hot tea he'd just purchased for her at the waffle cart parked on Central Drive. She had to be hungry as well, but at least he'd got her to agree to a hot drink.

'No thanks,' she replied.

He sipped the scalding black coffee he'd got for himself, inhaling the hit and stopping himself from reacting badly to her rejection of his offer. This wasn't about him, remember?

The last hour had been tolerable. Talking her through the family business had been easy. More personal things? Not so much. Telling her about their grandparents—Ken and Joan—had been bearable. But explaining their parents' relationship, that it had been strained with the desire for more children? He'd skipped those bits. She didn't need to know that, only that she'd been so wanted, so loved, by all the family. That was absolutely true. Telling her about his boarding school was straightforward enough, though honestly it surprised him that she wanted to know anything about Eldridge.

Then she asked about his personal life. His non-answer had been both guarded and guilty, because personal relationships were not a strength. But now she returned to it.

'So you said you and Alex got friendly at the prep school,' Ellie ventured. 'What was he like back then?'

Alex? Again? Roman frowned. 'Why are you so interested in Alex Costa?'

He stopped, facing her, because the colour had leeched from her cheeks.

'He didn't tell you?' she whispered. 'About us?'

'What do you mean *us*?' Roman stared at her. His mind computed and came up with a very *wrong* answer. 'Did Alex seduce you?'

Now colour stormed her face. 'No,' she said. 'We seduced each other. Not that it's any of your—'

'That son of a…' He raked his fingers through his hair, emotion flashing to fury. The woman was dealing with enough already. And *Alex*? 'What the hell was he thinking? I'm going to murder him. How dare he take advantage of my kid sister?'

He was shocked to the core. Because it wasn't like Alex to go for someone vulnerable.

'Wait a minute.' Ellie grasped his arm and tugged. 'Alex didn'a know I was your sister when we first slept together.'

Roman stopped dead but his brain exploded. 'What do you mean *first* slept together? How many times did it happen?'

He clamped his teeth together but it was too late—the question was already out. It was so inappropriate. Only that raging protectiveness was now unleashed. He'd always back Alex, but right now he had the strongest urge to smack the guy. What the *hell*?

'Again, not your business,' Ellie snapped. 'But we've been living together since he took me to his mansion in the Adirondacks for Thanksgiving weekend.'

'Living together?' Roman simply gaped and echoed her stupidly. '*You* and Alex?'

Living together? Alex? The guy who'd sworn he'd never see a woman in his house longer than three nights *max*? Now he'd moved a woman in with him for…what…? *Weeks!* Roman stood locked in place, feeling as though a tornado of puzzle pieces were swirling around him.

Alex. Eloise. Emotion.

At the heart of all the confusion he wished for Violet's calm eyes, her breathless chatter.

He recalled the strain in Alex's voice when he'd called yesterday. Roman had figured it was because he'd run the DNA test without dialling Roman in first but maybe it wasn't so much about that…as *this*.

'Yes, me and Alex. Why are you so surprised?'

She looked shocked and hurt, and Roman realised he had to be careful now more than ever. But he also had to be honest. He owed her that. 'It's just… Alex is a player. He doesn't do relationships. Not for as long as I've known him.'

So this didn't make sense. He was furious with the guy. As if Eloise didn't have enough to deal with! The urge to protect her stormed. 'And even if he did,' Roman added huskily, 'You're not his usual type. At all.'

Ellie's eyes flashed. Hell, he'd been too honest.

'So what is his usual type?'

Yeah, he shouldn't have told her that. 'I'm really not sure I want to be having this conversation with my sister.'

'Well, tough. You started it.'

'Okay, fair point,' Roman huffed. 'You said yourself you came straight from Moira to New York. I'm guessing there weren't a lot of eligible men back there.'

She nodded.

'All I'm saying is, Alex usually dates women with…' He cleared his throat awkwardly. 'Women with a lot of experience.'

It wasn't like Alex to get involved with someone unused to his lifestyle. Did Ellie understand a fling wasn't going to lead to rings, vows and for ever? But Roman was assuming again. Would Ellie even want for ever with Alex?

'I see.' Ellie frowned thoughtfully. 'To be fair, he didn'a know I was a virgin when we first slept together at Halloween.'

Roman shut his eyes. 'You were a…? Oh, hell. I seriously did not need to know that.' Completely discombobulated, he sank onto a nearby park bench. 'Now I don't know whether to kill him or torture him first.'

Surely Alex should have known *that*? Surely Ellie should have told him?

He closed his eyes, really not wanting to go there. Roman had known with Violet—she'd *told* him. She'd been honest. Now his own hypocrisy scorched his conscience. He'd teased Violet about her over-protective older brothers but here he was, acting as if he had any say over his own sister's choices! But he didn't want to see Ellie hurt. He knew Alex and this was *not* normal behaviour for him. Which meant maybe this wasn't a normal affair. Maybe it was something more. Confusion clouded everything and Roman didn't know what to think.

Maybe Ellie was right. Maybe this wasn't his business. But she was still his sister and, while it wasn't his business to *interfere*, it was his business to *care*—wasn't it? Maybe it was his business 'just' to listen in support… simply be there.

That was what Violet had said she wanted. Someone to be there—emotionally intimate, easy. Not judging. Not fixing. Not controlling. It was what she'd done for him. Because not everything could be fixed, controlled or made happier, better—let alone perfect. Not by one person— be it parent or other family, friend or even lover. Things couldn't always be sorted. That was sure as hell how it was for him and Eloise—*Ellie*. The past—their losses—could not be changed. But maybe they could move forward by just being here now. Being in each other's company.

Was that enough? Could it ever be?

Ellie suddenly sat on the bench close beside him. To his astonishment, she patted his knee—a gentle touch, as if he needed soothing, as if he was the one who needed compassion or protection this second. He managed a half-smile. Maybe he did need it. Maybe this was what *siblings* did— fought one moment and leaned on each other the next, like lion cubs in a den. They were just seriously out of practice.

God, he wished Violet were here. She was good with people—with a natural ease he didn't have. She'd get on with Ellie in seconds. She'd smile, they'd chat and probably unite to tease him. Part of him ached for that.

'Maybe we should keep talking,' he said when he saw Ellie check the time. 'You don't need to go in to work.'

He'd tried a smile to let her know he wasn't trying to *make* her. 'Never again, if you don't want.'

He really didn't want her to go and work in some bar. For one thing, it was hard work. Hours on her feet when she was already wrung out. At least now she had a little more colour in her cheeks, but she'd not eaten properly. Plus, this situation was soon going to reach the public, and the interest would be intense. But Ellie just smiled.

'Let's talk some more, soon,' she said.

Yeah. Life was going to change now Ellie knew her background. She was going to have decisions to make regarding her inheritance—even if she didn't want to face all that just yet. But all that had been waiting for her for twenty-one years. It could wait a little longer while she adjusted to the idea of it all. He could give her that time.

They rose simultaneously from the bench. With a small smile, she stretched up and gave him a quick peck on the cheek. Roman was neither quick enough to respond in kind nor—thankfully—jerk back in an unintended rejection. He just froze, unaccustomed to familial touch, the fragility of everything in this moment—most especially his own armour.

What the hell was happening to him?

He watched Ellie walk away and that hollowed out feeling returned. His objections had been futile, of course. She was going to her shift in that bar and more power to her. Because he had no real power. Not here. Not with her. Not, perhaps, with anyone. For all his money, for all his supposed social status. Hell, he mocked himself wryly, not even his title as New York's most eligible bachelor meant anything. He was just going to have to wait. Putting pressure on people only pushed them away and Roman couldn't lose Ellie five seconds after he'd finally found her. After *Alex* had found her.

He frowned as he tried to figure out that conundrum. Alex and Ellie? It seemed complicated—something neither Alex nor he were accustomed to. But Roman could hardly lay into Alex about it when he was the one who'd gone and got someone *pregnant*. And, if he couldn't get through a simple conversation with his sister without screwing it up and having to start over, how did he think he could sort out the mess that was his future with Violet? Realistically, what *were* his chances of being a decent husband or father? About nil. He'd already pushed her away.

He'd go to the office and set everything up with the lawyers so the second Ellie was ready the options could be presented. It wasn't good enough. *He* wasn't. Because he'd not just given up on finding Ellie—in believing in her survival—he'd given up on *himself* too. He'd pushed aside his own instincts, unable to trust anything or anyone, least of all himself. He'd gone for the rational approach. The measured 'research and reflect', unemotional decision-making. Compartmentalising—burying—emotional issues. All of which was fine in a business context. But the second it was something personal…

This last week was the first time he'd faced truly personal problems in years. And he really doubted he was up to it. If Alex and Ellie were involved, if it was complicated? Frankly, Roman knew no man as good as Alex. If he was serious about Ellie, he'd be good for her. He'd look out for her. Roman realised he hoped it *was* all that and more between them. Because after this one meeting between him and his sister… It had gone okay, yes, but it didn't feel enough. It didn't feel certain. Nothing felt quite *right*.

He wished, he missed, he wanted… Violet. To hear her laugh, her chatter, her thoughts. And there'd be no mistaking her feelings on everything. But him walking out yesterday had hurt her. Not including her in his decisions, not sharing his thinking—let alone his feelings—had all hurt her. Because she'd trusted him with her feelings and that had taken strength. He'd been autocratic and uncommunicative. He'd arrogantly assumed he could handle everything alone, make everything all better again, when that was actually *impossible*. He couldn't go back to how he'd been. She'd changed him somehow.

Yet the thought—the fear—of losing everything all over again swamped him. He had to pull back from everything. Because that was what he risked. In trying to make this all work, he'd put himself in the position of possessing things, enjoying experiences, that he'd never thought he'd ever have.

But that also meant there was the prospect of losing… *everyone.* His best friend. His sister. His lover and their unborn child. That risk was too much even to contemplate. It hurt to breathe. Every heartbeat hurt his ribs. He couldn't sustain this tension. Regulating his need to maintain control of a situation was almost impossible. And opening up and letting someone close…*really* close…?

He'd never allowed it. He still couldn't. But at the same time he didn't think he'd managed to stop it from happening. Not this time. Violet was right—he was a coward. And she deserved so much better.

CHAPTER FOURTEEN

VIOLET *WANTED* TO run away. She could find her way to a bus in the nearby ski town and leave today. She could bury her head in travel and adventure—see new sights, absorb everything new and avoid getting too deeply entrenched anywhere or with anyone. But that wasn't possible. First, she didn't have the funds. Second, she didn't have the heart. That wasn't hers any more, it was in bits. Part of it belonged to her baby. The rest of it had been broken and tossed back at her feet by Roman. But she was going to give it the chance to heal. Then she'd pick it up and carry on.

At least here she had some distance from him. Maybe soon she'd be able to control her emotions enough to make a plan. But right now she still didn't know how it could work. Her family lived on the other side of the world. He ran one of the largest companies in the States. His whole life was here. And she? She didn't have a life. Not one she'd made for *herself*. Not yet. And she wanted that, a life for her child and her. One that could be rewarding and secure… Honestly, she didn't need all the fancy things. She just wanted him.

She gritted her teeth. She wasn't going to have him. He'd made that more than clear. But she would never walk out on him. She wouldn't run away when he had so much else going on in his life that was so huge. Meeting Eloise was far more important for him to deal with, but Violet was hurt that he'd pushed her away so completely. He was so used to doing everything alone, to coping alone, to containing every emotion. Privacy, she understood, but such emotional isolation was sad.

And she worried for their child. Was Roman going to be an emotionally absent father who could give only *material* support? He'd shown it once again—his first priority had been to establish financial security for Eloise. And, while she respected his desire to give his sister her birth right, was there not more to be built? More that was more important? Just meeting her, building a relationship with her? Maybe it had only been one of his reactions. The only one he felt comfortable sharing with her.

But that said everything, didn't it? He couldn't open up to Violet about how he was really feeling. Couldn't admit excitement. Or fear. Couldn't share the things she really wanted to be able to share. Fears. Hopes. Dreams. He didn't *want* to.

She wanted a different relationship from that of her parents. Not trying to force some kind of perfection, of smothering protection and pretence that everything was going to be all right all of the time, while at the same time never confronting the fact that it might not be. Never addressing it. She wanted someone she could be fully honest with. And being that honest would be okay.

She'd thought for a moment they'd had that. That she could admit her fears and he would listen. Empathise. Support. But she wanted to do the same for him. Sharing one thing. Sharing all. The good and the bad. Richer or poorer. Sickness and health. Secrets, dreams, embarrassments, amusements…that was what she really wanted. True intimacy. She wanted to have it all. With him.

But he didn't. Not only did he not think he was capable of it, but he didn't want it with *her*. He didn't love her.

And he was the father of her child. She needed him to do better. But if he wasn't going to, if he was incapable, then she was going to have to step up even more. Because she didn't want her child suppressing her emotions the way she once had. Always saying she was fine, maintaining a brave face and covering up. No one could do that for ever. It wasn't healthy. Look at Roman—he was the example of that. An emotional ice box. So, yes, this baby was going to need more from her.

So she would stay. But he wasn't going to get it all. They'd become…*colleagues*. There was no other way to consider it. They'd be doing a job together, raising their baby. But they would not be friends. Their affair was over. She'd been a fool to continue it on the train. And she would never marry him. Nor would she marry anyone else. Not ever. The thought made her sick. At least she knew he wouldn't, either. He'd only considered it with her because he'd got her pregnant. That wasn't a mistake he'd make again.

But *he* might have affairs. She would have to cope. But she didn't have to *see* it. She could, she realised, stay here. She could take over the running of the lodge for Linda when she wanted to retire. It wouldn't be ideal to work for him, but it was one route. If he refused to consider it, she'd get a job in the village or at the nearby ski resort. For these early years, before school, this was a place she could adore. And, in her breaks, she could still travel a little. She could make a good go of it. She was bruised but she *would* be okay.

Met Ellie. Thanks for finding her but you should have told me about the two of you. WTH?

It took almost twenty-four hours for Roman to hear back from Alex. The first message he got was from Ellie, saying she wanted to meet and discuss the family and financial stuff early in the New Year. Roman was happy to make that timing work. He would have everything set up and perfect. Then Alex called.

'She wants to meet with the lawyers in the New Year,' Roman said but he suspected Alex already knew far more about what Ellie was thinking than he ever would.

'That's good,' Alex said.

It was. Ellie knew who she was, she was capable of looking after herself and Roman simply had to accept that. And he could. Maybe Violet had taught him how.

'You coming to the New Year's Eve party?' Alex asked.

Absolutely not. But Roman didn't want to drag Alex's mood down to his, so he was vague. 'I'm not sure.'

'Okay. Just let us know.'

Us.

Roman grimaced and smiled at the same time. There it was—weird as hell, but all the same he was pleased for them. Alex was solid. The best friend anyone could want. And Eloise deserved the best. He figured it was good they had each other.

But there was no message from Violet. Not that first day. Not the next. Nor with one after. That was good, right? No news was good news. Linda would keep an eye on her.

So now he just had to get through the next week. He didn't want to stay in town. He didn't even want to consider the New Year. Maybe he ought to head to one of the overseas offices again for a while. Except he couldn't think about travel without thinking about Violet. Violet who sought adventure. Who was curious and excited to see new places and meet new people, to see and do new things, even when she was a little afraid to. She revitalised him—made him want to appreciate it the same, all in a way he'd not felt for so very long.

He thought about Violet constantly. It annoyed the hell out of him because he still didn't know how to deal with their situation.

He avoided the hotel and went to the Fraser mansion instead—the place he'd offered Eloise. The place she'd refused. At least it was a place he didn't associate with Violet. Except she was still there with him. The dreams he'd had, they had changed. It was she who he saw now. Standing there—so proud, so angry, so honest. And on the fourth morning he lay alone in his big bed, in the big empty-feeling house, and thought about those moments he couldn't quite remember—the ones when Eloise had been taken.

Alex had told him that Ellie had said the couple who'd taken her had been caring. They'd never told Ellie the truth, but Alex wondered if they hadn't seen that Roman was still alive in that wreckage. Maybe they'd thought he'd died instantly—like his parents. It made sense if they had. Roman knew he'd been covered in blood, not all of it his own, but his father's as well. He'd been still. He'd been silent. He'd been broken.

For the first time he allowed himself to acknowledge that his attempts to call out hadn't only been to stop them from taking Eloise but to stop them from leaving *him* behind.

He didn't want to be left behind. Never again.

He'd *thought* he was okay. He'd thought he was living a full life, hitting so many targets—owning all the things, doing all the things. But he wasn't okay and what he really wanted now scared the hell out of him. He knew the fear was irrational but it had still been powerful enough to make him freeze—to render him silent at the most crucial of moments.

He tried to force his focus on work this week. He went to his gym room and pushed himself for hours. It didn't matter. He didn't sleep. He couldn't. But it wasn't the nightmares. It was the misery of his future. It had been the worst moment of his life twenty-one years ago when he'd wanted to say something but hadn't been able to. And he'd just done it all over again with Violet. But this time it was different. He wasn't ten. He wasn't pinned to the ground and injured. Here he was, *choosing* not to speak up. He wasn't helplessly watching someone slip away from him, because he wasn't helpless. This was his own stupid choice—not just to be silent, but actually to be the one to walk away.

He winced. *Losing* hurt too much. He couldn't take the risk. He'd wanted to stay safe. But what he *wanted* now was too intense and suddenly too strong. It hit him in an overwhelming rush. He couldn't live like this—not without having told *her* the truth. Not without her at all.

His own fear had constrained him and he'd been a fool. He had to see her. Had to do better, say more—say everything. He wanted to be there for his sister and Alex. He wanted to be there for his baby. He wanted everything. But he wanted it all *with* Violet. He wanted her most of all. So, this time, it wasn't enough to try to scream. This time he really had to move.

This time he actually could.

CHAPTER FIFTEEN

THE LODGE LOOKED stunning in the winter sun but Roman couldn't appreciate it. Maybe he should have messaged first but what he wanted to say had to be said to her face. He went straight inside and up to the private wing. But she wasn't in the lounge, nor the bedroom. He went back down and into the kitchen but it was empty.

He finally found her in the reception room. She was in jeans and a soft jersey, and she was leaning close to the main Christmas tree to take off an ornament. There was a strand of silver tinsel around her shoulders and a large open box at her feet. She had her headphones on and he realised she hadn't heard him come in. It was Bruce who gave him away. The cat crept out from under the tree and yowled at him.

'What is it, boy?' Violet turned and saw Roman. Her eyes widened and she pulled the headphones off with her free hand.

All the words he'd mentally prepared evaporated at the sheer relief she was there. 'I'm glad you're here,' he muttered.

'Of course, I said I would stay.' She set down the ornament and her headphones. 'And you've come back.' She shot him a look. 'You didn't say you'd do that.'

'I didn't say a lot of things.' His throat tightened.

Seeing her again made all his emotion rise. He'd missed her even more than he'd realised. He didn't want to be apart from her. *Never* again. The fear of losing her—having failed her once already—hit in a colossal wave. He couldn't say anything again.

'Did it go okay?' she asked.

He read the concern in her eyes—that calm caring, even though he'd hurt her. But her concern wasn't enough. It wasn't all that he wanted. He had to do better.

'Fine.' But he was literally unable to say more. All the words clogged his throat and, in his silence, she shrank a little.

'I've made a plan,' she said, because he left it too long. She glanced away, building a wall he didn't want. 'I like it here. I want to stay here. I like the view, the mountains, the snow.'

He swallowed, distracted. 'I thought you wanted to enjoy big city life.'

'If I live here, I can be near enough to you to balance childcare needs, but have space as well.'

She wanted space from him.

'I'd like to work. Linda and Dennis are looking forward to retirement. Linda can train me.'

'To look after the lodge?'

'Why not?' Her chin lifted. 'We can open it up more. I'm good with people. I could manage this place easily.'

Admiration filled him. She had courage and strength and she wasn't going to give up. Ever. She would make her plans and push forward.

'I'm sure you could.' He stepped towards her. 'But what if I don't want you to do that?'

Her focus darted away from him—seeking escape again. 'Then I'll get a job in the village. I know it might be a little messy for me to be your employee, but I had thought you could get over that.' Reproach filled her tone.

He had to take a steadying breath before he could explain. 'I meant if I don't want you to live so far away from *me*.' He never wanted to be far from her—never again. These few days had been too long. 'What if I don't want that?'

Her lips trembled and she pressed them together tightly. 'You won't miss out on time with the baby. You can be here as often as you want and you know it. You can work from here if you have to. But you like Manhattan. You like your hotel suite. You like your life there.'

He hated it now. He hated the soulless style and the deafening silence. 'You wanted to travel.'

'I still can. Maybe at some weekends, when you're in charge of the baby. Or I'll take her with me on adventures.' She glared at him them, daring him to deny her.

He couldn't. 'And your family in New Zealand?'

'I'll visit them. They can visit me. But I'll live here most of the time.' She nodded as if it was all perfectly reasonable, like it was a good solution.

She really had it all planned out. He didn't know whether he was impressed or outraged. Either way, the blood was beating back around his body and his brain was coming back online. 'What about your personal life?'

She hesitated. 'I'm going to be busy with the baby. Adjusting to life here. I'm not going to have time for…'

He waited but she didn't continue and he walked towards her. He couldn't stop himself now. The colour in her cheeks deepened with every step he took, and honestly it was the only thing that gave him any hope.

'No time for anything intimate?' he pressed.

She didn't answer.

'And *my* personal life?' he asked. Huskily. Desperately.

She shot him a look. 'Won't be any of my business,' she muttered. 'I don't need to know.'

'It's a sacrifice,' he said.

'It's a compromise.' Her lashes lifted and she stared at him directly—properly—for the first time since he'd arrived. She stared at him with such reproach, such emotion. 'One you need to match.'

His heart melted. God, he loved her. And he needed to step up and be worthy.

'What if I don't want to sacrifice anything?' he asked. 'What if I want it all?'

Anger flashed then. 'You can't have everything you want, Roman. Not this time.'

But he wanted it. *Everything.* With her. There was a sheen in her eyes that she couldn't hide…

'Won't you want more children?' He couldn't stop the questions now.

'Maybe I'll *have* more.' Hurt made her voice higher.

'With someone else?' Was that what she meant?

'*What* do you *want*?' she demanded furiously. 'Why are you asking me this? To torture me? You *know* this is the best we can do.'

'But it isn't.' He couldn't resist any more. He put his hands on her waist, finally holding her again. Heaven help him, he knew he'd never ever let her go.

Violet was struggling to claw back her emotions. He was back. Why was he back? Why was he asking these questions? Didn't he know they were tearing her heart out? While he'd been gone she'd been able to control herself enough to make a plan. But, seeing him, so much yearning, love and *hurt* flooded her. It was impossible to think clearly.

'It's not what you really want, Violet.'

What she really wanted was impossible. He'd already

let her know that and he didn't need to drag her through that denial again. 'Leave me alone, Roman. Why are you even here?'

Because, within that flood of emotion, *hope* had floated up. Stupid, foolish hope and she couldn't stop it. She desperately hoped that he'd come back for her. Because he was holding her now. Tightly. And it was a good thing, because now she was trembling so much she wasn't sure she could keep standing. Not alone.

'I don't want to be apart from you,' he muttered huskily.

She pressed her head down and her forehead hit his chest. She couldn't look at him. She couldn't believe in the tenderness in his eyes. But he carefully cupped her chin and lifted her face.

'Violet. Please listen to me.'

She closed her eyes because tears were already forming. She didn't want to hurt any more. Nor hope. Nor wish. Not any more.

'I'm sorry,' he whispered. 'I'm so, so sorry.'

'Don't,' she whispered. But she began to shake even harder.

'Don't tell you how I feel? Don't finally open up and admit how wrong I've been? What an idiot? Violet… please…please can you listen to me?'

She forced herself to hold still. To listen. Because his voice was a whisper. But it was a true whisper.

'I shouldn't have gone,' he said. 'Not after you…' He dragged in a breath. 'I never should have left you—'

'You had to,' she interrupted quickly. She couldn't bear to remember what she'd said—her admission, his rejection. Better to focus on his sister, right? 'How was it? How was she?'

He hesitated, then breathed again. 'You're going to like her, I think. She looks so much like Grandma Joan. But she doesn't sound… Scottish accent. I'll tell you more later. You'll meet her soon.' His fallen-angel frown deepened. 'But the way I left you… The things I said…' He closed his eyes. 'What I *didn't* say. I wasn't thinking. Wasn't coping. Violet…'

She waited this time, not filling the silence. Not trying to make it easier for him. Not trying to run from the depth of the emotion that swirled between them. It had to be acknowledged—and released. He needed the space, the time, to speak when he was ready. His eyes flashed open, he gazed right at her and she realised he finally was.

She shook and his hold on her firmed.

'I've always thought the worst moment of my life was when I was trapped in that car. When I tried to call out, silently screaming as someone I loved slipped away. It was awful. Had it even happened at all?' His body tensed. 'I couldn't trust anyone. Couldn't trust myself—my own judgement. I built barriers and defences. I never wanted to feel loss the way I did back then…' He lifted a hand and caressed her cheek. 'I lost everyone.'

She nodded. She knew. It was horrendously sad for him.

'I didn't stop to consider that it was happening again. That I wasn't just allowing it but actively letting…' He shrugged. 'I'm not used to speaking about personal things. About how I feel. But I have to. I need to work on it. It isn't fair otherwise. Not on you, not on our child.' He slowly swept his hand down to her belly. 'I can't expect you to be a mind-reader, that's not fair of me. I have to *speak*. I have to say something—the truth about how I feel—to stop myself from losing the most precious thing to me now.'

'You're not going to lose the baby. I won't leave. I won't take it away from you.'

Somehow he was closer still.

'I'm not talking about the baby. I'm talking about *you*...' he breathed. 'You told me you love me.'

'Yes.' She wasn't going to deny it.

He paused. That fallen angel frown lifted—just for a moment—and he was so handsome, her heart broke.

'I'm scared, Violet. The thought of having you—both of you—but then losing you would be the worst, the absolute worst thing. Because having you in my life is the best thing. So good that I...'

He trailed off, looked at her and gave a helpless shrug. 'You're the most genuine, caring person I've met. You're chatty and kind and beautiful. And when you let yourself fall into my arms, when you chose me, you smiled and told me your secrets and I've never had someone look at me, see me, smile at me, the way you do.' His breath shuddered. 'You were so trusting.'

'You mean so naïve.'

'I mean *brave*. You were fearless with me. You opened up, and your warmth?' He shook his head. 'I've never known such softness. Such laughter and heat. And then I hurt you. I tried to deny what it really was because it terrified me. If I didn't name it, it wouldn't become real and then I couldn't lose it. But I was lying to myself. Because I didn't just lose it, I pushed it away. I pushed *you* away—' He broke off. 'But you realised what you wanted and you fought for it. You told me how you felt and I couldn't listen. I refused you. I rejected you, and it was such a mistake. I'm sorry.'

'Roman...'

'I tried to forget you after Halloween but I couldn't. I had to come back. And then after that night on Thanksgiving...' He pulled her closer. 'Then on the train I tried to contain everything. But it didn't work. Instead I began to thaw. The past hurt—it still hurts. But the thought of a future without you?' He shook his head slowly. 'Whatever days I have here, I want to spend them with you.'

Finally, warmth began to flow through her. 'And the nights?'

'In you,' he said huskily with the smallest of smiles. 'I want to go to sleep locked in your arms, your body, your heart. I will make love to you every night for the rest of my life.'

And now she was quivering inside. 'You'd better.' She clutched him, her hands wide, her heart overflowing. 'Roman—'

'I love you. I'm sorry I couldn't say it before. I love you.' His head bent as he gazed into her eyes with pure intensity flowing from his. 'Please let me love you.'

'Yes, of course. *Yes.*' Tears coursed down her cheeks. 'I missed you. I love you. And you're not an idiot. You're strong and kind. You just…need practice at speaking up.'

But there was no talking now. His mouth was on hers and the message was so very clear—everything he'd just said and more.

Her heart soared. 'Oh, Roman…'

He toyed with the tinsel around her shoulders. 'You're my Christmas angel.'

'You know I'm not,' she half-chuckled. 'I was helping remove the decorations. Linda said she always takes them down before you arrive.'

'Is she here?' he asked.

'She and Dennis have gone into the village. They won't be back for a while and I'm not expecting them to come up to the lodge at all.'

'Great.' He breathed fervently. 'That's great.' But he suddenly glanced up at the tree. 'Maybe we should leave the decorations up a little longer this time.' He turned back to her. 'Seeing you here this Christmas Eve was the best and worst night of my life. It was everything. You were everything. Honestly, you freaked me out. Or…my feelings for you freaked me out.'

She smiled softly and put her palm to his cheek.

'I want a family with you,' he said. 'I want to enjoy all of it. I don't want to shut myself off from life any more. I want the celebration. I want the good stuff too.'

'So do I.' She nodded.

'Good. Because I want it all with you. Everything with you.' He suddenly moved. 'Starting now.'

'Now?' She chuckled. *Finally.*

'Now.'

He whisked her Merino jumper over her head. Desire deepened in his eyes as he gazed at her breasts, and she was so glad she'd been too lazy to bother with a bra that morning. She hated the time it took to shimmy her jeans and panties down her hips. Fortunately, he'd kicked his jeans off already, and now desperate hunger pulsed through her.

His laugh slid into a groan as she reached for him. 'Darling, I'm not going to last…'

'So hurry up and make love to me,' she ordered. 'I've missed you so much.'

In the split second before he kissed her, she saw his expression crumple—revealing all the raw emotion. The love. The need. The leap of joy.

Then his kiss was hard, deep and so hungry, and she met it, matched it. She was absolutely aching. They tumbled to the floor and there wasn't time for more. There was only the driving need to be together.

'It's not like anything else ever,' he muttered as he moved over her.

'I know.' And, as innocent as she'd been before him, she did know that there was no joy like this.

She wrapped around him, letting him love her like no one ever had. And she loved him too—chanting his name, her love for him, over and over until she was so overcome with ecstasy, she could no longer speak.

Long, breathless moments later, he pulled her to rest in his arms, his body cushioning hers.

'Alex found Ellie.' His chest rumbled when he finally spoke 'They're together.'

'Together?' Violet echoed, then lifted her head to look him in the eyes. 'You mean…*together*?'

He nodded, tenderness gleaming in his eyes.

'How do you feel about that?' she pressed him.

'I just want them to be happy.' His smile began to deepen. 'And, if they're half as happy together as I am when I'm with you, then they're very lucky.'

He drew breath. 'It's going to take some time, I guess, for everyone to get used to everything.' He ran his hand across her back, keeping her warm and close. 'I need to return to Manhattan for New Year's Eve. I really want you to meet them. Will you come with me?' He paused as he watched for her reaction. 'We can have another couple of days here first, though.'

'I would love to meet them,' she murmured. 'And I would love more time here first too.'

'I love it here too. But we're going to need to spend a lot of time in the city.'

'Fortunately, I love the city too.' She chuckled. 'And I'll be with you.'

'Yeah…' He glanced above her at the Christmas tree and regret tinged his features.

'What is it?'

'I never got you a Christmas present,' he said.

She reached out and retrieved the strip of tinsel that had fallen from her shoulders and draped it across her chest.

'*You're* all my Christmas and birthday presents rolled into one. I never need anything else.'

'Not even a little thing?' He shifted her just a little, only so he could reach his jeans and pull from his pocket a little box.

'Roman…'

It wasn't a little thing. It was a ring. A beautiful, gleaming piece of art.

'I've never seen a stone that colour.' She couldn't stop staring at it. 'It's beautiful.' It was set in platinum—a multi-faceted oval that drew her eye deeper into the stone.

'It's a violet diamond.'

Her heart melted. 'I didn't know such a thing existed.'

'There's not many of them.'

She glanced at him shrewdly. The man was underplaying it. He meant it was rare, and it was stunningly large, which meant it had probably cost far too much.

'Roman,' she queried softly. 'Does this stone need its own bodyguard?'

'An over-protective arrogant jerk maybe?' He grinned at her tenderly. But then his smile faded. 'Can you consider it a promise from me?' he asked gruffly. 'Whenever— *if* ever—you want, then I am right here, ready, willing, desperate to say *I do*. I want to marry you. But it's up to you—time, place, everything…' He ran his hand through her hair as he whispered, 'Just know that, no matter what, I am yours. Always yours.' He took the ring from the box and his fingers weren't quite steady. 'Please accept it,' he asked. 'Accept me.'

She understood that his need to give her this was part of who he was. 'You want to spoil me.'

'Want to give you everything.' He nodded, the look in his eyes almost shy now.

She placed her hand on his chest, feeling his quickened but steady heartbeat. 'You already have. But I will wear your ring. I will be your wife. I will carry your child. Our child. But you are *mine* too and I want everyone to know it.'

There was a strand of tinsel in his hair and a smile in his eyes. 'Oh, you do?'

'I do,' she said boldly. 'And there will be no more edible bachelor lists for you.'

He pulled her back down, holding her prisoner in his arms. 'Are you saying yes?'

'I will always say yes to you.'

He threw his head back and laughed with joyous delight. '*There's* a promise. Say yes to me now.'

She wriggled free of his hold only to straddle him. Sultry pleasure flowed through her veins. Oh, she did love him. She did love that he'd opened up for her. And, as he gazed up at her, that vulnerability unveiled again in his eyes.

'Love me,' he breathed.

She understood now how sweetly he loved her. How insatiably. How he ached for her the same way she did for him. And how it was the most terrifyingly wonderful thing for him too.

'Yes,' she promised him once more, understanding that right now he needed to hear it again and again. As did she. 'Love me back.'

'I do,' he promised. 'I will. And I will tell you, and show you, every day of my life.'

CHAPTER SIXTEEN

New Year's Eve, one year later

'AREN'T YOU READY YET?' Roman leaned against the wall and watched his wife run the styling wand through her hair. He loved watching her do that—especially when she was clad only in silk and lace underwear. But then, he loved watching her do anything, wearing anything, at any time.

Yeah, he was smitten, and he was going to run his fingers through that beautifully straightened hair within the next two seconds.

'Almost.' She breathed, her gaze fixed on the mirror.

'It's New Year's Eve,' he teased as he moved to stand behind her. 'We can't be late.'

He was looking forward to the evening ahead. To the *years* ahead. The decades.

A week ago they'd looked in at the Christmas Eve Ball at the lodge before retreating upstairs. There would always be a bittersweet element to Christmas for Roman, but spending it quietly with Violet made the sweet swamp the sadness. There would always be the memory of his parents and the accident, but now the season was also linked to the joy of finding his sister. Of seeing her happy with Alex.

And now, on New Year's Eve, he stood in his Manhattan town house. He'd just cradled his child to sleep and he'd come to find his wife. And his level of contentment was indescribable.

Violet's gaze shifted, drinking in his reflection. When he ran his hands down her arms, she instantly smouldered.

'Is that right?' A teasing purr, a promise of pleasure.

She leaned back so her lush curves pressed and turned him rock-hard and ready.

'She's asleep.' His voice was like gravel.

His daughter Lottie was a cherub when asleep. It just took a while to get her that way. Thankfully, she now was. Now his time was his own—to be spent with his woman.

Violet's eyebrows flickered. 'That's why you're looking so smug.'

Amusement lifted even as his need to have her intensified to the point of unbearable. 'I'm feeling far more than smug. For far more than one reason.'

'Oh?' His beautiful wife finally put down the styling wand.

He leaned closer and lifted his hand to mess through her sweet-smelling, silky hair. Oh, he loved it. Loved her.

She groaned. 'You—'

'Love it when I do this.'

Oh, she *did*. Violet shivered as he brushed aside her hair and kissed her neck. A second later, he unfastened her bra and pulled the lace from her warm, soft skin. The guy was smooth. But she met his gaze in the mirror and read the heat, the need and the love in his eyes. She couldn't stop her smile. Couldn't stop herself from arching into his touch as his hands slid to her panties and pulled them down.

'What happened to not being late?' she muttered

dreamily. 'We're supposed to meet Alex and Ellie in twenty minutes.'

'They won't mind if we're a little late,' he assured her firmly. His touch was equally firm.

'Yeah...' She wasn't sure what she was agreeing to any more. She just needed him to love her like this. Again and always. And he did—with every fibre of his big, strong, body. 'Roman...'

'I'm here. I love you.'

She closed her eyes and loved him right back.

'Not so very late.' Roman grinned at her ruefully when they finally got into the waiting car to meet Alex and Ellie just over half an hour later, leaving their nanny watching little Lottie.

Violet chuckled, but she knew their lateness didn't really matter. Roman held her hand as he threaded through the crowd in the stunning restaurant on the top floor of a Manhattan skyscraper. Alex and Ellie were ensconced close together in a private corner. The views were amazing, but the city lights couldn't match the sparkle in Ellie's eyes or the gleaming smile on Alex's face as they greeted them. The couple looked stunning, and it wasn't because of their beautifully tailored clothes. In fact, they looked so shimmery that Violet instinctively stopped before taking her seat.

'You two look even more...' She cocked her head and frowned at them. 'What's going on?'

'We can't hide anything from you, Violet.' Alex smiled at her, then looked straight up into Roman's eyes. 'Eloise is pregnant.'

There was no preamble and, while it wasn't exactly a shock, it was emotional. A sudden wave of happiness swamped Violet—but she turned to Roman, knowing he'd feel this even more deeply.

'Eloise…' Roman echoed softly. His hand tightened on Violet's.

She knew it pleased him immensely that his sister now sometimes used her original name. That Eloise was utterly, fully, herself meant so much to Roman and he looked at her protectively now.

And Ellie smiled at her big brother cheekily. 'Surprise.'

'I'm thrilled for you both.' Roman simply sank into the empty seat next to his sister. 'Thrilled. I get to be an uncle. Violet an aunt.' He breathed out as he absorbed it. A moment later a smile curved his lips. 'I can't wait to see you, Alex—' he suddenly laughed '—pacing with a new-born. Nappy changes. Pacing again…'

Violet watched her handsome husband tease his sister and his best friend, even as his fingers laced even more tightly through hers and she felt the pulse of his emotion. She loved that he reached to her for support, for celebration…that they shared *everything*. Several months ago, they'd gone back to New Zealand to meet her family and tell them their news directly. Of course, Roman had completely charmed them. They'd married there. It had been wonderful and then, a few months later, little Lottie had arrived. Alex and Eloise had married and now they were going to experience the joy of having a child too.

Violet blinked back sudden tears.

'Violet?'

All three were looking at her.

'I'm fine. It's just…good…' she half-gasped, half-giggled. 'All *so* good.'

As Alex and Ellie laughed, Roman pressed a quick, understanding kiss to her mouth. She melted against him. With friends and family like this, with her daughter

sweetly sleeping at home and her husband alongside her always, her life, her future, was so much more than full.
   It was heaven.

* * * * *

WEDDING NIGHT WITH THE WRONG BILLIONAIRE

DANI COLLINS

MILLS & BOON

With deepest gratitude to my editor, Laurie Johnson, who always seems to know what questions to ask me when I've literally lost the plot.

Without her savvy navigations these characters might have been stuck in the Bermuda Triangle forever.

PROLOGUE

June, Niagara-on-the-Lake, present day...

IT WAS SUPPOSED to be the happiest day of her life, but Eden Bellamy wasn't happy.

She *should* be. Her groom was a reliable, steady man, exactly like her father. Their marriage would save her father's company. She'd been stressing over how she would do that since Oscar Bellamy's death a year ago. She ought to be thrilled to her pedicured toes that she was finally resolving things.

She pretended she was happy. She plastered a smile on her face as her mother dabbed the corners of her eyes and wished Eden's father was here.

"Me, too, Mama. Go take your seat." *I want this over with.*

Her mother hurried away. Eden's heart seemed to follow, stretching out after her the way a child's might when their mother left them at preschool for the first time. *Wait. Don't leave me. Save me.*

The wedding planner secured the microphone to the sweetheart neckline of her gown and tried to lower Eden's veil. She stopped her.

"I need to see the stairs."

Nerves already had her so unsteady, she feared she

would tumble down them. Micah wouldn't let that happen, of course.

Her half brother was standing in as father of the bride. He wore his habitual stoic expression as he stood at the open doors to the terrace watching Quinn, Eden's maid of honor, coax the bridal party into their positions. She urged the flower girl to take the hand of Eden's adolescent cousin as they moved to the top of the stairs for the procession down to the lawn.

"Ready?" The wedding planner finished fussing.

"Is it working?" Eden asked, into the microphone, and heard her own voice come through the speakers outside.

With a pleased smile, the planner melted away. Seconds later, the music paused. The murmuring of the crowd went silent.

Eden's stomach curdled. A dire sense that she was making a colossal mistake condensed around her like a noxious fugue.

He doesn't want you, she silently screamed at herself, exactly as she had while lying awake last night. As she had every night, in fact, for months. For years.

She tried to recount all the reasons why marrying Hunter Waverly made sense, but her thoughts insistently drifted to that other man, the one who barely acknowledged she existed. The one standing beside Hunter right now.

How could seeing him be the only thing about this day that she looked forward to? She would stand near Remy Sylvain while she spoke her vows to another man and *he wouldn't care*.

Micah held out a crooked arm.

Tears pressed behind her eyes as she came forward to tuck her hand inside his elbow.

Outside, the lyrical notes of the harp invited her to step

over the threshold into her new life. Her heart began to pound so forcefully, the microphone might have picked it up. There was a rushing sound in her ears. Her feet tried to glue themselves to the floor.

I can't do this, she thought with abject panic.

"You!" a man's angry voice shouted down below.

It was followed by a plaintive tone from a woman. "Daddy, no! Please!"

"What the hell?" Micah muttered. He strode to the edge of the terrace.

Eden followed and peered down at the hundreds of assembled guests, all facing the pergola where Hunter was standing with his groomsmen and the wedding officiant.

A gray-haired man in rumpled clothes shook his finger at Hunter while his daughter, presumably, tugged his arm, begging him to leave. She held a baby, one new enough that she was protecting its neck as she cuddled it against her shoulder. The senior shook her off and continued berating Hunter.

"Dad!" the woman cried. "He didn't know, okay? I never told him!"

After a stunned pause and a charged exchange between father and daughter, Hunter's voice boomed through the speakers.

"Is it true?"

Eden's brain finally caught up and crashed into what was happening. That old man was claiming the woman's baby was *Hunter's*! Her knees nearly gave out.

Hunter tore off his microphone and handed it to an usher.

That's when she realized Remy was looking up at her.

He was wearing the same morning suit as the rest of the groom's party, but he wore it so much better. His white shirt and burgundy vest with swirls of gold were positively regal on his muscled torso.

If a man was capable of being elegant and beautiful while maintaining every shred of masculinity, that's what Remy managed to do. Always. His hair had been freshly cut into a midfade, his strong jaw shaved clean. His tall, muscled frame was powerful and unmoving, while his demeanor was more remote and contained than ever.

He wasn't shocked by what was going on, though. That's what struck her like a slap. He was watching to see how *she* reacted.

Had he *arranged* this? Had Micah been right? Was Remy willing to ruin her wedding? Her *life*?

Beside her, Micah muttered a string of curses. "I'll kill him. This time, I really will."

Down in the pergola, Remy nudged Hunter. Hunter moved his gaze up to her. So did the woman. Hunter's grim expression hardened with culpability.

The farcical energy crackled for two or three seconds longer, long enough for Eden's heart to twist and wrench inside her chest. Humiliation crept like poison from the pit of her stomach to ache in her cheeks.

The woman with the baby looked equally mortified. Her expression crumpled and she hurried away.

Eden's numb fingers released her bouquet. It fell off the ledge of the terrace. She dragged her gaze from Remy's unreadable expression and swept herself back into the honeymoon suite of the vineyard's guesthouse.

CHAPTER ONE

Paris, five years ago...

EDEN ALMOST LET Quinn go to the Louvre alone. She had
been to the museum before and it was always a crush of
people, especially around the most famous painting in the
world.

Culture wasn't her priority when she came to Europe.
She wanted to visit her brother and enjoy vacation pur-
suits, like sailing, shopping, swimming and snowboarding.

Quinn liked those things, too, but she hadn't grown
up with money. She was building her future on an education obtained through scholarship and maximized every
chance to learn.

Eden respected that. In some ways, she envied Quinn
her limitless choices. Eden's life path was set in stone. She
would finish her business degree, inherit Bellamy Home
and Garden and keep it flourishing. She was happy to do
so, but she needed a break from the pressure sometimes.

She and Quinn were best friends *because* they were
willing to go along with what the other one wanted to do,
though. Whether it was homework, browsing boutiques,
or craning to catch a glimpse of a painting through a sea
of patrons' phone screens, they wanted to hang together
and crack dumb jokes for the other's amusement.

"I thought it would be bigger," Quinn said, swaying on her tiptoes.

"Haven't you heard? Size doesn't matter."

It was a lame phrase they threw at each other more often than twelve-year-old boys declared, "That's what she said."

A snort of amusement behind her prompted Eden to glance back.

The breath was stolen clean out of her lungs by a man in distressed denim jeans, suede ankle boots and a mushroom-gray linen jacket over a green shirt with sunflowers on it. His collar was open, revealing a modest gold pendant nestled against the hollow of his brown throat. A protective saint, perhaps.

Confidence radiated off his tall frame. His wide shoulders spoke of physical power. He wore his jacket with the sleeves pushed back, exposing the Montblanc on his wrist. Above his high fade, his black curls were natural and short. His goatee framed his full-lipped mouth. The heavy-lidded gaze that lingered on her sent a gorgeous slithery sensation from her abdomen into places inside her that had never felt alive.

Her cheeks warmed and her breath shortened as she held his rye-whiskey gaze.

"Age matters, though," Quinn mused in her ear.

Eden sent Quinn a side-eye of "shut up" and returned his smile. She was nineteen, definitely old enough to flirt with someone in his midtwenties. This was Paris. It was kind of required by law.

"You speak English?" she asked, which wasn't exactly high-level flirting, but dozens of languages were competing in the din around them. It was a logical opener.

"I do. I'm Canadian. Like you."

"How do you know we're Canadian?" Eden cocked her head with curiosity.

"Halifax is hitting her *r*'s harder than a pirate." He nodded at Quinn. "And you said 'sorry' to the guy who crammed his elbow in your ear."

"Prince Edward Island, thank you," Quinn said, correcting him with mock indignance. "I'm going to try to get closer." Quinn inserted her shoulder into the crowd.

Eden held out her hand. "Eden. Toronto." She skipped the second *t*, the way most locals did.

"Remy. Montreal." He gave it the Quebecois pronunciation.

They held hands and gazes until Eden was nudged from behind. She took a step into Remy to catch her balance. Her hand pressed one of those sunflowers to his very firm, warm chest. He steadied her with a grip of her elbow.

"Sorry?" she said wryly, trying to cover up how her knees softened at being so close to him. The flutters in her midsection had become waves of heat that pulsed upward into her breasts and throat. Her cheeks were likely turning pink because she was tingling all over with acute warmth.

"No problem." The indent at the corner of his mouth was the most beautiful thing she'd ever seen, but his indulgent gaze was a teensy bit rueful. She heard the reserve in his voice as he released her. "Are you au pairs? Or is this a graduation trip? You don't strike me as backpackers."

He thought she was fresh out of high school? "I come every year to see my brother." She was going for sophistication, but probably came off as boastful. "He keeps an apartment here."

It was more of a penthouse and one of several mansions, villas and top-floor suites that he owned. And, yes, Micah was currently living there. He had arranged their flight and a stupidly generous budget, encouraging her to bring Quinn. Micah was sweet as caramel beneath his titanium crust, but he didn't want to stand around in boutiques debating chartreuse over pistachio-green. "Take both and decide later" had been his impatient contribution to their one and only shopping trip together.

"We're heading back to McGill University in September," Eden clarified.

Remy nodded, his restless gaze scanning her face with a hint of conflict.

Eden could tell he was trying to decide if she was too young for him. She was inexperienced in some ways, but sophisticated in others. She dated regularly, but men her age seemed like juvenile nitwits when compared to her brother, who set a high bar of dynamic intelligence and shouldered far-reaching responsibilities he had inherited too early from his father.

At home, her own father was a big fish in a small pond, but people still acted weird when they found out who he was—sometimes intimidated, other times opportunistic. She sidestepped revealing her male relatives until she got to know strangers better.

"You?" she asked. "Are you on vacation with your wife or…?"

His mouth twitched and his gaze delved more deeply into hers from beneath eyelids that grew heavy with interest.

"I'm single," he assured her. "Here on business, but I have family—" He winced and glanced at his watch. "I'm meeting my cousin, actually. Now I'm late. Are you in Paris long? My friend owns a nightclub. I promised to drop by on Friday. Shall I ask him to put you on the list?" He took out his phone.

"That sounds fun. Eden and Quinn." She didn't give him her last name, not wanting him to look her up. She didn't ask him to include Micah, either. Her brother was already behaving like a Victorian guardian.

"I'll arrive around eleven. Don't let me down. I want to see you again."

His point and wink gave her a sensual kick inside that kept her buzzing for days as she dragged Quinn along the Champs-élysées in search of the perfect dress. She settled on a silver metal-chain dress with a snug halter top and a fringe below the short skirt. Her shoes were four-inch, sequined sandals with straps that spiraled halfway up to her knees.

Quinn picked a strapless green minidress that she chose because it had pockets—big surprise from practical Quinn—but it suited her figure.

When Friday arrived, for once, Quinn wore her gorgeous red hair down, but she was radiating tension on their way to the club.

"Is something wrong?" Eden was so excited she could hardly sit still.

"I'm not sure. I—" She hesitated. Conflict and a desire to evade glinted in her eyes.

Eden prickled with apprehension, but she was distracted by the sign that flashed "Until Dawn" in French.

"That's it. *Jusqu'à l'Aube*," Eden said to Micah's chauffeur and pointed ahead.

"Long line to get in," Quinn noted.

"That means it's popular." Eden had been a tiny bit worried it would be sketchy, but it was in a lively, upscale arrondissement.

The parade of laughing twentysomethings were dressed in chic miniskirts and shiny suits. They sent a mixture of curious and hostile glances when the car stopped at the end of the covered walkway into the nightclub and Eden and Quinn emerged.

"They hate us. Why didn't we get let off at the end?" Quinn asked under her breath.

"We're on The List." At least, they had better be. Eden did not want to believe she had fallen for a scam to boost numbers at a club. Remy's interest in her had felt as immediate and strong as hers had been in him. If he wasn't here, well, she would be more devastated than she was prepared to admit.

She nervously gave their names to the greeter and they were escorted into the club. Inside, the crowd bounced to the DJ's pulsing music beneath flashing colored lights. Their hostess showed them to the VIP section, where Remy was holding court on a U-shaped sofa.

He truly was the most gorgeous man. He rose and flashed a smile, kissing each of her cheeks as if he was genuinely glad to see her. As if they were longtime friends. Or something more. He wore black trousers over neon pink sneakers and a black T-shirt beneath a blue silk blazer embossed with a pink paisley pattern.

He tried to introduce her and Quinn to his friends, but all Eden heard was that one was his cousin from the museum. The woman wearing long braids and glowing white nail polish smiled and waved. A couple rose and motioned that they were headed to the dance floor. Two men joined them, making room on the sofa for Eden and Quinn to settle beside Remy.

"Champagne?" Remy reached for one of the open bottles. "Or rum? Something else?"

They chose champagne and he poured. Eden leaned toward Quinn as she accepted hers. "This must be what it feels like to be rich and famous."

"You are rich and famous," Quinn teased.

"Not like this." This was Micah rich.

Quinn smiled her thanks as she took the glass Remy offered. She waited until Remy had topped up his own and clinked, then sipped.

Eden could hardly keep her glass steady. Her senses were on overload as the crush on the sofa had her pressed tightly against Remy, feeling his every shift and move. As he settled back and set his arm on the back of the sofa, his weight tilted her into him. He smelled as good as he looked, like summer and spice and maybe lust, but that might be her.

Their gazes tangled. She wanted to hear everything he might have to say, but she also wanted to stay exactly like this, simmering in sexual excitement. It was far more intoxicating than any bubbly.

His lips grazed her ear as he dipped his head and asked, "Do you want to dance?"

She nodded and glanced at Quinn. She waved at them to go without her, her mouth pursed in rueful acknowledgment that she was in the way. One of Remy's companions glanced hopefully toward her, but Quinn was already frowning at her phone.

Something *was* bothering her, but Eden's hand was in Remy's and she was too eager to dance. She would question her later.

Remy was so sexy! Being well-dressed, confident and wealthy wasn't enough for him. He danced well, too, sinking into the groove while his hands shaped the air around her. He rolled his body and kept his gaze fixed on her, making her feel like the most desirable woman alive.

She loved dancing. Nothing made her feel more beautiful than becoming one with the music—except possibly brushing up against Remy's chest and thigh, feeling his hand graze her arm and lower back and hip. He brought her hand up over her head and twirled her, then she backed into him, thrilling when he slid his hands down her sides.

This wasn't dancing. It was foreplay. She had kissed and messed around a little, but always in an experimental way, never feeling this level of potent attraction. Her desire to be closer and touch more of him, to press herself into him, was such a force, she thought she would burst from it.

When someone stumbled into her, the spell was nearly broken. Remy quickly drew her off the dance floor into a shadowed corner at the end of the bar, brow furrowed in concern. His touch skimmed down her arm as he leaned close.

"Are you okay?"

"Fine."

Now she was entranced by how their heads were tilted close, their lips *so* close.

Acting purely on instinct, she slid her hand up his shoulder and pressed lightly in invitation. His hand splayed on her waist, drawing her in.

She held her breath as the press of their bodies clicked like magnets connecting. A sensation of rightness, of completion, encompassed her as their lips met and slid, parted and sealed.

Joy blossomed within her. He was The One. She knew it from the way his arms closed around her in a way that was both gentle and powerful, crushing her into him in the most tender way. Claiming, but telling her she was precious and important.

With the colored lights glinting behind her closed eyelids and the thumping music amplifying her heartbeat, she transcended her human self. For a few seconds, they occupied one common dimension of time and space. There was nothing between them but sparking electricity and acute pleasure. It was perfect. Utterly perfect.

And so hot. She leaned into him a little more. His hand splayed over her bottom and his tongue tagged hers. She twined her arms around his neck and—

He jerked back a step, releasing her so abruptly she

staggered to regain her balance. In the same second, he swung around to confront someone.

No. He'd been pulled, she realized. Dragged into a confrontation that quickly turned into a shoving match, one that might have turned to blows, but she suddenly recognized who had attacked him.

"Micah!" she cried in horror. "Stop!"

CHAPTER TWO

Last October...

TONIGHT WAS THEIR coming-out as a couple.

Hunter's sister, Vienna, had introduced Eden to Hunter Waverly last month. They'd begun dating very casually. He was preoccupied by a court case that had threatened his national telecom business, Wave-Com, but the final judgment had come down a few days ago. Hunter was throwing a splashy soiree to celebrate his win and he wanted Eden by his side.

"I want people to know we're serious. You've stuck beside me through a rough time. That bodes well for our future."

Did he think she had so many prospects that dating him had been an act of loyalty? Given the jeopardy at her own family company, she was actually a liability. She had to come clean before things went any further.

"I don't want to misrepresent myself," she told him haltingly. "I need you to understand what you're getting into before you we talk about whether we have a future."

Eden had studied hard to prepare herself to take the reins at Bellamy Home and Garden. She had worked in the storefront at fourteen and moved to an entry-level position at head office when she turned sixteen. Through university, she had taken on greater responsibilities, running marketing campaigns and negotiating buyer agreements and working on inclusion policies with HR.

She had believed she had earned the respect of the board along the way. When her father had passed, she had thought she had everyone's support as the next president of BH&G.

Knives had promptly come out, however. She discovered that movements toward a coup had begun when her father's health had declined. As economic storms had battered the company, a handful of acquisitive shareholders had injected capital with a ticking-time-bomb sort of clause. If they didn't earn a guaranteed return by the end of next year, they would assume controlling interest.

They were already trying to oust Eden. If she didn't fight with every cell of her being, her family's legacy would be a pitiful headline bemoaning the demise of "another" Canadian institution. All options were on the table, including an arranged marriage.

"That's why I let Vienna introduce us. I didn't want to bring it up when you were battling your own dragons, but I can't keep quiet about it any longer."

Hunter listened with equanimity. "I do have experience with dragons," he said dryly, having just triumphed over one. "I'm sure we can work out a win-win."

For the first time in a long time, Eden allowed herself a shred of optimism. Her smile was natural as she stood next to Hunter, greeting his guests. Maybe she wasn't in love with him, but she had every reason to believe she *could* love him. Eventually.

Not a frothy, heart-twisting infatuation, either. She didn't want that awful thing that continued to strike a pang of yearning through her soul. Whatever she had *thought* she had felt that long-ago night in Paris had been a deliberate play by a scoundrel on her youthful pheromones. It hadn't been real so it shouldn't haunt her.

It did, though. *He* did. Every man was measured against that illusion, even Hunter. He was the first to come close, but even he was found wanting for the crime of not being *him*. Worse, even the times she did feel a smidge of curiosity about a man, she felt so humiliated by her gullibility, she didn't trust her own judgment.

If Vienna hadn't set them up, she wouldn't have trusted Hunter. Even then, she had made it clear she wanted to take things slow. They hadn't had sex and probably wouldn't until they were married. Hunter said he was fine with that.

Maybe if he had lit her fire the way Remy had, she might have lost her virginity by now, but the only man who had ever made her crave sex was her brother's mortal enemy.

It was confusing and made her wonder if she possessed some hidden kink that yearned for the forbidden.

"There he is," Hunter said with warm affection, excusing them from their conversation with a couple from New York and drawing her toward a man that made her entire body feel as though it iced over, became heavy and unwieldy.

"Eden, this is Remy Sylvain. Eden Bellamy," Hunter introduced, then added to Remy, "You'll remember I said Vi was setting me up? Turns out she has a talent for matchmaking."

Somehow, Remy had become even more freaking handsome. More mesmerizing. His beard was a narrow strip on his chin, his hair shorter, his face now more mature in the nearly five years since she'd met him so briefly in Paris. He still had obscenely great fashion sense, wearing a closely tailored suit in dark merlot over a black shirt and tie.

The flash of his dark gold gaze cut across her like a

scythe, practically taking her knees out from beneath her. "It's nice to meet you." His voice was cool. He offered his hand.

As it penetrated that he was pretending they had never met, she placed her limp hand in his, clammy skin burning on contact with his hot palm.

A lifetime of cultivated manners had the words "It's nice to meet you, too" slipping from her lips. It wasn't nice. It was a deadly shock. How was no one noticing that her jaw had fallen onto the floor?

He shook her hand in a perfunctory way. Not hurtful, but she felt his hardness toward her before he released her, as though *she* had burned *him*.

She *felt* hurt, which was so stupid! She didn't want to feel anything for him or about him, least of all rejected. He hadn't truly wanted her in the first place.

Her mind raced, trying to work out whether he would blurt something out in front of Hunter. Should she say something? She had only just gotten her life back on track!

She couldn't speak, anyway. Her heart was in her throat, cutting off her voice. Her breasts tightened and her cheeks were on fire.

The memory of Paris was detonating in her mind, but so was Micah's insistence afterward that she should *forget it happened*.

Also, Hunter hated scenes. His stepmother was notorious for them. He would dump her if he knew what a drama had unfolded back then. Eden would be back to square one, looking for a husband who possessed enough scratch—and enough courage—to save her company.

Her stomach knotted in anticipation of Remy saying something, but he kept his expression neutral and polite.

"Congratulations on the win," he said to Hunter, exchanging a more heartfelt handshake and shoulder squeeze with him. "You deserve it."

"Thanks. How's your family? Is Yasmine still in New York?"

Eden stood there in a fog, waiting for Remy to look her in the eye again while he and Hunter briefly caught up. Remy turned his head her way a couple of times, appearing to include her in the conversation, but he looked through her every time.

He was really pretending they were strangers! Even though his lips had been on hers. His hands had fondled her backside. She had felt his erection against her stomach.

The backs of her eyes stung and her heart pounded so hard she nearly swayed under the impact. It was Hunter's night, though. This wasn't the time or place to confront Remy about old wounds.

Why did those wounds feel so *fresh*?

"I hate to be the guy who fails to stick around for the toasts, but I have commitments elsewhere. I'll say hello to Vienna before I go, though." Remy scanned the room. "I'm happy you're finally able to put this behind you."

"Thank you. Us, too. Let's get a beer soon. I'll put Vienna on the hunt. We can double-date." It was pure facetiousness on Hunter's part and spoke to how close the men were that he would make a joke like that.

"Sure." Remy made a tight noise that held no actual humor.

Was she the only one who'd noticed? That cynical scrape of sound made her heart shrink in her chest.

"I'll text you," Remy said to Hunter, sending another streak of apprehension through Eden. He added an absent nod in Eden's direction before he slipped through the crowd to the other side of the room.

They were quickly approached by someone else, but

Eden was distracted. She couldn't imagine a more hurtful way for Remy to behave toward her. At least if he'd been angry or hurled accusations, she would have known he felt something toward her, even if it was hatred. His cool disinterest only confirmed what Micah had told her—that Remy had been using her as a tool of spite.

"Okay?" Hunter asked, perhaps noticing her silence.

"Tiny headache. I'll be fine," she assured him with a wan smile.

She felt sick, though. Her inner radar tracked Remy for the next half hour before he waved at Hunter on his way to the exit.

Hunter nodded and Remy melted away.

As much as his presence here had turned this party into a pressure cooker of anticipating disaster, now she felt bereft. Why? Why did she have to feel this way about someone she had only met three times? Someone who had cared absolutely nothing about her?

She lurched her way through the rest of the evening, mind churning with trying to work out whether she should tell Hunter that she had once kissed Remy in Paris.

At face value, it sounded laughably innocent. A kiss stopped by a protective older brother. The night had been more embarrassing than anything. It wasn't as if she'd given him her virginity or shared her deepest held secrets.

Micah had acted as though Remy had attacked her, though. He had shoved him and Remy had shoved back. Micah had made threats. Not the kind that communicated, "Ha-ha, I'll kill you if you touch my sister." No. Micah had been dead serious and things might have become truly violent if Eden hadn't thrown herself between them. Quinn had rushed up to grab Micah's arm. It had been *awful*.

Micah had never fully explained what had happened, only insisting that Remy had targeted her to strike at him.

We have history. It's not your fault. Forget this ever happened. When Eden got home to Toronto and brought it up with her mother, Lucille had been distraught, but also very cryptic. *Just leave it, pet.*

Eden had spent years trying to forget. She had concentrated on finishing school, worked alongside her father, cared for him and buried him, taking over at Bellamy Home and Garden after he was gone.

Now BH&G was hanging by a thread. As Hunter drove her home after the party, she tentatively asked, "How do you know Remy?"

"University. We shared some classes and a similar life experience, I guess. We were both taking over our respective empires. We don't have time to see much of each other these days, but it's one of those friendships where we pick up where we left off. I expect he'll be the best man at our wedding."

Her stomach tensed as if receiving a blow. His words sent her mind tilting off-kilter while the streetlamps flickered in her eyes.

Say something, she urged herself. *Say something now.* But she didn't want to malign his best friend. Was that why Remy had pretended he didn't know her? To protect Hunter finding out how low he could sink?

What if Remy turned it around and made it about her and Micah? Would he see this relationship as another chance to take a swipe at her brother?

"Am I rushing you?" Hunter asked with quiet caution. "I thought that's what we meant when we said we were serious."

"No. Um, I mean, a little. You caught me by surprise." She tried to brush away her misgivings and not ruin the opportunity before her. With a tremulous smile that was equal parts hope and trepidation, she said, "I would love to hear what you're proposing."

His mouth quirked at her pun. A few days later, he presented a detailed business proposal that included a prenuptial agreement.

That brought Micah flying into town, which worked for Eden. She cornered him before they left to meet Hunter for dinner.

"I should tell you something before we go. Hunter knows Remy Sylvain."

"I know." Micah slipped his phone into his pocket, giving her his full attention. His expression had hardened to granite.

"Did you have Hunter investigated?" she hissed with outrage.

"The Waverlys have skeletons falling out of every second closet. Of course, I peeked in the open ones." He shrugged, not the least bit remorseful. "Waverly and Sylvain are school friends. Aside from a weekend golfing last summer, they rarely see one another. They don't have financial ties. I don't think Sylvain is conspiring with Waverly to use you to get at me, if that's what you're worried about."

It had crossed her mind and she hated that she had become so mistrustful.

"There's nothing for Waverly to gain by that," Micah continued in his detached tone. "He needs the appearance of stability and wholesomeness that you bring to this union as much as you need his cash. A fresh scandal is the very last thing he wants. I'm confident he's acting in good faith, but I'll say again, you don't *have* to marry him."

She held up her hand, forestalling that heavily belabored argument.

"Just tell me one thing. Does Mama's refusal to let me

accept *your* money have anything to do with the feud between you and Remy?"

"Not really."

"A little?"

"Look." His eyebrows settled into a line of frustrated concern. "I knew your father was having money troubles a few years ago. I offered to help. Mama asked me to stay out of it. I understand her aversion to taking my father's money. His parents always believed she got pregnant on purpose and married him for his wealth. She refuses to fuel that misconception. I respect that, but you're in charge of BH and G now. You can make a different decision."

She sighed, wishing she could, but their mother had already told her she would rather lose the company than save it with Micah's father's money. Eden thought Lucille was taking pride a little too far, but she also wanted to respect their mother's wishes.

"And Remy? Why does he hate you?"

Micah hissed out a sigh. "Remy's father worked for mine. He stole proprietary information for our competitor."

"Industrial espionage?" Eden thought that was something that only happened in films.

"There was gossip that he was retaliating for an affair between my father and Remy's mother. All sides denied that and Remy's father has always claimed he was robbed. My father was never able to prove that he was paid to steal the schematics, but he moved his family to Canada and started an airline. You do the math."

"Okay." She took in that information and saw the bad blood it would create. "But that's history between your father and his. Why do *you* hate *him*?"

"He went after *you*."

Her heart lurched in remembered anguish.

"Don't you think…?" She felt self-conscious even saying it. "Isn't it possible we met by accident and he actually liked me?"

"No, Eden, I don't." Micah's voice was gentle, but heavy with reluctant truth, which made it all the more awful to hear. With another sigh, he hung his hands on his hips. "You remember when I was supposed to come live here? I started school and all the rest?"

"Yes."

"There was an incident with Remy back then. I don't want to get into it. It was kid stuff, but my father overreacted. As he was wont to do." His expression darkened. "The bottom line is, I knew it was between the two of them and let it go. Remy hasn't. Years have gone by and we have both taken over our respective companies, but do you think his will entertain a bid from us for any of their projects? Never." He sliced his hand through the air. "And that's fine. I don't care if he wants to be petty. I don't need work that badly, but a few weeks before that night in Paris, I bought a vineyard his family had been trying to purchase. I didn't know that. I was in the right place at the right time with the right price. He was obviously annoyed and *that's* why he went after you."

She hugged herself, stung afresh by the thought of being used.

"Should I tell Hunter all of that?"

"*I'll* tell him what he needs to know, which is that if he wants to marry you, he needs to find a different best man."

"Oh, *don't*." Panic stung her veins. She wasn't sure why. She told herself it was anxiety that the feud would only escalate, but it was more insidious than that. She didn't want to push Remy away. Deep down where she barely wanted to acknowledge her desires, she wanted to see him again.

"Let's be adults," she urged. "If Remy is prepared to act as if he doesn't know me—"

"You've seen him?"

"Briefly. And I don't want to sabotage what I have with Hunter by making him choose between me and his friend."

"You're determined to marry him, then?"

"Hunter?" *Of course, Hunter.* "Yes." She lifted her chin, trying to sound confident when she was still a scattered mess. "If he'll have me."

"Do you love him?"

"Not yet." She bit her lip. "Do you think that's bad?"

Micah snorted. "Romantic love is a pretty bow people put on things like desire for sex and fear of death. This kind of caring is what matters." He pointed between them and tucked his chin to send her a look of exasperated affection. "I will always look out for your best interests. I want you to be comfortable and content. I believe this marriage—not Hunter, per se, but the marriage he's proposing—will meet your needs. I'm glad you're going into it with a practical mindset rather than telling me you can't live without him. In that respect, it's good that you're not in love with him."

"Thanks, I guess," she said dryly.

"His poor taste in friends concerns me, though. I'll keep a close eye on Sylvain. If he steps one millimeter out of line…" He left the threat hanging.

In the end, she told Hunter a pale version of the truth.

"I met Remy years ago at a nightclub. It was one dance so I'm not surprised he didn't recognize me. He and Micah aren't on the friendliest of terms, though. I didn't want to make anything of it, especially at your party."

"I appreciate that," Hunter said solemnly. "I've had enough scenes in my life."

He seemed to let it go, but a few days later, Hunter said, "I spoke with Remy. He said his beef with Micah is firmly in the past. He doesn't want to revisit it, which is why he acted as though he didn't know you. He offered to drop out of the wedding if there's a conflict."

"Don't be silly. It's your wedding, too! You should have the best man you want." What was *wrong* with her? She didn't want to see Remy again. Did she?

If that was her motive, she was disappointed. He only appeared once before the wedding, at the engagement party.

Eden thought she had adequately braced herself to see him again, but the second he came into the room—before she even saw him with her eyes—a tingling sensation prickled across her skin.

She looked up and he was looking right at her.

The ground fell away. She was both soaring and plummeting, hot and cold, happy and aching with loss.

Once again, he was devilishly handsome and painfully indifferent. Once again, he made his excuses as he arrived.

"I'm flying to Martinique tonight, but I wanted to extend my well-wishes." He didn't kiss her cheek the way everyone else had, only shook her hand very briefly.

She closed her fist around the sensation to keep it lingering on her palm.

"We should honeymoon in Martinique," Hunter said, glancing at her.

Did Remy flinch? "Rainy season starts in June."

"Right. Forgot about that. Niagara Falls, then, since we'll be in the neighborhood." Hunter winked. It was a joke. Micah had already offered his island villa in Greece. "We're marrying at Niagara-on-the-Lake," Hunter explained to Remy.

"Oh?" Remy's tone was impossible to decipher, but it was weighted with…something. Remy held Hunter's gaze and Remy's eyes narrowed with— Eden couldn't tell what that was. Significance. A question?

Hunter's face went oddly blank. Something in the exchange made the back of Eden's neck prickle, but Hunter glanced at her.

"It was Eden's decision." Hunter was inviting her to fill in the blanks.

"Oh. Um, my aunt has a vineyard there." Eden's voice was thin and unsteady. Hopefully, the men attributed it to bridal nerves. "Weddings are her specialty." And it was the Bellamy family brand that they support Canadian merchants whenever possible.

"Do you have a lot of family attending?" Remy's hammered-gold irises flashed a spark into her eyes that left them stinging. A hot sensation filled her chest and swam up to her throat, suffocating her words.

"Most of my relations live in the Greater Toronto Area. My brother bases himself in Berlin these days." She fought to steady her tone. "He'll step in as father of the bride."

She waited, ears straining for Remy's reaction.

The silence went on a beat too long.

Hunter must have misread the thinness in her tone. His warm hand squeezed her shoulder. "I'm still kicking myself that I didn't call you right after Vienna suggested setting us up. Maybe I could have met him. Oscar Bellamy sounds like he was a good man."

It was her cue to say her father would have liked him, but she could only manage a weak smile. Her father never would have asked her to marry to save the company. He had fallen for her mother the minute he met her and waited as long as he had to.

"I'm sorry for your loss," Remy said distantly. His gaze flicked to Hunter's hand on her shoulder, then slipped past her. His cheek ticked. "I should say hello to Vienna."

Vienna is married, Eden wanted to scream for no particular reason at all.

"I'm arranging my own bachelor party. My PA is," Hunter said, correcting himself with a wry cant of his head. "Golf in the Okanagan. I'll have her send you the dates."

"Wouldn't miss it," Remy said with a tight smile. One final, flashing glance landed on her before he nodded and walked away.

Her brother had already said he wouldn't be back until the wedding, but Eden could have wept at the strain that continued to hold her taut. This felt like a twisted game of chicken, where Remy was calling her bluff, waiting to see if she would go through with marrying Hunter while she waited to see if he would interfere and disrupt it.

As the weeks toward the wedding counted down, she began to believe that Remy would let the wedding happen. She needed this marriage so she ought to have been relieved. She only grew more anxious.

When Remy missed the wedding rehearsal at the vineyard, the night before the wedding, she asked Hunter with as much levity as she could muster, "Are you sure the rings will arrive on time?"

"I have them. Remy texted. He's running late, but he's on the road. He'll arrive tonight. Everything will go smoothly tomorrow. I promise."

She smiled as if she believed him, but a jagged lump sat in her chest.

The lump stayed there, behind her breastbone, right up until the wedding planner said, "Ready?"

CHAPTER THREE

Present day

"EDEN—" VIENNA CAME into the suite behind her.

Eden whirled on her. "Is it *true*?"

Her voice reverberated through the speakers outside.

Quinn, ever the protective friend and efficient maid of honor, made a cutting gesture across her own throat. She unclipped the microphone the wedding planner had attached to Eden's neckline and turned it off, setting it amid the clutter that had collected on the bar.

"I don't know." Vienna's expression was a study in apology and distress. "I honestly wouldn't be surprised if our stepmother staged this. She's that spiteful."

As Eden's heart took a swoop between anguish and hope, she looked to Quinn. Quinn was as supportive as ever, but even though her expression brimmed with empathy, she shook her head, indicating this development was a death knell as far as she was concerned.

Micah finished shuffling the bridesmaids off the terrace and through the suite, instructing the teenager to deliver the flower girl to her parents before he closed the doors.

He folded his arms and cocked one dark eyebrow in a silent "I can still help you."

Any second, Lucille would burst in to keep Eden from

agreeing to exactly that. If she had allowed Eden to accept Micah's help in the first place, she wouldn't be in this situation!

I need this marriage. It was the mantra Eden had used to muffle all the misgivings she'd had from the time Hunter had proposed to this morning, when she'd struggled to keep her breakfast down.

Why? Evil stepmother notwithstanding, Hunter was perfect. He was even-tempered and smart, wealthy and good-looking. He understood she had responsibilities and aspirations and was ready to support her in achieving them without trying to tell her how to do it. He wanted a family.

She clenched her eyes over a hot sting.

Judging by five seconds ago, he *had* a family. A baby he had abandoned, if the accusations by the baby's grandfather were to be believed.

The young mother had said something about not telling him. Hunter wasn't one to wear his emotions on his sleeve, but his astonishment had been apparent, as had the fact he recognized the woman.

Has he been having an affair all this time? Am I still that blind and stupid?

Eden started to rub her eye before she remembered the makeup that had taken an hour for a professional artist to apply.

Was this even happening? Or was she in one of those too-real dreams brought on by anticipation of a big day? No matter where she was traveling, she always had a missed-my-flight nightmare right before her alarm went off. Maybe that's all this was.

She pinched her arm with her manicured nails, trying to awaken. Trying to convince herself she was sleeping late because she had tossed and turned past midnight, consumed with thoughts of *him*.

Curse Remy Sylvain! He hadn't been surprised by any of this. As she'd stood out there, aghast at the scene unfolding below her, the groom's *best man* had only lifted an inscrutable look to *her*.

"Let me help you out of this," Quinn said gently as she brushed aside the train on the layers of satin and tulle skirts that Eden wore.

Eden stiffened. "I can't change until I know whether it's true."

"You still want to marry him?" Micah's voice thundered with astonishment. *"Let me help you."*

"No." Eden thrust out her palm in a halt against the suggestion. "If you want to argue about that, go do it with Mama. In fact, go head her off. I don't want her in here." Was she blaming Lucille for this fiasco? Perhaps a little. She would also start to cry if her mother came in and wrapped her arms around her. She would ruin makeup, dress and day all in one go. "Tell everyone to stay calm. This is just a delay." *Please, God.*

Micah's eyebrows went up. He was not used to being ordered around, but Eden would play the bridezilla card as long as she could cling to it.

I need this marriage.

As the door closed behind him, Eden looked to Vienna. "Has he been seeing her all this time?"

Vienna's head went back with indignation on her brother's behalf.

"If he has, it's news to me. *When?* He was wrapped up in the court case, then you two started dating…" Vienna's defensiveness trailed off as she squinted into the middle distance. "He was here with Remy last summer, though, for a weekend of golf. That was before I introduced you two. Maybe he met her then?"

To Eden's eternal damnation, the lurch in her stomach

had nothing to do with her groom picking up women on a bro weekend. It twisted and shrank because Remy probably had as well.

Why? She was nearly twenty-five, but she was more obsessed with that vexing man than a preteen with a celebrity crush.

"The baby looked pretty young," Vienna said hesitantly. "Maybe six or eight weeks?"

"That math checks out," Quinn said with a pained nod, equally reluctant to crush Eden's hopes and dreams.

"I'll find out what I can. You can't stand here wondering." Vienna slipped away.

"And then there were two," Quinn murmured as she brought across one of the mimosas that had been delivered a few hours ago. "I'm sorry this is happening, Eden. Really sorry. But you wouldn't marry him if he has a baby with someone else, would you?"

"Maybe?" Eden sipped. The tepid liquid dripped like battery acid down the back of her throat. "Not if he's been with her all this time, but he looked pretty shocked. If it was just a—a fling and he only found out today…" She could hear herself reaching for justifications that would allow her to forgive him.

I need this marriage.

"It's not the way I planned to start our family, but we both want one." Her voice was strained by the growing tightness in her throat.

Had they wanted a family with each other, though? It struck her that Hunter had been as content as she was to put off sex, despite the ten months that had passed while they dated and became engaged. They had shared a few long kisses, which had been pleasant enough. Not earth-shattering, but warm enough she had thought sleeping with him wouldn't be a chore.

She hadn't really *wanted* to sleep with him, though. Not the way she *really* wanted—

"That's bargaining," Quinn noted quietly.

"Pardon?"

"The stages of grief aren't just for grief. A stalled car can trigger them and you're going through them now. You don't want to believe the baby is his because that means the wedding has to be called off. That's disbelief and denial. Now you're trying to tell yourself there's a way to make his baby fit into your life so the marriage can go ahead. It can't, Eden. I'm sorry, but it can't."

Eden clenched her eyes shut against her friend's kind but firm truth-telling.

"It's not like he's had a baby all along and you knew what you were getting," Quinn continued, saying what Eden knew, but didn't really want to hear. "The conditions have changed. At the very least, you need time to revisit the terms of your marriage before you go ahead with it. This wedding can't happen today."

"I don't *have* time," Eden cried.

"I know," Quinn noted with a frustrating level of patience and understanding.

"You have never supported this marriage," she accused Quinn, hearing herself resorting to anger, but Quinn didn't take it personally and maintained her calm tone.

"I don't support marriage as a concept. It's not personal to you and Hunter. I want you to have what you want, Eden—I do. But this isn't it. Not anymore."

"I need this marriage," Eden sobbed and swirled away in a rustle of tulle. The first few times she had picked up all these skirts, it had been like gathering clouds and dreams. Now they felt like heavy armloads of soiled laundry.

"Would your mother support you going to these lengths?" Quinn prodded gently. "Now? After this?"

"Go ask her!" Eden waved her hand in vexation. "I think there's more to her stubbornness than pride, but the fact she won't talk about Micah's father tells me more than if she did."

"What do you mean?" Quinn frowned.

"I've always suspected…" Eden hesitated to voice her ugly suspicion, hating to think of it. "I think Micah's father was abusive, but I can't ask her that. I can't ask Micah."

Quinn recoiled slightly and hugged herself, mouth somber and gaze dropping to the floor. "No," she replied. "I can see why you don't want to push her to speak about that."

Maybe her reasoning was more emotionally driven than logical, but Eden was grateful Quinn understood and supported her refusal to press her mother to talk of something so potentially painful.

There was a knock on the door that turned both of their heads.

"Eden, it's me," Hunter said.

Quinn's cheeks went hollow. She moved to let him in, stepping out to give them privacy.

"It's bad luck to see the bride before the wedding," Eden said, hearing the hysteria creeping into her tone. It was moving like poison through her arteries and nerve branches and lung tissue because one look at his grim expression and she knew. She knew it was true. She knew she wasn't getting married today.

In reaction, promises and assurances and angry retaliations burbled out of her. Very little of what she said was the result of having a spurned heart. She was humiliated, yes, but the acrid taste in her mouth was failure. She was not going to save her father's company today.

The iconic chain that her great-grandfather had started as a mail-order catalog of bulbs and seeds, the one that supplied middle-class families across the country with their home-and-garden needs, would gasp its last breath on her watch.

That was more shame than she was prepared to accept.

Hunter didn't stand there and let her berate him. He cut into her litany with a firm "I'm sorry," and walked out.

Quinn came back in as Eden was still swaying in shock, too devastated to even cry.

"Let me help you—" Quinn began.

"Go tell Micah to send everyone home. Or— They should eat the food, right?" She was now in the stage of trying to keep everything normal despite the fact a nuclear-size catastrophe had landed in her lap. "They've come all this way."

"I'm sure the wedding planner has dealt with things like this before," Quinn said soothingly. "I'll have an announcement made, then I'll come back to help you change."

Eden nodded and knocked back the last of her mimosa, brain firing with fight-or-flight chemicals. Mostly flight. She hated herself so much in this moment, she wanted to crawl out of her own skin. There was no way she could face all those guests, who would cast pitying looks at her.

She set down the champagne glass and reached for another, but noticed the fob on the bar with its I-heart-PEI key chain.

She didn't overthink it. Her purse was right there, her phone on the charger beside it. She scrambled everything into her bag and opened the door to the hall.

"Eden," her mother called. Lucille was coming into the suite from the terrace.

Eden ignored her and rushed out, sweeping down the inside stairs.

The voices in the breakfast room silenced as she appeared, but she didn't so much as glance to see who was gathered there. She shot out the main doors to the path lined with tall hedges that led to the guesthouse parking lot.

It was a dirty trick to steal her friend's car and not even wait for Quinn to catch up and come with her, but her friend would understand.

Eden burst from the path, already scanning for Quinn's blue hatchback—

Tires screeched and the nose of a black sports car huffed a breath against her voluminous skirts. The engine growled dangerously.

Eden hadn't even looked for cars before running straight out in front of this one. She was the proverbial deer in the headlights—paralyzed, unable to make sense of her own distorted reflection in the windshield.

The tinted window lowered on the driver's side. Remy's carved mahogany expression glared at her. Her heart was pounding so loudly, she barely heard his growled command.

"Get in."

CHAPTER FOUR

THROUGH THE OPEN window of his car, Remy heard voices in the distance, near the entrance to the tasting room. They grew more animated the longer Eden stood before him.

Eden glanced in that direction and horror solidified on her expression as she realized she was about to be spotted and photographed. She scrambled to open his passenger door and dropped into the low seat with an "Oof."

Then she gathered—and gathered—her billowing skirts into her lap, like piling snow for a snow fort.

"Is that it?" he asked testily when she finally dragged the door shut. His veins were still on fire at nearly striking her with his car.

"Would you get me out of here?" She reached for her seat belt.

No. That's what he ought to be saying. How the words *get in* had passed his lips was a mystery he wasn't ready to unravel. Fate and karma were not concepts he subscribed to, but his mother had always been very philosophical about life unfolding the way it was meant to. Given the way Eden kept landing in front of him, he was beginning to understand his own helplessness against such greater forces.

He finished making his way out of the smaller parking lot to the main one, crawling now instead of lighting up his tires because mad women were darting out of hedges.

At the exit to the main road, a Mercedes-Benz SUV turned out ahead of a handful of midsize vehicles. Remy assumed that was Hunter, leaving with Amelia, chased by paparazzi.

Remy had made a handful of executive decisions in the moments following Amelia's appearance. While the guests had been gasping at the accusations leveled by Amelia's father, Remy had been calculating the age of the infant she held. Hunter didn't kiss and tell—or make a habit of one-night stands—but Remy distinctly remembered the smoldering heat coming off the pair as he and Hunter had shared drinks with Amelia and her friend last summer. Remy had taken Amelia's friend home, allowing nature to take its course between the other two.

Apparently, nature had gone all the way. Amelia's baby was almost certainly Hunter's.

And, because Remy knew Hunter would never abandon his child, Remy had instantly known the wedding was off.

Firmly ignoring any personal feelings on the matter, Remy had done his duty as Hunter's best man. He had instructed the wedding planner to open the bar while they waited for the official announcement. He had ensured that the food would be served on time and the band would play their sets as scheduled. He quietly suggested to Hunter's grandfather that he take Amelia's father for a drink, since they were likely to be in-laws very soon.

Then, when he glimpsed Hunter wearing a grim expression as he headed purposefully toward the guesthouse, Remy had searched out Vienna, who gave him a grave little nod of confirmation. *She looks just like him.*

Remy informed Vi that everything was under control and urged her to call him if he could help in any way, but explained he had commitments elsewhere.

He didn't. Only the ones he had fabricated so he could

leave the wedding as soon as politely possible, but he sensed Micah Gould wanted to pin blame for today's farce on him.

Remy had some hard truths he would love to hurl at Micah, but Remy had promised his father he would keep his lips sealed on all of it. He decided to get the hell out of Dodge before he had a run-in with Micah, or did something equally stupid and spoke to Eden.

Even though he had a thousand questions for her. He had bones to pick, and accusations and defensive explanations he shouldn't feel an urge to make because his family was the one that had been wronged.

Or so he had told himself many times, especially in the last few months.

He turned in the opposite direction from the SUV and glanced at her, biting back a compulsion to ask if she was okay. She absolutely was not. She was pallid beneath her golden-brown complexion, eyes wide with shock.

But she was still so beautiful, she punched the breath out of him.

Eden Bellamy had entranced him from the first time he'd glimpsed her, flashing a dimple as she made a cheeky remark to her friend.

Remy had been killing a few minutes until meeting his cousin, who worked in one of the other departments of the Louvre. It had always been his game with himself to see how close he could get to the *Mona Lisa* without having to jostle through the crowd. He had never once arrived at the rope, but on that day, five years ago, he hadn't even glanced toward the painting. He'd been too enamored with the mysterious smile on the face that turned to regard him.

Eden was classically beautiful—he couldn't overlook that—but a gentle warmth radiated from her that he found even more compelling. On that day, she had worn a filmy summer dress that gave her figure the grace of a goddess in a glen.

Two nights later, she had delivered a heart punch when she turned up at a nightclub in a sparkling silver dress. Her hair had been a wild mass of glossy black ringlets falling around her elegant cheekbones. She'd been all legs and sensuous movements, eyes smoky and her entire being held together with an air of self-possession.

As fantasy-provoking as she'd been, Remy was very careful in how he treated women. They were not objects. He didn't make assumptions about their interest beyond a dance and a laugh. When she had leaned into him in a shadowed corner, however, and offered her mouth, he had greedily devoured her lips.

He'd been lost in a way he had never experienced, not before or since. He still avoided reliving that memory, however. It was too raw, switching so abruptly from all-encompassing passion to near violence. From acute pleasure to toxic aggression.

Things had come so close to violence, the music had been stopped. Bouncers had immobilized him and Micah. The fact that Remy's friend owned the nightclub was the only reason the police hadn't been called. They had both been asked to leave.

Remy was still stinging with affront and injustice at the way Micah's lip had curled in derision as he'd told Eden, "He's using you to get at me."

"How?" The accusation hadn't made sense. "Are you *with* him?" Remy was immediately appalled that they had locked lips. In those confused seconds, he felt he'd been set up and betrayed. Self-loathing had had him spitting out the taste of her lingering on his tongue.

"He's my *brother*." Eden recoiled from the suggestion that she and Micah were romantically involved.

Micah's sister? Even worse. Remy's heart lurched with agonized disappointment, a reaction that made even less sense. He searched Eden's features, not seeing much resemblance. Micah was distinctly white European, while Eden looked mixed-race.

In looking for the resemblance between them, Remy had become morbidly fascinated by the shape of Micah's nose and mouth and jawline. It churned up a different recognition, one that was knotted up with helpless anger and defensiveness. Apprehension that the secret he kept so diligently could be discovered if he spent any time with them.

"Don't pretend you didn't know she's my sister," Micah accused contemptuously.

Culpability at what he *did* know must have flashed onto Remy's face.

Micah misinterpreted it, and warned viciously, "Stay away from her."

He collected Eden and her wide-eyed friend. They disappeared from the club and his life.

Remy had breathed a sigh of relief on one score, but he had never fully shaken his memory of Eden. His desire for her. He'd been compelled to look her up and learned that she was a Bellamy, only related to Micah because her mother had briefly been married to Micah's father, Kelvin Gould. Lucille had remarried when she moved back to Canada.

If Remy had known Eden was associated with the Gould family, he never would have spoken to her. He had sworn to himself he never would again.

At least, that's what he'd told himself. Yet here he was, inviting her into his car today.

A muted buzzing sounded within the folds of her skirt. She fished through yards of netting and silk to reveal her purse, and opened it. As she glanced at the screen on her phone, she made a helpless noise then swiped to accept a video call.

"Where *are* you?" It sounded like her friend Quinn. Her voice was high and anxious.

"I had to get out of there. Tell everyone I'm okay—" She shot Remy a look as though it had just occurred to her that she might not be able to trust him.

As if *his* family was the dangerous one.

"Whose car is that?" Quinn asked with surprise.

"Um." Eden swallowed, then asked tentatively, "Is anyone else there with you?"

"Do not tell me she's with him." Micah's outrage was tangible enough to reach through the phone and ignite Remy's temper.

Quinn's exasperated "Micah!" sounded beneath his reply: "Tell him to bring you back."

"I'm not going to sit in that room taking visitors like I'm hosting a wake." Eden's voice was as vehement as it was fractured.

"What kind of car is it? Which direction are you headed?" Micah demanded.

"I'm not kidnapping her," Remy boomed. "If she wants me to leave her by the side of the road, I will, but she got into this car all by herself."

"Remy can drop me at a hotel. I have my wallet. I'm an adult. Don't worry about me," Eden insisted.

"Which hotel?" Quinn asked. "I'll meet you with your things."

"Thank y— Oh." Eden released a small curse as she delved into her purse. "I have your keys." She held them up. "I was going to take your car."

"You pack her bag. I'll meet her," Micah commanded.

"I really think this is a job for a maid of honor," Quinn argued.

"You two work it out. I'll text when I know where I'm staying," Eden muttered and ended the call. She dropped her phone into her purse and set it on the floor, where the incoming calls and texts were muffled by the weight of her skirt. "I swear those two need to have sex and get it over with."

"Is that what you'd like? For me to leave you at a hotel? Because my helicopter is waiting at the heliport near the falls."

"Oh." She frowned with confusion. "Isn't this your car? I thought Hunter said last night that you were driving in from Toronto."

"It is." It was a long story about wanting to get to the wedding as slowly as possible and away from it as quickly as possible. That's why his pilot had brought his two-rotor Sikorsky, capable of speeds near three hundred miles an hour.

Perhaps it wasn't that long a story. Perhaps it was perfectly obvious what his motives had been.

"I have commitments at home."

"In Martinique?"

"Montreal." Such was the perk of owning homes in many places. He could prevaricate with something close to the truth.

"I need to go home, too," she murmured, sounding as though she was speaking to herself. She turned her face to the window. There was a pang in her voice as she said, "I need to know, though. Was it part of your feud with Micah to set me up for this? To ruin my wedding *and* my company?"

"Wow." Remy tightened his hands on the wheel, reluctant to excavate his thoughts and feelings on the wedding and its train wreck of an outcome, but he damn well wouldn't be accused of sabotaging Bellamy Home and

Garden. "Much as I'd like to claim that much superpower, no. I was as shocked as everyone else."

"That's not true." Her head snapped around. "You recognized her."

A hard pulse shot through him. Not guilt. Not quite. But she was right.

"We had drinks with Amelia and her friend last summer. I didn't know it went beyond that between Hunter and her."

"You must have presumed, though. You brought him here to pick up women, didn't you? That's what Vienna implied."

"Is that what Vienna implied? That I arrange hookups for other men? There's a name for that and I'm shocked Vienna used it to describe me. I've always considered us friends."

Eden *tsked* and looked away. "I'm just saying you're the one who brought him here."

"And what's the minimum sentence for that, Your Honor? You and Hunter hadn't been introduced yet. What he and I did last summer had nothing to do with you." Hunter had mentioned Vienna was trying to set him up and Remy had commiserated because his own sister was forever matchmaking, but that was all they'd said on the subject. "You know what Hunter's legal troubles were. I brought him here to golf and drink craft beer. To decompress."

"Is that what the kids call it these days," Eden said with a sniff of disdain.

"Hey, if you want to blame me for your wedding being called off, go ahead. My conscience is clear."

"Is it? You're confident you didn't plant a baby of your own that will pop out of the woodwork any second?"

"That's not where babies come from."

She rolled her eyes and turned her face back to the window.

"And, yes. I'm sure." Remy loved sex and women had been throwing themselves at him from the time he topped five feet. He was now six-two, healthy, rich and rubbed elbows with celebrities. He also knew when a server was flirting because she'd seen his name on his Centurion credit card and was vying for a free trip to the Caribbean. Sex was never a currency for him. He had seen Amelia's friend home, thanked her for a nice evening and hadn't thought about her since.

"Why would you care if I did?" he asked, zeroing in on the most salient point.

"I don't," she assured him, stubbornly keeping her face turned away.

He heard her swallow, though. He smiled with grim satisfaction without letting himself wonder why.

They wound along the Niagara River in silence, rows of grapes flickering on the hillsides above her.

"You never told him," he noted.

"Who? Oh. I told him you and I had met. Once." She began to fiddle with the veil attached to her hair.

"But not about what happened at the club."

"It wasn't relevant."

"You don't think it would be relevant to your fiancé that you nearly got his best friend arrested?"

"You and Micah nearly got yourselves arrested. And Micah has told me repeatedly that your interest in me was *not* personal or sincere, so *my* conscience is clear."

Her veil came free and she pushed it into the back seat, shaking it off her fingers as though it was as sticky as spider silk. She began removing the fernlike pearl-and-sequin doodad from above her ear.

"You really didn't know who I was when you came on to me in Paris?" he asked with skepticism.

"You think *I* came on to *you*?" Her voice rose with outrage. "You were using me to get to Micah!"

"I want less than zero contact with anyone in your family," Remy said, because it was supposed to be true. It had to be.

He geared down with enough aggression to make the Audi's engine growl.

"Then why are you helping me?" she asked with a crack of wildness in her voice.

Why, indeed.

"Because Hunter is my friend," he said with a casual shrug. "He would have quietly called things off if he had known he had a child. A baby is more vulnerable than you are, so his priority shifted to where it needed to go. I'm confident he feels like a sack of dirt, jilting you so publicly. He would want me to help you if I could. He would do the same for me."

"Said another way, your loyalty toward Hunter outweighs your hatred of me and Micah?"

Did he hate her? Remy veered from prodding at that exposed nerve. "Hunter saved my life once. I owe him a favor, no matter how unsavory."

She made a noise that was halfway between being insulted and astonished. "How? Did he suck snake venom from your ankle? Catch a bullet with his teeth?"

"He kept me from freezing to death, if you must know." He rarely mentioned it, still feeling like a callow idiot.

"Really? Where? How?" Her tone had shifted to concerned curiosity.

"U of T. I skipped a year in elementary school so I was younger than the other freshmen. That didn't stop me from trying to keep up at the frat parties." He had lost his parents the year before and his grandfather's health had already been failing. "Hunter found me passed out in the snow. He got me back to my room and stayed while I lost my guts. Then he shared his notes for the two days of classes that I missed."

"But *you* didn't feel a need to tell him you had met *me*," she pointed out. "You waited until he brought it up."

He felt her gaze on the side of his face like a bonfire throwing heat and light.

"I thought about it." His shock on seeing her again, and his libido's quick surge of hunger that had only grown more insatiable in the intervening years, had prompted him to throw up a defensive wall. He had acted as if there had never been anything between them because there never could be. "Hunter hates drama. I didn't want to ruin his court win by publicly dragging his new girlfriend."

"You had other opportunities. The engagement party. The bachelor party. You could have dropped him a text anytime in the last eight months."

"Did you *want* me to tell him?"

"No. I don't know," she muttered, exhaling with frustration.

He waited, but she didn't add anything.

"In my perfect world, I would never cross paths with your brother again," Remy said. "But that wasn't reason enough to get in the way of Hunter's life plan. Whatever this feud is that Micah thinks we're engaged in, he's the only one playing."

"Really. Because that's what he said about you." Her tone was pithy. Her big brown eyes were swallowing her face, swimming in confusion.

"Damn." He almost missed his turn. "Do you want to come with me? I can drop you in Toronto." He pointed at the sign that warned of low-flying helicopter traffic.

"Oh. Yes. Thank you. I would really appreciate that."

He snorted. They were enemies, he reminded himself, and he only wished he felt it more deeply.

Remy drew to a stop outside a heliport where colorful flags hung motionless in the afternoon sun. A family picnicked on a table nearby and a woman pointed at Eden as she emerged from the car.

"Look! They're getting married in a helicopter!"

Not. But Eden didn't want to curdle everyone's ice cream with a glower so she picked up her skirts and followed Remy into the building.

"You're early, sir." A young man straightened from chatting up the pretty young woman behind the heliport's check-in counter. "I had a bird strike on my way in. One of the rotors is damaged..." His voice trailed off with confusion as he noticed Eden behind him.

"It's being repaired?" Remy asked.

"Not yet." The young man dragged his distracted attention back to Remy. "They didn't have a spare here. The replacement is on its way. Their mechanic can install it when it arrives, but I expected you to be three or four hours at least."

"I'll charter one of yours," Remy said to the young woman who had a name tag that read Andrea.

"All of our machines are in the air," Andrea said with an apologetic look. "We're fully booked for tours." She gestured at the family in the waiting area.

A boy was guiding his toy helicopter on a path around the coffee table. His adolescent brother studied Eden with puzzled curiosity. Their mother met Eden's eyes with a stare that both dared and pleaded with her not to disappoint her young family.

It had probably taken her all year to save up for this

treat for her boys. Eden was willing to tell her what kind of day she was having, though, to see if they could come to an understanding.

"Let me have a look," Remy said gruffly, shifting his gaze from the family to Eden. He flickered his eyes at the gown that was beginning to weigh on her like a soggy fishing net. "If I can't fix it myself, it's likely to be a few hours. Maybe call your friend to come get you?"

Seriously? He thought she would plant herself in that tiny waiting room eating dry popcorn until Quinn got here?

"Is there somewhere more comfortable where we could wait?" she asked Andrea as Remy walked out to the tarmac.

"We have some partner hotels who are very good to us. Let me make a call."

Eden had meant a private lounge, but Andrea was already dialing and, yes, she would prefer a hotel.

She took a quick peek at her own phone. There were a plethora of texts and voice mails—her mother, Micah, Quinn, Vienna and other guests from the wedding. Oof. Shareholders. BH&G's chief financial officer was also trying to reach her.

This was a seriously terrible, no-good awful day.

"They're trying to get off on their honeymoon, but there's a mechanical issue." Andrea's giggle penetrated Eden's awareness. "No. Not that kind! But they *are* anxious for some alone time." She winked at Eden's stunned expression. "Be a cupid— Oh, wait. Let me ask." She tucked the phone into her neck. "Budget?"

"Money's no object," Eden said flatly. The cost of her wedding was up in flames. What was one more hotel room on top of it?

"The best you have. Perfect," Andrea purred into the

phone. "They'll be there shortly." She hung up and scribbled out an address. "Ask for Jorge. Tell them Andrea sent you." She pronounced it *On-dray-yah*.

Eden accepted the chit of paper and wondered if one really could die from a thousand paper cuts, because she was ready to give it a whirl.

Remy strode in from the tarmac with a scowl of annoyance. "It's not something I want to risk. I'll have to wait for the repair."

"No problem. *On-dray-yah* booked us a room." Eden said it with an admirable lack of sarcasm.

"Great." He took the directions and they went back out to his car.

Eden dropped back into her seat with defeat. Exhaustion was catching up to her. Not only from her poor sleep last night, but also from the marathon that was the organization of a wedding and the fraught emotional journey of taking control of BH&G only to discover it was adrift on stormy seas.

"I kind of want to get drunk off my face," she said as he pulled away from the heliport.

"Fill your boots. I have to fly later so I'll stick to water."

Maybe she should stay the night after all. Quinn would happily get drunk with her.

A few minutes later, Remy pulled into the shaded portico of a ritzy hotel. A man in a hotel uniform hurried out to greet them. His name tag read Jorge.

"You must be Andrea's honeymooners. Let's get you comfortable." He took the duffel from Remy's popped trunk, then looked with puzzlement from Eden to the empty trunk to her parade float of a dress.

"Do you have a boutique in your lobby? Send up a selection," Remy said tersely. "Put everything on my card." He handed it over.

Moments later, they were shown into a top-floor suite.

"It's the only thing that wasn't booked. I hope it suits?" Jorge asked.

It had a full living room with an electric fireplace, a kitchenette, a bedroom with a king-size bed and a Jacuzzi tub with shutters that stood open, allowing the bathers to take in the spectacle of the waterfall beyond the floor-to-ceiling windows.

Eden paused to take in the massive wonder that she had never made the time to see before. It was a stunning sight. Frothy, green-blue water poured over a horseshoe-shaped ridge. Mist billowed off the heavy curtain and floated toward the cloudless sky.

Housekeeping staff were hustling around, setting out a bucket of champagne and gift baskets of fruit and other snacks. One paused to light some candles. Eden shook her head.

"That isn't necessary." Hysteria was threatening to explode out of her. "Can you all please leave?"

"She really is in a hurry," one muttered as they melted away.

The door shut and there was only the faint but distinct rush of water over the falls.

"If you laugh, I will throw myself off that balcony right now," Eden warned Remy.

"I'm not enjoying this, if that's what you're suggesting." He began unbuttoning his morning coat, then halted. His cheek ticked. "Do you need help getting out of that?"

"And wear what?" she cried.

"There must be a robe in the bathroom. Or..." He moved his duffel onto the sofa and dug through it, coming up with a gray T-shirt and maroon shorts with a drawstring.

Dear Lord, those looked so comfortable she could have wept.

"I'm about ready to cut myself free of this," she conceded. It was the foundation layer of shapewear that was killing her. "If you could just open the little catches…" She fiddled at the base of her spine, but the hooks and eyes were hidden behind a fold of satin.

She turned her back and he came up behind her.

"Your skirt is in the way." The satin shifted against her legs as he brushed it aside.

He stepped closer and pressed bunched silk to the backs of her thighs. Her skin tightened. Her scalp tingled with awareness of his looming presence. She thought she felt his breath against the back of her neck, but she was barely breathing herself. Her eyes drifted shut. His light touch grazed where the back dipped to expose the top of her spine.

"They're behind the—"

"Yes, I've worked it out." His voice sounded strange. Deep, but tight. His fingers slid under the edge of the satin, where it hugged the skin of her back. The bodice tightened slightly.

Her nipples stung and a weighted heat rushed into the place between her thighs. A noise like a sob tried to escape her throat.

There was the barest hint of release, then the squeeze again as he drew the gown tight so he could release the next hook.

"It's a pretty gown. It suits you."

"Thanks?" Was he not drowning in sensuality and absurdity, the way she was?

Another constriction, then another release.

"Does that hurt? It left a mark here." His thumb lightly grazed her shoulder blade.

"It's fine." Her voice was pitched three octaves too high.

Slowly, slowly, he freed her. When the front began to slip, she pressed her forearms across it. Her breathing grew more uneven as he worked. Her skin was so sensitive to the brush of his knuckles, she was bereft when the faint contact ceased.

She practically swayed where she stood. This was the part where her groom was supposed to take her to the bed and finish seducing her. *Kiss me. Touch me*, her body cried.

"Thank you," she said, forcing out the words. Her voice was barely a whisper.

She scooped up her purse and started for the bedroom.

"Eden."

Her name in his deep voice halted her.

Her head swam at the conflicting dictates between rational thought and carnal desires. She reeled at his calling her back, unprepared for whatever he was about to ask her.

"Yes?"

"Don't forget these." He offered his shirt and shorts.

She snatched at them. "Thanks."

Mortified, she hurried into the bedroom.

CHAPTER FIVE

REMY WAS SERIOUS about zero alcohol when he had to operate anything larger than a toaster, especially an aircraft, but damn, did he want a drink.

He settled for an icy bottle of spring water and drank it so fast he gave himself a throbbing ache behind his left eye.

Too bad it didn't numb the pulsing heat behind his fly.

Five years ago, the moment he had realized who Eden was, she had become more than off-limits to him. He would call this inconvenient desire *taboo* if it didn't sound so deliberately titillating. The fact that she had just ended her relationship with his best friend made her even more forbidden, but his libido didn't seem to care.

He rubbed his face, trying to erase the jumble of thoughts and emotions flooding into his head. The whole time she'd been involved with Hunter, he'd been trying to use their relationship to fuel some sort of repulsion in himself, but it had never worked. He hated thinking of her in bed with anyone, but in the grander scheme of things, he really didn't care whom she slept with. Everyone had a history, including him.

Nothing seemed to change how he reacted to her. The only thought in his head as he had stood so close to her while unfastening her dress was that she smelled amazing. Any man would be undone by the graceful line of her spine, appearing inch by inch. It had been all he could do not to dip his head and taste her skin where her neck met her shoulder, especially when he had noted her fine trembles. They had matched the unsteadiness in his hand, as though they were vibrating on the same wavelength.

His eyes drifted closed and he once again saw her smooth, narrow back. The gown's satin against the luster of her skin had mesmerized him. The edges had tickled his knuckles, making him want to draw out undressing her until they were both crazed with lust. He imagined the dress falling loose at the front, inviting his touch to slide around and cup her breast. Her flesh would be warm and weighty, filling his palm, firming the way his flesh was firming—

What the hell was this chemistry between them? Why was it so potent? It had poured into him from that first glimpse he'd had of her in the Louvre and had been simmering and sizzling within him ever since. It was maddening. Nearly irresistible.

He moved to the window, barely taking in the view as he considered whether to walk out on her. He could text Vienna to send Quinn or Micah here. There was no reason he had to stay, even though he had offered to take her to Toronto. *Just make the call.*

A knock at the main door broke into his brooding. As he crossed to open it, he braced himself to dodge a thrown fist, half expecting Micah to have found them.

It was Jorge with a rolling rack of clothing, apologizing profusely for interrupting. "I wasn't sure if I should…" He flicked his gaze around, looking for Eden.

"Thanks." Remy slipped him a tip, took back his credit card and closed the door.

If only he was about to have sex with Eden. If only. *Snap out of it.*

He took a cursory look through the options they had delivered, then released a sigh at himself before going to the bedroom door. He knocked and called, "The clothes are here. You don't have to wear mine."

No answer.

Now he was growing aroused thinking of his clothes against her skin.

He would leave, he decided. But he was done with this wedding suit. He peeled off his jacket and tie on his way to where his duffel still sat on the couch. A pair of low-waist trousers in pale green came to hand along with a short-sleeved shirt patterned with asymmetrical shapes in red, yellow, and green on an ocean-blue background.

He was known for his fashion choices, but his flair was by association. His sister had always been enthralled with textures and fabrics. She had begun designing the minute their grandmother had taught her to thread a needle. She worked for a top label in New York and used Remy as a walking mannequin for her creations. He didn't mind. He genuinely liked the colors and cuts she chose for him.

His sister. Thinking of her certainly killed his lingering arousal. She was yet another reason—the core reason—he shouldn't be anywhere near Eden.

He stripped, sighing in relief as the air-conditioned room brought down his temperature.

"Oh! I'm so sorry!" Eden's voice blurted as the door latch clicked open and slammed shut.

Remy swore and snatched up his trousers, keeping his back to the door as he shot his legs into them. As he adjusted himself and zipped, he called, "I'm dressed."

He hurried to thread his arms into the light shirt, hearing the bedroom door slowly reopen behind him.

"I didn't know if you heard me," he said, glancing over his shoulder to see she was wearing a hotel robe.

"I heard the door and honestly thought you left. You don't have to stay. I'm not going to do anything rash." She moved to the rack and began flicking through the sparse selection. She sounded as though she'd been crying.

His heart lurched. He turned to see she was holding a shapeless top in camel-brown against her front. The color leeched any vibrancy from her face. Her makeup was smudged and lines scored both sides of her unhappy mouth.

"You definitely need an intervention if you're considering wearing that," he said as he pulled out a silvery pink skirt and a sleeveless silk turtleneck in buttercup-yellow. "Keep it bright," he suggested as he hooked both across the top of the rack. "Don't let anyone see how much you're hurting."

Her thick black lashes lifted and her dark brown gaze flicked over the loud colors in his own shirt, then rose to meet his eyes. Hers were filled with questions.

"Or so I've been told." He walked away, shoving his hands into his pockets.

"I don't know how to feel," she said heavily. "I'm so angry, I want to punch Hunter in the throat, but the fact that his priorities are in order tells me I wasn't wrong to trust him, just underinformed. I keep telling myself none of this was my fault, but I'm the one who wanted the big wedding. That's why there were so many people there, witness to my disgrace. I'm so nauseous—"

"Are you pregnant?" A thick blade seemed to slice across his chest.

"No." Her eyes went wide with surprise at how intensely he had reacted.

"You're sure?"

"Yes." She shuffled a few more items on the rack, her complexion darkening with a flush.

She paced restlessly away without choosing anything, moving to pull the bottle of sparkling rosé from the bucket. "Maybe tequila would be better." She looked toward the bar and shoved the bottle back into the ice. "I should probably eat something first."

There was a cellophane-wrapped basket on the coffee table. She peered at the butter cookies and mixed nuts on offer, then pressed her hand to her stomach.

"You'd think I'd have an appetite. I've been starving myself for three months. And, yes, I know how unhealthy that is, mentally and physically. Again, I'm the one who wanted this pageant. Hunter told me flat out his preference was something quiet at a courthouse."

"His stepmother." That woman had been making public scenes as long as Remy had known Hunter and Vienna. Well before, from what Hunter had told him.

"He went along with what I wanted and I wanted the fairy tale. As if there is such a thing. I think I was compensating."

"For?"

Eden went back to the pink bubbly. It was from a local winery. She peeled off the foil to reveal a cut-glass stopper. As she struggled to pry it out, Remy started toward her.

She handed him the bottle and walked away.

"I don't really want it. I didn't want any of this. I didn't want to marry him! There. I said it." She dropped onto the sofa and hid her face behind her hands, buckling forward as though in pain. "My life is a disaster and I'm so humiliated I want to die, but I'm relieved."

Remy stared at the bottle in his hand. *Don't do it. You're flying later.*

"You don't love him?" There was a fine rattle in the depths of his chest.

She lifted a culpable face, then said defensively, "He

doesn't love me, either. It was an arrangement that had benefits for both of us."

Remy quickly saw how pairing with a name like Bellamy would have fixed a lot of Hunter's PR problems. He didn't know what she would have gained that couldn't have been achieved through the various business mergers they had already announced, though.

For some reason, learning that it had been a marriage of convenience, not real feelings, made him furious. He had accepted Hunter marrying her because his friend had had some terrible blows in life. Hunter deserved to be happy. At heart, he was a decent man, and Remy had known Hunter would treat Eden with care and respect.

But he hadn't loved her? Not even a little?

Was Hunter even *sorry* that he'd treated her so badly today?

There was a loud pop and the stopper flew across the room, hitting the ceiling before it dropped to the carpet.

Eden instinctively covered her head, watching as Remy swooped for a glass. He caught the foam as it began to overflow and offered the flute to her.

Her throat was an arid wasteland, but she waited for him to pour a glass for himself. He only set the open bottle back in the ice.

"Aren't you having any?" she asked.

"I said I'd fly you to Toronto," he reminded her stiffly.

"Right. So I can get back to work." She let out a long, heavy exhale, thinking of the marriage contract she would review. The agreements she and Hunter had signed were contingent on their marriage being finalized, but surely something could be salvaged.

All her problems were supposed to be solved by now!

This champagne in her hand ought to be a celebratory toast for saving the family legacy. Of winning.

The bubbles stung her nose and the alcohol was sour on her tongue.

"You're going back to work?" Remy had found the stopper and moved to plug the neck of the bottle. "I would have thought you had time booked for a honeymoon. Can't you use it to regroup?"

"That's what I resent the most right now! I'm not getting the honeymoon I was promised." She'd been pushing herself like mad, her vacation time the carrot at the end of the stick. Now she would have to work harder than ever not to lose everything.

Remy had gone very still.

Her words hit her ears.

"I mean swimming and reading." She gulped down another mouthful of cold, sizzling wine. "In Greece. I'm not hitting on you again, if that's what you think. I didn't in the first place. I'm babbling because I'm nervous. Leave if you want to. I'll phone Quinn to come get drunk with me and restart my life in the morning." With a giant hangover, but so what?

He cocked his head. "Why are you nervous?"

Because he put her on her back foot with questions like *Why are you nervous?*

"It's not the most comfortable thing to be trapped with someone who hates me."

"I don't *hate* you." His stoic expression didn't quite disguise the flash of forceful reaction behind it. "That is the issue, Eden. I should hate you. Or at least want nothing to do with you. It's not that easy. It never has been," he muttered and moved to the window, showing her only his rigid back.

She sagged, but not with relief. Not when she was nursing anxiety that this could be some ploy he had decided to enact.

"Can I ask you something? Will you please be honest with me this time?" she asked.

"I didn't know who you were," he said starkly, guessing what she was going to say. "I know why Micah thinks I was trying to use you. Our families have history. I don't want to get into that, but what happened at the nightclub, when we kissed—that was basic, mutual attraction." He turned his head to pin her with the golden spike of his gaze. "It *was* mutual, wasn't it?"

"Yes." She took another sip to dampen her whisper-dry throat.

"But nothing can come of it, Eden. That's why I didn't interfere between you and Hunter. I'll see you home because it's the decent thing to do, but that's all this is."

"Then we'll never see each other again?" She didn't hear the pang in her voice so much as feel it as it felt like a shard of glass lodged in her chest. At least when she was marrying his best friend, she had thought she might run in to Remy now and again. She had known she would hear about him through Hunter and know he was well.

Why did that matter so much to her?

She realized he hadn't answered her. He stood so still, so very still.

Her pulse throbbed unevenly in her throat as she replayed her own words in her head. *We'll never see each other again.* A rushing sound filled her ears.

"Remy?" She could hardly speak. "Am I deluding myself? Is it just me?"

"Eden." Her name was an imprecation. He dug the heels of his hands into his eyes. "Don't do this to me."

"Don't what? Don't tell you how I feel? Don't be *honest*? Why not? What do I have left to lose?"

"You have nothing to *gain*." He swung his head around and his flashing gaze warned her to stay silent.

Even so, the words left her.

"I think about you all the time. I always have." They didn't come out in a burst, but in a soft, faltering trickle. The emotions behind them were a river, though, one that brimmed its banks and flooded the room, soaking everything with her truth. "This is the first time you've properly spoken to me since Paris. If you had said something before today, I wouldn't have let the wedding get this far—"

"Damn it, *stop*. You want honesty?" He rounded on her, but his voice was fatalistic. "I want you, Eden. It sits inside me like a black hole that swallows up everything else. It eats at me so I feel empty all the time. *Hungry*." He set his fist against his diaphragm. "It hurts. I wanted to kill him for marrying you and now I want to kill him for scorning you. *This is hell*."

She covered her mouth, pressed back into the sofa by his vehemence. By his suffering.

"But it can't happen. Accept it. I have."

"It's just us here." The words slipped out of her, impetuous. Desperate.

A distant part of her urged her to show some sense. She knew Micah would never forgive her for so much as getting in Remy's car, but they had had something in Paris. It had been interrupted and the not knowing what could have been had left her with an ache of yearning that had stalled her in some way. If she couldn't have Remy then it didn't matter whom she married. All men were the same because they weren't him.

"No one would know," she added.

"Damn you, Eden!" He walked past her, snatching up his duffel on his way to the door.

"Remy!" She shot to her feet and cried his name exactly as if he was striding off the balcony and into Niagara Falls.

He stopped and stood there for one, two…three beats.

He dropped his bag and his hand shot out to slam the inner latch across the door so it couldn't be opened from the outside. He turned.

"I *don't* pick up women. Some of my relationships have been shorter than others, but I have relationships, Eden. I can't have one with you, though. Do you understand that? This would only be today. An hour. We couldn't tell anyone. Ever. If Hunter found out—"

"If Micah found out," she said with a catch in her voice. "I don't care about any of that. I really don't."

"After this, it goes back to the way it was, like we didn't even know one another. Is that really what you want?" His face twisted with conflict.

"No," she confessed with a chasm opening in her chest. "But I'll take it."

He closed his eyes, swearing as he fell back against the door with a defeated thump.

"Come here, then."

Eden ran across and he stepped forward to catch her. She was off her bare feet, secure in arms she hadn't known long enough to miss, but she had. When his mouth landed on hers, she was *home*.

Bright sunshine filled her, searing away her skin from the inside out so all she felt was him. His mouth drank at hers as though he was parched beyond reason. They were both wild and greedy and *joyous*. It was such a brilliantly perfect kiss, her eyes stung with emotion.

"Tell me you're sure," he said in a gravelly voice.

"I'm sure. Don't stop." She touched his jaw, steering his mouth back to hers.

How could a mouth, a pair of lips, be so firm yet so soft? So demanding, yet so giving? She reveled in the way he kissed her, as though she meant everything to him. This was what she had longed for the most. This feeling like she was *The One*.

In the same way that he was *The One*.

A thumping, terrifying urgency stalked around her as she clung to him, but she ignored it, letting herself sink into this moment. She memorized the feel of his strong shoulders beneath her palms and the soft abrasion of stubble coming in on his chin. His hands slid across her back, petting and massaging and pressing her into him, as though he wanted her impression to remain against his front forever.

She wriggled and stood on her toes, trying to get closer still. Her robe loosened and her thighs felt the rough fabric of his trousers.

He kept saying her name—"Eden, Eden"—as though he couldn't believe she was real. His mouth went down her neck and she flicked her tongue against his earlobe. His breath hissed and she smiled.

Then his hand slid between them and tugged at her belt, pulling it completely free. He drew back and watched her reaction as he let her robe fall open.

She didn't flinch with shyness. She probably should have. She wore only a slash of bronze lace across her hips, no bra, but she had been his all this time, if only he had noticed. If only he had grown solemn and his chest had shaken, while his reverent gaze slid down.

His hand rested on her bare hip while his thumb traced the edge of lace. It was barely a caress, but her stomach sucked in and she grew light-headed. A flicker of satisfaction touched the corner of his mouth.

She brought up her hands to begin releasing the buttons on his shirt, one by one.

He didn't move, letting her do it in her time. He held her gaze and the only sound was their uneven breathing and the muted thunder of the falls outside.

When she spread his shirt and splayed her hands across his firm abs, his breath rattled. He cupped the back of her neck and drew her in for a new kiss, one that was hot and slow and made her toes curl. Her bare breasts met the hot surface of his chest and such a hard jolt of pleasure went through her, she sobbed with delight.

His smile flashed once, then his eyelids grew heavy with need. He kissed her again, deeper, sliding his tongue against her bottom lip and into her mouth. Her knees shook and the rest of her went limp.

She wrapped her arms around his waist, stroking his back and learning the landscape of his spine and shoulder blades and the shape of his backside through his trousers.

It struck her how natural this felt, considering she'd never been this naked with anyone before. She nuzzled her face into the crook of his neck and let her body tell him how much she enjoyed the roaming of his hands beneath the robe, how much she craved more. So much more.

He cradled one of her breasts and slid his lips down the front of one shoulder, halting with his hot breath bathing the swell. He swore softly. "I don't have a condom."

"There's some in the bedroom." Andrea had stoked the impression of newlyweds in a hurry to consummate their nuptials. The hotel had delivered.

Eden stepped back and folded her robe closed, then took his hand, leading him to the basket beside the bed. Erotic ideas had filled her imagination when she had glimpsed the candles, massage oil, ruffle-edged blindfold, lubricant and condoms.

"They're ultrathin," she pointed out, trying to keep a straight face through her bemusement. "And vegan."

"And gluten-free, I hope?" He tilted the basket. "No handcuffs? It's our *honeymoon*."

They both chuckled unevenly. Hers held an edge of helpless, hopeless sadness that this wasn't such a thing at all.

"The energy drinks are," she pointed out. "Gluten-free. Gotta stay hydrated."

She leaned into him. He hugged her, but his expression sobered.

"Don't ask me again if I'm sure," she chided. "I am. Aren't you?"

His next laugh was a rough exhale that held little humor and a lot of frustrated desire. "I want this so much it terrifies me."

She smiled, but it didn't stick. She turned her face into his bare shoulder and kissed the hollow there, then lifted her mouth, yearning for his.

With a groan he dragged her against his front. They sank back into the delicious pool of passion.

Her sense of rightness expanded. It was odd how sure she was, given she didn't know him that well. There was a tiny concern still hovering that he might be using her, but in this moment, she didn't care if he was. He had been haunting her fantasies for years. If circumstances had been different, she had no doubt he would have been her first lover.

If she had had that affair in her history, she might not have felt so boxed in by her impending marriage. At least this way, she rationalized, she would have the memory of the growling sound he made as she slid her hands up his sides and around to his back while she brushed her breasts against his chest.

"Why do you smell so good?" His breath played across

her shoulder before he dipped and stole a hot damp taste of her nipple. "Like cloves and…"

Whatever he said was lost as he enclosed the tip of her breast and a moan of luxury rolled up from deep in her throat. The way he drew on her sent shots of heat fluttering through her belly and pulsing between her legs. She felt drunk on her own sensuality.

She was so hot! She let the robe fall off her shoulders and he made a sound of gratification, straightening to drop his shirt. His eyes were molten gold as he shed his pants. His gaze was so bright, so illuminated by lust, it was hard to hold his stare, but she couldn't look away. The throbbing between her thighs intensified.

"Tell me what you like." His fingertip traced the edge of lace beneath her navel then followed the seam at her hip. Slowly, slowly, he followed her bikini line, filling her sex with a heavy ache and a sensation of empty longing.

He watched his own caress with narrow-eyed intensity, voice deepening to a gruff, animalistic sound. "I want you so satisfied that I ruin you for anyone else."

A catch of helpless laughter left her. He already had.

His mouth twisted with self-deprecation. "I don't know when I became such a Neanderthal. Somewhere between the living room and here."

He was still tickling at her bikini line, but now he brushed a light fingertip across the front of bronze lace, teasing the plump flesh beneath.

"I want to taste you here. Take them off?"

"You can. If you want to." Her cheeks grew hot and her voice was a husk of itself. Her inhibition seemed to have equally eroded. She was shaking and barely able to stand, but she held very still as he eased down her panties to let them fall at her ankles.

His nostrils flared and he took her hand, helping her

step out of them, then he brought her hand to his mouth and kissed her fingertips, moving to the underside of her wrist and the inside of her elbow. He kissed her collarbone and the point of her chin, and his teeth scraped her earlobe.

"Lie back," he urged.

She melted onto the bed and he followed. His hot weight blanketed her as he kept up those hypnotizing kisses. Each one was tender and inciting, making her soft and tense at once. She relaxed, but she wanted more. She needed more.

"Remy."

"Not yet, *ma chérie*. I want to taste all of you." He rolled her onto her stomach and continued brushing his damp mouth across her skin, tongue dabbing at her spine and into the hollow of her lower back. "You have dimples here, too," he noted, kissing the top of each cheek.

His lips touched the backs of her thighs, the backs of her knees...

"Remy, please." She rolled to face him and he ran his hand from her knee to her thigh, squeezing her quadriceps.

"I only have this once," he said gruffly. "Let me do it right."

A jagged strike of lightning went into her heart. He leaned to press a kiss to her stomach, then shifted between her legs, easing one of her thighs over his shoulder.

Her scalp tightened. Here again, she should have been more self-conscious, but he was so reverent, so confident and so unhurried.

"Oh," she groaned as he slowly tasted her, deepening his caress in increments, working zings of pleasure from her center outward, nurturing them into stronger and stronger pangs of delight. She writhed in pleasure, lost to the earthy joy of it.

She was tempted, oh-so tempted, to let him take her over the edge like this. She was shaking, edging close to climax, but she wanted that other intimacy. The thing she'd been dreaming of for five long years.

"Remy, please," she moaned. "I want you inside me."

"I want that, too," he growled. He shed his underwear, then stood on his knees over her as he applied a condom.

He was very good at it, for a man who didn't make a habit of hooking up.

"Maybe, um, a little of the lubricant?" she suggested, suddenly nervous as she realized this might hurt. "It's not flavored, is it?"

"No." He anointed himself, then caressed between her legs with his slick finger, making her bite her lip as desire rushed back to a level of near combustion. "You have no idea how many times I've thought about this."

She shook, fighting not to climax, and held up her arms.

He loomed over her, bracing on his elbow. She bent her legs, catching her lip with her teeth as he guided himself into position.

It struck her that this was how many a bride felt on her wedding night. Eager and apprehensive. Aroused, but feeling a little awkward at how brazen this act was.

"Second thoughts?" he asked, flashing his eyes at her, perhaps sensing her tension. "We can stop."

"I don't want to stop. I'm wishing I was good enough at this to ruin *you* for anyone else." Her eyes stung. Her throat and chest heated at how true that was.

"What makes you think you won't?" His face tightened as he shifted slightly. His flesh prodded for entry.

She made herself relax, but her hands tightened on his shoulders.

"Does it hurt?" he asked, perplexed.

"No." *A little. Maybe more than a little.* "I'm nervous. Oh." There was a startlingly real sensation as his thick shape forged into her. The stretch stung quite a lot. She bit her lip again.

He froze. "This is hurting. I'll stop."

"No, I *want* this. Please keep going." She touched his back, urging him.

He pressed a little more insistently, watching her with concern.

The sensation was remarkable. So intimate, she blushed. So intense, she trembled. It hurt, but she experienced a silly rush of pride as she took him in. He filled her so deeply, his pulse seemed to beat within her. The sensation of being joined with him in such an indelible way brought bright tears to her eyes.

"Eden," he said through gritted teeth.

"It's okay. The hurt is fading. I like how it feels."

Myriad emotions flickered across his expression. "Damn it. Are you a virgin?"

"Are you mad?" she asked with apprehension.

"I'm—" He was braced on his elbows and hung his head so his scorched laugh of disbelief huffed against her chin. "Why would you do this? Make your first time *me*?"

He lifted his head and searched her gaze for answers. There were a thousand facets in the hammered gold of his eyes. Astonishment and suspicion, exasperation and tenderness, and such humbleness that he made her mouth quiver.

"Do you really have to ask?" she whispered.

He closed his eyes. "No. No, I don't." He cupped her cheek and set a very gentle kiss on her lips. "Don't let me hurt you."

Irony tickled at the corner of her mouth. He would hurt her. Maybe even devastate her. It was inevitable, given the deal they had struck to arrive at this point. He wouldn't hurt her physically, no more than the discomfort she had just suffered. She could tell he was remorseful about that. He was treating her as though she was made from eggshells, holding himself so carefully within her and kissing her so softly that it was a tiny bit frustrating.

In an hour or a day, however, he would turn his back and pretend they had never done this. That would crush her far worse than being publicly thrown over had.

At least they were together right now. She could provoke his rumbling purrlike growl as she stroked the back of his neck and ran her hands down his back. Her tickling exploration across his buttocks provoked a slight thrust of his hips, causing pressure against her most sensitive places, teasing her back to the intense arousal that had made her beg to have him inside her.

She instinctually widened her thighs and rubbed them on his hips, riding them up to his waist. Another shimmer of joyous sensations followed.

Now the noise he made was hedonistic and possessive. He gathered himself as he withdrew slightly and returned.

"Oh," she breathed, so dazzled by pleasure, he seemed to exist in a halo of dancing lights. "I didn't know it would feel like this."

"Me, either," he said gravely, drawing out his next withdrawal and thrust, making them both shudder under the power of it.

Eden lost herself to their lovemaking then, allowing the sheer cataclysmic pleasure of flesh moving within flesh to consume her. Nothing about it felt awkward anymore. It was like the most graceful dance, the most natural union. There was no tracking who caressed and who moaned, who kissed and who caught a sharp breath.

She could have lived forever in this wondrous place, but they were mere mortals who could only withstand so much. As the intensity redoubled on itself, the pleasure heightened to such levels it was excessive. She quivered on the edge of climax.

"Let go." His voice was a rasp of command and plea and exaltation. "I'll come with you." He thrust once more and golden light engulfed her.

CHAPTER SIX

ON HIS FINAL THRUST, Remy experienced a release unlike any other. It took all his control to keep from bruising her with his grip on her shoulder as molten heat and shivering silk and intense pleasure consumed him. It was so good, he nearly blacked out. His blood and nerves and bones were infused with sweet, sharp possessiveness and deep gratitude that this had happened. *Mine. Finally.*

Yet not. Even as his shaking frame sank weakly upon her, his haze of satisfaction was disturbed by... He couldn't call it remorse. Regret? Yes, but not because they were making love. Nothing about this felt wrong. No, he already regretted it could be only this. Once.

And it was over.

His heart was still trying to steady itself as he gathered his strength to lift his weight and withdraw from her. It had to happen, but the act was akin to stepping out of his own skin. His muscles were shaking, his body still damp with their combined perspiration. Everything in him resisted leaving paradise.

She drew in a startled breath as his relaxed erection slipped f—

He swore bluntly at the rush of cool air on his damp flesh.

"What's wrong?" Her hands dropped from his shoulders and her body went stiff with wariness.

"The condom broke." Why had he trusted freaking novelty skins with Honeymoon Helper stamped on the foil?

"Really?"

"Yes, really. Are you using anything?"

Her pupils seemed to explode, turning her dark brown eyes into inky black pools.

"Birth control? No. We were pl-planning to start a family right away." Her voice faded into a mumble.

Because she was supposed to be doing this with Hunter. His best friend. On their wedding night.

Remy found another handful of sharp curses and thrust himself from the bed.

In the bathroom, he discarded the split latex and splashed cold water onto his face, trying to soak some rational thought back into his head, but it was impossible. Not when there was a new, even more disastrous mess in front of him.

He wanted to crack his head against that idiot in his reflection. *What the hell were you thinking?*

He hadn't been, obviously.

"Remy? Could I, um, have the bathroom?" The quaver in her voice wrung a fresh wince out of him. She was new to this and he was behaving like—

He didn't know how to behave!

"Of course." He went back to the bedroom.

She was standing uneasily in the middle of the room clutching a pillow in front of her to hide her nudity. Maybe for reassurance. She had her thighs pressed tightly together and wore an expression of distress. Her eyes were smudged and smoky. Her hair was fraying out of its conchlike style and was curling behind her ears. The puffiness in her lips and the sleepy sensuality in her eyelids were erotic as hell.

All he wanted to do was drag her back onto the bed they'd wrecked, but she brushed by him and muttered, "Thank you." She threw the pillow on the floor as she closed herself into the bathroom.

He pinched the bridge of his nose and blew out a pained breath.

When he heard the shower come on, he took a step toward the door, wanting to ask if she was okay. Was she hurt? Upset?

Of course, she was upset. *He* had been turned inside out by this development.

With a final, jaded curse, he dressed, then he straightened the bed and left the clothes he'd picked out for her on the foot of it. He spared a moment to examine the condoms. They were within their use-by date and were actually made by a reputable manufacturer. Maybe it had been the wrong type of lubricant?

Did it matter? The condom had broken. That couldn't be reversed.

He went back to the living room and downed the wine that Eden had only tasted. It had gone flat and warm, but his need for a drink had overshot all his other concerns.

He checked in with his pilot, who reported that the repair part should arrive any minute.

I'll need you to fly us to Toronto, Remy texted as he refilled his glass. Text Alister to send someone for my car. Alister was his personal assistant.

The hotel would have to shuttle them to the heliport when the helicopter was ready, but so be it. Remy took another gulp of wine. At least it was cold this time.

He was thinking about opening something stronger when Eden reappeared. Her face had been washed clean. Her hair was tidied smooth, but still in its arrangement. The bright colors of the skirt and top suited her, making her look more confident and put-together, countering the wary vulnerability in her eyes.

"What happened to not drinking?" she asked as she noted the glass he held.

"My pilot was supposed to drive my car back to Montreal. I asked him to fly us. Someone else will pick it up." He topped up her glass so it wore a fresh head of bubbles.

Her mouth… Damn, she had a pretty mouth, especially when she pouted it that way.

"I've never needed one of those morning-after pills, but I think I can get one over the counter at a pharmacy. I texted Quinn that I would leave her key with the concierge. When she gets here, she can take me."

His heart lurched. "*I* can take you to a pharmacy. Is that what you want?"

"For Quinn to take me?"

"To prevent a pregnancy?"

"It's what you want." The dignity in her voice fractured.

He held his glass so hard it might have shattered in his fist.

"What makes you think that?" he asked.

"Wasn't that the point of the condom? To prevent a pregnancy? You're obviously horrified that it broke. You're pouring me alcohol—"

"Forget that." He snatched up the glass he'd poured and dumped the liquid into the bar sink. "I wasn't thinking." It was time he *started* thinking. He poured out his own. "I'm not *horrified*. I'm—" Seeing a reason to keep seeing her. That's what whispered at him like a devil on his shoulder. "I don't know how to react. This is a lot to process."

"It is." She sank onto the couch, hands in her lap, sightless gaze pinning itself to the middle of the floor.

She looked very young in that moment. Like the nineteen-year-old innocent he had met in Paris, the one who had looked at him with such bewilderment as her brother dragged her from the club.

Into the silence, her stomach growled.

With a pained sob, she set her hand across it and glanced at the abundant baskets of snacks.

"Let's eat. We'll think better." Remy started breaking into them, setting out rustic crackers on the dining table with spreadable cheese, tiny gerkins, stuffed olives and hummus. "Would you rather have room service?"

"No. This is fine." She collected plates and cutlery on her way to the table.

They sat and wordlessly devoured the snacks.

"I think we worked up an appetite," he said wryly as he reached for another handful of deluxe trail mix. "Do you feel better?"

"Yes, but now I want to bust into the one with chocolate."

He rose and brought it to the table. As an afterthought, he opened the door to the Juliet balcony so the sound of the falls and the mist-infused breeze floated in, then sat down again.

"This is actually really romantic," she murmured, wistfully staring at the falls. The corners of her mouth went down.

He knew what she was thinking. *If only this were real.*

"Eden—" He hesitated, but she needed to hear it. He needed to *say* it. "That was the best sex of my life."

An infinite number of emotions flickered across her expression. Amazement at his blunt honesty, shy pleasure at the compliment and profound self-consciousness that he would reference it so openly. Tremulous hope followed with something so naked, it stopped his heart. Then a shadow of anxiety as she remembered the consequences

they might face. Finally, her mouth quirked with self-deprecation.

"Me, too," she said huskily.

He snorted. But, yeah. It still didn't compute that she
had been a virgin.

"How...?" She was twenty-four. Twenty-five? Peer pressure tended to push people into sex long before now. "You
and Hunter were engaged." His friend might not be a se-
rial womanizer, but Hunter had had affairs. Amelia, for
instance.

"He was okay with waiting. So was I." Eden set down
the dark chocolate truffle she had bitten in half and wiped
her fingertips on her napkin. "Before him, I didn't date
very seriously. I was busy with school and working with
Dad. Also, Micah had convinced me that you had used
me in Paris. It messed with my faith in my own judgment
where men were concerned— Why are you mad?" She
sat back.

Remy tried and failed to erase the flare of temper from
his expression.

"The fact your brother thinks I would use a woman for
any reason says more about him than it does about me.
You realize that? Paris had nothing to do with y—"

"Oh, my *gawd*," she cried, throwing herself to her feet
so fast her chair toppled. "If I hear one more time that
Paris had nothing to do with me... No matter what you
were fighting about, I was still in the middle of it! One
second we were kissing, the next, you two were at each
other's throats. You two *put* me in the middle of it. And it's
the reason you and I can't..." She waved between them,
face flexing with anguish. "You're in a cold sweat over a
broken condom. Because you might become a father? Or
because *I* might be your baby's mother?"

Her anger crashed against his own, but it allowed him

to compress his simmering antipathy back into the box where he kept it.

"It's me. Isn't it?" she demanded with a tap of one fingernail on the table. "Because Micah is my brother. Say it."

Because Micah was Yasmine's brother. That was the shocking truth of it, but Remy had sworn to his father that he would keep that fact hidden. Forever.

"Given the history between my family and Micah's, yes. You and I are impossible."

"Why?" she cried. "Because of industrial espionage twenty years ago? That's why you're making me take a pill instead of—"

"I'm not making you take that pill!" he interrupted vehemently, also flinging himself to his feet. "If you—" Such conflict gripped him, he could hardly breathe. "Whether you take a pill or not is entirely your decision." He grappled for control of his voice. Of his composure. He was pro-choice all the way. "I'll support you no matter what happens. I'm not afraid to become a father. I always expected I would be one. Eventually."

"But not with me," she choked out with agony.

He moved to grip the rail on the balcony. Maybe he'd been holding out for her, which didn't make any sense whatsoever. He spun back into the room and closed the door.

"What do you want, Eden?" he asked as calmly and rationally as he was able to. "Forget all the rest."

"You haven't told me the rest!"

"Indulge me," he pressed. "Forget Hunter and Micah and even me. Ultimately, this comes down to whether or not you want to take a chance on being pregnant right now. On carrying a baby and delivering it."

Her mouth trembled. Her eyes glossed with emotion. "It's more complicated than that."

"Not really," he chided softly. "Everyone thinks there's a perfect time or circumstance to start a family. We all want to believe we're in control of our lives, but hell, look at Hunter. Life happens. Literally. Plans have to be adjusted."

"And you would adjust yours to accommodate me?" she scoffed. "Maybe nothing will happen. Maybe this entire conversation is moot."

"Maybe," he agreed. "What is the timing like?"

"My cycle?" She gripped her elbows. "I've always been a little irregular when I'm stressed. It's been a really difficult year. I know I don't want to have a baby by someone who resents me for it."

"With," he clarified. "Not *by*, *with* me. I would never blame you for getting pregnant. There were two of us in that bed. If a baby comes along, it's ours."

"Meaning you would want to be involved. See? That means I'm making a decision for both of us."

"No. If you let nature take its course and a pregnancy happens then, yes, I'll be right there with you, every step of the way. But you're the one who has to carry that pregnancy. Right now, *you* have to decide what's right for your body and whether pregnancy is a chance you want to take."

She shook her head. "You can't mean that. What if I decide to take the pill? Then what?" she challenged.

He'd be disappointed as hell, but… "I'll respect whatever choice you make, I swear."

"No pressure." Eden paced toward the window, but didn't take in the view. Her attention was turned inward, her body still simmering with sensuality from their lovemaking.

In that heated tussle, everything in her world had been utterly perfect. She could have existed in the aftermath of twilight joy forever, but he had sworn and pulled away, reacting with such fury, she had been flattened by rejection. And fear, as she realized what a precarious situation she was in.

I'll just take a pill had been her panicked thought in the shower. It was the great undo button, wasn't it?

It was also an action that couldn't be undone, but she had been certain that was what Remy wanted her to do.

Instead, he was saying it was up to her. That was a huge responsibility to carry! What if she did get pregnant? Micah would be furious. Hunter would be…well, who cared if Hunter had to weather another storm of unflattering publicity? Remy was the one who would be affected the most.

She bit her thumbnail, trying not to be swayed by his promise to be with her all the way. What if he was lying? What if this was exactly what Micah had warned her about?

It wouldn't matter, she realized with illogical clarity. She would want the baby regardless. She had always wanted a family. The family she had grown up in had been fractured by her mother's difficult relationship with Micah's father, forcing her only sibling to grow up away from her. When her cousins had started having their children, she had said goodbye to beloved grandparents, then her father. She had never imagined motherhood would be easy, but she had always known she wanted to have a child.

Remy was right about there being no real control on timing, either. Her life was a mess, so today wasn't optimal, but even if she lost the company, she was a very privileged person. She had enough resources that she could afford to support her child.

Most importantly, she didn't know when she would find

another man with whom she would want to make love, let alone make a baby. As first times went, Remy had made hers as near to perfect as it could be. She would have no regrets on how conception had happened.

If it happened. Her heart pounded with a mixture of anticipation and trepidation. What if it did? She would be bound to him for a lifetime. Was she ready to take that risk?

She turned to face him and knew she was. Why? Yes, he was handsome and so well-dressed it was blinding, but she wasn't that superficial. She had only interacted with him a few times so she couldn't claim to really know him, but… Was she delusional? She felt as though she knew him at a soul-deep level, even though she couldn't say what he ate for breakfast or whether he preferred cats to dogs.

She trusted him, though. Instinctually. She had climbed into his car in her moment of need because she felt safe with him. She wanted to *be* with him. Her entire being yearned for it, and had since the moment she had met him in Paris.

"I want to see what happens." What if he thought she was trying to trap him?

He paused in tidying up the remnants of their picnic.

"Okay." He nodded gravely. Then he continued using economical movements to close jars and stack the dirty dishes in the sink.

"Really? You're not going to react more strongly than that?" Reveal delight or dismay?

"I'm impatient to know whether it happens, obviously." His mouth twisted with self-deprecation. "But that will take a couple of weeks?" His whiskey-gold eyes fixed on her.

She nodded jerkily. "I think the early tests only work if you to know when you ovulated. I'm not sure, so…"

"So we wait."

She searched his expression because his equanimity didn't make sense.

"Are you *sure* you won't be angry if…?" *If I carry your child?* "You don't want a baby with me, Remy. I know you don't."

His cheek ticked and he turned away, veering from the open bottle of wine to the bar. He unceremoniously snapped the seal on a bottle of whiskey, twisting off the cap as though he was wringing someone's neck.

"It's not ideal," he said, tone so ironic she knew it to be a gross understatement.

She came to the other side of the bar and gripped it.

"Because of Micah. He said your father stole proprietary information from his."

Remy's reaction was to pour a healthy measure of amber liquid into a glass. Then he topped it with the smallest splash of sparkling water from the refrigerator. He offered her the rest of the water.

After the salty snacks, she was dying of thirst. Plus, her mouth was positively arid. She took the glass he offered and poured it out for herself.

"Your brother seems to think I have it in for him. The truth is, I don't think about him at all. If our paths never crossed again, I'd be thrilled."

Her hand unconsciously went to her midriff while a searing pain pinned itself through her chest. Her throat flexed, refusing to swallow the water in her mouth.

Remy had his back to her, so he didn't see her reaction, but now he turned.

"He seems to think my lust for you is retaliation." His matter-of-fact tone caused a flood of pained heat to rise in her cheeks.

Lust? That's all it was?

"The conflict should have remained between our fathers." His cheek ticked with tension. "Micah's father, Kelvin Gould, literally pulled me into it."

"Micah said something once, but he didn't want to get into it. You met his father? Where? When?" And how? Eden had never met Kelvin Gould herself. Micah's father had mostly stayed in Europe, only visiting Canada once that she knew of. Her mother had left her with Grammy Bellamy, her father's mother, while he was in town. Kelvin had developed dementia when Micah was in his late teens and died a few years later.

"It was a middle-school basketball tournament in Toronto."

"When Micah lived with us." She recalled Micah saying that, too. "You would have been eleven? Twelve? I was really young, myself. Not even in school. All I really remember is that Micah was supposed to stay with us, but he went back to boarding school. I cried for weeks and begged to be sent to boarding school when it was time for kindergarten. I thought it meant I would see him there."

"Cute," he said with a dry snort that she took as patronizing.

"I love my brother, Remy."

"I don't doubt it. Or that he loves you." He sipped his drink, gaze fixed on her.

"But," she prompted. "What happened at the game to get him sent back to boarding school?"

"I don't know why he had to leave town. It wasn't that big a deal." He came out from behind the bar and wandered to the window. "The game was much like any other at that age, clumsy and loud. There was a father on the other team's side who was riding his son pretty hard, but I didn't pay much attention. My father noticed, though. He was an assistant coach and chaperoned the away games. I'll never forget the look on his face when he glanced across and recognized Kelvin Gould. It was worse than seeing a ghost. It was a type of hatred that…" Remy swallowed some of his whiskey and there was a rasp in his voice from the alcohol when he continued. "It was murderous. My father was a very generous and loving man. I didn't know he was capable of that sort of lethal revulsion."

A chill settled into her chest. "What happened? Did he confront him?"

"Not immediately. He told me later that he wished he had pulled me from the game the moment he saw Gould. That we had waited on the bus, but I was playing well, having fun. Then Gould saw my father. He figured out which kid was his and started calling out some truly vile things at me. Racist remarks, which was hurtful enough, but I could tell he was doing it because he knew that going after someone he loved was the most effective way to hurt my father. I couldn't stand it. I tripped Micah."

"You said this feud wasn't between you two!"

"I tripped him in a game, Eden. We were kids. The only real damage was to his adolescent pride. But his father left the bleachers and came after me like a street fighter."

"Oh, my God." She touched her cold fingers to her lips.

"Next thing I know, I was waking up on the floor. Dad was over me. One eye was bloodshot and his lip was split. Gould had been removed and Micah was gone, too. My father took me to get checked at the hospital and I never saw Kelvin Gould again. I didn't see Micah until that night in Paris, when he seemed to think I was continuing what we'd started that day by making advances on you. I'm not that childish," he said derisively.

"He said you were mad that he bought a vineyard, one

your family wanted. And that you never let his company bid on your projects."

"That's business," he said, dismissing her suggestion with a flick of his hand. "For the projects we've had, hiring Gould Automation would be like asking a neurosurgeon to give us a haircut."

"So it all goes back to Micah's father thinking yours robbed him?"

"My parents were the ones who were robbed," he said forcefully. "Have you ever looked it up online?"

"I didn't find much." Basically, the story was exactly as Micah had related it. Remy's father had *allegedly* double-crossed his employer by selling proprietary information.

"The story you read was written by the side with the greater financial resources." Remy's spine was rigid. "My parents weren't poor, but they weren't on Gould's level. My father was born in Martinique, and my mother was Haitian. They met while schooling in France and both had family there so it made sense to marry and settle in Paris. My father took a position with Gould Automation as a robotics engineer. He was very talented."

Eden had no doubt. Micah had inherited the conglomerate that helped factories around the world become more efficient. The company had always been well regarded as innovative and profitable.

"The undisputed facts are that my father was a lead engineer working on a project in the Netherlands. His laptop and backup diskettes went missing from their home. Shortly thereafter, a Gould competitor poached the client and built them a system very much like the one my father had been designing."

"Was the competitor ever questioned?"

"They claim it arrived anonymously. Investigations

proved nothing except that my father didn't benefit financially. Even so, Kelvin Gould did everything he could to discredit and ruin him. The accusations followed him to Canada. Fortunately, Mom had family in Montreal who were trying to expand from selling package tours to the Caribbean into operating a dedicated fleet of airplanes. My father became a pilot and it all worked out."

Remy was still at the window, keeping his back to her, which gave her a vague suspicion he wasn't telling her everything.

"So Micah's father attacked you because he believed your father had stolen from him and got away with it? Then, years after that, Micah thought you were still nursing a grudge about his father's attack and came after me? I'm sorry, Remy, but it sounds like you two need to sit down and clear the air. It's not worth holding on to so much acrimony, is it?"

"Not to you. Or Micah. His father's company lost a hundred thousand euros, which is no small sum, I'll grant you, but my family was impacted far more personally and profoundly." He threw back the last of his drink. "So, no thank you. I do not want to kiss and make up with him."

She considered how his parents must have felt—uprooted. Their reputations were shredded and their careers stopped in their tracks. Did Micah think Remy was still covering up for his father? Why did he continue to be so suspicious of him?

The room phone jangled, startling her from her ruminations.

Remy frowned.

"The airfield?" she queried.

He picked up the extension on the end table next to where he was standing.

"Hello?" His expression went flat. He held out the phone to her.

No-o-o. Micah had found her? Eden took it gingerly.

"Hello?"

"Why are you in a room registered to him?" Micah asked in his I'm-willing-to-be-reasonable-but-don't-waste-my-time voice.

"What have you been doing? Calling hotels?" Infuriating man!

"He caught me catching a rideshare to come here." Quinn's urgent voice sounded in the background.

"You're *here*?" Eden had texted Quinn after her shower, but that had been two snack baskets and two deeply disturbing conversations ago. "For God's sake, Micah. I am an adult."

"And as such, you will give me your room number and invite me up to speak with you," he said with false pleasantness. "Or meet us here in the lobby."

"Why are you so—" She stopped herself and clenched her teeth in frustration.

Part of her wanted to force the conversation he needed with Remy, but one glance at Remy and her heart juddered to a halt.

Remy was watching her closely. Outwardly, his expression was remote and unaffected, but she sensed the explosive tension gathering beneath his surface. He hadn't told her everything. She knew that instinctually.

She also knew that Micah would again accuse Remy of playing on her feelings and using her as an instrument against him. She wouldn't be able to hide from her brother that she had made love with Remy. She definitely couldn't stand here and listen to Micah berate him.

"Is the concierge there? Let me speak to them. I'll ask them to let you up."

A man's voice came on the line. She gave him their room number and hung up.

Still holding Remy's inscrutable look, she said, "We have to go."

CHAPTER SEVEN

EDEN RATTLED QUINN'S key fob onto the coffee table. Then—with a wild look of panic—retrieved the "honeymoon" basket from the bedroom.

Remy took it from her as she thrust it at him, even though he was not in the habit of fleeing with evidence from the scene of consensual lovemaking. Nor was he afraid of Micah. He had steeled himself to be around the man today, willing to keep their family history from overshadowing his best friend's wedding.

That was, of course, before he had taken Eden's virginity and courted an unplanned pregnancy. Somehow, he didn't think Eden's naive vision of his breaking bread and mending fences with her brother could be built on *that* new information. She was right. It was best he left.

He refused to leave her to make explanations on his behalf, though. He held the door while she hurriedly tied herself into her shoes.

The white heels didn't go with her outfit at all. They were embellished with sparkles and a satin ribbon that hung in a bow at her ankle, but they did what heels did and piled sex appeal onto an already knockout figure. Her hurried strides pulled at the narrow skirt so it slithered against her ass and thighs, and he saw a flash of her shins.

His fascination with her had gone far enough, however. The implications of what they'd done went beyond a possible pregnancy. He had only scratched the surface on the events of twenty-eight years ago when the rivalry between their families truly started, but some secrets were meant to stay buried.

He would worry about how to *keep* it buried if Eden actually turned up pregnant.

Eden set the internal locking lever so the door remained cracked as they left.

"I'll text Quinn to make herself at home." She turned away from the elevator. "We should take the stairs— Oh. That's convenient."

Midway along the hall, a wide, carpeted staircase led them down to a deserted, multifunction floor. It held a closed bar and a handful of locked breakout rooms. At the far end, there was an elevator that would take them straight to the parking level.

"I've been drinking," Remy recalled as she pushed the button for the basement. "My keys are with the valet." He set the basket on the floor of the elevator and pulled out his phone to call the front desk. There was a text from his pilot. "They're replacing the part right now. That answers where we're going."

"I'll tell Quinn I'm going to Toronto. Micah can meet me there if he's that anxious to see me." Eden sent her text and hurried from the elevator into the parking garage. "Hi! Hello! Excuse me!" Eden trotted forward a few steps, waving at a woman climbing into a hatchback. "Are you leaving? Would you be interested in driving us to the heliport for…" She glanced at her purse. "I think I have forty dollars. I don't carry much cash," she told Remy.

"Make it a hundred." He had a half dozen currencies on him at all times.

The woman warily agreed. Eden put her at ease on the

short drive, encouraging her to share that she worked in catering and had two kids. Her husband worked at the US-Canada border. When she asked about their reason for needing a lift, Eden brushed away her question.

"It's a long story, but let me give you my card. Please reach out if you need anything at all. I have a lot of resources at my disposal and you've been such a lifesaver."

"You realize she'll go to the press once she puts together who you are and what happened?" Remy asked as Eden waved her off. "Micah will know you left with me. Everyone will."

"The media storm is already throwing hailstones," she said starkly. "I authorized my assistant to confirm the wedding is off, but I have to prepare a press release so Hunter's people can coordinate with my team then...ugh. Ride it out, I suppose."

Him, too. Remy was realizing that it had been one thing to be seen with her in the moments after the wedding had fallen apart—that had been a favor to his friend—but any enterprising paparazzo could trace them to that hotel room and draw salacious conclusions.

"Oh, you're back," Andrea said as they strode into the heliport. "And you've changed." She waggled her eyebrows. "I guess you enjoyed the room."

Salacious like that. What the hell was wrong with some people? Eden blushed chokecherry-red and tried to stammer out a thank-you for the woman's earlier assistance.

Remy cut her off as he demanded, "Status of my machine?"

"I believe they're working on it," Andrea said, sobering as she read his dismay.

"Good." He grabbed Eden's hand and tugged her out to the tarmac with him, refusing to leave her there to suffer that woman's speculation even though his possessive, protective attitude basically confirmed they had "enjoyed" the room.

None of this was supposed to have happened. He was furious with himself and could only think that they needed to keep a lid on it. He couldn't drop her in Toronto to ride out the wait alone, though.

"The mechanic is finished, sir. We're fully fueled and can take off as soon as we're cleared by control," his pilot said.

"Good." Remy nodded for him to continue his preflight preparations and squeezed Eden's shoulder to draw her attention from the phone she was double-thumbing.

She lifted a distracted expression. Lines of tension had come in around her mouth and anxious shadows invaded her dark brown eyes.

"You were leaving for Greece directly from the wedding, weren't you? That means you have your passport?"

"I do." She hugged her purse under her arm. "Why?"

"Your home in Toronto will be staked out. I'll take you to Montreal. We'll fly from there."

Her eyes went wide with shock. "To where?"

"Martinique."

"I thought it was rainy season." She made it sound as though she'd caught him in a falsehood.

"That's why it's a quiet place to stay."

She blinked in befuddlement before her eyebrows came together with caution. "By myself? Or…?"

"Together. But let's keep this—" He searched for a way to describe whatever this was between them. Obsession, maybe? Spending more time with her certainly wouldn't help him dampen his lust, but that's what he would have to do. "I want to know as soon as you do. If nothing transpires—" he couldn't help the twist of his mouth as he found such a lovely euphemism for the hot mess they would be in if she was pregnant "—we go back to Plan A."

"One and done," she said in a hollow voice.

"Yes." He ignored the sharp knife of electric heat that jolted through his chest and left a scorched sensation in the pit of his stomach.

"Sir?" His pilot closed the hatch, where he had stowed Remy's bag, and opened the door to the passenger area of the helicopter.

Remy held out his hand.

Eden didn't know if she was being cowardly or desperate as she settled into the plush leather seat facing forward. Her phone was still blowing up with emails and voice messages that she was eager to avoid, but she felt bereft as Remy moved into the copilot's seat in the forward cabin.

He left the door open, but she was so sensitive, she felt rebuffed. The helicopter was close-quarters, not cramped. He could have taken the seat across from her without their knees touching beneath the table between them.

He didn't want to be with her, though.

If nothing transpires, we go back to Plan A.

She had agreed to that, but it seemed like a thousand hours ago. She had foolishly believed the ache of yearning for him would somehow be satisfied if she slept with him once. On the contrary, she now knew what he could make her feel and was even more drawn to him.

As the helicopter swayed ever so slightly as it lifted off, she looked toward the sliver of Remy that she could see— his shoulder and the headphone that covered his ear. She silently begged him to reveal again the man who had said, *I feel empty all the time.*

That's how she felt, so intensely hollow she could hardly breathe through the desolation.

That man had disappeared, though. He was distancing himself. Shutting down and shutting her out. He was trying to hide his association with her because he was embarrassed—ashamed?—to have slept with her.

This schism hurt so much, she ought to have insisted he take her home, where she could begin reassembling her life, but there was that other irrational part of her that would settle for this scant contact. For a few more days with him, remote as he might be.

Truthfully, he wasn't wrong to hide their relationship, such as it was. She wasn't ready to face whatever questions would come up if she went home. Her mother wouldn't understand this reckless desire that gripped her. Micah would see it as outright treason.

Which didn't make avoiding them right, but it certainly made it easier to put off the inevitable reckoning. Almost all of it. She had a press release to craft.

With a sigh, she picked up her phone again. Her PR team had suggested a slant that threw all the blame onto Hunter and the wedding crasher, Amelia.

Eden sidestepped taking such an easy way out. There was an innocent baby involved. She couldn't throw a single mom under the bus and, honestly, she didn't feel like a victim, just collateral damage.

As she glanced out the window, where the shadows of the rotors chopped across the sunlight, she considered how little rancor she felt toward Hunter. Today had been awful, but in some ways, she couldn't relate at all to the woman she had been this morning when she had been buttoned into her gown.

How had she imagined she could marry Hunter Waverly when Remy Sylvain existed in this world? Marrying anyone else seemed like a ridiculous delusion.

Not that she expected to marry Remy.

With a small sob, she slouched deeper into her seat.

Believing they were soul mates was a delusion, but as she lifted her gaze to the back of his shoulder again, she felt a nearly irresistible desire to move closer and touch him. Not to get his attention, simply to touch. To have the right to caress and share a moment of physical connection.

Why was she pulled so inexorably toward him?

And why was it so terrible for them to see if they had more than sexual attraction? Remy's explanation about Micah's father had helped her understand a little, but it still seemed like an overreaction. She almost wished she had hung back to ask Micah why he continued to hold on to so much antipathy toward Remy? Because of her? She was fine.

Sort of.

She checked in with Quinn, texting to ask if Micah had blown his stack when they got to the empty hotel room. Three dots briefly came up, but disappeared just as quickly.

Eden thought about trying a video call, but she didn't know how to explain to her friend why she was fleeing the country with the one man no one would approve of. Better to focus on her press release.

She sent it to her assistant as they landed. Remy helped her down the steps to the tarmac and they walked directly across to a private jet painted in an abstract blend of metallic green, purple and tropical blue. Remy waved her to precede him up the stairs.

Inside, it looked more like an exclusive nightclub than an airplane. The furniture was low and cut along curved, ultramodern lines. The lighting was subdued gold, the colors mimicking white sand and blue-green seas. They moved past a dining nook with a wraparound bench and Remy indicated one of the recliners that faced a big screen showing a welcome message and a Wi-Fi code.

He moved forward through an oval door that blinked like an eye, like something in a spaceship movie. Leaving her to travel alone again, she supposed.

She turned her pout to the window, where the midsummer sun was descending, turning the shadows long as the day stretched toward evening.

"Ms. Bellamy?" A male steward held a tray with a damp facecloth, a small dish of mint candies and a glass of ice water. "I'm Antoine. I'll be serving a meal once we're airborne, but may I bring you a refreshment before takeoff? Champagne? A cocktail, perhaps?"

"I would love a Caesar, but make it a mocktail, please." She kept the facecloth and the ice water, feeling modestly revived after she had washed her hands and rehydrated.

Remy returned as Antoine brought her drink.

"I'll have one of those," he said as he eyed her Caesar.

"Virgin?" Antoine asked.

"Promiscuous. As morally objectionable as you can make it."

Eden hid her smile against the spiced rim of her drink, enjoying the tang of clam-flavored tomato juice with a shot of tabasco and a hint of dill.

Was that what she was now? No longer a virgin, therefore morally promiscuous? She turned a wistful glance to the window, unable to say she was sorry about it. The memory of their lovemaking brought goose bumps to her arms and shivers of pleasure all over her body.

She realized Remy's aloof gaze was fixed on her. She rubbed at her arms, cheeks stinging at how obvious she was.

"I should have got my suitcase from Quinn," she lied. "I hope there'll be some sort of shopping when we land?"

He opened a hatch beneath the television and shook out a sweater with wavy bands of sunset colors knitted into it.

"If that's too big, my sister may have left something in my stateroom."

The sweater was massive on her, but it smelled like him and felt so consoling, Eden snuggled herself into it. But—

"Is this *your* plane?" She realized he had changed into a lighter pair of pants and loafers without socks. "Like, not a charter or a corporate jet?"

"Why is that surprising?" He took his seat, stowing his phone into the cup holder without looking, as if it was something he'd done thousands of times. "I own a fleet."

"I guess that's why I'm surprised. I assumed you would jump aboard a flight whenever you need to, not keep one parked like a car in the garage."

"My sister occasionally steals the keys," he said dryly. "The rest of the family fly standby, but my schedule requires more flexibility so I keep this ready."

Antoine brought Remy's drink. "If you're comfortable, sir, the pilot has instructed me to buckle in for takeoff?"

Remy nodded and Antoine disappeared through the spaceship door.

"You sound like you're close with your sister," Eden mused gently, wanting to know more about him. As the president of Can-Carib Airlines, Remy had a presence online that was heavily curated toward business reporting, but was readily available to access. The rest of his family seemed elusive by comparison.

"We are." He took another long sip and exhaled to cool whatever burn it had lit in his throat. "She texted me earlier, asking if I would take her to France with me. My aunt and uncle are celebrating their fortieth wedding anniversary next week. I told her I was headed to Martinique and would leave from there. She's in New York so she'll have to find her own way." He tapped his glass with one pensive finger.

"You'll, um, go without me? If we don't know by then?" Eden was a big girl. There was no reason she should feel so abandoned.

"We'll see, won't we?" He flashed her a look. "I imagine you'll dominate the gossip sites for the next week or two."

"For what it's worth, I didn't mention you in my press release. Have you texted Hunter? Does he know we're—" Her heart swerved away from the word *together*. "That you're helping me?"

His mouth flattened. "That can wait."

It's not like he'll care, she wanted to say. She looked out the window to hide the dampness that rose against her lashes. She'd been so frustrated by this long day, she could hardly keep tears from overflowing.

When she had control of herself, she texted her team that she was taking her honeymoon time as vacation and instructed them to schedule a board meeting for her return. Then she checked in with her mother and her brother, telling them the same thing.

Her mother texted back, Micah said you left with Remy Sylvain. Are you home?

Eden glanced across at him. No. He helped me avoid paparazzi by flying me to Montreal. Now we're—

She backspaced.

Now I'm on a plane to the Caribbean.

Where, exactly? I'll meet you.

Eden chewed her lip, reluctant to tell her mother that she was with Remy. Lucille would disapprove. She was sure of it. When Eden had returned from Paris five years ago, deeply hurt by the belief that Remy had targeted her,

her mother had grilled her in a way that had seemed like maternal concern at the time, but now Eden wondered.

"Put it behind you," Lucille had insisted before she had a long conversation with Micah behind a closed door.

Lucille had also been concerned when Eden had revealed that Remy was Hunter's best man. "What did he say?"

"He acted like we'd never met."

"Then you should do the same," Lucille had said firmly. "Let sleeping dogs lie."

Eden wished she could ask her mother for more details on what might have transpired between Remy and Micah's fathers, but Lucille rarely talked about her first husband. Eden doubted her mother would tell her anything, so it wasn't worth stirring up old hurts.

I need some time alone, Eden texted. To work out how to solve the BH&G situation.

It was an open-ended nudge for her mother to relent and allow Micah to help, but her mother only replied, I'm sure you'll come up with something. Let me know when you've landed safely.

Eden put her phone away, thinking her mother had more faith in her resourcefulness than she did in herself.

CHAPTER EIGHT

A CRACK OF thunder and a flash of lightning had Eden sitting up with a gasp.

For a moment, she was dizzy and disoriented, heart racing with alarm. Slowly she made sense of the furniture illuminated by the dim glow from the night-light she'd left on in the adjoining bathroom.

Martinique. Remy.

She closed her eyes in a twinge of disgrace, both in going away with him and for putting herself in a position of needing to. The debacle of her wedding flew straight onto the pile of her chagrin, along with the weight of BH&G.

Her entire life was a scorched, sticky mess and she was alone in the middle of it.

Without checking, she knew the other side of the mattress was empty, not that she had expected Remy to have come to bed with her. Did she want him to? She shouldn't, but she felt tremendously lonely.

At least during the flight, Remy's steady presence had kept the worst of the doom at bay. They had eaten spinach-and-artichoke puff pastries in their seats along with rice cups that held a scrumptious bite of tandoori chicken. Then they moved to the dining table for their main course, roasted lobster with whipped parsnips and a watercress salad. They finished with a light strawberry mousse.

After that, they watched a forgettable action movie, then, just as she was nodding off, they began their descent. The rain had eased and the freshly washed night had reflected the sparkling lights of Fort-de-France.

"There's something magical about arriving somewhere at night, isn't there?" she had said dreamily as the hatch was opened and a fresh breeze wafted across her face. "It's like a Christmas present still in its wrapper. You can't tell what's inside and you have to wait to find out."

"That's very poetic. Are you secretly a romantic?"

Since that hadn't been the first time she'd been accused of being one, it probably wasn't a secret, but she deflected, and said, "I've never been to the Caribbean before. It feels exciting."

"We have a few nightclubs, but on the whole, island culture tends to be very laid-back." He walked her to a wine-red convertible waiting on the tarmac for them.

"Different, then," she said once they were nestled inside it. "I've been to Florida for the amusement parks, and Micah brought me to Europe two or three times a year. I've seen Mediterranean beaches, but most of my family vacations were in Canada. BH and G's motto is 'It's great to be home…and garden' so camping in the Rockies was more on-brand than visiting a tropical all-inclusive. I'm dying for sun and sand."

"Sand, I can promise, including in places you don't want it," he said dryly as he steered the car onto a highway. "Sunshine will be hit-and-miss."

Traffic had been light and Remy knew the roads. He had zipped in and around other cars, taking a route inland that climbed and wound into dense tropical forest before descending toward an expanse of black ocean and charcoal clouds on the horizon.

Her arduous day must have caught up with her because the next thing she knew, Remy had asked, "Are you awake?"

The car had been parked and her cheek had tingled with the sensation of a light caress.

"Do you want me to carry you in?"

Of course, she did. She wanted to be coddled and petted and told everything would be all right.

"Don't be silly." She'd walked into the villa, taking in an impression of burnt-orange shutters against Tuscan-yellow walls and a wraparound veranda.

Had she also heard the rush of waves? If so, it was muffled now by the rumble of thunder and the steady patter of rain on the roof.

She was thirsty, so she rose and retied the sarong she'd worn to bed.

This was Remy's sister's room. He had told her to help herself to whatever she needed, but his sister was a fashion designer and most of the clothes looked to be her own creations. They seemed too well-tailored and personal to borrow. Eden had limited herself to the sarong and a silk sleep bonnet still in its package.

She padded out and followed the soft glow toward the living room.

The villa wasn't as extravagant as she had expected, given the luxury of the jet. It was more of a charming bungalow, reminding her of her Grammy Bellamy's farmhouse in its eclectic, comfortable decor. Eden nudged a rattan rocking chair on her way through the living room and picked up a mango from the bowl on the dining-room table to smell it.

Oh! Family photos.

She moved behind the table to study the mosaic of framed photographs on the wall.

There was Remy, maybe five years old, deeply tanned

and wearing a checkered shirt and a big smile as he held an infant she presumed was his sister. His parents were a cute pair of young professionals in double-breasted suits with thick shoulder pads, looking fondly on their children. Other relatives were captured in dated photos wearing fashions from bygone decades. In one beautifully framed, hand-colored photograph, a couple stood in formal attire from the early 1900s, their expressions somber.

"Do you need something?"

"Oh." Her heart flipped as she turned. She self-consciously touched the sleep bonnet.

Damn. Remy was wearing hardly anything at all, just drawstring shorts tied low on his hips and a whole lot of naked skin over well-toned muscles. Her gaze swept down to the narrow trail of hair below his navel and jerked back upward.

She swallowed and crossed her arms to secure the sarong, instantly aware of her nakedness beneath the light cotton.

"A glass of water?" She lifted a sheepish shoulder since there was an L-shaped counter between her and the sink. "I couldn't resist looking at the photos. This is a family home?"

"My father's grandparents built the original and raised their children here." He moved to the kitchen, where he'd left a light burning over the stove. He opened a cupboard to the left of it. "We modernized ten years ago, but the laws are strict when it comes to exterior changes. We were more interested in preserving what we love than turning it into a palace, anyway. My sister and I are the only ones who use it. Tap okay? Or would you prefer bottled?"

"Tap is fine." She followed him into the kitchen and accepted the glass he poured. "Do you spend a lot of time here?"

"As much as I can, given the size of Can-Carib and my many responsibilities and other family obligations. My father's relatives are here so I try to visit a few times a year. I share a housekeeper with my aunt. She'll know I'm here and will expect me to drop by."

That sounded like a warning. Eden lowered her glass.

"Will the housekeeper tell her you're not alone?"

He leaned his hips on the counter and folded his arms across his bare chest, drawing her eye to the curve of his biceps and the ball of his shoulder. The compulsion to set her lips against his burnished skin was nearly irresistible.

"She might. And since I've never brought a woman here before, I imagine she'll read into it."

Eden tried to swallow past a sudden dryness in her throat. *Don't think that makes you special*, she cautioned herself. He had only brought her here for expediency's sake.

"What will you say if she finds out?"

"I don't know." His mouth twisted.

Another crack of lightning made her jump. Thunder rattled like a convoy of semitrailers across the roof.

She looked up with alarm while the lights flickered.

"You should be here during a hurricane."

"Have you?"

"Yes. And I take back recommending it. It's exciting in the wrong way."

She liked that quirk of his mouth when he was being ironic. Their gazes caught and locked. Whether it was the gathering of ions outside, working toward another lightning strike, or the ever-present chemistry between them, she didn't know, but the air became charged. All of her pricked and her lungs grew tight.

"Is it not fair to say that you're helping me dodge a publicity problem?" she asked, feeling the tension that flexed in her throat. "That that's all this is?"

"Sure," he drawled. "I can give that a try."

"Your aunt won't buy it? Because it's not as if we're... carrying on." Had she really used one of Grammy's old-fashioned expressions?

If she was honest, she definitely wanted to carry on. Longing was buffeting her like those winds outside, gusting and pushing and swirling—

The world went black. Utterly absent of light.

Above them, the cascade of rain on the roof increased.

She blinked and widened her eyes, but saw absolutely nothing.

"I left my cellphone in the bedroom." She reached for the edge of the counter, planning to set down her water. Her fingers bumped into the warm skin of Remy's tense abdomen.

He caught her hand, held it firmly.

"Mine is in my room, too." His voice was tight.

He started past her, but she held on to his hand, shuffling behind him past the furniture and into the hall. She trailed her free hand along the wall as they made their way past the opening to the first room. It had looked like an office when she had briefly glanced in on her way to the kitchen.

He stopped and held her from bumping into him with a light pressure on the hand he still held. "Can you get to the bed from here?"

She could feel the heat radiating off him. Her ears were trying to pick apart his tone. Was he angry?

"I wonder if this is what it feels like to be untethered in deep space," she mused, hand reaching into the nothingness.

"We have oxygen."

Yet she couldn't breathe. As metaphors went, the vacuum of space epitomized her future. Formless and empty. Unsurvivable.

"I'll get my phone so you can see," he said.

Before he could step away, without letting herself overthink it, she turned into the only thing that felt real. Him. She reached for his strength and pressed herself into his warmth, sliding her arms around his waist. Her face found the hard plane of his chest and she rubbed her cheek against the taut silk of his skin.

"Eden." Her name was a tight, hot roar of fire.

"I'm sorry." Her chin grazed his hard nipple as she tried to push away.

He didn't let her go. His arms clamped around her. "I can't take another chance."

"I know. I just wanted to feel you."

"Feel, then," he said in a guttural voice. He scraped her hands across his chest and swept them behind his back again. Then he cupped her face with his firm palm and his mouth was on hers. Hungry. So hungry she moaned in ecstasy at feeling her own yearning echoed back to her in this greedy, encompassing kiss.

It felt stolen, kissing like this in the pitch-dark. His image formed in her mind from her questing hands. From the indent of his spine and the firm globes of his butt and the ripples of his rib cage as she trailed her hands across him. She found the taut tendon connecting his neck and shoulder. His earlobes were as neatly formed as the rest of him. His tight curls prickled her palm as she pressed the back of his head, urging a deeper kiss.

He seemed equally determined to discover and memorize, squeezing and caressing as he swept his hands across her back, hips, breasts and waist.

"Let's find the bed," she urged.

Instead, he slipped away from her. His lips touched her collarbone, then he was sliding from the arms she had twined around his neck.

She sobbed with loss, only to realize he was dropping to his knees. Her back met the doorjamb. Her sarong was an ephemeral thing that was brushed away like a bridal veil. His mouth branded kisses across her abdomen and across the tops of her thighs and into the aching center of her.

Gasping with acute pleasure, she clung to his shoulders and moved with the rhythm of his kiss, moaning unashamedly, thrilling and rising so quickly to her peak, it ought to have been embarrassing, but it was too good. Too, too good.

He didn't stop. She was still pulsing in climax as he pressed his finger inside her. He continued kissing and laving, and the gentle thrusting of his finger drove her to an even higher pinnacle. She nearly screamed when she arrived.

Shaking, she would have collapsed, but he rose to gather her and somehow shuffled to the bed and set her on the rumpled covers.

With a half laugh of bemused joy, she stroked her touch over his arms, eager to feel his weight come down upon her. She wanted him *in* her.

He evaporated into the dark.

"Sleep. I'll see you in the morning." His words rasped across her sensitized nerves.

"Remy." She sucked in a breath of betrayal and rose onto her elbow, but only heard the door closing behind him.

Pressing her still trembling thighs together, she rolled onto her side, hugged a pillow and buried her crumpling face into it.

After feverishly appeasing the lust-driven barbarian within him—alone, with his fist—Remy slept in. He woke with a head full of sawdust and recriminations ripe in the back of his throat.

In those sightless, humid moments in the night, he had told himself it was enough that he didn't risk another pregnancy, but his attempt to slake his thirst for her had only been stimulated, not satisfied. He wanted her more than ever.

He stepped under a blast of cold water, swore, but was no longer erect, so he dressed and followed the aroma of coffee to the kitchen.

Beyond the open doors to the veranda, the sun shone brightly on the thick tropical vegetation that spilled bright blooms around the gazebo. The rest of the backyard was mostly sand and almond trees, with a boardwalk beneath their shady branches that led to the beach.

Eden stood in the open wooden gate at the end, facing the ocean. She had switched out last night's bonnet for a yellow-and-blue head wrap and had changed into one of his sister's T-shirts and a pair of loose board shorts, both a size too big.

Remy heard a noise and realized it was him, groaning. He only needed to look at Eden and he was right back to wanting to touch and taste and take. Last night had been the backslide of an addict, but oh, had it been worth it. Her trembling thighs and writhing hips and cries of exaltation had nearly tipped him over the edge, all from touching her, not himself.

Somehow, he'd kept himself from taking yet another reckless chance, but craving her had returned with a vengeance.

So stupid. It wasn't fair to say she had reached for him first, either. He knew she was going through a lot. He never should have let it get as far as it had. It was a damn miracle he had walked away last night, but he had heard her gasp of shock right before he'd closed the door between them. She had been hurt by his exit.

He had turned what could have been a tense, but civilized, sharing of a living space into a powder keg of bottled emotions.

There was no hiding from it, though. He poured himself a coffee and walked down to join her.

"Thinking of starting your day with a swim?" he asked as he came up behind her.

She stiffened and sipped the coffee she held, eyes staying on the ocean.

"Maybe later, when it's hotter. I don't feel like being cold and wet right now." Her voice was thin and strained.

His ears rang, hearing too much significance in that statement. Then he thought, screw it. He wasn't going to pick apart what they'd done or leave himself open to jabs.

"Your Canadian is showing," he said and set his cup on the top of the gatepost. He brushed past her, striding unhesitatingly down the kelp-littered beach and into the surf.

The water here was always a tepid, silky bath. Diving into a wave submerged him in homecoming, washing away whatever troubles had driven him to the place of his roots.

Today, his troubles waded cautiously into the water behind him.

"It's warm!" she said with an astonished smile that hit his heart like an exploding rainbow.

"You said you'd been to the Med. It's warm, isn't it?"

"Sure, but I've also been in the Atlantic. I never got past here in PEI." She cut the side of her palm against the outside of her thigh. "This is fabulous."

She sank to her shoulders. Her head bobbed as a wave rolled in to pick her up and move her toward the beach.

They swam for twenty minutes before they waded ashore. The T-shirt hung off her shoulders and clung to her chest. She plucked it away so her bra wasn't so visible through the fabric, but he'd seen it. It was imprinted in his brain now, exactly the way she was. Indelibly.

"Iguana," he said, forcing his gaze down the beach and pointing.

"Get out." She walked a little closer to the driftwood, where the stocky, brownish-gray lizard was perched. Waves rhythmically frothed around their shins. "Do they bite?"

"I've never been close enough to find out. He'll disappear pretty— There he goes." It skittered up the beach into the brush, leaving only slither marks in the sand.

"Too bad they didn't see it." She looked toward some children who were coming onto the beach with their father. Tourists, Remy surmised, since he didn't recognize them. "This was your childhood? Swimming before breakfast and spotting lizards?"

"This was my winter. I don't even know what a white Christmas is."

"Lucky."

He was. He knew that. But not always, he thought, as her profile grew troubled again.

"Can I ask you something?" It had been bothering him since the hotel room.

"What?" She lifted her gaze and wary shadows came into her expression.

"Why did you want to marry Hunter if you didn't love him?"

"Oh." She looked at her feet, bending to pick up a broken shell. "Lots of reasons, all very practical. Being impetuous has never served me well. Where's the harm in meeting a man at a nightclub?" She lifted a disparaging eyebrow. "Where's the harm in sleeping with him *once*?"

Once. His heart swerved. He didn't look at her, but

he knew she wasn't looking at him, either. That word—
once—had been closing like walls around him, suffocating him in its limitations. That's what last night had been.
Once *more*.

So foolish, but he couldn't seem to regret it. Not enough
to swear it wouldn't happen again.

"Being impetuous got my mother into trouble. Literally. The same kind," she added with amused despair. "A
tale as old as time, right?"

"Is that why she married Gould? She was pregnant with
Micah?"

"Yes. She was a small-town prairie girl backpacking
in Europe with a friend. He swept her off her feet and
she immediately turned up pregnant. She was so relieved
when he agreed to marry her, but she quickly regretted it."

"Abusive?" he asked with a stab of suspicion. Stronger
than suspicion. Fatalistic certainty.

"I'm not sure about physically." She frowned into the
distance. "She doesn't talk about him. My take is that he
was very insidious in how he dismantled her self-worth.
His family piled on. Mama wasn't born into money and private education and aristocratic lineage. His parents thought
she was a gold digger. They insisted she have a nanny, then
Kelvin used that against her when she left him, saying she
had never bonded with Micah in the first place."

Kelvin Gould had been a monster.

"When did she leave?" Remy was pretty sure he knew,
but he wondered if Eden did.

"When he cheated. Of course, the prenup favored him."
She worked her thumb on the smooth inside of the shell
she still held. "She signed it very naively, believing him
when he said it would protect her. She wasn't entitled to
anything and didn't want his money, anyway. She wanted
to bring Micah to Canada. She didn't have any money of

her own, though. Nothing for a lawyer and no qualifications to get a job that paid well enough to afford one. She had to work minimum-wage, entry-level stuff. Kelvin said she couldn't support Micah in the standard he was entitled to and left him in Austria with his own parents. He threatened such an ugly fight, Mama settled for Micah visiting a few times a year, when Kelvin deigned to send Micah to her. Her boss found her crying about it one day. He bought her a coffee and a few days later he gave her a promotion and a raise."

"Your father?" Remy asked, guessing.

"Yes." Eden smiled with affection. "They still didn't know each other that well when he proposed. Mama wasn't keen at first, having already been in a marriage that went south, but Dad could see how desperate she was to have Micah in her life. He loved her practically at first sight—"

Her voice faltered briefly and Remy's breath stopped in his lungs, but maybe she'd just been affected by discussing the loss of her father. He didn't even believe in things like love at first sight, let alone imagine it was hereditary.

"Dad was also very pragmatic and sensible, so it wasn't the same whirlwind that had got Mama into such a bad situation with Kelvin. Dad wanted a family and they already worked well together. He said if she married someone as well respected and wealthy as he was, she would have more leverage against Kelvin, which was true. She was able to fly him over more often and eventually got him to live with us. Briefly."

Her voice halted again as she perhaps remembered what he'd told her about that time.

"Anyway, they loved each other very deeply. That encouraged me to believe I could have the same strong and healthy marriage if I found the right sort of partner."

Was that really what she wanted? Something about that

didn't ring true. He couldn't claim to know her well, but she was lively and whimsical and had leaped into his car very impetuously. She was here with him, barely twenty-four hours after she was supposed to marry another man, and could possibly be pregnant with his child.

Eden struck him as someone who led with her heart. It didn't make sense that she would settle for a dispassionate and pragmatic arrangement. No, Remy was sure she would prefer to marry for love.

"Bonjour," she called warmly in French.

They had come up to the children, who were turning over a rock.

"What have you found? A sea star? Oh, a baby crab." Eden expressed the right amount of fascination. They invited her up the beach to see some other small wonders.

Their father hung back with Remy, asking if it was safe to let the children swim or if there were rip currents to watch for.

Remy said it was safe and gave him tips on where to snorkel and hike with his young family.

He was absently keeping one eye on Eden and the children as they bent to examine a pool of water. Eden was smiling as she rose to stand, but her expression dropped into a surprised sort of blankness. She staggered once and her knees collapsed.

"Eden!" Remy started running, but couldn't get any traction in the sand.

Even as she put out a hand to catch herself, she crumpled limply to the beach.

"Eden!"

The children stood wide-eyed as Remy dropped to his knees beside her. He rolled her onto her back. She was completely unconscious. Breathing, at least, but his own lungs had shrunk to airless sacks. His entire body flooded with adrenaline.

"What happened? Did something sting her?" The father came up, breathless.

The children shook their heads, fearful.

"Run to that house with the red gate." Remy pointed. "Tell Celeste that Remy needs her." Would she be home? It was Sunday. Church.

Damn it.

He touched the backs of his fingers to Eden's cheek. Heat exhaustion? There was still a fresh morning breeze, not the full humid heat of the afternoon.

He examined her hands and feet, looking for bites or scratches. His mind was running through all that they'd eaten. She hadn't had breakfast yet. Was it low blood sugar? Was she diabetic?

Why didn't he know everything about her?

"Come on, Eden." He squeezed her shoulder. *"Wake up."*

CHAPTER NINE

"Remy!"

Eden heard someone call his name, but was too confused to make sense of who it could be. She was on a warm, lumpy bed that was both comfortable and not. Cool, but in a nice way.

She opened her eyes and sunlight shot straight into the back of her brain, causing spots behind her eyelids, which she'd reflexively clenched against the brightness.

How many people had she seen? Three? Four? Remy and some children?

"No," she groaned, recalling how her vision had gone white. "Did I faint?"

"*Yes.* No. Stay there." Remy's heavy hand pressed her shoulder, forcing her to remain on the sand. "This is my auntie Celeste. She's a doctor. This is Eden, Auntie."

Eden peeked against the sun and glimpsed a buxom woman in her late sixties wearing a yellow dress and a madras headscarf. She was sinking down to one knee beside Eden.

"Bonjour, Eden. Let me check your pulse."

"I'm okay," Eden insisted. "Please don't be alarmed."

"I'm actually retired." Celeste picked up her wrist. "Too old to be running down a beach, so let's both take a moment to catch our breath." She took a slow inhale, rolling her free hand to encourage Eden to breathe with her.

They took three or four breaths together, then Celeste released Eden's wrist.

"Your pulse is a little weak."

"I'm fine. Honestly," Eden insisted.

"Pregnant?"

"No."

"Possibly," Remy corrected grimly.

Celeste's glance toward Remy conveyed about a thousand questions, emotions and layers of parental disapproval, but her voice remained reassuring as she asked, "How far along would you be, Eden?"

"It's low blood pressure," Eden said with a grimace of embarrassment. "It's not serious. It happens sometimes when it's hot, if I stand up too fast. I take salt pills, but..." She risked a glance at Remy. "I didn't take them for the last week because I didn't want to retain any water." For the wedding.

Remy made a noise of disgust and pushed to his feet, looking as though he was warming up to lecture her into a watery grave.

"You need an electrolyte replacer," Celeste said.

"I have some tablets at the house." Remy helped both her and Celeste to stand. "Thanks for coming, Auntie. We won't keep you." He kissed her cheek.

"You'll come for dinner. I'll cook for you after church." Her stern look at Remy suggested he could use some churching himself.

"We'll be there," he promised, but Eden could feel the tension radiating off him. She wasn't sure if it was because he was still rattled by her fainting, or by what he'd let slip to his aunt.

"See, I'm fine," Eden reassured the children with a smile. "Maybe I'll see you here tomorrow."

If she survived whatever fallout was about to happen from Remy's blurted announcement.

"Will she tell anyone?" Eden asked him when they were back in his home and Remy was stirring rehydration tablets into a glass of water.

"She doesn't gossip, especially about someone's health history, but she'll have questions." He handed her the fizzing glass and began efficiently preparing breakfast, setting fish cakes the housekeeper had left into a frying pan and chopping mango that he put in bowls with yogurt and muesli.

She should have offered to help, but the last thing she needed was to bump elbows with him again. She sat at the dining table, where she could watch him without being too obvious about it.

"What will you tell her?" she asked.

"It's more what she'll tell me," he said sardonically. "She's my father's older sister, the matriarch on his side of the family and traditional in her views. That's a Catholic church she's attending today. She sees it as her place to ensure I live my life right and she also misses my father. She wants to see him reflected in the next generation. That means I ought to marry and start producing little Sylvains. I respect all of that."

But not with you, Eden heard silently tacked onto the end of that.

I can't take another chance, he had said last night. He hadn't wanted to up their risk of pregnancy.

For a few minutes on the beach, she had quit obsessing over what had happened between them and simply enjoyed what the morning and his world had to offer. Now her thoughts were drifting back to what had almost felt like a dream, if she hadn't awakened to see her half-empty glass of water on the counter.

"Can I take your car after breakfast? I need to pick up a few things," she said, purely because she needed an escape from this pressured awareness.

"Salt tablets?" he asked.

"And clothes. Maybe a laptop so I can work. A salon." She could take out the clip-in extensions herself. She had planned to do it on the flight to Greece, but what she really needed was space and time away from him.

"My sister has one she likes. I'll make a call to get you in. I'll take you to the boutiques she likes, too. Let me know the specs on the laptop. I'll see what I can find while you're getting your hair done."

Great. More time together.

"Finish that," he said sternly, as she started to set aside her glass.

"It's honestly not a big deal. I've fainted on a beach before and I still live a rich and fulfilling life." She had also fainted in the shower once and wound up with a goose egg, but she kept that to herself.

She broke their staring contest first, noticing in the daylight that the wall of photos had an empty hook. Weird.

The buzz of Remy's phone and the cynical snort he released distracted her from asking about it, though.

"What's wrong?" she asked.

"Hunter is asking if I still want to be his best man."

"He's marrying that woman?" Amelia? Was that her name?

"Tomorrow."

"Wow." It wasn't that shocking, but it was awfully fast. And it really blew out the last candle on the Hunter-will-save-BH&G cake.

"Are you upset?"

"No." She caught him eyeing her with skepticism and realized with a crumple of her last shred of pride that she would have to tell him the rest. "I had another reason for marrying him. BH and G is in trouble. Serious trouble. He knew," she said quickly as Remy's eyebrows shot up. "We talked about it when we started dating. He and I worked out that expansion of his network technology using our store properties as part of our marriage agreement."

"RuralReach. That's off now?"

"My team is confident they can rescue it, but new terms will have to be worked out. It's definitely delayed. Hunter was planning a substantial investment as well. I was okay with sharing ownership with him when I was planning to have his children. Now he's just another business partner and I'm less comfortable allowing him so much influence in my company." She swirled the dregs of the hydration tablet in the last of her water and knocked it back. "That will happen, anyway, if I can't come up with another option, though."

"Why hasn't your brother bailed you out?"

"Mama refuses to let him! She has scruples against taking Kelvin's money even though he's *dead*." She rubbed at a chip in her nail polish. "I won't go against her wishes, though. I'm having some of our personal properties assessed, but that takes time and probably won't raise enough capital. Not as fast as we need it, anyway."

"Are you asking for my help?" He brought their dishes to the table.

"*No*. I'm arming you with a reason to tell your aunt why we can't marry. I'm a money pit."

"What if you're pregnant?"

"I didn't plan for that condom to break, Remy."

"I know that," he said evenly, reaching back for the

cutlery before taking his seat. "I'm simply exploring what might happen if you are."

"Marrying for money did not work out for me," she noted bitterly.

"Because you didn't marry."

"Quit acting like this is something you would consider doing!"

"I'm obliged by my position as president of Can-Carib Airlines to evaluate all opportunities that are presented to me. Hunter is a shrewd businessman. He wouldn't tie himself to a sinking ship. There must have been benefits that went beyond using the Bellamy name to clean up Wave-Com's reputation." His flickering gaze across her shoulders and throat said, *Besides the obvious.*

Her stomach pitched.

"Will you send me the contract so I can review it?" he asked.

"What are you thinking? Travel agencies within the store to book tropical vacations? I don't see it, especially out west. Hawaii is a shorter flight and Mexico is cheaper. Also, our brand is stay-cation. Camping and outdoor sports like hiking and hockey."

"Martinique's economy is too reliant on tourism. It needs to diversify. A fresh distribution market through a trusted franchise in Canada would allow the export sector to expand."

"Hmm." She tucked her chin in her hand. "My father always played the buy-Canadian card. It was the way we differentiated ourselves from the big-box, lowest-price chains. Things are so global now, it's been hard to stick to that. What kind of products would we carry?"

"Let's see." He looked to the ceiling. "Spices. Hammocks. Plants," he said with a tone of discovery. "'Can't get away this winter? Bring a taste of the tropics into your home with an orchid or a hibiscus.'"

"'Bring the garden into your home.' That works." She nodded. "But are you really willing to throw a pile of your own money at my company to make that happen? A *lot* of money?"

His expression shuttered and he stabbed a bite of fish cake. "If you're pregnant with my child? Absolutely."

If she was pregnant. Her heart twisted and she looked to her own meal.

Back to wait and see.

Remy could have left Eden at the pharmacy, but he stuck around to ensure they had what she needed to increase her blood pressure. Once he was reassured she wouldn't faint again, he left. The salon was only a block away and he had to drive across the island to the computer store.

He brooded the entire way.

He was glad to finally understand why Eden and Hunter had gotten as far as they had, but he was also annoyed. He was really freaking irritated that Hunter had roped her into an arranged marriage to save her business, then left her in the lurch. He was even more irritated that he cared. It was not his job to solve her romantic or business problems.

On the other hand, if he did have a baby with her, he wanted to be prepared. While he waited for the laptop, he sent some messages, setting up a discreet team to explore opportunities with Bellamy Home and Garden and forwarding to them the copy of the marriage contract she had sent him.

Marriage. He already knew that's what Auntie Celeste would suggest. It was very much her belief that if you took a chance on making a life with someone, you ought to be prepared to make a life with them.

In other circumstances, he would be.

Remy shook off that childish wish. *This* was his circumstance. It wasn't only his aversion to her brother, or the promises he had made to his father and himself, promises to love and protect and support his family. He wasn't a perfectionist—okay, he was—but he forgave himself the mistake of kissing Eden years ago. He hadn't known who she was then.

He expected more honorable behavior from himself now, though. Still, he had made love to her, knowing she was off-limits, and he was her *first* lover. That came with its own set of expectations he hadn't been prepared to meet.

Last night? What the hell was that if not pure self-indulgence? He could rationalize all he wanted that they hadn't risked pregnancy again, but what he had done was not exactly heroic.

Eden was dangerous to him. She had hung around in his head for years and, when he was around her, he abandoned his core principles. If she wasn't pregnant, he definitely couldn't marry her.

If she was... Hell, he didn't know what he would do.

He was still ruminating on her and self-control and what made a man a man as he visited the bakery near her salon, then set his purchases in the back seat of his open convertible.

His masculine eye was snagged by a woman walking toward him, swinging a few shopping bags. The wide skirt of her simple blue dress stopped midcalf and a line of buttons all the way down the front broke up the block of color. Her lips were painted a shimmery pink, her eyes were behind cat's-eye sunglasses and her hair was in shoulder-length braids.

His whole body twisted with such craving, he had to

bite back a groan. Maybe he hadn't recognized Eden right away, but his body had. Her. It always had to be her.

"Perfect timing." Eden set her bags in the trunk as he popped it. "That's everything, except I'd like to get something for your aunt."

"Done." He pointed toward the back seat.

"Merci." She shook back her braids. The gold cuffs on the ends clicked together cheerfully. "I love that everyone speaks French here. Well, and Creole, obviously. I overheard some at the salon, but didn't catch any of it. I'd love to learn, though. I think I love everything about this place."

She radiated such happiness, he wanted to taste it. He wanted to cup her face and seal his mouth to hers and drink up her bubbly bliss. He wanted to kiss the hell out of her in the middle of the street.

He moved to open her door. "We should get home and unpackage your laptop. They always have to run a bunch of updates before they're any use."

Her bright mood faded slightly, but she only nodded as she slipped into her seat. "Good advice."

Yeah, he was chock-full of practical ideas. Too bad he wasn't capable of following any.

"Can I help with anything?" Eden offered when they arrived to find Celeste cooking on her outdoor stove.

"No, you sit. I make this fricassee in my sleep." Celeste waved her to the patio, where there was a table with four regular chairs and a rocker nearby. She had changed into a more casual, loose-fitting dress and had switched to a lightweight turban-style head wrap in robin's-egg blue.

"You're supposed to ask the housekeeper to cook," Remy reminded her, dropping a peck on her cheek. He reared back right before he got a wooden spoon in the kisser.

"Flore-Aline cooks for company. I cook for family. Fetch the salad from the refrigerator. Wait." She eyed the boxes he was carrying. "What did you bring me?"

"Macarons."

"That's why you're my favorite nephew. Take them inside or I'll eat them now. Tell me about yourself, Eden." She turned her wide smile on her.

Eden leaped at the opportunity to reassure Celeste that she and Remy were *just friends*. She gave her an abbreviated version of her wedding disaster, playing up the drama of Amelia arriving with a baby, and turned it into a joke at her own expense.

"As you can imagine, my groom disappeared very *unceremoniously*."

Celeste chuckled, appreciating the pun, but shook her head, agog. "That was *yesterday*?"

"Yes." It seemed like a lifetime ago.

Remy appeared with a round of water and gave Eden one with the orange fizz of yet another electrolyte tablet. Seriously, Celeste was going to ask her next if she had a UTI because he had become Mr. Hydration and it was going right through her.

Eden obediently sipped and made sure he saw it before she continued.

"Remy was kind enough to save me from the worst of the publicity by bringing me here."

"Oh? Are you famous?" Celeste paused in her cooking to look at her.

"Not really. My father's father had a number of radio shows throughout his life, so the Bellamy name is familiar in broadcasting circles. Years ago, he recruited my mother to a call-in show for gardening tips. She still does it, but it's more a promo thing for the family's chain of home-and-garden stores. I recently inherited the company. No, the *famous* one—maybe I should call him infamous?—was my groom. Actually, do you know Hunter Waverly?" Eden cocked her head. "Remy's friend?"

"You were marrying Hunter Waverly?" Celeste's voice went up several octaves and she shot a look at Remy. "Would he be the father of your—" Her spoon drew a circle in the general vicinity of Eden's middle.

"No," Eden and Remy said together.

"It's complicated, Auntie," Remy added.

"I'll bet."

Eden bit her lips together and kept her gaze on the paving stones beneath Celeste's feet.

Celeste went back to her pans and soon dished up. Conversation switched to lighter topics while they enjoyed a delicious meal of conch fricassee with rice and spicy avocado balls.

Afterward, Eden excused herself to the washroom. She heard Remy's and Celeste's murmured voices through the open window, but they were speaking Creole. She wished she knew what he was saying, but supposed it was best to let him make their explanations however he saw fit.

She came out of the washroom and was confronted by a fresh wall of family photos. She immediately became lost. Why these sorts of displays fascinated her so much, she wasn't sure, but she was always a sucker for them. Maybe it was because both her grandmothers had had them. They felt like home.

They also told interesting stories with their fashions and hairstyles, the backgrounds of gardens and homes and the style of the photos themselves. Mostly, she loved the emotions. Here was naked affection between siblings on a beach, the water and sky faded by age while their love was still clear and vibrant. There was an earnest smile from a child to her photographer, her closed lips suggesting she was self-conscious of lost teeth.

Eden remembered that feeling and smiled with sympathy.

"Eden?"

"Oh, I know, I'm sorry. I couldn't resist. You look so much like your father and his brothers, don't you? And the girls all look like your aunt. This whole side of your family stamps everyone out like carbon copies. I don't know why I find that so endearing, but I do. Your sister takes after your mother, though. They're both so pretty."

Except— The strangest thing happened. A trick of light on the glass of the frame over a preadolescent snapshot triggered the most bizarre, random sense of... *I know that face.*

Eden had seen Yasmine's photo online with Remy. They were all pictures of her as an adult with her tall, curvy frame, her ultrachic clothing, her hair in locs and her femininity emphasized with bold eyeliner and thick lashes, and lip colors like blue and mauve. She was clearly artistic and effusive.

Yasmine had her mother's skin tone, too—lighter than Remy's and his father's. Lighter than her mother, actually. As Eden stared at a nine-or ten-year-old girl, she saw another, similarly aged face. One that was Caucasian, before he had grown facial hair and thick eyebrows and a hard jaw and an Adam's apple.

"Oh, my God." She backed into the opposite wall and leaned there, afraid she would faint again for an entirely different reason.

"Eden."

Remy's voice came from the other side of the universe, but it was so quiet, it might as well have been inside her own head. He knew what she was seeing. He knew that she knew and she knew that he knew.

She began to shake. "Does Micah know?"

Remy seemed to be holding himself under such pressure, she half expected him to split out of his own skin. His head jerked once in negation, but it was his only movement. The rest of him was held in paralytic stillness, the way one stood when facing a deadly viper looking for an excuse to strike.

"No one does," he rasped. "Yasmine doesn't."

Why not? Eden tried to say it, but the ugly truth hit her like a meteor—jagged and explosive. Devastating.

CHAPTER TEN

"EDEN DOESN'T FEEL WELL," Remy told his aunt. Neither did he.

Auntie Celeste was a medical doctor, but she was also a woman shrewd enough to glance between them and understand something emotionally catastrophic had occurred.

"Take her home to rest then," she murmured.

Remy did and, once there, followed her into the living room where she sank, zombie-like, onto the sofa. He was too restless to sit and felt her gaze follow him as he paced.

"How…?" Her voice strangled on the word.

Remy began to talk without making the conscious decision to do so.

"After my dustup with Micah, my parents were worried Gould would start harassing them again, impacting the lives they'd made in Canada. That's when my father told me the first part—the part I told you. He insisted they'd been robbed and told me not to get into any more shoving matches with Micah." *Stay as far from him as you can.*

"The next time we had a game with that school, Micah was gone. I mostly forgot about the whole thing. A few years went by, then Yasmine got sick. It turned out to be a blood disorder that she has since learned to manage, but at the time they thought it might be leukemia. By then I was closer to fourteen, capable of researching what a bone-marrow transplant was. I said I wanted to donate mine. My mother brushed me aside. It was…" He pinched the bridge of his nose, still hurt at how abruptly she had dismissed him.

Don't be foolish. You can't.

"It was trying times for them. Obviously. My mother wanted my sister to be well, but I overheard her arguing with my father. What if they had to ask *him*. What if he *took* her?"

"Oh." Eden breathed in a sense of discovery.

"Yes. That was their greatest fear, right from the beginning. I cornered my father and he completely broke down, terrified that he would have to go crawling to Kelvin Gould to save his daughter's life. Terrified that Gould would let Yasmine die, rather than help her, purely out of spite. He swore me to secrecy, of course. Then Yasmine came out of hospital and I carried that secret with him." *For* him. "I never even told my mother that I knew."

He rubbed the center of his chest where the weight of it felt heavy enough to crack his sternum.

"It wasn't an affair, was it?" Eden asked sadly. "Did your mother go to the police?"

"No. She didn't even tell my father right away. He was working in the Netherlands, finalizing that prestigious contract. He was on top of the world when he came home. She had recently been awarded a lucrative research grant. He could tell she wasn't herself, but she made excuses. She told him later that she was trying to pretend it hadn't happened. She couldn't keep pretending once she realized she was pregnant. She honestly didn't know if Gould or Dad was the father."

Eden released a sob of agony. "Can you imagine that decision?" she asked in a voice scraped thin with anguish. She pressed the heels of her hands into her eyes. "I'm so sorry, Remy. So sorry she went through that. That you all did."

"It's not all tragedy. Yasmine is a gift. We all love her. It's not her fault that—" He couldn't finish.

"I know," she murmured. "I can tell you love her with everything in you."

"I do." He rubbed his face, trying to work feeling into his numb skin. "But loving her doesn't mean my parents weren't angry. Mom couldn't stay where she might see Gould. She suggested the move to Canada and my father agreed, but it was too much for him to let Gould benefit from what he'd developed. He struck back the only way he could. The only way that mattered to Gould."

"Money," Eden said, guessing.

"Yes. He threw his laptop in the river and sent the backup files anonymously to the competitor."

She nodded slowly, taking in all of what he'd said while tangling her fingers in her lap. Her thick lashes lifted.

"But all of them are gone now. Why haven't you told her?"

"I can't." His voice grew unsteady just thinking it. "I don't care where the DNA came from that made her. She is my sister in all the ways that matter and I will protect her with every fiber of my being. Even from—*especially* from—information that could destroy her."

Eden started to say something, but thought better of it and swallowed it back.

"You took down her photo." She pointed at the wall. "You knew I would guess."

"I forgot about the ones at my aunt's house." Had he, though? Or was he so weary of carrying this heavy secret, he'd allowed her to discover it?

He went long periods without really thinking about it,

but lately it had sat like a pearl in an oyster, growing bigger and more intrusive the more he tried to ignore it.

Because it stood between him and Eden?

This was why she was such a danger to him! He had not only broken his father's confidence, but he had also broken it with *her*.

"Remy." Her voice was very quiet. Very grave. "Micah needs to know."

"No." He swept his hand through the air with finality.

"He can't keep thinking your family is the one who wronged his."

"Have I just made the worst mistake of my life by trusting you?" he asked in his hardest voice.

"I won't tell him." She sat straighter. "But you know I'm right. This feud has to stop."

"No. He has to grow up and leave me alone. We all have to keep our distance." He pushed his hands through the air, feeling a pang in his chest as he included her.

"I disagree." She swallowed and sat even taller as she seemed to gather her courage. "I think we should marry."

"What?" Remy's eyebrows crashed together.

Eden's heart flipped over. Her thoughts were tripping over each other, taking in crimes and astonishing outcomes, so much pain and blame and protectiveness and love. At the heart was an innocent woman who deserved to know her kin, even if she didn't know he was kin.

"We have to become a family. *She* has to become Micah's family."

"Yasmine doesn't need a family like his," Remy growled.

"Micah can't help the family he grew up in." Eden rose to pace off her agitation. "My mother did what she could, but he was his father's heir. He wasn't given a choice about stepping into his father's shoes and running an empire—"

"He had a choice," Remy interrupted scathingly. "We all have choices."

"Yes. I have the choice to walk away from my father's legacy, too." She waved a hand. "If I don't want to marry for money, I can sell off rural branches and doom small communities to driving out of town for their housewares. The choices we're faced with aren't always good ones."

"That is why you want to marry me." His pointed finger stabbed the air. "To save your company. Don't pretty it up."

His words went straight into her like a blade, but all she could think of was Micah and the emotional deprivation of his childhood. She and her mother had poured love all over him when they could, but it hadn't been enough. That's why he was such a hardened cynic. It broke Eden's heart that he had missed all those years with his other sister. That Yasmine had missed getting to know him. That she had been taught he was the enemy.

"I want to right the scale." Eden's voice cracked under the pressure of her emotions. "This feud has to stop. Micah and your sister deserve to know each other, even if they don't know they share genetics."

"They'll figure it out if they're sitting across the dinner table, won't they? Then she has to learn what his father did to our mother. No, Eden. It can't happen."

"Remy." She wanted to stamp her foot, but settled on rubbing her eyebrows with her thumb and fingertip, trying to find a delicate way to say this. "In the same way you believe your baby would have a right to your fortune, I know that Micah would feel Yasmine has a right to a share in his."

"She doesn't want a cent of that." His lip curled in disgust.

"That's not your decision to make, is it? She's an adult. You're treating her like a child."

"She doesn't need anything from him," he insisted. "She has a vibrant career and she already has a brother who will step in if she needs anything she can't get for herself."

"Careful. You're starting to sound jealous."

The dangerous flash in the grim bronze of his gaze chilled her blood, but she continued making her point.

"Micah knows his father was rotten to his core. He has made countless changes—at his own expense—to repair things and ensure the company is more ethical moving forward." Micah had returned ill-gotten art and donated questionably obtained properties to the indigenous people they'd been appropriated from. There had been an infamous "winter cull," when a number of executives had been fired for various harassment complaints and other corruptions. "By refusing any part of Kelvin's fortune, you're allowing him to continue avoiding the consequences of his actions, even after he's dead."

Remy bared his teeth in a snarl of dismay, rejecting a truth he didn't want to hear.

"Micah would want to do what he could to right this wrong. He would want to compensate your family for your parents' lost careers and damaged reputations. I understand why you want to distance yourself. You want to protect your sister. I will respect that, but at least let me make reparations on his behalf."

"This has nothing—"

"Don't tell me it has nothing to do with me!" she cried. "If that history hadn't happened, you and I would have a very different relationship right now. Wouldn't we?" Her voice dropped to a more tentative pitch.

He looked away, not confirming or denying, which left her heart trembling in her chest.

"I'm in the middle of this cold war whether I like it or not," she said, pretending she hadn't needily asked him to tell her he wanted her. "Let me try to fix it."

"By letting me buy in to your company?" he snorted. "Gee, thanks."

"It will be to your advantage. I'll ensure it." She crossed her arms, trying to stem the ache emanating from the pit of her stomach at the risk she was taking. "You'll have enough control that you could annihilate my company. You can exact your final revenge, if that's what makes you happy. You can also ignore my situation and let my company go to hell and leave Micah to stand by helpless as it happens."

"I'm not like that," he growled.

"I know. I trust you. And Micah will be suspicious of whatever arrangement we come to, but this is my company and my decision. He'll have to accept it." She could already feel the weight of her brother's disapproval. Her mother's shock and concern. "At least there would be a cease-fire. Then, as you bring Bellamy back from the brink instead of ruining us, Micah will start to believe you don't have it in for him. If Yasmine were ever to find out, do you want to still be at odds with Micah? Or on civil terms?"

Remy made another animalist noise of discontent, turning away as he asked, "What would you get?"

You.

Was that her real motive? To spin out her time with him as long as she possibly could?

"I get to keep my company instead of watching it be stripped for parts." She hugged herself harder. "Our marriage doesn't have to be forever. It could be in name only and we could divorce in a year, if that's what you want. You would still have a stake in BH and G and Micah would still have to behave himself."

"And if you are pregnant, we'll marry, anyway."

She flashed him a startled look, heart swerving in her chest.

"You had to know that's what I would want, Eden." He turned to face her. "What was my alternative? Watch the mother of my baby lose her company? Live apart from my child? Hide them? No, I was putting off saying it out aloud because..." He grimaced and rolled his wrist to encompass all he'd just revealed.

Was that really all he felt for her? Possibly the mother of his child, but not...more?

His hands landed on his hips and he hissed out a sigh. "I don't expect you to sacrifice yourself for someone else's actions. Gould wasn't your father. It's not your debt to pay."

Sacrifice. She bit the tremble from her lips.

"Micah is my brother. I know you haven't seen his softer side, but he has one. He's angry with you because of me. If he ever learns he has another sister, well, good luck being the only pit bull in the yard."

Remy brushed that aside, not wanting to consider that scenario. Right now, he was more concerned with keeping the secret of his sister's paternity so she wouldn't be hurt.

Eden had a point, though. If Yasmine ever found out, it would be a softer blow if he and Micah had found some common ground first.

Or was that a rationalization so he could get what *he* really wanted?

"Would we...?" He searched her expression. "Continue trying for children?"

Her stomach sucked in and she swallowed. "If you want."

"It has to be something *you* want," he replied with such force she took a step back. "Consent is mandatory." He had just explained why.

"Sex and babies are two different things." Her lashes swept down to hide her eyes. "I assumed we would have sex. I wasn't sure about the babies." She hugged herself and cleared her throat. "But consent goes both ways, obviously."

Good God. He ran a hand down his face while his heart fishtailed in his chest.

This was madness. Madness.

If there hadn't been such an urgency to resolve her business problem, he wouldn't rush into it. They might have had a quiet affair until this lust had burned itself out. In a corner of his mind, he knew that marrying her would ignite multiple bushfires in both their families, not to mention impacting his friendship with Hunter. He knew his relationship with his sister could be changed forever.

All so he could openly bring Eden into his home and his bed.

"Are you prepared for the kind of pushback we'll get?" he asked, fearful she wasn't clear-eyed to the repercussions.

"It's the right thing to do, even if we're the only ones who know it."

He wasn't strong enough to say no.

"Then we'll marry as soon as possible."

CHAPTER ELEVEN

REMY HAD SUCH a calm, unruffled persona, Eden had un-
derestimated how fast he moved when he decided on something.

She supposed she had seen it before, when he invited her
to that club after exchanging a handful of words. Also at
the wedding, when he ordered her into his car without any
waffling and when he had made love with her very sponta-
neously, then brought her to Martinique at the last second.

None of that made their decision to marry seem any
less reckless than it was. At least with Hunter, she had a
solid friendship with his sister and had dated Hunter long
enough to get to know him a little.

Her relationship with Remy continued to be a headlong
rush toward possible disaster. What if Micah had been
right all along and Remy was out to destroy her while she
was too infatuated to see it?

Knowing Micah would presume exactly that kept her
from telling her brother what she was planning. Her mother
would be equally alarmed, so she kept her in the dark, too.

The secrecy heightened her anxiety. It made her feel she
was doing something wrong, but there was value in keeping her nuptials under wraps. Those investors who were
rubbing their hands with greedy glee, expecting to oust
her, would be ambushed by her announcement. She would

throw the switch on their takeover before they had time to make any other dirty ploys. In fact, with her stock price down, Remy was buying up as much as came available, helping her cement their combined ownership.

As for the contracts, they modified the agreements she had negotiated with Hunter. Her groom would still own a huge chunk of BH&G, but unless she was incapacitated, Remy was obliged to support her leadership.

All of that should have reassured her, but Remy moved with such lightning speed and determination, she felt pounced upon. His decisions were made like a blade cutting through inconvenient obstructions, forcing a path toward his goal. Yes to this paragraph, no to that. Chop, sweep, get us *there*.

In the midst of her double-checking the legalese on the new contracts, he broke in with fresh information.

"Martinique has a month-long residency requirement. So does France. We can marry in Gibraltar within a day, so we'll tie the knot there after we attend my aunt and uncle's anniversary party. Where is your birth certificate? I'm chartering a flight for my assistant to meet us with my own documents."

"It's at my apartment." She blinked in bemusement. "Quinn might be there. She offered to take my suitcases to my apartment. I told her to stay there if she wants to."

Quinn usually spent her summers working in PEI, where rent costs were lower, but she had begun her doctorate and was looking for accommodation closer to the university.

She picked up the video chat right away. Her red hair was in a messy bun, her freckled face clean of makeup, and she was wearing a loose-fitting T-shirt with stars and moons on it. Eden's kitchen was behind her.

"Are you okay?" Quinn asked without even saying hello.

"Yes." Eden was taken aback by her urgent tone. "Why?"

"Because you were publicly thrown over two days ago! You're allowed to be an emotional wreck."

"Oh. Right." Eden spared a moment to take stock. Her veins were stinging with the stress of having a lot to do, her emotions were reeling over the news that Micah had another sister, but her mind was clear and her heart... Her heart felt stretched in every direction. "I'm not *great*. These last two days have been a lot." Understatement of the year. "But I'm doing well enough."

"Okay. I'm glad." Quinn didn't sound convinced. "Because I can come if you need me. Just say the word."

"Thank you. I—" Eden was genuinely touched. She loved her mother and brother with everything in her, but Quinn was like a sister. "I actually need your help. And I have to ask you to keep it a secret."

"I'll put it in the vault with the rest of them," she vowed promptly.

"You're the best." Eden curled her legs beneath her. "Can you go into my office? There's a key under the plant on the windowsill. It opens the middle drawer on the desk. I need my birth certificate."

Quinn was no dummy. She set down her mug and her expression became very grave.

"You know I'll do anything for you, Eden, but it's been *two days*. At least you got to know Hunter. Even at that, you didn't know enough."

"I know it sounds impulsive, but it's for the company." That was partially true, at least.

"Your dream was always to marry for love," Quinn reminded her. Pleaded almost. "That's why I was so hesitant about you marrying Hunter. You have always wanted what your mom had with your dad because your childhood was so much better than Micah's. Saving BH and G shouldn't come at the expense of your own wants and needs. You know that, right?"

"It won't," Eden insisted, even as her stomach clenched with fretfulness. "It's complicated, but can you please trust me when I say I'm in my right mind and doing what needs to be done?"

"I trust *you*."

"But Micah has poisoned you against trusting Remy." Eden sighed. "Was he awful when you got up to the hotel room in Niagara Falls?"

"He wasn't pleased." Quinn started down the hall.

"I'm sorry I jumped ship. Please tell me you enjoyed the room at least."

"Erm." Quinn plonked the phone onto the desktop so all Eden could see was the ceiling. Quinn's voice sounded higher, almost strained, but maybe she was simply pitching her tone so Eden could hear her as she moved to the window. "He did his yeti act, blamed me for being your best friend rather than his informant. I finished the wine and had a bath. Enjoyed the view."

"Good."

"Which is pretty much what I'm doing here. There's paparazzi downstairs. They know I know you and keep trying to come up. But, hey, Vienna lives in the building. You never told me that. We're having drinks later."

"I thought you knew. But their apartment is a convenience. They live in Calgary."

"Really? I must have misunderstood her. Okay, I found the certificate. What now?" Quinn came back on the screen to show it.

"Put it in an envelope, lock the drawer and—"

A noise at the door made Eden glance up. Her heart lurched when she saw Remy there. How long had he been listening?

"Would you like her there?" Remy asked quietly.

"Where?" Eden frowned.

His head tilt said, *You know.*

Their wedding? Eden swallowed and nodded jerkily. She wanted someone who loved her at her wedding, seeing as her groom didn't.

"There's room on the flight. Tell her my assistant will send her the details." He walked away.

Ridiculously moved, she blinked her hot eyes as she asked Quinn, "Would you like a free trip to Europe?"

"Always. But seriously, are you okay? Be real." Quinn frowned with concern.

"I am. I promise you, I am," she lied. "But I have to go. Remy's assistant will be in touch."

She ended the call, her chest tight with emotion. It was nothing for Remy to add a body to a flight and cover a few nights at a hotel. Such a small gesture shouldn't mean this much to her, but it did and she knew why.

Quinn was right. Eden *had* always wanted to marry for love. It was hitting her that she was. It was too soon, way too soon, to believe herself in love, but she was halfway there. Remy was considerate. He was protective and valued family. And the more she got to know him, the more she was convinced that he was *worthy* of her love.

Even so, she felt as though she was sliding down a well-greased slope, careening at an uncontrolled speed toward… The unknown. A broken heart maybe?

Remy still regarded her as an enemy of sorts. At best, they would be business partners with benefits.

Now would be the time to call a halt to this madness, but she wouldn't. Couldn't. She had never been able to forget him, and marrying him, being with him, felt bigger than necessary. It felt done. Whether they went through the legal process of marrying or not, whether she had his child or not, she was linked to him forever. She was his and had been for a very long time.

It made for more hot tears against her eyes. They blurred the future she was sketching for herself. What if she was making a horrible mistake?

They flew overnight to Paris.

Eden was still feeling raw, aware that her attraction to Remy was far beyond fantasy and infatuation. It was a very earnest yearning for him to feel as she did. To want her in the same all-encompassing ways she wanted him.

They shared a light meal, talking of incidentals to do with the contracts and what sort of gown she should procure for the party, but the air crackled with discordant tension.

When they were finally left alone, Remy said gravely, "I heard what Quinn said, about your wanting to marry for love. Is that true?"

Eden wished she could make some quip about love being a luxury she couldn't afford. She wished she could downplay her dream as a childish whim.

Instead, she asked unsteadily, "Isn't that what most people want? Don't you?" She tried to make the question a mild one, but her heart was tripping in her chest.

He took his time answering, voice heavy when he said, "Love makes you so damned vulnerable. I've never wanted more than liking and respect."

His words went into her like twin stilettos. How could he like and respect her when she was related to his enemy and needed his money?

This was exactly how she had felt after Paris, when she

had put herself out there, been open and receptive and excited and suffused with attraction, only to be struck back with a hard knock from reality. Five years ago, Micah's words had made her feel callow and wrong to want so much from Remy. Today was the same, as she reckoned with his not having any real feelings for her. And he didn't want to have them.

Each of her breaths burned inside her lungs.

"I would argue that I am marrying for love," she said and heard his sharply indrawn breath. "Micah doesn't know that I'm doing this for him, but love isn't transactional. It's something you feel by giving, not getting."

As she sat in the truth of her words, some of her misgivings dissipated.

"I don't want to hurt you, Eden. Then I would be exactly what Micah is warning you against—someone who used his sister to get what he wants."

"What do you want?"

"You," he said with pained remorse.

A pang of agonized pleasure went through her.

"You already have me." She felt positively naked as she said it, barely able to meet his eyes, but she needed him to know this was about more than money and family secrets and potential babies. She needed it to be about *them*.

He held her gaze with facets of bronze and copper and gold all churning in his eyes.

She swallowed and had to look away, but as he rose, her heart swerved in her chest, swooping and dipping, then soaring as he held out his hand. She set her fingers on his palm and watched them disappear in the gentle crush of his grip.

He led her into the jet's sumptuous stateroom, where a pale bar of indirect light glowed above the bed. When he closed the door, the click of the lock sounded like the mechanism on a vault.

The way his gaze slid over her made every inch of her burn.

"I don't want to fall in love because even this…" He cupped her face. "This craving consumes me. I don't believe in witchcraft, but it's like a spell. I don't want to be helpless to it."

She dropped her gaze to his throat. His Adam's apple bobbed as he swallowed. Her mouth must have pouted with her disappointment because his thumb slid across her bottom lip.

"That wasn't blame. I'm trying to tell you to be careful. Don't see this as more than it is."

"You think I'm not cursed in the same way?" she asked with a trace of bitterness. She tilted back her head in time to see him flinch.

Then his mouth was on hers, his kiss long and thorough, not rough, but not gentle. There was a taste of regret when he drew back enough to look into her eyes.

"It feels like something bigger than I can control. That makes it destructive." His voice was quiet, but his words reverberated in her ears, leaving her trembling, but not in fear. In excitement.

Her hands rose to grip his wrists. "Destroy me, then."

Their next kiss was all the more powerful, imbued with the desperate longing that had gripped her ever since he had kissed her in a nightclub then glared at her with betrayal.

That anxious yearning had her pressing closer, fingers clenching into his shirt while her body flowered with need as she absorbed the warmth of his. She needed to take all of him into her. *All of him.*

He made a noise that seemed equally tormented and

his arms hardened around her. He crushed her close and she reveled in that small ache of her bones and joints and flesh in the vise of his embrace. She gloried in the enormous hunger that drove him to do it.

They dropped their clothes away and it was all about contact. Touching and caressing, claiming and tasting and sighing at the sheer bliss of holding each other. They rolled back and forth as she splayed herself across him, legs interlaced with his, breasts loving the friction of hair on his chest. He pressed her beneath him and pinned her hips with the weight of his thigh, then teased her ear with his tongue and scraped his teeth against her throat. She pushed him onto his back and his hands skated down her waist and hips, claimed her backside and swept up for the weight of her breasts.

Wisps of doubt floated in her periphery, making her wonder if they would burn each other to cinders, but she brushed away the thought, letting the miasma of sensuality engulf her. In this moment, they had and were everything. She worshipped the heat of his neck and the hollow beneath his ear and the scorch of his hard shaft against her damp, aching sex. She gloried in the way his palms drew circles at her waist and hips and buttocks, while his mouth drank from hers again and again.

She loved his smell.

She loved him. She loved him so much.

A skeptical voice asked, *How?* But a stronger voice countered, *How could she not?* He had so many admirable qualities. Sexy and physically strong, but strong in character, too. Protective and principled and loyal. He was funny and capable of forgiveness, and he stilled to cup her face, forcing her to meet the banked lust in his gaze while he asked huskily, "Are you still with me?"

"Yes." She wanted to tell him she was falling so deeply in love, she would be with him forever, but she feared he would push her away. Her eyes were wet and she felt foolish for being so emotional, but... "I really want this. You."

She wanted to pour her love over him so she could wallow in the beauty of it.

She melted onto him and ran her lips across his chest and stomach, and lower, making him groan. His hand squeezed her shoulder, cupped her neck, caressed her cheek.

"No more," he finally said in a husky, tortured voice that thrilled her.

He dragged her upward until she straddled him again.

"Condoms are in the drawer," he said.

Their gazes locked. She wanted to say it wasn't necessary. She wanted to marry him and have his babies and grow old together.

She did as he asked and retrieved one, then tried to put it on him, only to hear him as he rasped, "Are you trying to destroy *me*?"

With a soft laugh, she let him take over rolling the condom onto his length, then rose to guide him into her, so deliciously satisfied when she was finally connected to him again. She splayed her hands on his chest and felt his heart beat against her palm. The strong, uneven rhythm traveled up her arm, made her own pulse skip, then filled her heart to overflowing.

This was love. It had to be because it was too perfect to be anything else. It was generosity and sharing and vulnerability. It was such incredible dedication to ensuring the other's pleasure, it could only be that beautiful, all-powerful force.

It held her in its tender, unbreakable grip as they began to move in flawless synchronicity.

Despite their exhaustive lovemaking, Remy didn't get much sleep.

He reached for Eden in the night, half-lost to a heart-stopping dream that she wasn't there. She slid close and murmured sweet nonsense. Moments later, they were immersed in passion and his dream was forgotten.

She woke him a few hours later, returning to bed chilled from a trip to the bathroom. Her cold foot found his shin and she ruefully apologized for waking him. Then her hand found his hardening flesh and she said, "Since you're awake…"

He couldn't seem to get enough of her.

Which worried him. It felt a lot like the way people hoarded necessities right before the supply was cut off. He felt as though he was storing up all the memories he could, from the explosive orgasms they gave each other to the sound of her breath when she was relaxed against his side, so he would have something when he had nothing.

They were marrying, though. She had said he already had her. Did she mean her heart?

He hoped not. He didn't want to hurt her, but he couldn't let himself fall for her. There would be an inevitable choice—her or his family. Such a split of loyalty would tear him apart.

He was already tense as hell at her meeting Yasmine at the anniversary party.

Perhaps Eden sensed it, or perhaps she was apprehensive as well. She was quiet through the day as she was fitted for a gown and went to bed early.

Remy made some calls, forewarning his aunt Hanameel whom he was bringing as his plus-one.

"You can't bring her here, Remy," she scolded. "After all that trouble she caused you and your cousin? She's one of *them*."

He drew a subtle breath of patience, understanding her concern, but he said, "Please don't judge her until you've had a chance to meet her, Auntie."

She *tsked* and acquiesced, but Eden was equally unsettled when her stylist arrived.

"Are you sure about this? I don't want to get between you and your family on your aunt and uncle's special day. If you'd rather leave me here…"

They were in a trendy apartment he owned in Paris, big enough for a bachelor who traveled frequently, but not ideal for a couple. Remy was already thinking about where they might look for something that would feel more like a home.

"I want them to meet you so it won't be such a shock when we marry. If they make you feel unwelcome, we'll leave."

"I don't want that!"

Neither did he. "We'll make it work. I promise. I have to run out for a few minutes, but I'll be back in time to change."

He went to a jeweler, where he bought her some earrings—diamond waterfalls in four columns that ended in a taper. He was thinking they would bring out the silver detailing in her gown, but he was unprepared for how well the gown would suit her.

She almost knocked him out of his tuxedo and into the wall.

Her hands fluttered against her strapless neckline and down the fitted silk against her hip. Long sleeves ran from her upper arms to her wrists, leaving her golden-brown skin naked across her shoulders and chest. A slit in one side of the skirt revealed her smooth thigh, her shapely calf. Lower, he took in her black suede sandals with silver heels. The hem of the gown was beaded with silver patterns that licked upward like flames.

"Is it okay?" She started to touch her hair, then thought better of it. She had released her natural curls so they were a bouncy, glossy halo with a side part.

"You're beautiful." He had to clear his throat. "I should have bought you a necklace, too." He opened the box and offered the earrings.

"You didn't have to— Oh." Her eyes widened. "I have these hoops." Her hand went to the thin gold he hadn't even noticed.

"Call it an engagement present."

"I still have to return the ring Hunter gave me," she murmured absently, seeming mesmerized by the earrings.

"Give it to me. I'll do it," he said in a surge of unmitigated possessiveness. "Will you wear these?"

"How could I not? They're stunning." Her look up at him was admonishing, but filled with helpless delight.

Minutes later, they were in the back of the car. He couldn't help angling to see his earrings glinting and sparkling through the shadowed interior, filling him with intense satisfaction that she had accepted them. That she wore his diamonds, not Hunter's.

Not that he was the sort of man who needed to put a stamp on "his" woman. He was genuinely relieved she wasn't in that marriage. She would have been deeply unhappy and he was sick with himself that he hadn't stopped it sooner.

Could he make her happy, though? He kept telling himself this was a business arrangement with a benefit of slaked lust, but what if his family rejected her? For Yasmine's sake, he wanted the hostility with Micah defused and hoped this marriage would do it, but walking into the actual party was a delicate dance on a minefield.

Eden was a naturally warm and gracious person, however. No matter how stiffly she was welcomed when he introduced her to different people, she smiled and showed genuine interest and soon charmed even his aunt Hanameel.

"She's easy to like, I'll grant you," she conceded when

they had a moment on a balcony, where they were catching a breath of air. "But what is your endgame, Remy? An affair with her will only stir up her brother against us. Do you love her? Is that it?"

She sounded so disapproving, he quickly said, "No, of course not."

It felt like a lie. His heart lurched, but he said it again, more firmly.

"I don't love her, but I can help her in ways that will put our feud to bed once and for all. That has to happen, Auntie. It can't continue."

She searched his gaze and he had a sudden thought—*she knows*. His heart swerved again. She was his mother's sister and perhaps had been his mother's confidante, but he looked away, refusing to confirm his own knowledge. It was too painful to consider.

"Secrets are as heavy as grudges. You know that, don't you?" She squeezed his arm.

A sensation hit his throat, one that made it seem as though all the air had been sucked from his lungs.

"You're neglecting your date, Remy," Yasmine said, forcing them both to turn to the open doors, where Yasmine as standing with Eden. Yasmine was her colorful, effusive self, wearing a wildly radiant and flowing pantsuit. Her locs were draped loosely around her shoulders, her lips were painted gold. "I could see her from across the room, standing here waiting for you to ask her to dance."

Eden gave him a wan smile. "I didn't want to interrupt."

With his joints feeling rusty, he made his excuses to his aunt and invited Eden onto the dance floor. She was stiff in his arms.

"If you overheard—"

"I like your sis—"

They both stopped speaking. He nodded to invite her to speak first.

"I like Yasmine a lot. She's so bubbly and hearing how she talks about art… She sounds like a creative genius. Your cousin said that fashion might be her bread and butter, but she can make bread and butter look like a masterpiece."

Remy forced a smile of amusement. "I can't disagree."

"Yasmine said her propensity for being consumed by art contributed to her recent breakup. It sounds like it was serious." Her lashes lifted as she tilted a look of deep understanding at him. "I see why you'd hesitate to hurt her, especially now."

He nodded in curt acknowledgment. Her recent heartbreak did make him that little bit more protective. So did that disturbing exchange with his aunt. Yasmine was no more vulnerable than the average Black woman. In fact, she had an incredible safety net in their large, wealthy family, but he wouldn't want her to feel as though any of that didn't belong to her or had slipped beyond her reach.

"Do you want to…?" Her lips rolled inward. "Invite her to…?"

Their wedding? It was partially for Yasmine's sake.

"Maybe."

One of his uncles cut in on him, eager to tell Eden about his award-winning roses. They didn't talk about it again until they were aboard the flight the next day.

"You decided against inviting Yasmine?" Eden asked cautiously when they were in the air.

Her heart was still stinging at overhearing him last night, when he had assured his aunt that he didn't love her.

"I didn't want to do it at the party. Too many people around. I texted her this morning, but she probably stayed late and was still asleep. I made arrangements for her to catch up with us if she wants to. There's time before the wedding tomorrow."

Technically, they could have married on arrival and stayed overnight to fulfill the residency requirement, but this way they had time to relax in their suite, make love then lazily rise and enjoy the setting.

Eden texted Quinn, inviting her to join them on their terrace for an aperitif, then stood at the rail to take in the view.

Across the placid sea, the muscled coastline of North Africa was silhouetted against the reds and golds of sunset. A light breeze rippled the caftan she was wearing. Her whole body felt like warm honey, her mood expansive and light.

Remy joined her, wearing only a pair of drawstring joggers that hung low across his hips. He braced his forearms on the rail and cocked one knee.

Eden nearly swallowed her tongue at how casually sexy he was. She set her hand on his shoulder and skated it across his sun-warmed back, purely because she could.

And because she liked hearing him catch his breath and feeling him twitch with pleasure under her touch.

"Where will we marry?" she asked, hearing her voice waver with the potent emotion taking her over.

"In the garden. There's a gazebo near a fountain. We're the eleven o'clock. They do this all the time." He turned his head. "Do you mind that it's small?"

"Gosh, no! As long as you show up, it will be the best day of my life." It was a lame joke at her own expense, but so true that she experienced a sharp ache in her chest. At the end of the day, that's all she would ever need. Him.

"I'll be there," he promised with a laconic smile. His

eyelids grew heavy and he straightened to drew her into his arms.

He needed a shave, but she liked the scrape on her palm as she cupped his jaw.

Everything in this moment was so perfect—the man who was soon to be her husband, the intimacy of this moment, the sureness inside her that this was meant to be—she couldn't stop the words from tumbling out of her.

"I love you."

He didn't move, but she felt the stillness that came over him. She saw the warm light fade from his expression.

"I...thought you should know." She felt as though she had stepped off this balcony and was now only held up by his strong arms—arms that were falling away from embracing her.

He licked his lips.

"I was hoping this could be a real marriage," she said hurriedly. "One where we plan to stay together all our lives, not just for now. One that's about *us*—"

"Eden, *stop*. You know I can't think like that. For God's sake, we barely know each other. This chemistry..." He waved between them. "That's all this is. You have to know that."

His words were such a blow, she stepped back and tried to swallow past the jagged ache in her throat.

"This *chemistry* has lasted five years. For me, at least," she added weakly. She turned her hot eyes to the horizon. "I wasn't asking for you to say you love me, only that maybe you could. That you *wanted* me forever."

"How can I say that when wanting you goes against what's best for my family? I've let myself be carried along by this...madness." He flicked his hand through the air. "It's selfishness on my part. I'm trying to convince myself I can have you, have sex, without consequences. Now you're telling me it will impact you in ways that—" His profile winced with deep torture. "I don't want you to love me. Why did you have to say it?"

She didn't have a response for that angry accusation. She was so hurt, she wanted to hurt him back. She wanted to say, *Because I don't lie. Because I don't hide things from people just because it's hard for them to hear it.*

That wasn't love, though.

She stood there encased in pain, mouth quivering, trying not to cry. Trying not to make it worse, but what could she do? What would *they* do?

Into the charged silence, she heard a knock on the interior door.

She seized the excuse to walk away from him. Maybe in the back of her mind she thought it would be Micah, but she should have known it would be Quinn.

"Hi!" Quinn's bright smile dropped off her face. "What...?"

"Take me to your room? Please?"

"Of course. Let's go."

CHAPTER TWELVE

REMY CAUGHT THE brunt of Quinn's accusatory glare as she swept her arm around Eden, but Eden didn't look back.

The door closed with a heavy click, leaving him with a knotted stomach and a sick taste of bile in the back of his throat.

How could she believe she loved him? How? It was too soon. She had to know that.

Yet he felt as though he had broken her heart. His own was tangled in canes of thorns.

This chemistry has lasted five years. For me, at least.

He pinched the bridge of his nose. Had he led her on, telling her how longing for her had gripped him all these years? It was physical, though. Wasn't it?

The jangle of the room phone crashed into his tortured ruminations.

He snatched it up, thinking that if it was Micah, he would gladly let the man kick his ass for hurting Eden.

"Remy?" It was Yasmine. "Can we talk?"

"You're here?" His heart nearly came out his throat. "Where? I'll come to you."

She told him and he quickly pulled on a shirt, trying to muster a semblance of clear thought at the same time. What should he tell her about asking her to come here? Was his marriage even still on?

Eden's need of financial help remained, but their marriage was also supposed to defuse the feud. It was supposed to bring Micah and Yasmine together without having to tell her the truth about her conception.

Everything in him balked at relaying that deeply painful truth to her, but his aunt's words came back to him. *Secrets are as heavy as grudges.*

He leaned against the wall of the elevator, nearly buckling under the weight of this one. Yasmine *was* an adult. Eden had gotten that right. He didn't want to tell his sister the truth, but he was starting to think he would have to. Not for any reason except that she deserved to know.

The doors opened and he moved with pained purpose down the hall, then rapped on her door and gathered himself for the difficult task as she opened it.

She was wearing torn jeans and a loose blue T-shirt. Her locs were gathered behind her neck with a yellow scarf and her face was clean of makeup. He might have dismissed her plain appearance as a slow start and a mild hangover, but her eyes were red and she seemed almost gray beneath her usually healthy glow.

"What's wrong?" he asked as she led him into the sitting area of her studio suite.

"Auntie Hanameel told me."

"Told you… What?" The words gusted out of him as though he'd been punched.

She nodded, seeming shell-shocked.

He did the only thing he could. He wrapped his arms around her and hugged her as hard as he could, feeling her trembling, but maybe that was him.

"I wanted to tell you myself. I didn't know how," he choked out.

She nodded jerkily, sniffing and holding on to him.

"It doesn't change a thing about who you are to me."

He was clenching his eyes against a sting of tears. "You are my sister and I love you. Always."

She nodded.

"How are you doing with it?" He drew back a little, trying to see her face.

"Shocked," she mumbled and wiped at her wet cheeks. "Maybe not as shocked as I ought to be. I always thought there was something different about me."

"You're perfect. Okay? Believe that? Please?"

She nodded, blinking her wet lashes, mouth still unsteady as she sank into a chair.

He folded into the one opposite.

"Why…? I only realized last night that Auntie might know." His voice was a dry layer peeled off his heart. "Why did she think today was the day?" He ran his hands up and down his thighs, guilt a heavy mantle on him as he suspected his bringing Eden to that party had been her impetus.

"She asked me to come see her this morning. She wanted to know if I thought you were serious about Eden. I said I imagined so, since you had texted me to meet you two in Gibraltar."

"You told her that?" He bit back a curse of remorse.

"I was excited. She said it was time I understood what the animosity between you and Eden's brother was really about." Her voice was unsteady. "Remy… Does he know?"

"Micah? No."

"Does Eden?"

"She guessed. She—" He rubbed his brow. "It's complicated. We made it complicated. I was trying to protect you, trying to end this feud, and really…" He shook his head as he opened his eyes to reality. "I think we were just trying to find a way to rationalize marrying and being together when our relationship isn't rational. I don't want to hurt you, sis. I've been trying to find a way to make it okay that I'm involved with someone who is related to…" He searched her face, not wanting to say it aloud.

"The son of my biological father? It's not Eden's fault. It's not Micah's. I'm going to need some time to put all of this right in my head, but I know there will come a time when I want to meet him to…" She shrugged. "See if… I don't know, if we have things in common? It's weird. It's like I found out I was adopted. I have questions, but I also need time."

"Of course." He reached across to squeeze her hand. "It's enough that I don't have to hide it from *you* anymore. I won't say a word to anyone."

"And Eden?"

"She wants him to know, but she won't tell him. I'm sure of that," he added as he read Yasmine's skepticism. "She's…" Eden was *good*. She was kind. She was loyal and so heart-forward it scared him.

It made it really easy to stand right on her softest feelings and grind them to dust.

He hung his head in his hands. His elbows dug into his knees.

"Did Auntie send you here to stop us marrying?" he asked.

"She didn't know what to think of you two, but I pointed out how you had barely taken your eyes off Eden all night. That you're in love with her." It was a statement, not a question.

"I am," he admitted to her and himself, realizing only as his inner being shook under the impact that he'd been plunged fathoms-deep over his head. "It doesn't make sense because we barely know each other, but I think I fell for her the moment I saw her. I don't even believe in love at first sight."

"Because you're like Daddy, wired for mechanics logic. You have never believed in things you couldn't see and touch. You think planes fly because of physics, never wanting to admit physics is an incantation."

He ran his tongue over his teeth, letting her have that one because her teasing meant she was coming out of her tailspin.

He wasn't. It was hitting him that he had pushed Eden away for exactly the reason she had just said—he didn't understand how his love for her had happened, so he struggled to believe it was real.

"Is love magic?" he asked with a break in his voice. "Can I conjure it back if I've ruined things with the only woman who will ever make me happy?"

She wasn't pregnant.

Eden had thought her situation couldn't get any worse and, logically, she knew this simplified things, but when she came out of the bathroom, she was even more devastated than when she'd gone in.

The thought of having Remy's baby had been such a sweet one. Losing that possibility was a hard blow, one that felt very final. She was really freaking *sad*.

Quinn hugged her and tried to console her, but it didn't help.

"I thought he was The One," she told Quinn through her tears. "I thought we were soul mates. I know that sounds delusional."

"It's not," Quinn soothed. "Not for you."

"Because I'm immature? I wanted to believe destiny kept bringing us together. It was just coincidence and fixation. Lust. Micah always says that love is a lie people tell themselves to justify having sex. He's right."

"Your brother is a very cynical man. I'm pretty cynical myself, but we both love you and your big-hearted optimism, don't we? It's not immaturity to see the world in a brighter light. It's necessary. Otherwise we'll all sink into bleak pessimism. If Remy is too blind to see what a gift you've offered him with your love, then he doesn't deserve you."

"He does, though! That's the worst of it. He's a good man, Quinn. He's honest and strong and caring. He loves his family so much, but he doesn't love *me*. He can't."

Quinn's brow furrowed. "Because of Micah?"

Eden took a breath, thinking...*kind of.* But that would open up more questions and she couldn't reveal the secret Remy carried about Yasmine.

Her breath left her in a sob of despair. She curled herself tighter into the sofa, feet on the cushion next to her, whole body leaned weakly into the back.

"Oh, sweetie." Quinn rubbed her shoulder. "We're going to take this one minute at a time, okay? I'll make some tea." She glanced to the kettle and coffee maker on the sideboard.

Eden wasn't thirsty. In this moment, she really didn't care if she evaporated from dehydration, but she could tell Quinn felt deeply helpless.

"Water is fine," she rasped.

Quinn nodded and rose, but halted when her phone rang. They shared a look, both aware it was likely Remy.

With a wince of persecution, Eden nodded that it was okay for her to answer.

"Hello? Yes, she's here." Quinn held the receiver to her breast. "He wants to know if you'll meet him in your room?"

Eden briefly dropped her brow onto her upraised knees, but the one thing she had learned from her first wedding was that it was better to cancel it rather than hang on to whatever expectations she'd had for her future.

She nodded and forced her feet to the floor. "I don't have my card for the elevator."

"I'll take you up with mine. She'll be there in a minute," Quinn said and hung up, then said, "If you need to, pack your things and come back here. Or call me to help."

"I will. Thanks." She lifted empty hands as she realized she hadn't even put shoes on before she had fled.

With her mouth in a flat, sympathetic line, Quinn picked up her own key card and led Eden to the door.

Outside, they heard a woman speaking. "Call me when you can."

Then it sounded like Remy's unmistakable timbre. "I will. I love you."

Quinn's eyes goggled with outrage.

Eden was so shocked she could only watch in horror as Quinn flung open her door to see if it was really him.

It was. Remy was embracing—

"Excuse us," Quinn said stridently.

"It's okay!" Eden squeezed Quinn's arm, holding herself upright as shock and relief collided within her, making her feel punch-drunk. "She's his sister." What a farce!

The startled pair in the open door across the hall broke their hug to stare at them.

"Hi, Yasmine." Eden's smile was an act of bravery and very poor one. Yasmine must have rushed to fly in for their wedding and now it was yet another disaster.

Eden wanted to hang her head and scurry into the swamp. If any of this wound up in the press, adding to her first humiliation... Oh, who was she kidding? The paparazzi were probably outside right now.

She couldn't even look at Remy as they started stiffly to the elevator. Inside, a freshly married couple in full wedding regalia were beaming and staring with adoration into each other's eyes.

Eden was downright sick by the time Remy opened their suite and they walked into the luxurious rooms. The space still wore the stamp of their messy occupancy—a tossed shirt here, a pair of discarded sandals there. The doors to the terrace were still open so the warm breeze wafted in with the hush of waves against the shore.

Night had fallen, though. The rooms were shadowed and everything felt dark and empty.

Remy flicked on a light. "Eden—"

"I'm not pregnant," she blurted.

"Oh." Remy straightened and squeezed the back of his neck. His voice became deeper. Heavier. "Are you okay?"

"I've had my period before. I'm pretty sure I'll survive it." She cringed, immediately regretting her snap. "What I'm saying is, we don't have to marry." She paced a few steps, but didn't know where to go. "I'll honor all the negotiations with the business. I still want Yasmine to have…" Her voice trailed into a pang as she felt completely adrift.

It struck her that she really didn't care what happened to her company. She and her mother would be fine. Not great. It would be a loss financially and a terrible blow to Eden's sense of confidence in her ability to run a company, but BH&G had been in trouble when she took it over. She hadn't caused the dire straits it was in. She was simply failing to rescue it.

"Yasmine knows," Remy said, voice not quite steady.

"What? How? I didn't say a thing," she insisted as she flung around.

"I know. It was my aunt. Which makes me feel like a coward for not being the one to tell her." He pinched the bridge of his nose. "But she knows now and that's a good thing."

"Is it? Is she okay?"

"She will be, I think. She's not ready to tell Micah."

Eden nodded and hugged herself. "I can help when she is ready. If she wants."

"Thanks." He nodded and licked his lips, searched her eyes.

There was a long awkward pause that asked, *Where do we go from here?*

"Once she's ready to tell him, he can make his own offers of reparation." Eden realized with a sick jolt. "You don't want to go through with this." Why would he? "I completely understand. Neither do I."

She swept her hand through the air, pacing again. Moving on because it was the only choice she had, but she was walking across the broken shards of her own heart, making every step an agony.

"I'm disappointed," Remy said. His hands were fists at his sides, his expression agonized.

In her? So was she! Hot tears rose to her eyes.

"I'm devastated that you're not pregnant," he continued, voice urgent. Unsteady. "It makes no more sense than any of this, but I wanted a baby with you." He pointed at her, then waved at the world around them. "I wanted all of this. The marriage, the future that lasts forever. I wanted to help you fix your father's company. Not for Yasmine, but for *you*. I want your love, Eden. I love you."

Cupid's arrow went straight into her heart. It rose to throb in her throat and she was blinking hard, trying to clear her vision. "But—"

"But I thought I shouldn't want it. That I had to protect my sister. I was protecting myself. Love for family isn't the same as what I feel for you. That love is not this crashing force that damn near knocked me down the minute I saw you. Do you know that when I walked away from you in the Louvre, I kicked myself for not getting your number? But then I stopped worrying about it because I knew that I'd see you again. I just *knew*. Make sense of that for me, will you?"

She bit her trembling lips and shrugged. She couldn't, but it had been the same for her. She just knew.

"When I asked my assistant to meet us here, I had him go to my home in Montreal and get this." He strode to the safe in the bedroom closet.

She went to the door and saw him withdraw a velvet box. He opened it and offered it to her.

"These are my mother's rings. I wouldn't give these to a woman who isn't my forever, Eden. I knew that in here." He tapped the spot on his chest over his heart, then his temple. "I didn't know how to put that knowledge into what I knew up here."

"It has been fast," she murmured, still trying to see him through her blur of tears. Bemused ones now. Bordering on joyous. Great bubbles were expanding in her chest.

"It's been five years," he said helplessly. "Do you have any doubt that you'll feel the same in five more? In fifty?"

"No. I think you're the only man I'll ever love like this. After we're both gone, I'll look for you in heaven. Or in the next life and the next."

"What about here and now, though? Are you prepared to spend the rest of this life with me?" He came to where she was standing in the doorway and went down to one knee. "Will you marry me? Not for any reason except that we love each other?"

She cupped his jaw and lowered to sit across his thigh, never breaking eye contact as she did, even though her whole body was trembling and unsteady. "It would be my honor to marry you, Remy Sylvain."

With reverence, he tried the ring on her finger. It was a little big, so he moved it to her index finger, then said wryly, "We'll get it sized later."

"We'll make all the adjustments we have to." She looped her arms around his neck, so filled with love, she felt made of it. "The important part is that we'll do them together."

"We will," he said solemnly and gathered her closer, sealing their vow with a tender kiss.

Yasmine teased Eden that she would never forgive her for not letting her design her wedding gown, but she heartily approved of Eden's choice.

It was a small wedding, so Eden had picked a minimalist style while she'd been in Paris. It was the opposite of the confection she'd worn for her wedding to Hunter. The body-hugging slip dress with a cowl neckline was classic and elegant. Instead of a veil, Eden chose a modest crown of silk delphinium blossoms.

Yasmine wore a wide-legged pantsuit in a darker blue. Quinn put on an ice-blue dress, cheekily musing that she should have worn the bridesmaid dress already owned.

The pair had chatted while Eden and Remy were working out their differences.

"She came across to assure me he really loves you," Quinn told Eden. "Then we cracked a bottle of wine and talked about the sad state of our own love lives."

"Do you know how happy I am that my best friend has already bonded with my new sister-in-law?" Eden was brimming with happy tears and now had to dab a tissue beneath her eyes so she didn't ruin her makeup.

A few minutes before eleven, the women went down to the gazebo.

Eden had no fear of being left at the altar this time. Remy looked up from his watch and his love for her was like a wall of bright sunshine that fell hot and bright against her as she walked toward him.

Eden was vaguely aware of Remy's assistant and the officiant, but couldn't see anyone but her groom. He'd shaved and wore a simple gray suit with a vest shot with silver threads on royal blue silk. When he took her hand, her knees went weak.

"That's Mama's engagement ring," Yasmine breathed with awe.

"Do you mind?" Eden bit her lip.

"No. I just…" Yasmine blinked emotive tears and bit her wobbling lips. "It tells me how much you mean to him." She hugged Remy and Eden.

Impossibly, Eden's heart expanded even more. She could hardly breathe.

"Oh. Old, new." Quinn pointed at rings and gown. "Take this." Quinn worked off her bangle, one with blue sapphires that Eden had given her as a birthday gift years ago. "Borrowed and blue."

"Careful. I'm going to start thinking you're sentimental."

"Guilty. I want that back," Quinn said and they all laughed.

"Ready?" the officiant asked, waiting for nods before beginning to read from a small book. "Today we witness…"

This was really happening. With each word, everything between Eden and Remy changed. She placed her absolute trust in him. She gave him her future and herself, but he gave himself to her in the same way. The words—vows that they repeated very solemnly—were sincere, but also irrelevant. They were already one.

They were joined in ways that no force could put asunder.

In moments, she was startled to find herself placing a band on Remy's finger. He put his mother's on her and a fresh bubble of joyous laughter rose in her throat.

"You are married," the officiant declared simply. "Kiss, if you wish."

Remy's warm hand settled against the side of her neck. Eden tilted back her head and looked into his eyes. She felt such calmness and certainty, such rightness, she closed her eyes to savor it.

His mouth settled against hers. The kiss was chaste, but so deeply imbued with their love, fresh dampness gathered on her lashes. She loved him so deeply, the words formed on her lips as they clung to his.

Into their exquisitely perfect moment, a furious male voice cried, "Eden!"

"Oh, my God," Quinn gasped.

With a hot jab of adrenaline, Eden broke away from Remy and spun to see Micah striding up the flagstone path toward them.

"Oh, my God," she echoed. "I know you are not here to ruin my wedding." She moved to the rail of the gazebo. "No one in this world would be cruel enough to do that to a woman shortly after the last time it happened to her."

"Did you tell him?" Remy snapped at Quinn.

"That you were here? No." She looked and sounded as shocked as Eden was.

"No, she didn't." Micah sent a scowl of betrayal in Quinn's direction. "I figured it out all by myself when you two were all over the headlines after that party in Paris, but I couldn't find you the next day. Flight plans are public record and there's only one reason you would bring her here. It's not to see the Barbary macaques."

"Micah." Eden gripped the rail of the gazebo. "This has to stop."

"No, *this* has to stop." He pointed at the gazebo. "Have an affair if you have to, but leave it in the Bermuda Triangle. In fact, don't even do that. He's exploiting you when you're vulnerable, Eden. He's trying to get his mitts on your company. Come. We're leaving."

"No, he's not," Yasmine defended hotly. "They love each other."

Micah's gaze shifted to penetrate the shadows of the gazebo.

"We're married." Remy stepped up behind Eden. He squeezed bolstering strength into Eden's upper arms, feeling her tremble, but also used his bulk to shield his sister from Micah. "It's time for you and I to put down our swords and move on."

"When you're pulling stunts like this? Like. Hell."

Remy felt the jolt that went through Eden. Odious as he found the man, he didn't want to get between his wife and her brother. Or his sister and her other brother, for that matter.

"You *hypocrite*." Quinn suddenly threw herself forward to stand next to Eden. "Get off your high horse. You're upset about your sister getting married in secret? What about *your* secret?"

Micah's head went back. "Stop right there, Quinn. That has nothing to do with this."

"Micah and I have been having an affair. It's been on and off for ages," Quinn announced.

"What?" Eden breathed.

"Why are you doing this?" Micah's temper was condensing like a nuclear reactor getting ready to blow. "Why here? Now? Like this?"

"It was completely consensual," Quinn quickly assured everyone. "I'm not accusing him of anything more than *appalling* double standards. Your sister is allowed to marry whomever she wants. She can save her company however she wants. She can flush it all down the toilet if she wants to. You are not the boss of everyone just because you think you are!"

Micah stared so hard at Quinn, she should have incinerated on the spot.

"It's me you're angry with," Remy began.

"No. It's not." Micah gave one cold blink that dismissed Quinn. His expression became so ruthlessly implacable, Eden pressed backward into Remy. He closed his arms around her in reassurance.

"Are you coming with me or not?" Micah asked.

"We're married. I love him."

"You really believe that?" Micah choked on a humorless laugh. "You can all go to hell, then." He pivoted and stalked away.

"Micah!" Eden cried.

Eden had never felt such a tear of allegiance. She wanted to go after her brother to smooth things over, but when she glanced at Remy, she saw he was looking at Yasmine, who was wearing a look of teary shock.

Yasmine was staring at Quinn. Quinn was staring into the space where Micah had disappeared. She had such a devastated expression, Eden reached for her.

Quinn shook her off and pressed a pained smile onto her lips.

"I'm okay. I picked him because he would never hurt me." She flicked her gold-red hair over her shoulder. "It wasn't serious. We only kept it from you because you've always said you wanted me to marry him. I didn't want to give you false hopes. You know my feelings on marriage. For *me*. This is totally fine for you." She was forcing cheerfulness that was clearly false. *"Congratulations."* She hugged them both, short and hard. "But I'm going to take a beat…" She thumbed over her shoulder then hurried away.

"Quinn!" Eden started to go after her, but Yasmine touched her arm.

"I'll go. She did that for me. I told her." Yasmine shrugged helplessly. "We had some wine and she said she knew Micah. I didn't realize she *knew* him. You two just… be happy. Please?"

Eden let her go and looked in the other direction, but Micah was long gone.

"Regrets?" Remy asked.

She took a deep breath and sighed. "No." She slid her arm around his waist and leaned into him. "Just sorry that I've hurt him. That Quinn felt such a need to protect me that she's hurting now, too."

"We can go back to Paris," Remy suggested. "Or wherever he's headed."

"He'll need time to cool off. Let me call my mom. I want her to know that I'm genuinely happy and excited to start our life together." She was.

His smile kicked up at the corners, exactly the way that she adored most. "Me, too. We should probably talk about where that life will *be*, though."

"There's an idea," she said on a small chuckle.

They pressed their smiles together, then enjoyed a longer kiss before his assistant cleared his throat.

"The, uh, next couple will be here shortly, sir."

"Right," Remy said wryly, drawing back and taking her

hand. "One pair of many. I'd say we aren't special, but we damned well are."

"Damned straight we are."

Laughing again, he scooped his arm behind her and they started down the path toward their future.

EPILOGUE

One month later...

EDEN STARTED TO enter the elevator at her Toronto apartment building, planning to race upstairs with her new purchase, but she came face-to-face with Vienna, Hunter's sister.

Vienna had on her running gear and removed her earbuds. "Oh, my God. Hi! I thought you moved to Montreal?"

Within seconds, they had ditched their plans so they could catch up over brunch. Vienna didn't even bother to change since they walked to a nearby café that catered to yoga moms and entrepreneurs.

"I am in Montreal now," Eden said once they were seated. "Remy has a gorgeous Victorian greystone on Avenue Laval."

She smiled every morning at the joy of waking next to him, but the sunlight that bounced off the gleaming gold of the maple floors didn't hurt, either. Light poured through the etched glass in the partition doors and a curved staircase led to a second floor, where the original four bedrooms had been converted into a master suite with its own lounge, a massive bathroom with an infrared sauna and a private balcony. The top floor held a den, two guest rooms, a rooftop patio and a hot tub.

"I've been working from home while we create some executive spaces at the BH and G building there. I'm only here to see Mama and finalize a few things here." Like replacing the problematic board members.

"Quinn said you had offered to let her stay in your place here this summer, but I haven't seen her. Of course, that was when she thought you would be moving in with Hunter. Has she gone back to PEI?"

"She's still in Europe." And not communicating much. She wasn't ghosting Eden as ruthlessly as Micah was, but every attempt to reach out was met with a mention of research that was keeping her very busy. "How is Hunter?" Eden asked cautiously. "Remy actually went to meet him today, but you probably knew that. Is everything okay with him and…everything?"

"He and Amelia are actually great together. Peyton is a *doll*. I hope you're okay hearing that?"

"Relieved, actually. I feel like I should send her a thank you gift," Eden joked. "I wouldn't have been as happy with Hunter as I am with Remy. I hope you don't mind hearing that."

Vienna gave a little "hmm" of amusement, but looked into her latte.

"Are you okay?" Eden frowned with concern.

"Better than a year ago, but… Do you want to hear a secret?" She wrinkled her nose. "Neal and I have been separated since your engagement."

"Seriously? I had no idea. I'm so sorry."

"I'm not. It's…" She shook her head. "Complicated. It's simpler when I live here and he stays in Calgary," she said dryly, then her brow furrowed. "I haven't had the heart to tell Hunter, not when he was going through everything with Amelia and you and Remy. You know what the press will do to us. He doesn't need yet another scandal about his sister's marriage falling apart."

"I'm sure he'd understand. He's your brother. He'll want you to be happy."

"I know. It's just hard."

Eden knew. She had disappointed her brother and didn't know how to fix it. Whether Micah would let go of his anger once he knew about Yasmine remained to be seen, but even though Yasmine was starting to talk about meeting Micah, Eden and Remy weren't rushing her.

Eden and Vienna walked back to their building, promising to catch up again very soon.

That was when Eden remembered what she had run out to buy hours ago. She quickly did the test and was beaming when Remy arrived home a short while later.

"How did it go?" she demanded. She was bursting with her own news, but she genuinely wanted to know how it had gone with his best friend. Former? Or forever?

"Good." Remy nodded, still seeming introspective. "I told him a little more about the history between my father and Micah's. Not everything, but I wanted him to understand better how you and I happened. That we would have happened five years ago if history hadn't been in our way."

"I saw Vienna. She said he seems happy with Amelia."

"He said as much. In fact, I've never known him to be so enthusiastic about anything. He was acting as though becoming a father is akin to landing a man on the moon. He's only been one for five minutes."

"I'm sure you won't be like that at all," she teased.

"I don't need to become a father to tell people how happy I am. I have you." He drew her into his arms and gently squeezed her. "Whether we make a baby or make our family another way, that will all be icing. I have everything I want or need right here." He kissed her nose.

COMING
SOON!

We really hope you enjoyed reading this book.
If you're looking for more romance, be sure to
head to the shops when new books are
available on

Thursday 8th
December

To see which titles are coming soon, please visit

millsandboon.co.uk/nextmonth

MILLS & BOON®

Coming next month

THE COST OF CINDERELLA'S CONFESSION
Julia James

From the back of the church, footsteps – like nails striking the flagstones of the aisle.

A voice – harsh and strident, breaking the hallowed silence. Heads turning, breaths intaking across the congregation.

A voice calling out –

Announcing. Denouncing…

Luca felt his head turn. Felt his gaze fall on the figure of the woman walking down the aisle. A red suit, exposing every curve of her voluptuous body. A matching pill box hat with a black veil concealing her upper face.

A veil she threw back as she approached.

To his side he heard Tomaso give a snarl of rage, start forward.

But he himself did not move. Could not.

Could only level his eyes on her, with a fury he had not known he could possess, that should strike her to silence if there were any justice in the world – any decency.

But there was no justice, no decency. There was only her voice, ringing out like sacrilege. Freezing him to the very marrow of his bones.

"He cannot marry her!" she cried out. "I am pregnant with his child!"

Continue reading
THE COST OF CINDERELLA'S CONFESSION
Julia James

Available next month
www.millsandboon.co.uk

MILLS & BOON

THE HEART OF ROMANCE

A ROMANCE FOR EVERY READER

ODERN
Prepare to be swept off your feet by sophisticated, sexy and seductive heroes, in some of the world's most glamourous and romantic locations, where power and passion collide.

TORICAL
Escape with historical heroes from time gone by. Whether your passion is for wicked Regency Rakes, muscled Vikings or rugged Highlanders, awaken the romance of the past.

EDICAL
Set your pulse racing with dedicated, delectable doctors in the high-pressure world of medicine, where emotions run high and passion, comfort and love are the best medicine.

ue Love
Celebrate true love with tender stories of heartfelt romance, from the rush of falling in love to the joy a new baby can bring, and a focus on the emotional heart of a relationship.

Desire
Indulge in secrets and scandal, intense drama and plenty of sizzling hot action with powerful and passionate heroes who have it all: wealth, status, good looks…everything but the right woman.

EROES
Experience all the excitement of a gripping thriller, with an intense romance at its heart. Resourceful, true-to-life women and strong, fearless men face danger and desire - a killer combination!

To see which titles are coming soon, please visit

millsandboon.co.uk/nextmonth

LET'S TALK
Romance

For exclusive extracts, competitions and special offers, find us online:

 facebook.com/millsandboon

@MillsandBoon

@MillsandBoonUK

Get in touch on 01413 063232

For all the latest titles coming soon, visit
millsandboon.co.uk/nextmonth

JOIN US ON SOCIAL MEDIA!

Stay up to date with our latest releases, author news and gossip, special offers and discounts, and all the behind-the-scenes action from Mills & Boon...

 @millsandboon

 @millsandboonuk

 facebook.com/millsandboon

 @millsandboonuk

It might just be true love...